The Guardian

Book 1 of The Guardian League

Steven J. Morris

The Guardian of The Palace
Book 1 of The Guardian League
Steven J. Morris
Copyright © 2021 by Steven J. Morris
All Rights Reserved.

1st Edition

ISBN 978-0-578-84133-5

Prologue

Corpses patterned the ground as far as my eye could see, a patchwork quilt of death.

I stood atop a skeletal tower, overlooking the broken ruins of an ancient civilization, so very far from home. I envisioned the beauty that the soaring arches once held, the bridges between the constructs reaching out with broken arms, buildings leaning against one another like ancient lovers in a final embrace. Crumbled remains powdered the bases of former statues, and, everywhere, all of it was littered with the dead.

Like a phoenix, I stood, bathed in fire. An Angel of Death. Not *the* Angel of Death—he was an ass.

A part of me wanted to go down and see for myself. Maybe just to make sure... to make sure I had done my job... and killed everyone that used to inhabit that world. The magic I was wielding should have destroyed them all— something inside of me could *feel* that it had—but I wanted to *see* it.

Yet I knew that was unrealistic. I didn't have the time. There were other worlds that needed my infection, and Earth was on my shortlist.

Chapter 1

Red - Day 20, Sunday, the day after the attack

"Ms. Hernandez?" a muffled voice called from a distance, accompanied by a gentle rapping on a door. My consciousness registered the interruption as a nuisance and pulled me back under.

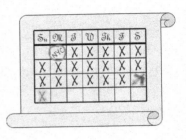

What seemed like seconds later, the rapping came again, more insistent. "Ms. Hernandez."

Ms. Hernandez was my mom… why were they bothering me?

Then a scraping sound, and an alarmed voice. "Ms. Hernandez! Are you okay?"

Some scrambling, some grunts, more scraping… shit, I was going to have to wake up. Why couldn't they just let me sleep?

I tried to answer, but my throat was dry and nothing came out. Coughing, I attempted to sit up, not wholly returned from my trip to dreamland. "I'm here. I'm okay." Was I though? I wasn't sure.

I was in my flat. Not the desert. My door was partway open, and a slightly overweight man had paused in the act of pushing his way in. I recognized him, but his name escaped me. Swinging my legs off my cot, I did a quick modesty check. I was fully dressed, though rather tragically, in some semblance of civilian fatigues—muddied, disheveled, and a little bloody.

The reason came screaming back to me. There had been creatures, unearthly *monsters*, in The Palace. They'd done things I could not explain by any of the rules I knew. And they'd beaten the hell out of me and then patched me back up in a matter of seconds. I'd blown the head clean off of one of them and fled the scene.

Not my smartest move.

Still trying to pull pieces together, I recalled the name of the man barging into my flat. Gil. Gil Rosenberg was a security guard I'd worked with, back when my biggest concerns were *normal*—how to redistribute deliveries so we could increase throughput at the delivery bays. Solid guy. Part of the sane world that had been mine a day before. Relatively sane, anyway.

Gil visibly relaxed, then looked embarrassed. "I'm sorry to barge in, Ms. Hernandez. There's been some... well... some weird stuff happened at The Palace. They tried to call you and you didn't answer. Then we found your phone down in the sublevels. They were worried and sent me over, and I found your door broken. I just wanted to be sure you were okay..."

I waved him off. "You're fine. You're fine."

He'd mentioned my phone. I'd lost it. Why? Oh, yeah. My boss had asked me to check on a camera that had gone out. While checking on it, I'd been knocked out and dumped in Central Park. At least the pieces were clicking.

I stood up, waited for a wave of dizziness to pass, then walked the few steps to the door. I moved the chair that had wedged it closed and let Gil in. Light from the hallway brightened my flat.

"Wow. What happened here?" Gil's eyes went from the disaster of my door to the disaster that was me. "What happened to *you*?"

I should have been worried about letting a man into my flat. Gil seemed trustworthy, but what did I know? Still, I could take him if I ended up being wrong.

5

"I need coffee," I said, turning to the adjacent kitchenette. "Would you like some?" My back was to Gil, but I heard him fumbling to close the door and replace the chair.

"No, ma'am."

I hit the button to start the coffee-maker heating and took the opportunity to close my eyes and lean against the counter.

"Are you sure you're okay, Ms. Hernandez?"

I slowly opened my gritty eyes. "I will be," I decided. I popped my coffee pod into the machine, slid in one of my two mugs, and pressed start. "If you can give me a minute, I'll go back with you. I was in The Palace earlier," I said, choosing my lie, "but got attacked and dumped in Central Park. I think I got a slight concussion out of it."

"We should get you to the doctor then."

I smiled ruefully. "Not my first concussion. I'll be okay. I can go back to The Palace first and report what happened, then get checked out."

Gil looked taken aback. "You're determined to have that cup of coffee?"

"I am."

"Well, then, I'll join you," he said, still staying out of the kitchenette, giving me my space. I pulled out my second mug.

"I don't have any cream or sugar," I said, hesitating before inserting a second pod.

"That's fine."

I activated his coffee and took the first sip of mine. Liquid heaven.

My only chair was holding the door closed. I offered him the cot, but he refused it. When I handed him a mug of steaming coffee, he stepped back a few feet. I appreciated that. We sipped in peaceful silence.

"I should get cleaned up," I said.

Gil shrugged. "Yeah, you're kind of a mess… is that blood in your hair?"

I reached up to my short, brown hair and poked around. Something crusty met my touch, but nothing hurt. "Could be," I shrugged.

"Clothes are pretty muddy… and what's that black goop?"

Oh, yeah. Those creatures. One had been cut in half by a goliath with a battle-axe, and the gore had splattered me. I found a spot on my sleeve and sniffed at it. "Oh, yuck. That's not mud. I'm gonna take a quick shower."

Gil nodded. "I'll let Alex know you're okay and that we'll be heading in soon. Go clean up. I'll keep an eye on your flat."

I gulped down my coffee, then reached under my cot for a bin of clean clothes. Careful not to touch the short blade I had hidden under some pants, a souvenir from the previous night's battle, I gathered what I needed. Gil didn't need to know about the blade.

He was already on the phone with Alex. I locked the bathroom door, turned on the water, and climbed in the shower. There was no way I could hear the rest of Gil's conversation with the noise the pipes made. I wondered whether he thought I was crazy. Or lying. Or concussed.

Ten minutes later, I returned to the living area, dressed and ready to go, with my dirty clothes soaking in the tub.

"Wow, that was fast," Gil said. He hadn't even finished his coffee, but he scrambled to his feet.

I walked to the door and moved the chair, allowing him to leave first, then exiting and wedging the chair back in place as best I could.

"That's not the most secure entry," he said, "which strikes me as ironic given your job…" He trailed off at my scathing look.

I led the way, and he followed. "When the guy dumped me in the park, he didn't leave me my keys or phone. I broke the door in."

"Did you consider calling the super?"

"On the phone I didn't have?"

"Well, yeah, but you could've asked a neighbor or something."

I sighed. "You're right. I wish I'd been thinking more clearly." *Nice opportunity to reinforce that concussion theory.* "Should I call the super, or do it myself?"

"Looked like the frame broke. It isn't a super-easy repair. But you probably don't want to wait for the super to get to it. I'd pony up the cash for someone to repair it. I can give you a name."

"Please."

"I'll get his number for you while you're at work. Oh, and thank you for the coffee."

I nodded, and we walked on in peace. Or it might have been awkward silence. Whatever it was, I was okay with it.

Chapter 2

The northwest building of The Palace was abuzz with activity. The night before it had been deserted, but that morning we walked through a cavalcade of police and government cars. Security was ratcheted up several notches above normal.

"Badge, Ms. Hernandez?" the security guard said nervously.

"She's your *boss*, Randy," Gil threw in for me.

"Ummm, let me get you a temp badge?" Randy suggested.

Okay by me. I wasn't in a hurry.

"ID number?" Randy asked.

Gil growled and walked over to the computer. He clicked the mouse a few times, typed something in, grabbed a temp badge, and swiped it, handing it to me as we moved through security.

As we walked to the elevators, I thought through my defense. They had found my phone in the building, so they knew I had been there. But Hon-chi, in charge of weekend security, had called me in, so I had a solid alibi. I still didn't know what had happened to the guard that had been watching my back.

The elevator ride to the second floor took forever. Had I left a trail? Had Scan missed some video when he was trying to erase it? I just wanted to sleep.

If the building was abuzz, Sec Ops was the hive that

had lost its queen bee.

Gil moved through the crowd toward a cluster of people standing near a console. I saw Alex, the head of security, dressed in casual clothes instead of his uniform—an all-nighter for him. He was standing over Phillip, our software security guru, who was digging madly into the digital security of The Palace. The video feeds were back up, and the monitors showed the atrium to be eerily empty. I saw no evidence of the bodies I had left behind there, except some tape on the ground.

Rocks watched everything from the back of the room—giving me a slight nod while he talked with a government official. Hon-chi was there as well, but he ignored me. Alex turned, and seeing me, he walked closer. "Ms. Hernandez," he said brusquely, then quietly, "come with me, please."

I followed him to a nearby conference room. We sat down opposite each other at one end of a table that could seat ten. I put my head in my hands and rubbed my face. I'd have killed for another cup of coffee.

"Tell me what happened yesterday, please, Ms. Hernandez."

I looked at him, and he didn't look accusatory or angry—just concerned. I took a breath, then dived in. "I came in late to fix one of those wireless cameras. Hon-chi called me, asking me to come. He said a bunch of people were out, and they were running on a skeleton crew. It was the first camera we set up," I said, to jog his memory. "It had lost connection."

He nodded for me to keep going.

"Anyway, I went down there, saw that the Ethernet line had been cut, and then somebody hit me on the head. I heard more than one person talking, I think. But I'm not sure, and I have no idea what they said. I don't think it was English, but I can't swear to it."

Taking a few breaths, I thought through whether there was anything else helpful to add, but came up empty. So I moved on.

"I woke up in the park, muddy. Maybe concussed. I couldn't think straight. I made my way out of the park. Sometime in there, I realized my phone, badge, and keys were gone. When I got home, I had to kick in my door. No keys. I should have gone to the hospital." I shrugged. "Like I said, I wasn't thinking straight. I'm still not sure my head is screwed on right. I don't feel great, though I'm just tired now. And thirsty." I smacked my lips. "Any chance of some coffee?"

"Yeah, I could use some too. Just wait here, okay?" He walked out, then came back in a minute later. I barely had time to lay my head on the table.

"I asked Charlie to bring us a couple."

"Thanks. Are you able to tell me what happened here?"

"Not with a great deal of understanding, no." He stared into space for several seconds. "I can say this— there's reason to believe The Palace, the building whose security *I* am in charge of, was attacked last night." He paused. "The government is all up in here now. Homeland Security, FBI, even a little CIA, to cover all the bases, I guess." Another pause. "I'd like to tell you more, but it wouldn't be wise. Oh! I can tell you this—it'll be on the news anyway."

He had my full attention.

He took a big breath, like he was about to plunge into depths without air. "There was almost no one here when it happened. The ones that came in, left early. Others turned back without ever getting into the building. They all had reasons, reasons they swear made perfect sense, but no one can make sense of their reasoning now."

"Like Hon-chi? And the guard who was with me

when I was checking out the downed camera?"

"Yes, Hon-chi's son had a toothache, and he thought it was more important to leave the building unguarded than have his son take some Tylenol." I didn't know Hon-chi had a son. "And the guard—Richard was his name—left because he heard a *noise*. He followed it outside and then wandered off. He can't explain it."

"That's crazy," I thought, and said so out loud.

"Right? Get this, it was the same at the Owaie building the night it came down. There was almost no one in the building, just a few security guards. Everyone else had left. It hasn't made the news, but Homeland Security—or maybe it was the FBI—confirmed it. The folks who left, they think it was a miracle. Our government agencies think it's some kind of drug, but they can't connect the dots."

Thinking out loud, I muttered, "Some airborne drug that makes you more open to suggestion… but where is the suggestion?" Or *magic*, I thought, but had the sense not to say it aloud. That robed figure, the one that had made the lights dance around, and Healed my ribs with a touch and some muttered words… well, I could hardly deny that there was something beyond my understanding at play. Calling it magic was as valid—and seemed more accurate than—assuming some super-advanced technology.

Alex shrugged, telling me, "You're going to get some scrutiny."

I raised an eyebrow.

"You're the only one who has directly encountered whoever did this. And I can tell you that *someone* interfered with whatever they were attempting. There were… some dead bodies found in the building. No way to ID them though."

Yeah, because they weren't human.

"They'll want to know every little bit of what you remember." He glanced at me and softened his tone. "You

12

look really beat. Maybe we should send you to the hospital to make sure you're okay." He waved vaguely at my head. "CT scan or something to check for a concussion."

"That's not a bad idea," I conceded, "though I think I'm past the worst of it."

There was a knock on the door. We saw Charlie through the small window, a coffee in each hand. Alex waved me to stay seated, and he retrieved both of our drinks. "I'll go let the agencies know you're here," he said, handing me mine. "Just wait here. I'll also schedule a doctor to come in and take a look—let him decide what to do, and give you a break from the questions."

I nodded, mouth full of mediocre coffee, and mind full of second-rate thoughts.

Chapter 3

Red - Day 20, Sunday, the day after the attack

Alex left the door open and headed back toward Sec Ops. I sat in silence and sipped my coffee, eyes closed, tuning out the bustle in the hallway and losing myself in the soothing aroma.

Before long, a woman in her forties came in, her short brown hair and fierce green eyes marking her as all business, her FBI jacket telling me which business she was in. Though her hair and skin were a couple of shades lighter than mine, her build was but an older version of my own, and I warned myself not to be influenced by that similarity.

"Ms. Hernandez?"

I nodded and slowly rose to my feet to shake her hand.

"I'm agent Terry Smith."

My forehead puckered while I tried to dig up why that name sounded familiar.

"Yes," she said, "'Agent Smith' from *The Matrix*. Some days I seriously consider using my mother's maiden name, but that's so much paperwork."

We shook hands. I never would have come up with that reference, but Agent Smith was probably ten years my elder, and *The Matrix* fit her timeline.

She sat, and waved for me to do the same. "Please, you look worn out—sit. Long night? Because mine has been."

I sat down, sighing, "Not long enough to get the

sleep I'd like."

Agent Smith gave a rueful half-smile. "Why don't you walk me through it, please."

It wasn't my first time to be at the wrong end of an interrogation. "You're *the man* in charge?" Tired and irritable, I'd lashed out for no reason. No reason she would know.

She grimaced; I'd hit a sore spot. "Agent Rogers is in charge. I'm just one of several agents interviewing people."

Fair enough. I reined in my irritation and told Agent Smith my story, using more or less the same words I'd used with Alex. I had to go back a little to explain some bits Alex already knew, like the extra security cameras.

"Ms. Hernandez," she said, when I finished. "You are former military, correct? One of only a few women who have been through special forces training, I believe."

"Yes, ma'am," I replied, but not with the crispness I would have used when I was still in said military.

"So you know how to use a gun."

I pictured two bullets going into the gullet of a monster standing in a beam of light.

"Not as well as many of my fellow soldiers. It wasn't my expertise."

"That's right," she said. "In terms of combat, hand to hand was your expertise, specifically knives."

Well, wasn't she thorough? I thought of another beast, carved in half by an axe-wielding troll. She surely didn't think that had been accomplished with a knife. Though the knife the troll had thrown at me was as long as my forearm and might be able to do the job. It would be a stretch though, and I doubted Agent Smith knew about the knife, which was not-so-safely tucked away in my unlockable flat. Oh well... what could I do?

I stared at her. "That's right, ma'am."

"Look, Ms. Hernandez. There were dead bodies

found in the building. Your training suggests you are capable of having been involved in their demise. We have every reason to believe the, uh, *bodies* we found were attempting to destroy this building. If you were involved, we just want to know more. I promise you there will be no prosecution."

"I'm glad to hear you don't plan to prosecute someone who saved my building."

"*Your* building?"

"Well, my *job* then."

We stared at each other in silence, then I broke eye contact and looked into my cup as I took a swallow of lukewarm coffee.

"I suspect you were involved," she told me. "I don't want to force your hand and make you say you were not. You'll be less likely to come clean later." She paused, and I remained silent. It seemed the wisest course of action. She rose. "Your phone, though the screen is broken, is still operational. I won't lie to you—we've already pulled everything from it, and you're clean... so you can have it back. It will be waiting for you in your Sec Ops." She pulled out her phone and clicked around. "I've texted you, sent you my contact info. You can reach me if you need to. It was a pleasure to meet you, Ms. Hernandez."

I nodded silently and finished my coffee as she rose to leave. She opened the door, just as a man was attempting the same from the outside, and he stumbled. He was of average height and build for a man, though big-bellied, but that still made him bigger than me or Agent Smith. He put a hand out to catch himself against Smith's arm, and after a brief, startled reaction where she helped him get his balance, she pulled away. What I thought was a blush of embarrassment on his face turned out to be cheeks burning with anger. Or both.

"Agent Peters." Agent Smith's tone was devoid of

emotion.

Even under good circumstances, the man would be deemed unattractive. With a mottled, red face, and a scowl that only grew as the seconds ticked by, he became downright ugly. "Hernandez was assigned to me," he barked, then sniffled.

"You were busy interviewing Ms. Wei," Agent Smith answered calmly, but with a hint of something hard in her voice.

"You have your people to interview, and I have mine. Now leave me to *my* work." He sniffled again. I doubted he knew he sniffled, because if he did, he would stop. It detracted from his anger and added to his nastiness.

Ugly inside and out. But I'd had plenty of experience with ugly.

"She's done," Agent Smith said, her voice going from a little hard to rock solid.

They stared at each other for several heated breaths. Finally, the newcomer sniffled and turned away, grumbling, "Rogers will hear about this."

"Shocking," she mumbled with an eye-roll and a sigh. She turned to me, gave me a nod, which I returned with a tired half-grin of thanks. I could have handled him, but I was glad to miss the opportunity. I decided I liked Agent Smith.

A doctor interrupted my musings with some quick tests using a flashlight, asked about my pain levels, and declared me "banged to hell, but free of a concussion." He rushed out, even though the only other injured beings in the building were also quite dead. Jerk.

I shrugged to myself, resigned to the fact that I had to live with being banged up. The moment alone gave me pause to think about what to do next—I thought of the other music I still had to face. With a two-hour time difference in Texas, my mother would be hearing the news soon. I decided to get *that* conversation over with. When I finished,

17

getting grilled by the FBI didn't seem so bad. I headed back to Sec Ops, ready to either help, or, if I couldn't help, excuse myself and go get some rest.

Chapter 4

"The choices we make, the paths we take, sometimes send us around such a bend, that it becomes hard to look back and see our former selves."

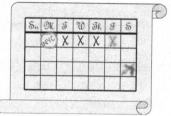

Oh, god, was he *serious*?

"Though we know we came from the other side of yon rocky outcropping, we can't remember life before the knowledge gained on this side of aforementioned rock."

I snorted, a most unladylike sound, and spit a mouthful of beer all over the table.

"Sorry, Scan," I said, "I didn't mean to laugh."

The rest of my crew chuckled at both of us as, cheeks flaming, I clumsily wiped up the beer. With a little drink, Scan could get poetic and long-winded for a techno-geek. While mopping, I told the guys, "That's his fancy way of saying, 'You can't go home again.'"

It was Friday night, but there weren't enough customers to keep the bar in business. I imagined the place came to life as the night deepened, though I didn't know that from experience.

"No home to go to." That was Bear, a giant of a man, pinning small-framed Scan into their side of the booth. I wasn't entirely sure what Bear meant, but I suspected he missed the camaraderie of our old unit. Some of us were struggling to adjust more than others. Bear did not say a lot—ever. Those words were a surprising soliloquy.

I sat next to Rocks, who had a middlish frame like me. Just then, he eased himself out of the booth, saying

19

with a smile, "Well, I have a home to go to, and a woman a damn sight more cuddly than Red to snuggle up with."

I frowned, but the sting of such barbs had faded years ago. While it was Scan's turn to blush, presumably out of embarrassment for my sake, Bear let out a deep chuckle. "More cuddly than Red. Har!" It would have hurt more if Rocks coddled me—the teasing was familiar and I had missed it in its absence. I knew very well that I could be... cutting? A little edgy at times? Difficult in a close relationship for sure. "Cuddly" would never work. Still, a specter of sadness lurked in Bear's eyes. But we were getting better.

We bid Rocks farewell, knowing we had a general arrangement to meet again in a week. My back was to the exit, but I could hear the step-tap pattern of Rocks's artificial leg as he crossed the tile floor. He said something friendly, as he passed the bar, to its tender, whose name he'd undoubtedly learned. I heard the door close, but the step-tap pattern of Rocks's exit haunted me long after.

Bear wasn't the brightest, but he was a mountain of a man and, if you gave him a job to do, he damn sure did it. And Scan had found a job for both of us. We were celebrating our first week providing security to a construction site—a far cry from our work overseas, but it was a step toward adjusting to civilian life.

I kicked Bear under the table, not getting much oomph behind it, which made him grunt and smirk all the more. "I should head home, too," I said, quaffing the last of my beer. Good IPA had been impossible to find on our last tour, and I enjoyed its return. "I've got nothing cuddly waiting for me, but I need to get some things done this weekend." I rose and threw a few bills on the table, covering more than I drank.

"That's too much," protested Scan.

"It's the least I could do for your landing me that job.

You never explained how you did it."

"I know a guy who knows a guy."

I raised an eyebrow at his obvious deflection.

"Okay, It's possible I bumped your chances a bit," he said. "You'd think the firewall for security for the biggest high-rise going up in NYC would be a little stronger. I mean—"

"Don't," I interrupted. "Just don't." I paused, looking down. "I appreciate what you've done for me, for *Bear* and me."

Bear grunted.

"But you don't need to put yourself at risk. We would have found a job somewhere."

"And you will," Scan said. "I'm just giving you a head start is all. Easy job assisting security at a construction site. Your résumé gets built up, and your starting point for whatever you want to do next is that much easier."

"Hmph. Give me your word you won't do it again, *Stan*." My using his proper name caught him by surprise. He knew I was serious. He hated that name, and I rarely used it.

"You've got my word, *Red*." A nickname our unit gave me. "I won't breach any firewalls for your sake— unless you ask me to," he added with a grin.

I had to smile in return. With a half-assed salute, I turned and strolled toward the exit. I looked back once, seeing Bear switch sides of the booth. Guess they were having another round. More power to 'em. I nodded at the bartender on my way out—I wasn't Rocks and didn't know his name—and he returned the nod as I entered the streets of Manhattan.

***

The August night was pleasantly cool, and I decided to walk back to my flat. It was dark, but not very late, and the city was still bustling. It was a ten-minute walk home, which gave me time to organize my thoughts while saving Uber-money for something better. I scoured the passers-by for threats, but spotted nothing that worried me.

I appreciated the jobs Scan had found for Bear and me. Working, keeping busy, was important, and I didn't want to screw up the chance to kick-start our new lives. The operations of our former unit were special—not easily explained or orchestrated—and while Scan was brilliant with electronics and computers, he was not so masterful at navigating the world of people. I was the one who had to manage the tactics—and sometimes even the strategy—for accomplishing our mission. It was ironic and irritating that Scan had landed me work before I had found it myself.

While behind the curve on the details, I could not afford to treat my new job any differently than our old missions. So I needed to learn more, and quickly. In charge of an entire watch, second in command to the security lead, I had a great deal of responsibility. I had just gained my security access, and I wanted to go scrub internal intel. Scan could have hacked his way in and gotten me the same, but there was no need for the risk.

As I neared my flat, my eyes automatically sought the brief parting of the buildings that gave me line of sight to the mammoth structure where I worked. The scale was distorted from that distance, with only city lighting to illuminate it, but in my mind, it looked like a monstrous rib cage, rising out of the corpse of a giant left behind on an apocalyptic battle field. I knew it was a modern marvel of engineering, but it put me in mind of death, not birth.

I entered my building and climbed five flights of stairs. The flat was new to me, and my rooms almost empty, but nothing in the building could be considered *new*. The stairs and hall were dingy and smelled of mold, with cracks in the walls and occasional bulbs out in the halls, but

I had been in much worse. I passed a young couple coming down the stairs. They were my age, but looked young to me. Innocent.

I put my key in the lock, wiggled it to get it to turn, pushed the door open, and then closed and locked the door behind me. Having a space all my own was strange and a little exciting, but also uncomfortable and a little scary. I owned nothing that would be considered personal. I had a cot folded up near the single window. A foldable card table sat between the door and the cot, with a foldable chair against the wall.

My entire life was foldable.

I had my laptop—yep, foldable—on the card table, along with some files and papers I had accumulated during the week. I flipped on the computer, and walked the few steps it took to get to the mini-kitchen. The kitchen was separated from the living area by a half-wall, and the only other room was a bathroom whose entrance was opposite the kitchen. I opened the fridge and pulled out a plastic pitcher of water, filling my coffee mug that sat next to the sink. I drank a bit, then topped off the mug, refilled the pitcher, and put it back. Water on Friday night… alone in my foldable flat… some life.

I looked at my single indulgence—a coffee-maker and a box of magical coffee goodness in the form of individual pods of coffee—and considered making myself a cup, but decided against it. I just wanted to get started learning about The Palace, not pull an all-nighter.

Such was my new civilian life and, while I wanted to do a good job, I was forever through with pushing the limits. I *would* carve a life out for myself, not just respond to the forces around me. I'd had my fill of living my life to fix other people's problems.

Chapter 5

Red - Day 4, Friday, fifteen days before the attack

I sat down with my mug of water and started poking around the web for information on La Penbrook Palencia, aka The Palace. I'd read it before, but wanted to have it up as I looked 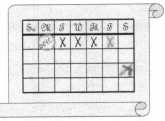 at internal info that came from security training. The general press statements from the Penbrook Corporation had two key ideas they were pushing.

   The first was the sales pitch to New Yorkers that The Palace was a building you never had to leave unless you wanted to. One write-up read, "Taking up multiple city blocks, the lower floors in each block have enough shopping and food venues to satisfy any appetite, and the floor that spans four city blocks will house a park-like arena, complete with running trails and a swim center!"

   I chuckled at the lunacy of putting a swim center— what—five... six... stories up?

   The second idea came in the form of a sales pitch to New York City—creating new livable, sellable real-estate. The population could increase with an amazing jump, with the promise of more jobs and more money coming into the city.

   "Penbrook Palace would be a vertical city unto itself. With floors dedicated to schooling, healthcare, and even entertainment, the mini-city would cause negligible tax on the city's transport systems." So, money for New York City without pushing the limits on its infrastructure. *Everybody wins, right?*

I switched to some internal docs I'd received during training. I knew they'd brought me in as they transitioned from Phase One to Phase Two of construction. Why?

"The construction of The Palace was phased in order to make this mini-city more financially viable. The four bases, and the first several floors that spanned the bases, were complete and usable after the completion of Phase One." I'd already been on a tour of those bases—they housed restaurants, stores, medical services, and similar businesses.

The northwest building housed the Security Operations Control Center, aka Sec Ops. My second home for the foreseeable future.

"Four base buildings were designed to support a massive amount of residents, who will come after the tower being built in Phase Two is completed. During Phase Two construction, the existing businesses will earn money from use by nearby residents and those willing to travel to see The Palace, the greatest engineering marvel of our time, being built."

That meant we needed to let visitors into the buildings, in order to get their money. So with Phase Two, security had become much more complicated. That explained my job.

The training docs showed me five floors in each of the four buildings. Above that, the buildings connected over the streets of New York, creating a truly monumental engineering feat of a single floor spanning four Manhattan blocks. They earmarked floors six through eight to house a massive park. Then there were three floors dedicated to white collar businesses—prime real estate—and finally, the "atrium" on floor twelve. The atrium was complete, but not fully operational. Businesses at that height were not yet open; venues were not yet staged. The docs clarified that the investors wanted the atrium to be a tourist attraction as soon as possible.

My job was to protect the building during construction, and potentially after. They needed the public in there, dropping coin, but not interfering with construction. Tough job. They'd hired me as a watch manager, second only to the security lead, Alex Hamdell.

"The most obvious threat is terrorism, mostly from outside the U.S.," our instructor had informed me as I sat in the small training room with twenty other new recruits earlier that afternoon. His PowerPoint slide displayed a world map with hotspots of concern. "Homeland Security sends updates that some of you will be digesting and funneling into our database. We will use that information to protect our building."

I'd raised my hand then, and the instructor had nodded his go-ahead.

"Forgive my bluntness, sir. I just came from military service overseas." I pointed to the map. "How do we keep people in our building safe from terrorist attacks without violating civil rights regarding racial profiling?"

You could have heard a pin drop.

"I'll return the favor and be blunt with you... *Ms*?" he said, raising his eyebrows.

"Ms. Hernandez," I said.

"Ah, Ms. Hernandez," he said, like he knew all about me. "The truth is, it will be *very* difficult. The building cannot afford negative publicity. That means we cannot be seen as performing racial profiling. We also cannot have terrorists blowing up the building. We will train you on what to look for in terms of *personality* profiling, and we can show you current hotspots of terrorist activity. We brought *you* in because you have some experience in this area."

The instructor nodded to me like he'd answered my question. He hadn't. At least not directly—what he *didn't* say told me a great deal. I knew from his response that the topic couldn't be discussed openly or directly, that it *was* a problem, and that they didn't have a brilliant answer.

"The next biggest threat is protesters—either a general 'You are wrecking the beauty of our city' type, or someone protesting 'fat cats getting richer.' The financial protestors are the least threatening, fighting through courts and lawsuits and political arenas. However, that doesn't rule out crazy acts of violence when somebody loses a legal battle."

I had only met the security lead a couple times. Once during the interview, and another time during the previous week's training. A dark-skinned man in his late forties, he had a sharp mind, and stayed on top of potential hazards. He had a tech guy, Phillip Roswell, who had designed the compute infrastructure of The Palace. Phillip was a slightly overweight white guy who thrived on recognition—I'd already witnessed an ego-pumping session from Alex. Part of my job would be to boil threat information down to actions consumable by the security details, sometimes pictures of people to watch for and why. Maybe it wasn't racial profiling if we targeted specific individuals? Even then, we would keep our eyes on those folks, not keep them out.

I spent a couple of hours taking notes for follow-up and called it a night.

I slept poorly, dreaming of *a city whose architecture was alien to me. Soaring stone arches with flowering vines lined a street cobbled with stones, but the stones were cut and placed so precisely that the road was smooth. No vehicles were on the street, and there were no people nearby, only in the distance, looking frantic, like a mound of ants that had been kicked. On the ground were two bodies, neither of them human. One was a child... hurt, bleeding... her features were strange, but as happens in dreams, did not seem strange... blond hair revealed pointed ears and pronounced cheekbones. She wore tan robes with flowered vines similar to the ones on the columns, a crimson stain rapidly spreading across the belly of her robe. The other figure was small and green-skinned, with sharp teeth and claws, hair tufting its long ears that matched its long, jutting jaws. It lay dead, a bloody knife having fallen from its hand. The knife was ornate—a dagger—with nightmarish faces carved into the hilt and etched into the blade. Through the blood on the knife, a menacing red light emanated from faces screaming in pain. Over the two bodies stood a figure, gleaming with white light. I stared, fascinated, frightened, wondering... why not me?*

I awoke sweating, confused, and disoriented about where I was. After floundering for a time, I calmed myself down and eventually fell back into a dreamless sleep.

Chapter 6

I arose the next morning and started my day with a jog. From the Upper East side, there was some stop-and-go movement to get to Central Park, but once I reached it, I could run several 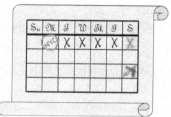 miles without having to slow. I'd only been in NYC a week, and had tried a different route each day, but I was ready to find a pattern to run. Having to decide with every fork of the trail which path to take—it kept my mind engaged on the jog, which was not always what I wanted.

What I wanted that day was to disconnect from my thoughts and get lost in the motion. I had been doing short runs that week, but the morning offered me a chance to do a full round of the park. Some sections were quite wooded; I couldn't believe they existed amid the concrete and metal jungle of Manhattan.

I found a place that looked safe to pause and do some core strengthening. I knew I would eventually want to find a space where I could practice some of my combat training, but until I did, the middle of Central Park would do. Maybe a punching bag could be my next home purchase?

After finishing a round of old-fashioned push-ups, I walked for a minute. I headed through a section of the park that looked less used, but quickly decided it didn't look safe and changed directions. When I continued south, I saw some movement out of the corner of my eye in the direction I'd avoided. Turning to look, I saw nothing, but a creeping sensation crawled over my skin, and I was glad I hadn't headed that way.

When I returned to my flat, I enjoyed a shower, but wondered if pipes should make that much noise. Finally, I had myself a cup of coffee while I followed up on some online leads from the night before.

Digging into the money aspect a little more, I found that the funding for the Penbrook Palace came via a deal brokered by The Penbrook Corporation, of which the majority shares were still held by the Penbrook family itself. I'd always had a penchant for history, and, intrigued, I kept reading.

Several generations of Penbrooks had grown the family business, and over those generations, each patriarch had shown his own strengths. Started by the great-grandfather of the current owner, the business was already sizable when the grandfather took over. The grandfather was not as much of an entrepreneur, but involved himself in politics—in "special interests" efforts. He steered the governmental and political arena in ways that expanded the family's interests. The father of the latest generation was another businessman, with little interest in the public spotlight. The man behind the business venture that began The Palace had several children, but there was little information available on them. All I could find was that the oldest son was taking over The Penbrook Corporation, but leaving The Palace to be built by his father. That single venture was big enough that it warranted such attention.

The rumbling of my stomach interrupted my studies. I didn't have any proper food, so I headed down to the street. Knowing from experience it was a bad idea to go shopping on an empty stomach, I stopped at a food stall and grabbed some street tacos. At the store, I stocked up on sandwich fixings and some more coffee pods. I did some mental math and frowned. I needed to find a cheaper solution to my daily coffee, but postponed that effort. I needed to learn to cook more too, but again... I wasn't ready.

Once home, I unloaded my meager groceries and sat back down at the laptop. I took a different research tactic and found the blog of someone protesting the construction of The Palace. "It's a lie that The Palace won't stress the city infrastructure," the blogger stated, claiming that, "With the food deliveries, utilities consumed, and waste produced, it would be a tremendous hit on the city's infrastructure!" According to the blogger, Amazon was planning to build a small distribution center *within* The Palace in order to support the expected deliveries. Sounded good to me, but I got the point—there was no such thing as a free lunch.

Other blogs shared similar views, but I also found some supporting The Palace, saying, "The Palace is being built to handle the deliveries, the utilities, the waste, and will bring in more money to the city, enabling improvements beyond The Palace itself." So, no free lunch, but at the scale of The Palace, the menu was bigger than The Cheesecake Factory's.

The blog sites had ads running through them— financial advisors, coffee-makers, dating services. *Damned web algorithms!* There were news blurbs about military actions overseas and even a monster attack in Manila, the Philippines. I tried to stay away from the ads, but eventually they became more interesting than the blogs themselves, and I took a break. After all, I had a pretty complete picture of public sentiment regarding The Palace.

I looked around the room and tried to decide if I was ready to make the place more of a home. Some pictures of my parents and sisters to hang on the wall? I didn't actually *have* any pictures that weren't digital, but I could get them printed. I flipped through my phone. Not a lot from before the military, but I paused on a pic of my army family—

Rocks, Scan, Bear... and Murphy. Murphy, who didn't make it back.

It took me some time to peel my eyes away.

Shrugging off my unease, I told myself I didn't have a hammer to hang a picture anyway. Or a wrench, which I was sure to need given the noise of the pipes. Real people had couches, and dining and coffee tables, not fold-up chairs and card tables. They had bookshelves and nightstands… with books and magazines to fill them!

I sighed, knowing I needed to try harder to fit into the civilian world. I had promised myself. But how did it work? Was I supposed to go buy things I liked, displaying who I was as a reflection of those things, or did I have to decide first who I was, and then furnish the flat to reflect my identity? Sighing again, I stood up to do something about it. Surely I could find a book or a magazine. Baby steps.

As I started out on my purchasing adventure, I was reminded of a quirk of my mother's. Whenever she was agitated or upset, she would slip in a DVD of the movie *You've Got Mail*. She wouldn't necessarily watch it, but you could hear it playing in the background, and she knew the dialogue by heart. I did a quick web search and learned that Fox Books didn't actually exist, but "The Corner Bookstore" did, and it reminded me of "The Shop Around the Corner" from Mom's calm-me movie. I headed south to check it out, detouring a little to head through Central Park.

The stroll through the park was relaxing. I took my time and noticed things I hadn't when jogging. It struck me again just how much of nature was being preserved in a city where real estate was so prized. As I passed the section where I'd felt uneasy during my jog, the threat of danger drew my eye, while, simultaneously, I thought it wise to stay away. I felt better once it was behind me, and I let the peace of nature buoy my spirits for the rest of the walk.

The bookstore looked like I'd envisioned—filled with

lots of homey books. *What kind should I get?* If I was sticking with my current identity, that narrowed it down to a book about the military or self-defense. But wasn't it time to leave that behind, to recreate myself into something more domestic? Like a book on home decor, or a cookbook?

I strolled around the center counter, looking at book after book. World Culture? I liked world culture, but that felt like a nod to my past. Cooking? I wanted to be there, but could that single book define my flat? Business? That seemed the most appropriate for who I was right then, but business books were so dry. If I could find a book that was both dry *and* empty...

I was getting frustrated. Who was I kidding anyway? I was struggling to find the book *right* for my flat, that *said* something about me, but who would it say anything *to*? It wasn't like I would actually have any visitors.

Suddenly irritated by the whole misadventure, I turned and left the store.

The beautiful day was soured. Everywhere I looked, there were couples, often with little knee-biters running around them screaming playfully. They had their lives together, as families, flats full of decorations and books, telling the stories of their lives and growing old together. I turned away from the park and started home via the business roads. A proverbial dark cloud hung over me the rest of the evening as I sulked my way through some web-based news updates. I did not spend the time well, dwelling on things I had started to hope for—things stolen away from me.

Eventually, I found some sleep. It was marred by dreams of *the world aflame, my vantage point from atop a building providing glimpses through the smoke to the anarchy below. Monstrous beasts scoured the beautifully cobbled streets, tearing apart the rapidly thinning band of people trying to escape. I felt a ripping of a cord inside of me with every death, some final pains more horrifying than others. How could there be so many of the beasts... how?!?*

The disturbing nightmare lost its grip on me and faded to more normal dreams, giving me a chance for rest.

I awoke early, as was my habit, and felt a little distance from the previous day's dark mood. I went for my run, which cleared my head even further. There was nothing like endorphins and sweat to help you fight your way out of a stupor. Feeling renewed, I shopped at a nearby store; bought a frying pan, eggs, sausage, cheese, tortes, and some salsa; and then headed home to make myself breakfast. It wasn't as good as Mom's, but it rivaled Dad's. Once done, I spent the remainder of the day at the American Museum of Natural History, where I lost myself in all the artifacts and explanations of our world's past.

That day, I floated in a cocoon of contentment—I hadn't found the perfect book to decorate my flat, but a frying pan was an excellent start.

Chapter 7

Red - Day 18, Friday, one day before the attack

It was the end of my third week of work, my first week being largely training, so really two weeks of *proper* work—that was the day things started their descent into madness. On Friday, around

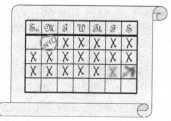

three, as I was wrapping up for the week, a pop-up on my notepad told me to head to Sec Ops.

Sec Ops was already feeling familiar, perhaps even more like home than my flat. I'd spent the first week on my watch visiting each of the security checkpoints where personnel and cargo entered the buildings. The second week, I'd proposed and implemented some changes—I'd had to push hard on Alex to get him to give my ideas a chance, and I'd worked closely with Phillip to get the software changes I needed. So I'd spent a good bit of time checking in at Sec Ops.

When I walked in, I found the room bustling. Several people were manning consoles, not just Phillip. The rat-a-tat-tat of keyboard strikes created a baseline racket atop which rode multiple quiet discussions as monitors flashed through screens of destruction.

I spotted Alex the same time he spotted me, and we beelined to each other. "Ms. Hernandez. There's been an incident that has us on alert. A building under construction in Hong Kong was destroyed. Not one of ours. Motivation unknown."

He paused, and my mind raced. An unknown risk. Clearly, if they had destroyed a building, the perpetrators were willing to do severe harm! I had so many questions.

"We don't know much yet," he said, reading my mind. "The building collapsed inward, limiting damage." He pulled me over to a live feed showing the view from a chopper. It reminded me of the feeds from when the Twin Towers came down. The major damage was confined to the block where the building had been going up, but the debris scattered for many blocks. The feed caption read that rescue operations were underway, but that human casualties were unusually low for such devastation.

Alex left me alone for a little while to watch the feed. They eventually flipped to a repeat of the cameras on nearby buildings showing the fall of the construction site. It was night there, but the city lights, like in NYC, kept the city aglow. From the outside, the building looked largely complete, though the scaffolding told the truth behind that misperception. The cameras showed the entire building lighting up, reminding me of black-and-white footage I'd seen as a kid of atomic bombs going off. Unlike that footage, which had a mushroom cloud sprout out of nothing, the video before me showed the reverse. The building collapsed in the middle first, like a handheld radio antenna, and once the middle vanished, the outside walls fell in. It seemed impossible that so much mass could compress to a mound only several floors high.

"No one is claiming credit for this destruction." Alex said, breaking my focus on the monitor. "There was nothing obviously contentious about the building. It was a massive housing complex."

Just like ours, I thought.

"The financials differed from those of The Palace, but not significantly so."

"So what you're telling me is that a building very much like ours just got attacked and destroyed for reasons we don't understand."

"Yeah," he said, shaking his head.
What in the hell was happening?

Chapter 8

Red - Day 11, Friday, eight days before the attack

Bear and I left work together at the end of the day and headed to Tom's for a relaxing evening with Scan and Rocks. We walked in companionable silence. I was feeling chipper with the prospect 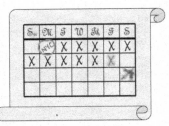 of implementing improvement plans I'd proposed to Alex.

"Good to see you smiling," Bear said.

That made me frown. "I *smile*," I said defensively.

"Har!" he said, grinning. I'd never been able to stay angry when he grinned like that.

"Fine," I said. "This isn't terrible. I kind of like my job." Bear put one of his massive arms around me and pulled me next to him in a short, still-walking hug, then let go.

We walked on in silence for a bit before he said, "Met somebody."

That news surprised me, and so did the stab of jealousy I felt. I couldn't help myself. "Girl?"

"Har!" he laughed. "*Woman.*"

He was still softly chuckling, and I was a mixed bag of emotions. It worried me that someone might take advantage of Bear—he could be *really* gullible. I felt a twinge of envy that he might have found someone. And I even felt a bit of fear that a new relationship would pull him out of our little circle. But I didn't want him to know any of that.

"So what's she like?" I asked him, a little too chipper. "How did you meet her?"

"She's nice," he said. There was that grin again. "We

met at the gym."

The gym? Great. The gym might as well be a meat market and all the customers, hungry carnivores. I didn't like Bear's odds. I refused to be a mother hen about it though.

We reached the pub, and I opened the door and held it for Bear. Music spilled out of the bar as he smiled and entered. My eyes soon adjusted to the room lighting. Scan and Rocks sat at the same booth as last time, opposite each other but with no drinks yet.

We worked our way to the table, navigating between a couple of people seated at the bar and some empty coat hooks on the wall behind them. It wasn't quite coat weather yet. When we reached the table, Scan scooted in to make room for Bear, and Rocks stood to let me in. It was easier on Rocks if he could keep his artificial leg on the outside of the booth.

"I ordered a pitcher of the IPA," Rocks said as Bear and I sat. I smiled, and Bear grunted. They all knew it was my favorite.

"Tell us how it's going at The Palace, Red," Scan said.

"I *think* it's going well. I have some ideas for helping things move faster and getting some credit for the security team."

The guys all chuckled. They'd worked with me before, and they knew I liked to find—and fix—things that were broken in a system. Or take a system that was working—to someone else's advantage—and flip it on its head.

"Need any hardware or software help?" Scan asked.

"Don't know yet. There's a guy, Phillip Roswell. He's getting me the software updates I need."

"Uh huh," Scan said. "He should be able to."

I raised an eyebrow.

39

"Sorry, I couldn't help but poke around a bit. Had to make sure you had some talented people."

"Uh huh," I replied, mimicking him. "And what are *you* doing with *your* time?"

Scan grinned. "A bit of this, a bit of that."

Another raised eyebrow from me.

"You know I've always been skilled at acquisitions," he said. "Sometimes it's information, sometimes hard-to-find items, sometimes the acquisition is a video feed. The item itself is never illegal to have," he quickly added.

"But your means of obtaining that item..." Rocks said.

Scan didn't even blush. "I research my clients. You know that. Most of the work is a no op."

"No op?" I asked.

"I mean that there is no question of right or wrong before or after the exchange. When I am asked to do something I find questionable, I turn down the request."

"But how do you *know*?" I asked. "How can you know you haven't been tricked? That someone won't use what you've gotten them for harm?"

"I can't, but how can I know that harm would not happen in the hands of the previous owner, or that some good might come from the new owner? I can't *know*."

The bartender arrived with a pitcher and four beer glasses and set them on the table, saying, "Any food tonight?"

"Hey, Mike," Rocks said. Rocks was great with names. "How's business tonight?"

"About normal. It'll pick up quite a bit soon. Our Friday night crowd usually starts a little later."

"Hope you have a lucrative but calm night," Rocks said, completely sincere. "I'll take a cheeseburger. Anyone else? Red?"

The bartender-turned-server cocked his head at me

and my brown hair and light brown skin. *"Red*?"

"Stupidest nickname ever," I muttered, and the guys chuckled. I didn't feel like explaining it… I never did.

We each ordered a burger, and Mike punched it into a tablet back at his bar. It impressed me that even a little hole-in-the-wall like Tom's talked to the kitchen through electronics.

"Anyway," Scan said, "I don't feel bad about what I do. I make sure the bad guys don't win, and if I'm wrong, I fix it." He took a slug of his beer and dared us to question him. I wished I had his confidence. I still struggled with the morality of some of our past actions. Rocks did too, but I didn't think Scan had the same moral compass. Bear's compass was the strongest, but it was all heart. I loved the guy, but he didn't have a lot going on upstairs.

"If any politician could ever sway you, he would be set," Rocks said to Scan.

"Snowy day in hell," Scan replied. "Okay, smart guy, how are you spending your days?"

"A bit of this, a bit of that," he said, drawing a scowl from Scan. "Okay, okay. Cynthia has her work at the library, and I tried volunteering there to see if I could be useful, but I got bored. The pace is relaxing, but it wore on me. My dad is trying to get me involved in the family business—some real estate and investments. I can't be as physically active as I used to be, but I'm hoping I'll find business more exciting than helping in a library."

Scan and I exchanged a look, and I saw Bear frowning.

"No," continued Rocks, "I will not work security with you. Other people can see it as they choose, but I won't put others at risk because I fail to secure an area due to having lost a leg. Maybe someday, when I've gotten better at moving around with it, I'll feel differently. But not now."

"Rocks," I said, my voice overly calm, "not every

41

detail has to do patrol—"

He cut me off. "No. It would drive me more nuts to be that close to my old life and not able to do it." He grimaced, then smirked. "It's funny. I purposefully walked away from my family. My oldest brother—"

"You have a brother?" Scan asked, eyebrows raised. Rocks scowled, but Scan continued. "What? I don't remember you talking about a brother—*ever.*"

"I have three," he said sheepishly. Then he grinned. "And a sister."

The rest of us looked at one another, palms up, shoulders shrugging, a chorus of "Whaaa?"

Rocks waved us back into quiet. "Yeah, yeah, yeah. I said I walked away from them. Makes sense that I wouldn't have mentioned them, right? My older brother was groomed to inherit the family business, and my younger brothers and sister all had their own... *related...* interests." He took a long drink of his beer. "I was always a bit of an outsider. So I followed a path that made sense to me."

He was as serious as I'd ever seen him.

"Now I find the prospect of a so-called *normal* life less disturbing. Less off-putting. I can't really explain it." He shrugged. "With my physical limitations, I'm more game for a cerebral challenge."

I kind of wanted to hug him, but I lightly punched his arm instead.

"Anyway," he said, breathing deeply, "for now, things are fine. I'm learning about the family business and finding a place where I can fit in. I've got enough money to play this out for a while, and if worse comes to worst... I know I've got you guys." He managed to time his statement with the arrival of our food. Rocks had always had a knack for timing.

We all laughed as the server expertly matched each burger with its owner. I took a bite of my cheeseburger with the works, and my eyes drew up to the TV over the back wall.

"You're kidding me," I said, mouth full.

"Twenty Killed in Hong Kong by Monster," read the caption at the bottom of the screen. I watched as a group of young adults were brawling on a street corner at night, the footage looking like it came from a shop's security monitor. There was a movement as something sped into the frame, moving in the general direction of the camera. The closer it was to the camera, the more grainy the picture became, until it was impossible to make out anything. There appeared to be rapid movement in several directions, and then the picture just as quickly cleared up. Instead of people moving about, there was nothing but corpses.

"What the hell?" I muttered. Was it a hoax? A news spoof on a TV show? I couldn't wrap my mind around it.

Rocks followed my gaze to the screen and turned to Scan. "She's watching the Hong Kong reel," he said. "Crazy. Did you poke on it any?"

"Wait, this is *real*?"

"I did." Scan answered Rocks, ignoring me. He also kept eating. "It has all the watermarks of being actual footage, just can't tell what the hell I'm looking at. I grabbed some other feeds, and that weird graininess is in there too. Just as brief—and hard to see."

"Some new tech that screws up cameras?" I proposed.

"Could be. Maybe if you do LADAR bursts at a camera or something." he said. "The news says the folks killed were random."

"So... a high profile target in there and the rest had to be taken out to make it *seem* random?" Rocks said.

"Maybe," Scan acknowledged. "But, if there *was* a high profile death, it's being covered up. From the reports it looks like nothing more than straggling partiers on a street

43

corner near a pub that had closed for the night."

The news moved on to some local issues, and I lit into my burger and beer.

We chit-chatted for a while longer and, after one last round of beer, ended our night. We promised to meet again the following week.

As I was walking home, I realized I hadn't followed up with Bear about his girlfriend. I made a mental note to ask him about her when we met after work the following week. I felt silly that I'd let fake news of monster attacks distract me.

Chapter 9

I texted Bear, Rocks, and Scan not to expect me for beer, and sent them a link to a news clip on the Hong Kong building implosion. They'd piece it together; at least Rocks and Scan would. And they'd explain to Bear.

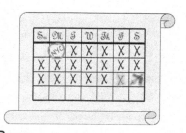

I watched news highlights repeating on the Sec Ops monitors. Somewhere in there, I caught the name of the building that had collapsed—the Owaie. It had come down at 2:33am Hong Kong time—12 hours ahead of us in New York. Even at that hour of the morning, there were enough city lights for the cameras in other buildings to pick up the destruction of the Owaie, especially with that strange light that flashed just before the building imploded.

Phillip was doing his best to dig deeper into the financials of the Owaie and searching the internet for clues. Scan was probably doing the same.

There wasn't much left that Alex and I could do, so we started working on contingency plans.

"Let's assume our building is a target," Alex said. "It's a Friday—we *might* convince the board to lock down the building for the weekend. But what could we actually do with that time?"

"Security sweeps," I said on autopilot. "Dogs to sniff out explosives." We had a call in to Homeland Security to ask for an expert opinion on what took the Owaie down. We doubted we would get info in time for the weekend.

"*Anything* we do is going to get us pushback from the

financial guys," Alex said.

"Can't slow down construction," I said, "even if it means the building might get destroyed."

"How can we increase security without slowing down entry to the building?" The question was semi-rhetorical. "Metal detectors? Wands for all the folks that didn't pass the detectors? Conveyor belts for scans of personal items?"

"Those will all slow down entry *and* cost money," I said, though I knew he knew that.

"I'll go in and argue for those things," he said, sighing, "but don't get your hopes up."

The reality for security was that the board would fight any change that would slow construction or increase budget. Bottom line? Our hands were tied.

It was a tough bottleneck—generally, the kind of problem I liked.

"Let's attack the problem from a different angle," I suggested.

Alex nodded his head, inviting me to go on.

"What if we look into weaknesses in the structure of our building?"

He thought about it briefly and nodded his head again.

"Phillip," he said, "can you get us the name of the lead engineer?"

His name and phone number were in our internal security database, but neither of us expected him to answer his own phone. He not only answered, he came in within the hour.

For a lead engineer of the most complicated housing structure ever built, he was pretty unassuming. He wore jeans and a nice shirt, but no tie. Glasses adorned his face, and his hair was greying and thinning out, but he was neither exceedingly fat nor thin—in better shape than the average engineer.

He looked around the room and headed toward Alex, Phillip, and me. I wondered who he was actually targeting—Phillip, the only person at a computer and the obvious engineer? But I would never know, as Alex stepped up to the newcomer and asked, "Can I help you?"

"I'm Ray," he said. We had guessed the pronunciation right. Rej, I corrected myself. "I'm trying to find Alex."

Alex smiled, reaching out a hand to Rej. "I'm Alex. I have to tell you—you were remarkably easy to get a hold of."

Rej took the hand and shook it. He had yet to smile, but neither did he seem angry nor irritated. "You wanted to talk about the vulnerabilities of my building, correct?"

My building? Okay, that was odd, but my time with Scan had prepared me for engineers that didn't fit social norms. "That's right," I said. I immediately realized my faux pas—I answered instead of deferring to my boss. Though I blushed, which I hated, I could see that Alex knew exactly what I was thinking, and he smirked but let it go.

Rej turned to me. "Can you bring up schematics from here?"

Phillip clicked a button, and the schematics popped up on the monitor closest to us, replacing a feed from Hong Kong. The Hong Kong feed moved over a monitor, and I couldn't follow if anything else switched screens. Phillip pointed at the console in front of us. "That one is connected to the schematics now."

Rej nodded to Phillip and sat down at the console. He tapped keys and popped up menus, which he thumbed through, then he started clicking again, and the image jumped out to a distant view of The Palace. He continued to play with the keyboard, and the schematic view of the building panned around, zooming in and out. "Nice, you mapped the hot-keys," he said.

That meant nothing to me, but it made Phillip blush.

The screen suddenly jumped to a view of one of the street level constructs and removed the stones to show girders—the skeleton of the building. Then it flipped among the other three bases. "Most people don't get how important it is to work out these details. They just live with having to use the menus. It's like having to go to the reference cards in a library to find a book. So much time lost."

Phillip blushed an even brighter shade of pink.

Rej stopped pressing keys. "Okay," he said. The screen was showing a view of the girders, focused on the street level views. "You've got five critical points in the structure. There's one in each base, and then one that's in the center of the tower." He pointed at the screen. "This building is a base, one of four. Take out any of the bases, and the tower will fall. Each base has a slightly different weak point, because we had to work with the city infrastructure that was already in place. Don't misunderstand—you could take out some other point and shift the weak point... more than one way to skin a cat... though I've never poked on why that would matter..." Rej started clicking, and a window popped up with a web search on "more than one way to skin a cat." It sat there a few seconds, then disappeared with a muttered, "sorry," from Rej. "I can send you a list of the most likely weak points for each of the bases," he said, looking at me.

"Um, that would be very helpful. When do you think—"

He didn't let me finish. "I'll sit and do it as soon as we finish this conversation," he said. "It makes no sense to work this hard on constructing The Palace and then ignore potential threats." He nodded toward the replay of the Owaie building collapsing on the next screen and looked at the display with interest. "I wish I knew how they did that. Never seen anything like it. Like the building *imploded*."

Alex cocked his head at Rej, some idea percolating. "Rej, would you be willing to talk to the board with me about increasing security?" Ah, he thought he'd found a valuable ally.

Rej waved a hand at him. "I don't do well with dip-shittery." *This guy is something.* "I'm more likely to say something inflammatory that will make your situation worse. They try not to let me talk with people." I wondered who "they" were—probably the people with the money. "If you want to take a shot at it, I can be there, but it won't end well."

Alex frowned but nodded. I had no idea what that nod meant.

"Okay, so the fifth weak point is the fulcrum of where the four triangles that form the pyramid meet," Rej said, moving on. "The pyramid is the structure on top of which we will build the tower. Take that out, and the tower comes down. I can get you the location for that point as well."

Rej waved toward the video of Owaie. "However they did *that*... it can't work the same with Penbrook Palencia. If you collapse the center point, the tower would collapse, more or less like what you see with the Owaie. But it would collapse onto the street beneath it, and it would leave each of the four bases relatively intact."

That made sense. He kept going.

"If you collapse any of the bases, the tower will topple sideways, like a broken chair leg would cause the chair to fall in that direction. We had to account for that... *I* had to account for that. If a base collapses, the cross-beams are rigged to fold, to literally spring up, and compression springs between the bases will push them apart. The three remaining bases will then lean out, allowing room for the tower to come down. The tower will crush the inner corners of the remaining three buildings, but will not disperse the tower widely."

He sounded so casual about something so destructive and deadly. After Phase Two, that tower would be full of people!

"If someone wanted to take out The Palace, they could take out any of the corners or the center." Rej pointed to a diagram on the screen. "I'll work on getting you the weak points."

Knowing the weak points was a start. But how did we use that knowledge to keep people safe?

Chapter 10

Alex and I huddled while Rej worked. "Well," I said, "the least we could do is mount some cameras around the locations Rej gives us."

"True," Alex said. "Phillip, what do we have that we can use short term for video cameras?"

"It depends on the location," Phillip answered, "but we could hit almost anywhere with some wireless cameras. The quality won't be as good as our wired cameras, but wired would take too much time. I'll go get the wireless cams."

Alex and I turned back to the Hong Kong feed, where the sun was starting to illuminate the rubble. I checked the time on my phone—6:34pm—and saw I had a text from Scan.

`Call when you can.`

"I'm going to step out to make a call," I told Alex. He nodded, and I left, calling Scan as I went.

He answered immediately. "Hey, Red. I don't have a lot for you, but what I *don't* have is odd."

"Okay, I'm listening."

"There's no digital trace of an attack plan on the Owaie building. There's chatter on claiming credit, but none of it looks like it's based in reality, just posers hoping to rise in the terrorist world."

"Okay, a small group then," I thought out loud.

51

"Also, the Owaie had an off-site backup showing who was in the building, and the count is amazingly low. Just a handful of people, all security. It's like everybody knew not to be there. And here's the other weird thing. Remember that strange blurring of the cameras from the footage where the people were killed in the street?"

"Yeah?" How was that information relevant?

"You can see the same blurring across a set of cameras leading to the Owaie building, just a few minutes before the building collapsed. Whatever tech is interfering with the camera feeds, it entered the Owaie."

"Okay," I said. "I'm not sure what to do with that yet."

"I hear you. Be careful, Red." He hung up.

Phillip came rumbling back down the hall with a cart full of equipment. I stared at him as I held my phone at my side. How was I going to relay the intel I knew to Alex? Was there any way to point him in the right direction and let him find the information on his own?

I joined Phillip as he wheeled past me into Sec Ops.

Chapter 11

Red - Day 18, Friday, one day before the attack

Alex, Phillip, and I gathered around his cart of equipment. Phillip pulled out some simple cameras, the kind you might find in a home or small office.

"Every one of these cameras is wireless," Phillip said. "We use them as temporary cameras for sections of the building not yet plumbed with wiring. The trick is getting a wireless signal to the camera." He pulled out a camera with a router Velcroed to it. "Each of the cameras is already paired with a router." He pointed to stickers on both the camera and the router. "Wireless network name is marked on the router and the camera, just in case they get mixed up. You've got to get the router plugged into an Ethernet port, within about 100 feet of the camera. I'll know when you've added one. With me so far?"

I nodded.

"From your notebook, you can connect up to each wireless router as you go, and you should be able to bring up the camera feed. That's just to check that the camera is connecting to the network. So connect up a router to a port, plug the camera into the wall, and test on your notebook that it's working. Okay? Got it?"

"Yes, sir!" I got it. It wasn't my first time to deal with wireless cameras, and Phillip had made it pretty simple, just as Scan would have.

"Okay," Rej interrupted, "I've sent you three a list of the locations closest to the weak points. There's one main

53

one in each building, then a secondary listing for each building, and a primary location in the tower."

I popped open my email and found the data. "You'll see that a few are in heavily trafficked areas, and you probably already have cameras there. Some are not—they're in the supporting access tunnels or maintenance areas."

"Why don't I take a few of these cameras and get started?" I suggested. "We can't get them all in tonight, but we should try a few and see how hard it will be to patch them in."

"You've already put in a full day, Ms. Hernandez," Phillip said, looking at Alex. "We should wait and start tomorrow."

"I'm good," I assured him. "If I can get at least one going, I'll have a better idea of how to instruct others. It'll go smoother."

"Okay, let's get one in place," Phillip conceded. "Rej, is there one here in the southwest building?"

Rej pointed at my notebook, and I handed it to him with his email opened. He scrolled through the table and pointed at a line. "This one. It's a secondary weak point, but it is close and an excellent test."

He pointed out a hallway in the underground level two of the building we were in—the level we used for transporting cargo between buildings. I was very familiar with those tunnels from the procedural changes I had worked to implement. I grabbed a backpack from a supply room, stuffed a couple of camera-plus-router combos in it, and some Ethernet cable. "Anything else you can think of that I'll need?"

"For maintenance tunnels?" Phillip asked. "Rat traps." I smiled and headed for the stairs. Two flights down to the ground floor, through some security doors, then the two flights down into the tunnels.

I'd been in those tunnels dozens of times. I was just going to set up a camera. So why was my heart racing like I was about to step into a combat zone?

Chapter 12

Red - Day 18, Friday, one day before the attack

The stairs opened into a short hallway next to the brightly lit main transport corridor. The tunnel formed a roughly octagonal ring underground, connecting the four buildings.

There were nooks near each of the large freight elevators, to give room for others to pass while waiting for an elevator.

Service doors sprinkled the main hallway. I studied my electronic map to get oriented. Second door on the left, then take a right turn after about twelve feet, then another twelve foot section and there should be a room the size of a master bedroom in Texas—or my entire flat.

My security card unlocked the door, and I opened it to a completely dark hallway. I fished in a pocket for a penlight, which revealed a corridor lined with pipes, ending in a right-hand turn. No light switch, just emergency lights.

Damn.

My phone didn't work down there, so I pulled out my radio. I spotted a camera in the main transport hall and made a show of waving the radio and then two fingers. I set the radio to channel two and said, "Phillip, this is Garnet Hernandez. You there?" I fought the urge to say "over."

No response.

I waited a minute and tried again. Still nothing. They were probably busy. I didn't like the idea that no one knew where I was. If the door closed behind me and jammed from the inside, and I had somehow gone into the wrong corridor, I could be stuck there for a while. I had my

TASER, my phone, the radio, and my penlight. I propped the door open with my phone at the base. It wasn't doing me any good as a phone—*might as well make it a doorstop.*

I walked down the hall, moving my penlight back and forth between the walls, looking for any sign of an Ethernet connection or power. The light cast creepy shadows, like fingers reaching out to grab me. An odd dripping noise on top of an increasingly loud thrumming made the sensation worse. I reached the corner and shined my light around it, revealing a closed door at the end.

There were plenty of pipes along the wall on which I could mount the camera—and electrical outlets—but no Ethernet. *Wait, is that someone speaking?*

I paused and listened, leary of continuing onward. Despite the spooky drip, I saw nothing wet. No voices, just thrumming. I'd been in more hazardous situations, but the hairs on the back of my neck were standing up. Why the hell would you make a corridor with no lights?

The odd dreams I'd been having crept from the recesses of my brain—magic and monsters escaped the corridors of my mind and hid in the shadows of the pipes. I wanted nothing more than to turn around and get the hell out of that hallway.

Sighing, I started toward the door to the mysterious room, scanning the walls with hopeless desperation for an Ethernet connection. Nothing.

The door had a simple knob, no security card. Presumably the previous door was the only one that needed it. The door I'd jammed open with my phone. *Damn it.* I'd bypassed the security by doing that. I shined the penlight back down the hall I'd come from. Empty. Why did I leave my phone?

I closed my eyes, berating myself. It was just a maintenance hall. I'd been in far worse.

Turning back to the little room, I opened the door, shining my light in.

Electrical room. The mechanical thrumming increased in volume. Sturdy metal boxes lined the walls, dimly illuminated by small readouts on some of them, with a large piece of equipment in the center of the room. A pump for Willy Wonka's chocolate river? A turbine for a steampunk floating pirate ship? Scan would know. I didn't.

But the room had a light switch! I let out the breath I hadn't realized I'd been holding, and I flicked it on.

"POP!"

Jerking back into the hall, momentarily blinded by the flash of light, I heard a tinny buzzing like a fluorescent trying really, really hard to activate, but failing.

Shit!

My heart was racing. I flashed the light back down the hall, and it was all clear, though the penlight beam over the pipes made every shadow seem to grow. I flicked it into the room to the same effect.

Taking deep breaths, I calmed myself, moving the penlight more slowly between the pipe-filled hallway and the metallic-box-filled room. Finally calm enough, I reached in and flicked the light switch off. The tinny buzzing stopped. I flipped the switch back on. That time, just the buzzing. I turned the switch off again and started into the room, shining my light slowly and thoroughly around. I landed on the light switch. Right beside it was an Ethernet port.

Thank God.

I huffed, pulled off my backpack, and rummaged through it. I grabbed the Ethernet cable and plugged it into the wall, then brought it down to the floor so it could go under the door. Later we could poke a hole through the wall if we needed to. I shined the penlight up—some pipes were not tight fits to the sheetrock. Hmm, could I use those gaps?

I unplugged the cable and poked it through the wall on the top of a shoulder-high pipe. I pushed a couple of inches of wire through, then from the inside, jabbed at the sheetrock with the penlight base, enough to poke a hole. I could feel the cable with my fingers and clumsily pulled it through. Plugging it in, I knew I would be able to close the door, and nobody would trip over the wire. I grabbed my backpack and closed the door behind me, glad to be done with the creepy-as-shit room. Assuming the Ethernet port was active. *Please, let it be active.*

I walked back down the hall toward the corner, wrapping the wire around the pipe as I went. When I got to the electrical outlet closest to the corner, I set down the backpack, pulled out the wireless router, plugged the router into the wall, and plugged the Ethernet cable into the router. I used the Velcro on the router to attach it to a pipe. I plugged the camera into the same wall outlet and thought about how I wanted to mount the camera as I let them both boot up. I plopped onto the floor, setting the camera and penlight down and pulling my notebook out of my backpack.

What made sense, I told myself, was to point the camera at the door that led to the main corridor. We would use the camera to watch for people coming into that area. On the other hand, my gut told me I should monitor that creepy-as-shit room with the thrumming beast and the light-popping switches. I laughed at myself, looking at my notebook to see if "WIRELESS12" was showing up yet. It was, so I joined the network, then tried to find devices. The camera was there, so I clicked on it to bring up the feed. All dark, which made sense. I picked up the penlight to point it in the same direction as the camera, looking at my screen.

I could see the light, with a small lag, bringing the hallway into view, showing the… what the heck… the door… the door to the creepy-as-shit room was open!

Hadn't I closed that? I could feel my body drum up the adrenaline.

I dropped the notebook to the floor, rising while pulling my TASER out. Penlight in my other hand, I took a step toward the room. The TASER was not as comforting as my familiar knife handle would have been.

"BWAAAAAAA!" A blaring horn blinded and deafened me.

I covered my eyes with the hand holding the penlight. The horn stopped for a second, then fired up again, and I recognized it as some kind of emergency siren. My eyes adjusting, I could see there was nothing in the hall ahead of me, and I turned back toward the hallway leading to the transport halls—just in time to see the door closing, my phone gone from the doorway.

Then the lights died.

Chapter 13

Heart pounding, I stared at the
door to the transport hall, penlight
pointed that direction, but my
eyesight hadn't recovered. I
stood stock still, listening as
intently as I could. The blaring

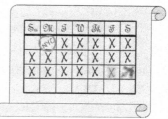

horn had been loud. I doubted I could hear if someone else
was moving in the hall. I flicked off the penlight and
crouched in the corner.

I heard no movement, nothing but the thrumming
and that occasional enigmatic drip.

It was probably only seconds later, though it felt like
an eternity, when the emergency lights flipped back on.
That time, no sirens.

I stood, backed into the corner of an empty hallway,
door to the creepy-as-shit room standing open like a dark
maw, ready to snake out a tongue and pull me in. In the
other direction, the door that led to freedom stood closed.

I stayed still, panting, reacting to the adrenaline. My
brain was trying to process everything. The lights—Phillip
must have turned on the emergency lighting, activating the
emergency siren, then flicked them both off and brought up
just the lights.

I looked down at my notebook and saw a text
message. "Hey, you got the camera working… that looks
creepy."

The camera was still pointed at the electric room,
and I thought, "no shit."

But I picked up the notebook and typed, "Thanks for

the lights." I was glad I was not on camera, my fear visible for anyone to see. I set the notebook down, took up the camera, and Velcroed it to a pipe. I checked the notebook. The image showed the transport hall door, which was the logical thing to watch. Yet, a voice nagged at me, telling me to watch the little room instead. But that didn't make sense, so I ignored it.

I picked the notebook back up and typed, "You'll have to keep these lights on if you want to use the camera." The notebook went back in my pack, which I put on, ready to get out of there.

I walked to the creepy-as-shit room and closed the door, feeling pity for the guys who had to work on the steampunk engine—or fix the broken lights in the room. Even with lights on, the room was foreboding.

On the way out, I stopped and waved to the camera, then opened the door and saw my phone on the floor about a foot away from the door. I picked it up and stared at the shattered screen.

I had convinced myself the phone had slipped. That the vibration from the siren had shaken it loose and the door had closed. But, no. Someone had stepped on my phone.

Chapter 14

Red - Day 18, Friday, one day before the attack

I hurried into Sec Ops, shadows and ghosts tailing me the four flights out of the pit of the tunnels. Once inside, I shut the door, leaning against it, feeling safe—I'd made it back to base. It  put me in mind of playing Green-Eyed Ghost as a kid, getting to base before the designated ghost-kid got me. I laughed quietly at myself as I tried to take slow, calming breaths..

"You okay, Ms. Hernandez?" Alex asked. He and Phillip were both staring. Rej was nowhere to be seen.

Get your shit together, girl. You've been through much worse.

"Just ran up four flights of stairs," I said, taking another calming breath, "Guess I'm not in the shape I thought I was."

I pretended to be winded, but I couldn't kick the feeling that I'd narrowly escaped. The safety of being in Sec Ops quickly faded, and the lingering sense of averted disaster grew. I couldn't afford to lose my job—I needed to get out of there while I still looked sane.

"Things will go more smoothly if you can be sure the lights are on for the other locations that need cameras," I said.

"Will do," Phillip said.

I didn't offer to do more cameras that night. No matter that it made little sense—*something* had been down there with me.

"I'm going to call it, gentlemen," I said. "We've got the process figured out. I'll work on more tomorrow."

We exchanged pleasantries, and I did as I said and left work.

I walked outside to find rain muting the evening, narrowing my visibility to a tight circle. I walked home, looking over my shoulder. There was a familiar wariness, reminiscent of my time overseas, and everything took on a strangely foreign cast. The lights buzzed, and I felt myself flashing back to that room. The signs on every eatery seemed written in other languages, unreadable and uninviting. Voices sounded harsh and abrasive, and the car horns blared echoes of the emergency sirens.

I skulked into my building and waited inside the hallway for a minute—to make sure no one followed me in, and to give my nerves a chance to settle. The coast stayed clear, and I climbed the stairs to my flat. I keyed my way in, and my lights took their sweet time flickering on. "Et tu, Brute?" I said to them and locked my door behind me.

Behind my locked door, alone and safe, I grabbed a beer and settled in, letting my nerves untangle in privacy. After a few minutes, I examined my phone. It was still usable, but irritating to read with the shattered screen. There were unread texts, but I wasn't ready to tackle them. Dang, I didn't have the time nor the money to get a new phone. How could I have been so stupid?

I opened my computer. A text from Scan immediately popped up on one of the messaging apps.

`Ping`

I sighed. I didn't want to share my cowardly evening with my old team any more than I wanted to share with my new team. "There was this really creepy room, and mysterious doors that opened and closed on their own." Yeah, that sounded sane. Hell, I'd been in *combat*. And I feared an empty maintenance hall?

I buried my head in my hands, trying to get it back on straight. I took a few calming breaths, then started typing.

> Hey, Scan. I couldn't find
> a way to bring up your
> observation about the
> cameras in Hong Kong...
> without sounding crazy.

Um, so you didn't bring it up,
or you brought it up and
sounded crazy?

> Didn't bring it up.

Ok. I have nothing new or
better. Think you'll get any
time to talk tomorrow?

> Doubt it. We want to add
> some cameras, so I'll
> probably spend a few hours
> doing that. We would like
> to do more, but we think
> the guys building this
> place will push back hard.
> I expect to lose some
> battles this weekend.

The screen didn't update for a minute, then Scan wrote back.

You're having trouble getting
security to be a priority over
construction, correct?
Financial issues driving the
need to deprioritize security?

Roger that

There was a longer pause before Scan replied.

You might get an unexpected
ally. Come up with some solid
ideas.

I raised my eyebrows but didn't need to know more. Scan had some... *unusual* connections.

Ok. I need to get some
sleep.

Roger that

His response made me smile—the familiar phrase a soothing balm.

I assumed we had finished. Scan would convey any info to Bear and Rocks.

With my beer emptied, I turned off the lights and crawled onto my cot. I was beat but wracked with worry. I closed my eyes, and though sleep remained elusive for a long time, I finally captured it...

The funeral pyre consumed the shrouded body, air spinning the flame, water encircling the base, the earthen stones holding the lifeless form in traditional death robes. It was the first death of someone close to me, and I ached with the emptiness it left in my soul. The flames darted in patterns reaching high into the night sky, licks of fire dancing with the stars that blinked down from their infinite height.

Chapter 15

I woke up from confusing dreams
of warfare and knife fights,
machines with long tongues that
pulled people out of hallways into
their hungry mouths, darkness
and light, sirens and deathly

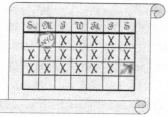

silences. Feeling no more rested than when I'd sunk into
slumber, I rose and fumbled my way to the kitchen, turning
on the lights and squinting as my eyes adjusted. The sun
wasn't up yet, and judging from the rain sluicing down the
windows, I believed it would not make an appearance at all.
I filled my coffee-maker with water, and while it warmed up,
I headed off to the bathroom.

     Minutes later, I sat down at my computer, "Hello,
Darkness, my old friend" coffee mug in hand, filled to the
brim with hot goodness. There were no significant updates
on the Owaie collapse, and searches for "monster attacks"
returned nonsense.

     6:00am, and my coffee was gone. I took a quick
shower and put on my combat boots. It was my day off. I
could wear what I wanted. Besides, my boots had room to
tuck away a knife, which made me much happier than that
TASER.

     I walked to The Palace.

     6:34am.

     I swiped in and nodded to the folks on weekend
security, who greeted me with a quick wave. Sec Ops was
pretty empty. A young Asian woman was manning the
computers in Phillip's place. With black and purple hair,

67

multiple ear piercings, and tattoos of, well, lots of things, going down her arms, she was a stark contrast to Phillip's geeky white engineer look. She subtly bounced her head to music I couldn't hear. Headphones on, she nodded to me in greeting and kept working.

Alex wasn't there, but I didn't need anyone else to get started. I picked up my notebook and prodded it to life. I sent Phillip and Alex a quick email, letting them know I was installing the cameras. Also that I needed to talk with Alex about some increased security we had already discussed. And, lastly, that I'd set the radio on channel two—no point in going through the same mess as the day before.

Most of the locations were underground, levels one through three, except for the one on the 12th floor—the atrium. Since the atrium was already on camera, I didn't need to do anything up there. I took the entire cart of supplies, as it would fit in the main halls and elevators just fine.

I started with the building I was in, figuring it was easier to learn in that building that I was missing some supplies than to learn it out in the next. The location was on sublevel three, and despite being deeper in the earth, the location was not so off-putting as the room the day before. It was a storage room, already lit—*thank you, Phillip!*—and there was both an Ethernet and an electrical outlet available. The entire operation took about twenty minutes. I couldn't count on them all being that easy, but with only six more to go, and even a good bit of walking between buildings, I would finish before lunch.

Alex pinged me on the radio around 9:00am. I was working on the first of the two cameras for the last building. "Morning, Ms. Hernandez."

I stopped and picked up the radio. I had not finished the camera and wireless connections yet, so there was nowhere for him to see me. "Good morning, Mr. Hamdell.

Over." Old habits. At least I didn't say "Sir."

"How is it going?" Slight pause. "Over."

I smiled. I'd train them yet. It just made sense.

"It's going well, sir. I'll be done in less than an hour, and we need to talk. I have some ideas… really it's just *one* idea... but it can wait 'til I finish. Over."

"Okay. I'll be here. You've got six camera feeds coming in so far. Is that what you intended?" Pause. "Over."

"Yes, sir. Six down. Two to go. See you soon. Over."

I finished the final two cameras without incident and headed back.

Chapter 16

Red - Day 19, Saturday, the day of the attack

When I got back to Sec Ops, I parked the cart in a corner and then moved to the computer consoles. Headphone-girl still sat there, bobbing her head to her tunes, and Alex was poring over 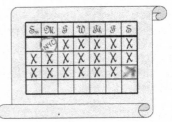 some data on a screen, taking notes with pencil and paper. I walked toward him, brought out my notebook, and set it down next to him. I plugged it in to juice it back up, then brought up the displays of the new cameras, starting with the last one I'd installed and circling backward to the first. They all displayed properly. The last image, the hallway leading to *that* room, made the hairs on my neck stand on end.

Sheesh.

"That one is unnerving," Alex said, looking sideways at the screen.

"How so?" I genuinely wanted to know—I couldn't put my finger on it.

"Don't know exactly. It's just a door. But it gives me the heebee-jeebees."

I nodded once. He couldn't pin it down either. "Can we talk now?"

"Yes. Let's. I'm stumped as to how we can make a proposal for increased security that people will agree to. I can't find one that even makes sense to *me*."

"I had some time to think about that while I was putting in those cameras this morning. We're thinking about it wrong."

"How so?" Alex asked. "We need increased security at the personnel entrances to protect the building and the people inside."

"Maybe," I said enigmatically. "Think about this—we've already identified the weak points in the system. People go in and out of buildings all day—we already accept a certain level of risk in *that*. Almost all the *weak points*, where we mounted cameras, have *security gates*, except one in building B and the one in the upper floors where the buildings come together—the atrium."

"So," Alex said, following my train of thought, "we just need to add a security door in building B. The upper floor will need some special attention, and we tighten the security on those doors." He paused briefly in thought. "We add security classes that explain what is and is not allowed through those doors—and why—and you have to pass the classes to get your badge activated. Plus some kind of personal approval by us. Or we escort people in when they have to work in those areas."

"You think all this is feasible?" I asked.

He ignored my question. "So, we don't increase security at the personnel entrances. We just tighten it at the critical points. That's much better. I feel silly now. I've been laser focused on personnel entrances."

"That'd be best if we could do it," I conceded. "But I don't see how we can."

"Agreed. That's what all this paperwork shows. So, what's the cost now? A new door, which is next to nothing, some training or time lost escorting people—it's all in the noise of our budget." He sighed. "I can't decide whether to be happy for having a solution, or irritated about all the pointless work I did and the sleep I lost."

I smiled ruefully. "It's a stressful job watching out for the safety of others, while trying to keep their lives worth living. Don't be too upset—your paperwork might come in handy. After all, we don't yet understand what happened to the Owaie."

"True," he nodded sadly. He gathered his pile of papers. "Can you pull up the location of the weak point that didn't have a door? We can get the work order in for that. And I'll add a guard posting there in the meantime."

I brought it up on my notebook, and Alex showed me how to bring up the same on a monitor in Sec Ops. We identified where we needed a security door, and Alex put in a work order, teaching me how to do it for the future.

I looked around. "Well, can you think of anything else we need to do to get ready for Monday?"

"No," he said, "I'll mark the exposed area in building B for a security rotation. You know what needs to happen there, so you can explain it to whoever gets the rotation. I think we're done for now. Thank you for coming in."

"You're staying?"

"For now. Hon-chi covers for me on the weekends, and he is doing some rounds. When he gets back, I'll take off. Go. Enjoy what's left of your day."

I nodded and turned to leave. Not having any specific plans, because I'd thought I'd be at The Palace all weekend, I pulled out my busted phone and texted the guys.

```
I can meet this evening if
y'all are free. 5:30.
Usual place.
```

It didn't end up being the relaxing evening I'd hoped for.

Chapter 17

Red - Day 19, Saturday, the day of the attack

Bear had recommended a gym—
the one where he'd met a girl—
and I had a few hours, so I
burned up some energy working
out. I liked the gym, and signed
up to become a member. Plus,

maybe I'd meet Bear's new girlfriend, and make sure she
checked out? I hit some weights, knowing I would be
pleasantly sore the next day. Also, I learned about a martial
arts class, and the thought of keeping some form of
defense training appealed to me. Tuesday for the class—I'd
try to remember.

After my workout, I swung by my flat and cleaned up,
then met the guys at Tom's. The crowd was different on a
Saturday—there were more families instead of the young
working crowd. Knee-biters bumped the noise level up. The
tavern boiled over with racket and activity, but Rocks and
Scan already had a table. Bear joined us soon after.

I told them about my week, and Scan brought me up
to speed on what he had dug up—he found those weird
camera distortions from Hong Kong in a few other
metropolitan areas. As far as he could tell, no one was
connecting them up as related events.

"So you don't think you need influence on the
business side anymore?" Scan asked.

"No. I think I'm okay, so you can call off whatever
you had in motion."

Scan and Rocks exchanged a look.

"Can't," Rocks said. "Too late."

I put my head in my hands. "What have you done?"

"Old Man Penbrook announced his retirement from the board of La Penbrook Palencia. It happened yesterday. The news became public a few hours ago. There's a new member on the board."

"Already? How is that possible? You engineered this?"

Rocks and Scan exchanged another glance—a guilty one.

"Seriously? How could you possibly pull that off? Do you have some kind of dirt on—"

Rocks interrupted, "Well I have tons of dirt on Old Man Penbrook, but I didn't have to use it."

I gaped at Rocks. Scan reached across the table and gently pushed my jaw closed.

"What the—"

Again I didn't get to finish. "Here," Rocks said, "just read it for yourself." He handed me his cell phone, opened to a news site.

"Clinton Penbrook, Heart and Soul of The Palace, Retires from the Board of Directors," read the headline. There were images of The Palace, and the man Rocks had referred to as "Old Man Penbrook," who looked to be in his early fifties, hardly retirement age for his line of work in such a driven family. I continued to read, "The seat on the board was handed down to his second son, Reginald Penbrook, whose time in the military Clinton felt certain would lead The Palace through the storm of safety concerns, after the disastrous destruction of the Owaie building in Hong Kong." The picture below showed the fifty-ish-year-old man shaking hands with a younger man... with an artificial leg.

I was stunned. "Seriously?" I said, looking at Rocks. "Your real name is fucking Reginald?"

"Just Reginald," he said, eyes dancing. "Only

Cynthia calls me 'fucking Reginald,' and only in the heat of passion." He winked.

I laughed, but was struggling to wrap my mind around the news. "You're rich. Not just rich, you're *filthy* rich."

"My *family* is rich. There's a difference."

I looked at Scan. "You obviously knew." I turned to Bear. "Did *you* know?"

"I still don't know," he replied. "What are you talking about?"

Normally it was my job to do explanations for Bear, but I sat quietly, stunned. I didn't really listen as Rocks explained. How could he have gone all that time without mentioning his family was *rich*? True, I never talked about my sisters or parents, but that was different. Wasn't it? Did I really even know Rocks at *all*?

I decided I couldn't deal with his secret-keeping right then. Or maybe I didn't like being reminded of my own skeletons in the closet... or maintenance hall. I slapped my hand on the table and changed the subject. "Okay, Bear, tell us about this woman you've met."

All eyes turned to Bear. Clearly that was also news. Bear looked at everyone. "I met a girl I like. Akira Tanaka. She's Japanese-American."

My mind was already spinning. Bear's gym had consisted of bodybuilders at the weights, and martial artists on the mats. I hadn't seen any Japanese bodybuilders, so one of the martial artists?

"We've been out a few times, and it seems to be going well."

Just then, my phone vibrated. I picked it up and saw that it was a call from work—Sec Ops. "Sorry, Bear, this is work." Covering my other ear, I pressed the answer button. "Hello?"

"Ms. Hernandez?"

"Speaking."

"This is Hon-chi Nguyen, from work. I wanted to see if you could help with something. A camera feed went out. We already sent someone down, and there does not seem to be actual trouble, so no cause for great alarm. I have someone posted by the entrance to that hall. The notes say you installed the cameras, and no one here knows the details. Could you help us get the camera going again?"

"Where's your tech guy? Or girl?" I hastily added the latter.

"Almost everyone is gone. I don't know if it's the weather or what, but the building is practically empty, and even a good bit of security called in sick tonight. We've got just a skeleton crew here."

The idea of going back to The Palace at night filled me with dread, but I felt a sense of duty regarding my work. Plus, at the thought of being scared away by shadows, I became angry with myself. "I should be able to help. Give me an hour, and I'll come in."

"Okay. Thanks. We appreciate it."

I clicked off my phone and asked Rocks to get me some water, needing to dilute the alcohol in my system. I ate my fries, drank my water, learned a little more about Bear's girlfriend, and tried to joke with my friends.

But I couldn't stop thinking about that camera. I knew exactly which one had gone out.

Chapter 18

After fighting another battle through driving rain, I entered The Palace and checked into Sec Ops. I let Hon-chi know that I would have channel two open on the radio, then took the

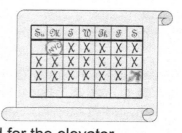

equipment cart with me and headed for the elevator.

I found a guard out in the transport hall, protecting the door into the hallway. After a quick greeting, I explained that I was there to fix a camera, and swiped my badge to unlock the maintenance hall door.

Of course the lights were out.

Holding the door open, I asked the guard, "Were the lights out earlier?"

"Yes, ma'am."

He looked nervously at the door, drumming up his courage. I had a sneaking suspicion that no one had actually gone all the way in to check the camera.

I should have grabbed a better flashlight.

Nodding to the guard, I shined my penlight into the corridor, then turned and backed into the hall, blocking the door open with the cart.

Turning back around, I picked up the radio and asked Hon-chi if he could figure out how to activate the emergency lights. He said he would try, but I could tell that neither of us expected that to happen. I grabbed my notebook and walked into the hell... the *hall*... I went into the hall. I couldn't understand how walking down that hall took longer than made sense. The familiar thrumming

77

became louder, as did my old friend, the drip. I found the camera still mounted, and its electrical cord still plugged in. The wireless router with the Ethernet cable was out of my line of vision, around the corner.

As I approached the corner, I shined my penlight around it. The door was blessedly closed. I pulled the camera down, and I could see that it was on, and at least *trying* to work.

Since the camera worked, I put it back. I could test the wireless with my notebook. I found the network and popped onto it. After a few clicks, I brought up the camera. On my notebook, connected to the wireless network, I could see the video feed of the light coming from the transport hall.

If the wireless and camera were up... I picked up my radio, "You've still got no image coming from this cam in Sec Ops, right? Over."

"No. Just an empty screen."

Damn. "Okay. Over." And it felt dreadfully over, because the only possibility remaining was the Ethernet cable, which meant I had to go back into *that* room.

I double-checked—the cable connected soundly to the router. And I could see it going into the wall where I had punched the small hole.

Geez, I really didn't want to go back in there.

I walked down to the door, creepy shadows following me like before. It shouldn't have mattered, being down in the tunnels, but the shadows somehow knew it was night, and they had free rein. I stood there a second, my nerves rattled as hell, but something felt wrong. More wrong than the last time.

Trusting my gut, and fighting my fear, I turned off my light. I let my eyes adjust to the darkness, trying to slow my breath and calm my nerves. I looked back toward the corner, seeing a hint of light penetrating the gloom from the transport hallway. Not a lot, but a little. Looking at the door before me, I also saw a whisper of light—up near the small hole for the Ethernet cable.

That was wrong. There was nothing in there bright enough to cast a flickering light through that hole. I put my hand on the knob, slowly and noiselessly turning it, then cracked the door wide enough to see that there were indeed some lights glowing inside, reminding me of the low illumination of fireflies, or distant stars. I pushed the door open far enough to snake my head and shoulders through, hearing that damn thrumming but something else as well.

Birdsong?

Chapter 19

Red - Day 19, Saturday, the day of the attack

My brain struggled to process what my eyes were telling me. The simplest piece was the figure with his or her back turned, robed and chanting in a foreign tongue, arms slowly moving along with 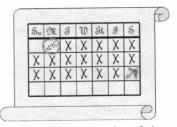 the chant—performing an eerie musical in the bowels of the earth. Its vocal range was somewhere between male and female, and in a less freaky context, it would have been quite lovely. The figure's location perplexed me, as it stood right where the massive piece of thrumming equipment had been the last time I had been there. In fact, I had a confusing vision of both images existing at once before my brain made sense of it and left me with just the robed figure. The machine wasn't there at all—just open floor.

If my skin was already crawling, the rest of what I saw made it get up and walk away. Glyphs of light floated in the air, dancing around the figure. Each glyph differed from its neighbors, some curvy and elegant, some harsh slashes of light, but they all circled around, moving with the rhythm of the chant, very Disney-like.

The light cast from the glyphs danced off the walls in a kaleidoscopic array. The room had the heavy odor of scorched metal in a weld shop mixed with the scent of bare earth.

Involuntarily, I mouthed "what the fudge?" and the figure froze. Had it heard me? Was I in danger? Knowing I had likely lost the element of surprise, I yelled the first thing that popped in my head. "Freeze!"

The figure stood still, its back to me. The dancing glyphs slowed and dimmed like the batteries had run out of a nightlight. What would I do if I lost the light?

The figure spoke, in a sing-song language I didn't know—that was the birdsong I'd heard! The robed hands moved slightly, and I tensed. "I said freeze! Don't make me shoot you." Not that I had a gun.

The figure chuckled, and I felt a strange sort of echo. I heard the voice continue to speak the foreign tongue and, at the same time, heard, "Okay, I wasn't sure that would work."

Was that *English*? Just looking at the robed figure, I didn't expect English.

The lights dimmed even more. I needed to act before my target slipped away—or caused me harm—in the dark. But as I stepped forward, my head exploded with pain.

Everything went black.

Chapter 20

Red - Day 19, Saturday, the day of the attack

I groggily came back to awareness. Muddled and confused, I still thought I heard voices overlapping—English and birdsong. "There, I've Healed the worst of her injuries."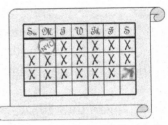

"Why?" said an unfamiliar voice, low and rumbling. I heard both a guttural almost-growl, with the same voice uttering that single word in English.

"Because we are here to save them!" the singsong voice answered with exasperation.

After a pause, the guttural voice replied, slowly, "We are trying to save their *world*." Another pause. "You know there will be losses."

"I know!" the singsong voice said irritably. "But I could have handled this one. You needn't have bashed her skull open."

That explained the sudden pain. The pain had vanished, replaced by extreme weariness, and I longed to slip back into slumber.

"You are the one who chose this particular tactic," spoke the low, guttural voice. "You know there will be injuries and death as a result. 'A small price compared to the numbers that will be lost if we do not,' you said."

"I know what I said! You needn't quote me to myself." The voice sighed, a bird's mournful cry. "I know I make no sense."

"Worry not," said the guttural voice. Worry not? Who says *worry not*? "It is better that you struggle with sacrificing

82

pawns. I have seen when your people have no care, and it is unfathomably worse. Though your newfound conscience makes things... *difficult*... at times."

The birdsong sigh sounded again, followed by, "You are truly the strangest," another bird-chirp noise, "that I have ever met."

The guttural voice made a choking noise, and said, "I would that you had met more of my people. I will remove her body, somewhere safe... where she will not be harmed by your work... or by me."

"Thank you," another nonsensical sound, "...don't take too long. You know where I will be, and what will be coming."

There was an acknowledging grunt, and seconds later, I felt my body being lifted. The blood rushed to my head, causing my slight hold on consciousness to slip away.

Chapter 21

Red - Day 19, Saturday, the day of the attack

I awoke on the ground…. literal earth… I smelled the grass and the soggy soil. It was dark, still night, and while it had stopped raining, I could feel the storm looming.

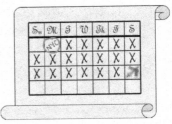

    I was lying face down, with my head to the side. A sudden flash of lightning revealed a hulking figure walking away. I tried to follow, but my body wouldn't obey. I haltingly climbed up onto my hands and knees. The world wobbled, and I held still. I then crawled my way to a nearby tree and used it to help me stand. It all took too long. The figure was getting away, and in the darkness there was little chance I would find him again.

    I took a few fumbling steps in the right direction, then my clumsy muscles and head stopped cooperating. I leaned against a tree and earned a downpour of cold droplets that startled me into wakefulness. A few more steps and I paused at another tree, producing another unintentional shower. I moved more steadily, hoping I still headed the right way. The only logical place I could be was Central Park, but I was in a thickly treed section, and the ambient lighting was sketchy.

    I could see a break in the trees, and as my body was responding better, I hurried toward it. The trees opened up to a trail. It looked like a part of North Park. I saw a few people out during the break in the rain, but no one coming from my direction. No one looking suspiciously like they had just left a body in the woods.

I'd lost him.

I'd also lost my phone, and my wallet was in my locker at work.

Shit.

Time to start hoofing it.

Weary, but full of anxious energy, I pushed myself, clumsily loping toward the northeast, following the trail until I hit the road.

I usually saw police around, but not that night. My legs steadied, and I jogged toward The Palace, but I wasn't sure what to expect. My head struggled to beat back the fog of what I'd heard and seen. Whatever those conspirators were doing, it wasn't worth killing me to get it done. Industrial espionage? Or taking down the building?

How had they even gotten in? What had they done to the guard stationed at the transport hall? Had they bribed him or dumped *him* in the woods too?

I couldn't think what to do. God, I was tired. I shouldn't have been that tired. I was so weary it was hard to think. Without my phone I couldn't get ahold of anyone.

Wait, I thought. From my apartment, I could reach Scan on my computer. Was it better to get backup, or would that cost precious time?

I changed course, heading for my apartment.

I didn't even know what time it was—nine, ten, eleven pm? As long as my guys hadn't stayed at the bar drinking, I could ping Scan, and he would mobilize the others. Bear had a badge; he could get in the building directly. I'd need his strength based on the size of the guy that left me in the woods. Sometimes size matters. Rocks could justifiably show up as well in his new role. Scan didn't need to be there—at least not physically. His skills were cyber and engineering, and if he could find his way into the security of The Palace, he could help.

I felt a little calmer with the beginnings of a plan in

place. But, with that calm, the adrenaline faded, and I realized just how bad I felt. I had pulled all-nighters in the army, and it felt like those. That blow to my head must have been bad—probably a concussion. Pushing through the weariness was hard, but I had to go on.

I reached my apartment building, tailgated in behind a couple too preoccupied with each other to notice me, and climbed the stairs. *Shit. No keys.*

But I needed the laptop that sat inside.

Damn.

I kicked my own door in.

Exhausted, I dropped into my chair, went online, and pinged Scan.

> Scan, I need help. Phone is gone. See if you can have Rocks and Bear meet me at the SW entrance to The Palace.

Within seconds he pinged back.

> Can do. Two things. Please wait a minute.

I waited, trying not to nod off.

> One - I'll have someone at the same place with a burner phone for you.

> Two - those camera distortions we saw in Hong Kong. I'm picking them up in New York as of a few hours ago. Be careful. Over.

> Roger that

Everyone needs a friend like Scan.

I closed my laptop, and stashed it on the top shelf of a kitchen cabinet, out of sight. It was the only thing worth stealing in my whole flat. I grabbed an energy bar, then a second one, and left, propping my only chair against the door as I closed it. Was there any chance my laptop would be there when I returned?

Assuming I returned.

Chapter 22

Red - Day 19, Saturday, the day of the attack

I stood across the street from the southwest entrance to The Palace. There I was, alone, dried mud caked onto my clothes, standing in front of a coffee shop.

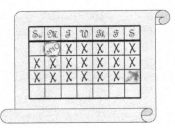

Not suspicious at all.

And the energy bars hadn't done their job.

A silver Honda Civic drifted to a stop on the corner. The passenger window rolled down. A man—Indian, if I had to guess—leaned over from the driver seat. "Red?"

I nodded.

"What am I bringing you?" His voice was wrought with suspicion.

"A phone."

He raised his eyebrows but reached out a hand toward the window. I took a couple of steps toward him and grabbed the phone. Without a word he raised the window and drove off. Seconds later, the phone rang.

I clicked the answer button. "Red here."

"Red." It was Scan. "Bear will be there shortly. Rocks is farther out. Get me up to speed."

"We had the lead engineer for The Palace identify weak points for the structure. I set up cameras for the locations, and one of them tripped this evening—that was the call I got at the bar earlier."

"With you so far," Scan said.

"There was something about that room, Scan. Something strange was going on. When I arrived, I saw only one person, but I took a blow to the head, so there must have been more than one. I blacked out and woke up getting dumped in Central Park. Ran back to my flat and pinged you."

"Geez, Red! Are you okay?"

"I'll live," I answered, letting myself feel, just for a moment, the total weariness I was trying to ignore.

"What was the strange thing going on?" Scan asked.

"The man I *did* see seemed to be performing some kind of ritual."

"A ritual? Like a sacrifice?"

"I saw nothing to sacrifice, but I remember hearing birds. And there were these lights, floating around the room." I suddenly felt very stupid. Why had I called in the troops again? "Look, I know this doesn't make sense—"

"No worries, Red. You don't brain-bash someone and drop them in a park for charity work. And we've got your back even if you turn out to be wrong. Got a plan yet?"

"I don't know what happened to the other guard. And I don't know if there are people on the inside or not."

I paused. He'd asked me for a plan, not my laundry list of cluelessness. I needed a plan.

"I'll send Bear in first," I declared. "Given the skeleton crew on tonight, he can get me in through a back door. I'll start walking to the northwest building right now. Have him go there once he enters, then tell him to call me. I know a place he can let me in." There was a service door he could open from the inside. It would register his doing so, but maybe Scan could erase that.

"Okay, I'll let Bear know what to do. Be careful." The line went dead, and I started toward the specified building.

The phone rang again. "It's Scan. Just go in, Red. Bear says there were no guards on duty, no sign of a fight. He just walked in."

"No guards on duty? What in the hell?" I started running. "Have him meet me in Sec Ops—the control

89

room."

I heard him talking away from the phone. Then he was back. "Done. I'm hacking into the building security."

I ran inside. Bear was right. No guards. The station looked abandoned. My badge had disappeared with my phone, so I leaped the waist-high station—I would skip the alarm sensors if I did it right.

Once inside, with no alarm, I realized my mistake. To get to Sec Ops, I would have to head down two levels to the underground tunnels and connect back up in the southwest building. I should have turned around and run back when I was still outside. I considered going straight to the maintenance room where I'd been bushwhacked, but I'd lose phone connection and have no way to let Bear know how to find me. So I did what I had to—I ran down a couple of floors, dashed through the transport tunnel as fast as I could, and took the stairs up four levels to Sec Ops. The climb up required a pause to catch my breath—I was not on my game.

Bear was waiting there, alone, with radios and guns. I looked at the monitor with the special cameras. No activity—and one dead channel. I put on my headphones. "This is Red. Do you read me?"

"I read you," Scan said.

"Still here," Bear said, and I heard him both in my headphones and right beside me. Flashback to the robed figure with dual voices.

"Scan," I said, "get Rocks to call Alex, the head of security. Let him know something is going on here. I don't believe he is in on this, and if I'm wrong..." I paused, reconsidering. What if Alex *was* involved? "Send the information anonymously, so it doesn't tip our hand."

"On it," he replied.

"Guns. Lights. Radio. Let's roll," I said.

Bear followed me out, back down the stairs to sub

level two and the maintenance hall. I wondered if I would have to shoot my way through the door, since I'd lost my badge. If they'd already tightened security, then Bear's might not work. Bear scanned his badge, and I heard the door click. I pushed it open and found the cart with the security cameras sitting inside.

The hallway was dark, but it did not have the sense of foreboding I was expecting. It was just a hall with pipes. I stepped carefully, but swiftly, around the corner, with Bear covering me. We arrived at the maintenance/electrical room. I opened the door, head low in case someone inside was armed and twitchy.

The room looked empty. I moved in, Bear covering high behind me. I flashed the light around but saw nothing. No giant piece of machinery out of some sci-fi movie, no robed and chanting figure from a fantasy film. The middle of the room was empty. There was a strange earthy incense smell. "Do you smell that?" I asked Bear.

"Smells like Christmas at Aunt Judy's," he answered.

I hadn't imagined the whole thing after all.

Out of curiosity, I flashed the light at the Ethernet cable. It was plugged in. But, following the cord up, I could see it was severed, dangling over a lower pipe, with the other end of the cut sticking out of the wall. The wall had a gash near the cord, like something big and sharp had hit it, though I saw no obvious broken pipe or metal strut that might have committed the crime. Whether intentional or not, the result was the lost camera feed to Sec Ops.

"Scan," I said. "There's no one here."

"I'm still trying to get into the system. Your buddy, Phil, has mad cyber skills. Anywhere else the bad guys might be?"

"Negative," I said. "All the other camera feeds were working. I looked before we came down." Then it hit me. "Except one."

Shit.

"Come on, Bear. Back to Sec Ops."

He grunted and followed me back out and up the four flights. I was breathing heavily when we reached the ground level and had to stop. "Sorry, Bear. I'm not feeling so great." He nodded and waited. When I was ready, we continued up—more slowly than before.

Looking around at the monitors in Sec Ops, I did not immediately see what I was searching for. Somewhere in there was a feed showing the upper level atrium. I walked down the line of monitors, looking ahead faster than I could walk. Nope. Nope. And there it was. Multiple feeds in fact. The room was large, and right in the middle of it was my robed person, chanting.

Bear saw what I was looking at and grunted.

"What?" asked Scan.

"We have eyes on them." I moved over to the monitor, hoping I could see more. I looked down at the controls. Could I operate them?

"There's a big open area on the twelfth floor. They call it the atrium. The robed guy, he's in there, up on a stage set in the center of the room, chanting." Lights danced around him, as before. I pointed at a shadow. "There," I said. "There's someone in that shadow. We have to assume there are more."

"I'm almost in, I think," Scan said. "Rocks called Alex. They're both moving. So, backup is on the way, though not exactly the cavalry yet."

"Understood. Bear and I will head up."

I inhaled deeply—in through the nose, out through the mouth—but it did nothing to calm the pounding in my chest.

Chapter 23

Red - Day 19, Saturday, the day of the attack

We reached the 12th floor via the stairs, with multiple rests along the way. Though I had climbed some tough terrain in my time, I couldn't remember feeling more exhausted. But walking out of the

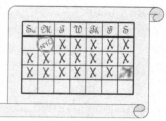

elevators would have been a dead giveaway—literally.

Coworkers had informed me I should take one of my work breaks in the atrium, just to *see* it, but I hadn't yet. If not for the threat to The Palace, I would've happily taken a break right then. I could see with my own eyes what I had learned from Rej—the atrium was there because of those four huge beams forming a pyramid at the top of the room. On that floor, they took up so much space that the architect made them part of the design. The important part for me was that, while there were four staircases clearly visible from the center stage, there were another four concealed by the beams. We had chosen a concealed stairway, but it put us farther from the action.

The stage had amphitheater floors sloping up and away from it. There were no seats at that point, just wide open space. No concealment. There were plans for concerts, or investor meetings, or expo displays, or whatever. Right then, it hosted a lone figure, chanting, glyphs of light dancing around him.

"I'm in the system," Scan said over the headset. "Trying to get to the camera feeds."

I signaled, and Bear and I split at the stairs. He moved to the right, and I went left. I had no sense of where that colossal figure hid in the shadows. So we each crept around one side of the beam whose stairs we had climbed. I could hear the birdsong chanting, which meant we would be audible if we spoke. I didn't hear the "double voice" in English, just the chanting.

"Okay, I've got the feeds," Scan said. "My god, that's a lot of cameras. And that place isn't even done yet. Let's see… this is probably a floor number. So one of these… yeah, okay, I have eyes on you, and the stage. Looking for more."

I paused. Having recon from Scan would be better than exposing myself to look around.

"I see only two others," he said. "One gargantuan man. The lighting is bad, but he seems to have strange tattoos, or facial deformities… or both. He's definitely armed, but not guns… *knives*… one in each hand… took a lesson out of your playbook, Red… and get this, he's got a damned axe on his back. Like something from Worlds of Warcraft. He's between the two of you, closer to Bear. I'd say let Red distract him, then Bear comes from behind."

"Roger that," I whispered. An axe—the cut cord and damaged wall in the maintenance room!

"The other guy is across from the giant," Scan continued. "So you'll both be completely exposed to him. Red, go back and swing away from Bear to the next entrance. Come out closer to the short guy."

I started back, crossed the aisle in some deep shadows, and crept around to the entrance Scan thought would be better.

"And he is short," Scan reported, "but wide, with a beard reaching down to his waist. He's carrying… well, I guess it's a club… looks very unwieldy."

Knives? Axes? Clubs? What were we walking into?

"I don't see anyone else. Or any guns… nothing with a range except those knives, if Big Guy throws them. Their setup seems like a crappy way to defend a position. Hold on. Let me check on Rocks."

I heard shuffling through the radio as I moved into position. Scan came back on. "Rocks is there. He's outside, waiting on Alex... who is probably the other guy I see coming up the street. *Shit*."

I froze. I couldn't ask what was wrong—I was too close to the enemy.

"Sorry, guys," Scan said, "but that distortion we saw in the Hong Kong cameras? I just saw it on the cameras here. It was moving fast, headed to The Palace. No casualties, but it's in the building. I don't know what you should expect, but if you want to act, now is the time."

I wanted to neutralize the immediate threat before confronting the next. Knowing Scan would see me, I nodded.

"Red is nodding yes," Scan said. "Be ready, Bear. Red, see if you can draw Big Guy out a few feet."

The birdsong chanting had gotten louder, and the light grew brighter.

I stepped around the corner, gun pointed toward the robed figure, trying to find the "tiny bearded man" in my peripheral. "Freeze, Snow White!" I shouted, walking forward.

For a second, everyone froze.

Then they all moved at once.

The figure in robes clapped its hands above its head, and a beam of light shot out from the floor, surrounding the figure and blasting up to the vaulted ceiling. There, the light hit the beams and began crawling its way back down them in a way I'd never seen light behave.

The giant across the chamber moved faster than humanly possible. I'd pulled him forward, but too fast—he was too far out of range to make an easy target for Bear. I could see flashes of light off a knife flying toward me.

To my right, I saw movement as well, like a small train barreling my way.

I took a step back to avoid the knife while drawing a bead on the approaching train. Taking the shot on the robed figure would have left me exposed. I didn't intend to die for a beam of light.

Wait, hadn't the Owaie building been surrounded by a light before it imploded? Shit!

I fired at the figure racing at me, hitting him square in the torso, but it didn't slow him at all. He held a Thor-hammer out in front of him like a shield and smashed into my chest. I felt ribs snap as I flew backward, landing twenty feet away in the empty seating area. I could barely breathe. But I didn't need breath to fire my gun. The little man moved toward Bear and the giant, but I was facing the wrong way to see what happened. My headpiece had popped out of my ear but was dangling close enough that I could still hear Scan. "I've lost visuals. The whole tower—all cameras are out."

I lay crumpled on my side and took aim at the Disney Princess on stage, ignoring my excruciating pain. I paused when someone rushed Disney from behind. The assailant crashed into the princess, sending her flying in my direction, a little past my feet.

I didn't watch to see if she stuck her landing, instead keeping my eyes on the new figure in the light beam. I finally had to let go of my tenuous grip on reality. The thing in the light was clearly not human, skin dark as night—hell, *absorbing* the light—taller than most humans, and it roared soundlessly. It not only sucked in the light coming from the ground, it pulled down the magical light that had burst upward—drawing the light into the place where a mouth should have been.

I took no time to dwell on the unreality of my circumstance. I emptied two chambers into the hideous creature's gullet, hoping to send the bullets out through its brain cavity.

The creature's head exploded, and it crumpled in a heap. No time to celebrate. I turned to Bear. He was still upright. The colossus and the short man had moved away from him and were charging toward me at breakneck speed.

Before I could raise my gun, the giant was over me with his battle-axe. I expected sharp pain, then quick death, but it didn't come. The giant's trajectory was off. He aimed above me with a crosscut, not the top-down slice that would've instantly decapitated me. The axe embedded itself into the chest of another of those creatures, and its upper body flew past me, splattering me with ichor.

Giant Axe shifted position to tower over the body of Disney Princess. Short Hammer watched the shadows in the corners of the room, putting his back to the giant's. The light from the beam on the stage faded.

Bear started toward us, and neither the giant nor his companion seemed concerned. The giant grunted, which drew my attention to his face. Instead of eyebrows, he had rocky protrusions. His nose was wide and flat, his jaw large, his face lined with cracks like the sun-beaten ground. His other exposed skin—on his arms and hands—was similarly patchy, like stones cobbled together.

The short bearded man kept scanning the shadows, then reached down and touched the robed figure's hand with the top of the hammer, and muttered something. His hammer glowed blue, then faded, and the figure by my feet stirred.

Bear approached cautiously, gun drawn and aimed at the larger figure. I tried to motion to him that I was okay—or at least not feeling threatened. They were looking for monsters, not trying to harm us.

I struggled to breathe. I knew I had broken ribs, but

my lungs were intact. As I struggled to sit up—and failed—the robed figure rose slowly to its feet.

Bear had stopped moving forward but still had the gun pointed at the giant. Disney looked around, turned to me, and walked over. Bear redirected the gun to point at Disney, but the giant moved to block Bear's aim, ready to take the bullet himself. Disney reached down and put a hand on my face. I wanted to swipe the hand away, but moving would have hurt too badly. The lighting was terrible—I couldn't pick out hair color or eye color, but I could see the light hairs on Disney's hands. *I think I got the princess's gender wrong.* He chirped a few words, and there was a flash of blue.

Oh my god, I could breathe again! I literally felt my bones reattach, felt the minor cuts stitch up. Dumbfounded, I climbed to my feet, ignoring the hand being offered to help.

Disney chirped a few more words, hands waving slightly, then the giant spoke. "You Healed her. Again. Why?" Again, guttural grunts and a voice overlapped.

"I don't know, *chirrup*," Disney answered. "I'm right that she blew the head off that *tweet-chirp*?"

"She did," said the short bearded man.

"And she pushed through the wards more than once?"

"She did," grunted the giant.

"And she got back in the fight after a resurrection, correct?"

With a grumbling sigh, the giant said, "She did, but she was also very easy to kill. Human skulls are like eggshells."

What? I died?

Instead of responding, Disney kept the questions coming. "And was the Guardian moving for *her* or *me*?"

"The Guardian!" laughed the giant, mirthlessly. "In

what world…"

The robed man put a hand to his head. "Sorry, my head hurts." He did look rattled, but who wouldn't after the hit to the noggin he'd taken? "Who was the creature attacking?"

"Her, *old* friend." The giant hit the word *old* hard— some shared history or joke?

"Okay, then. Probably worth having her on our side."

"On our *side*?" the goliath laughed again. "It is her job to *stop* us. She aimed her weapon at *you* before the *snort-growl* knocked you out of the *grumble*."

The dialogue was hard to follow. For most things I would hear two sounds. One was English and the other depended on the speaker—chirps and tweets from Disney, grumbles and growls from the giant, and a kind of rumble from the short man. It was like I had Google Translate running in my ear, with glitches on the tough words.

"I can aim my gun at you again, if needed," I threatened. Even in the poor lighting, I could see the giant's smile. Behind him, Bear tapped his ear. I grabbed my loose earphone and put it back in.

"Red here," I said.

"Video is back," Scan said. "I think I've got the controls for the lights. Be ready."

The robed figure spoke. "She's got comms." Then a pause. "The wards are blown. People are coming back."

"Do we have time to—" the giant started to ask.

"No," interrupted Disney, "nor do I have enough energy. We should go. Get close."

Ignoring the robed figure, the short man spun his hammer around and threw it toward the ceiling where it hit one of the four beams. The result was sparks and a thunderous gong, then the hammer fell back to the man's arms. He nonchalantly caught it, grumbling, "I'd like to meet the engineer that designed this…"

99

The robed figure returned to the stage and gathered his belongings. The giant and the short man moved in close to the robed figure. All three looked at me. "We will talk again soon, 'Red'." I could hear the quotes around my name. "We are trying to save your world, but we are going to need your help... and you are not going to like it."

He waved his arms and chanted something that did not get translated. With a distant pop, the lights flashed on. I had a brief, but clear, image of the three of them. The giant—looking more than ever like a construct of rock cobbled together—reminded me of movies and stories about trolls. Battered brown leathers covered his legs and torso, the shirt smothered with pockets like cargo pants meant for one's chest. Oversized jewelry adorned his neck and wrists, using chains that would have protected a bike from anything short of bolt-cutters, normal on his mighty frame.

The short man—too wide by far to be human—flexed massive rock-crushing arms as he secured his weapon to his back. *Dwarf*, my mind decided—Dwarf wielding a big freakin' Hammer. He wore leathers like the troll, but black, lacking the plethora of pockets, and the center of the shirt was tied together—a weak point if I ever needed to slip in a dagger.

And the robed figure in the middle—thin, with smooth, elegant musculature and golden wavy hair, pointed ears peeking from beneath. His golden pupils matched his hair. A *Lord of the Rings* elf. His robe flowed like silk, green and brown with glyphs in a lighter green, mystic leaves on a vine.

Just then, light flared brightly from the stage, and the space where the triad had been stood empty.

Chapter 24

Red - Day 19, Saturday, the day of the attack

I moved to the vacated space on the stage, and Bear angled to meet me there. I could still smell the aroma the others had left behind—earthy and minty like I'd smelled in the tunnels below The

Palace. There was nowhere to hide, no wall they could have fled behind that quickly. Had they hypnotized me and just strolled away? I didn't think so, but as long as there were otherworldly beings roaming the world, and sudden healing of bones, why not teleportation?

Bear and I looked at the dead monstrous bodies, one with the top of its head removed, and one that had been severed mid-chest. They had neither eyes nor mouth, but there was skin stretched tight where those peripherals should have been. No protruding nose nor ears, but tiny holes in their places. No hair. Skin black as night, though, in death, they didn't absorb light the way they had when alive. Their hands were taloned, fingers four to six inches long, the last inch sharp, bony protrusions. Not good for anyone who had to fight those things.

"I guess we just wait for people to show up?" I asked. Bear shrugged.

Scan chimed in over the headset. "I don't know, Red. I imagine you're not supposed to have brought those guns into The Palace. And they're going to wonder why you didn't call anyone else in. I could clear the tapes, but I think you used Bear's badge, didn't you?"

Bear nodded.

"I can clear that, too, but it's a whole different system. I'd have to get moving. What's your call?"

I wouldn't be able to explain the situation to other people without sounding insane. Plus, I'd be a suspect. "Clear the tapes. C'mon, Bear, let's roll. Does it matter where we exit?"

"Nope. Any way out is fine. I'll torch the footage. Okay, hitting the badge storage. This'll be tricky. Get out. Fast. Alex won't notice I'm here, but I'll have to bail once Phillip shows—he will see me for sure."

One last thing—I wasn't leaving without a souvenir. The troll's thrown blade was still implanted in the wall. The length of my forearm, it had flowing symbols carved into the metal, and a curvy blade with notches for catching other blades.

"Take it," Scan said in my ear. I grabbed the hilt to pull it out, saw a flash of blue in the blade, and felt an espresso-like jolt of energy.

"Alex and Rocks are in Sec Ops," Scan said. "But I've got the video feeds. They can't see you. Get going."

We fled down the stairs, and Scan continued to feed us information, while carrying out some cyber infiltration. "Alex is calling in his guys, and has Rocks helping with the government agencies—police, Homeland Security..."

Descending the stairs was less tiring than climbing them, but I was beyond tired. Scan's chatter was a helpful distraction.

"Interesting firewall. Okay, now... today's data... I need to corrupt it without deleting it. There's usually some debug fields that someone has left in... there we go... oh, geez, they left a test field. I'm setting them both and jumbling the badge IDs. Does that look corrupted?"

"How would *I* know, Scan?"

"Yeah, that'll do. Oh, wait, let me clear the locations too. That's better. 'Someone did something somewhere tonight.' That much is obvious from the dead bodies of whatever those things were." Sure, except I doubted anyone would believe those monsters hacked the building security.

Bear and I had made it out of the building. I tucked the knife into my belt, and when I let go, I immediately felt exhaustion hit me. "Okay, Bear. I think it's time to part. Thank you for this."

He gave me a silent hug.

"Give Bear your gun and the burner phone," Scan said. "We'll have to get rid of them."

I did as I was told, then started walking toward my flat. The whole walk home my mind replayed scenes from the strangest night of my entire life.

The door to my flat was still closed when I arrived. I wiggled it open, edged my way in, then closed the door and put the chair under the knob. As tired as I was, I needed to hide that blade. I pulled it out and felt again a burst of energy. But not enough to keep me going. I slipped it under my cot, burying it in a basket of clothes and throwing a blanket over it. Then I lay down and slept the sleep of the dead.

Chapter 25

Having been pronounced "okay" by the emergency doctor, I shuffled back into Sec Ops, my gaze taking in the entirety of agitated people and their attempts to piece together the previous day's events.

Agent Smith conversed with another FBI agent, both of them across the room from me. I caught her eye, and she held up her phone, then pointed toward a console at the back. My shattered phone sat atop it. Could I have struck a bargain? *If I admit I killed a monster in the atrium, and watched characters from* Lord of the Rings *kill another one, can I get a new phone?* At least they'd charged it. I slipped it into my pocket.

I made my way over to Alex and asked how I could help. "You can help by getting some rest," he said, frowning.

"As tired as I am, I wouldn't be able to sleep," I said, though my body called me out as a liar. "Not in the middle of a crisis like this."

"Ms. Hernandez," Alex said, lowering his voice, "there's really not a lot to do. The feds will keep asking questions until we're hoarse. Phillip is going nuts because he swears someone has tapped into his system. I don't think you can help there?"

I shook my head no. I was steering clear of that one.

"Then go home. I'm just monitoring the ant hill. Get some rest. Come back in tomorrow. We can plan our next steps when you've got a clear head."

He turned and walked away. Before I left, I needed to talk to someone. I scanned the room for Gil and didn't see him, so I left Sec Ops and strolled the halls nearby. I eventually found him looking at his laptop in a conference room, taking notes on a pad of paper. Someone stood watching over his shoulder, but I couldn't see who it was from my angle. I tapped on the door, and he waved me in.

"Interruptible?" I asked. The other guy looked up at me, and I recognized him as the guard outside the security door when I had been hit on the head. What was his name? Gosh, he looked as uncomfortable as I felt, his eyes snapping back to his shoes, and his cheeks could have led Santa's sleigh.

Oblivious to our discomfort, Gil answered, "Yes, ma'am. Just going over deliveries for tomorrow. I figure, since I'm stuck here, might as well be productive."

My eyes widened in surprise. "You're working on our throughput improvement? Now?!?"

"Yes, ma'am. Is there something else you need me to do?"

Gil finally noticed the cloak of awkwardness draped over the conversation. He looked back and forth between us. "Ms. Hernandez, this is my friend, Richard Wales."

I nodded.

"Richard, this is Ms. Hernandez, whom I know you have met before." Gil was grinning, amused with himself.

"Mr. Wales—" I started, just as he also spoke.

"Ms. Hernandez..."

I let him talk.

"I am *so* sorry for having abandoned my post. There's no explanation. I've never done anything like that before! I can't make sense out of it even now. There was this noise. And I followed it. And before I knew it—"

"Mr. Wales," I interrupted. "The building was

abandoned. It happened at the Owaie building as well. Maybe some kind of airborne drug that makes us open to suggestion, then some subliminal message to leave. I don't know, but it's not your fault. It's *not* your fault."

Gil was smiling and clicking away on his laptop. "I told you," he muttered to Richard.

Richard visibly relaxed. "Thank you for understanding," he said. "That's such a relief."

"Ah," Gil said to me, "you wanted my contact for the door repair."

I nodded.

"I called him and asked him to go take care of it. He's over there now."

Reading the concern in my eyes, he waved his hand. "No worries. He will respect your privacy. You're safer having him over there than leaving the door broken open."

I supposed that was true. "How much?"

"On the house. He owes me a favor or two."

I wanted to avoid being indebted to Gil, but I couldn't exactly say that. I paused, lips pursed, trying to think of how to explain my quandary without offending.

"Ms. Hernandez, I'm just squaring up."

"Squaring up?"

He sighed. "Look, I've been here since construction started. There's been three different watch leads in your role. Every one of them got chewed out by the business arm of the construction effort. Every one of them turned around and chewed out the grunts. We were always too slow. It was always *our* fault that the watch lead looked bad. They might yell at us, throw us under the bus, and every one of them ended up trying to micromanage us, which just slowed everything down because we would have to run every decision by the watch lead."

I just stared at him. He hadn't been that effusive before.

106

"Then you come along, and it's a whole different ball game. 'How do we make this a win-win, increasing throughput *and* security?' In one week, you pushed authority *to* us instead of taking it away. When we make mistakes, you absorb the fallout and give us a chance to try something different. The difference is night and day, Ms. Hernandez, and I owe you a favor or two. Don't you worry about that door repair. And, if you need anything else, you know who to ask."

"Wow, I don't know what to say."

"That goes for me too," Richard said, blushing. "You can count on me. I won't let you down again, Ms. Hernandez."

"Okay," I said, smiling wearily, "and I thank you for that. But please stop calling me Ms. Hernandez. My friends call me Red."

I ignored their confused looks. "Thanks again for the door repair," I said as I left the room.

I grabbed my flat keys from my locker and made my way out.

I trekked home, found the door jamb repaired, and my key opened the lock. My laptop had managed to stay hidden above my cabinet—I moved it back to my card table. I checked on the dagger under my bed. Still there. Wrapping my hand around the hilt, I felt that addictive energizing jolt. I tucked it back away and checked on the clothes I'd left soaking in the tub. They needed some scrubbing, until I declared them clean enough for combat, and hung them up to dry.

I was ravenous, but exhausted, so I scarfed down a couple of energy bars, downed a glass of water, and climbed back into bed. Gil's kind words were like salve on a wound. I replayed them in my mind, and the world faded around me.

Chapter 26

Red

I awoke Monday morning and felt... good. Finally rested, I was a new woman. Whatever illness or injury I had been suffering from had passed.

I geared up for my morning run and left. Thinking part way through Central Park that it was probably unwise to push myself too much, I cut east and started back. I realized shortly that the path would take me through the same unsafe section of the park, so I veered north, cutting my run even shorter.

It proved a wise move, as I tired out sooner than expected. Still, a respectable run. I hadn't re-injured myself—just normal tiredness. After, I cleaned myself up, scrambled some eggs, and sat down at my foldable home office.

From my laptop, I scanned the headlines. "Attack at The Palace," "Will The Palace Fall?" and the like. There was no meat to the stories, just reports and pics of all the government and police cars around the building on Sunday. There were statements about the situation having been handled, that the perpetrators were neutralized, and that the investigation was ongoing. No further details would be revealed at that time.

Duh. Oh, yes, and we found the bodies of two eyeless, mouthless creatures with Freddy Krueger talons in the atrium, one with a hole shot through its head, and the other sliced in half by an enormous blade.

Authorities had deemed the building safe, with security precautions taken to ensure that such an incident did not happen again. I spotted a video clip of Rocks—

Reginald Penbrook, I corrected myself—doing his best to reassure people. "I've spent the last day with building security and a plethora of government agencies," he said, smiling at the camera. "I can assure you, The Penbrook Palencia is as safe as any other building in New York, and safer than some."

Nice, I thought... security at other buildings would *also* have failed in stopping a mass brainwashing exodus and monster attack. Still, it would be good to understand why The Palace was singled out. The Owaie was also new construction. What was the common thread?

I walked to work pondering that question, but there wasn't enough information. The crowd waiting to enter The Palace was thinner than a normal Monday, despite the media's reassurances that the building was safe. I found Alex in Sec Ops. He was in uniform, so he must have gone home at some point, but he looked worn. He turned as he saw me come in. Nodding, he said, "You look a hundred times better today. I'm glad you got some rest. You've seen the news?"

"Some," I said, blushing. "I've been asleep most of the time since I was here last."

"Well, there's not a lot that the government is letting out. I expect there will be many people that don't show up today. We need to work on ways to make them feel safe again. We came up with one security increase to address the specific MO of the two attacks we've seen. Let me show you." He walked us over to a console showing a 3D map of The Palace.

I studied the screen to get my bearings, then noted, "There are bright spots near all the security checkpoints."

"That's right. What you're looking at is RFID markers in the security badges. They're passive, so the range is not far. We put radios at each entry point—and here in Sec Ops—that ping the badges. The data feeds into the

109

computers, and we get a count of who is actively at these security points."

"This is to prevent an exodus of the security team?"

"If the number of security personnel in one of those areas drops below a threshold, we all get pings—including the new board member, Mr. Reginald Penbrook. I spent most of yesterday with him." He looked at me sideways. "Not that I'm complaining, but it seems he's a contributing influence to why you have this job."

"Oh," I said, genuinely surprised.

"You didn't know?"

"I had assumed one of my army buddies helped me get this job, but I thought it was someone else. I only just learned that... Reginald... was a Penbrook." It hadn't been Scan that had landed me the job; it had been Rocks. Scan had even lied, pretending it had been his doing, to cover Rocks's involvement. "I hadn't connected those dots."

"Well, you might be cautious with that information. Some people will play it up as special treatment."

"But not you?"

"No, ma'am. Part of life is who you know. The other part is what you do. You've done well here. That matters."

I nodded. I didn't like the idea of people thinking I hadn't earned my right to be there, but at least to some degree, I didn't care. They would never know what I had done to earn my place.

"So you've engineered a way to detect if we are ever driven out of the building again," I said, steering us back on topic. "Let's hope our being here matters."

Alex looked perplexed.

"I mean, there are two reasons they could have driven us out," I continued. "One would be so we don't catch them. Our being here might counter that. The other is that they are trying to take the building down while minimizing human lives lost, in which case having security

110

here would only cause them angst about extra lives lost."

"That's a rather disconcerting thought."

"Sadly, I'm ripe with disconcerting thoughts."

Alex had been an early arrival on the scene after the attacks. He had most likely seen the bodies of those inhuman creatures that were slain. He couldn't tell me, because he didn't know I knew. I couldn't tell him, because I had decided that fleeing the scene would give me more opportunities to stop the enemy than turning myself in. He didn't know about the mystical creatures though... they had fled before he arrived.

There were pieces of the puzzle before me I could not assemble, no matter how I turned them. It was a picture of a black panther at night, and I couldn't find the edge pieces to even get the outline. The mythical creatures had killed one of the dark monsters. They were clearly not friends. The "elf" had indicated that they were trying to help. Were they saving the building from the dark creatures? What could possibly motivate those beasts to destroy the building? But there was at least a chance that the mythical beings had been the ones to drive people out of The Palace, saving them from the attack of those beasts.

About half the people who were supposed to report to work actually showed. There were very few absences from the security staff. The businesses, however, were understaffed, and the construction crews were suffering as well. I watched press conferences where Rocks, from inside the atrium, defended the security of The Palace.

A part of me wondered if people would be more, or less, worried if they saw the bodies of the slain beasts. Yes, they were frightening. The *idea* of them was frightening. They were also dead—slain, as far as anyone knew, by human hands. Surely that would be reassuring. I suspected fear would win over confidence in our ability to protect ourselves. The outcome probably depended on which theory would give the media more clicks.

I ended my day feeling downtrodden by my own spiraling thoughts. When I got home, I had a verbal chat with Scan through my laptop. He let me know that he'd told Rocks everything that had happened with those beasts and the mythical creatures. A picture was worth a thousand words—Scan had captured a snapshot of the trio when the lights had come on, before they had disappeared in a flash of light. He shared it with me over the connection.

"Troll, elf, and dwarf," Scan declared.

"Are you serious?" I asked. Hearing someone else say it made it sound... well, just as ridiculous as it did in my head.

"Which one of us has played more Worlds of Warcraft, Red?" Scan replied, as though I'd doubted his accuracy.

"Then why'd you call the hammer a club?" *Ha! Gotcha, Scan.*

"Lighting was poor. My brain wasn't really looking for a Mighty Hammer of Thunder... a club seemed to fit what I was seeing."

"Touché," I said, dismissing the topic. "And you've got no problem believing we saw an orc, elf, and dwarf?"

"*Troll*, not orc. Get your fantasy creatures straight, Red. Hell, yes, I have a problem with it, but I saw what I saw, and I don't just mean their appearances... I mean the way they moved, the way they disappeared, the fact that *anyone* could wield that frickin' hammer at *all*..."

"The elf Healed me," I interrupted. "My ribs broke when the dwarf hit me. I couldn't get up; I could feel the bones moving, loose. They hadn't punctured a lung, but it was bad. Then the elf spoke some words and touched me, and I could feel my bones knit. The pain faded." I paused. "Looking back, I suspect he did the same after they attacked me in the basement, before dumping me in the

112

woods. I think the troll hit me hard, and the elf had to Heal me to keep me alive." Another pause, as I contemplated the words from the elf about my own death. "They may not be the bad guys, Scan."

"Let's hope not. I'd rather they weren't. And they said they would find you, so I suspect you'll hear from them."

"You're covering our tracks on this conversation, right?"

"Of course. Look, Red, just carry on. Rocks will work the financial and political world. You keep up the strategic security, I'll handle the cyber, and Bear will prep for combat in case this stuff goes sideways, which seems at least possible."

"Roger that. Problem is, it's hard to strategize when you know so little."

"This isn't your first rodeo, Red. It's just way the hell out there. There's no one else I would rather have working on it."

"Thanks, Scan. Changing topics, are we ever going to have a burger and beer with Rocks again?"

Sighing, Scan said, "Doubtful. At least not for a long, long time. He won't be able to get out of the public eye."

"Poor Cynthia. She seems like she'll hate that."

"*I* hate that," he replied. "But whatever Rocks was going to do, it was not going to be quiet work in a library. No, opposites attract, and there's something in each of them that the other needed a bit of. I think Cynthia gives him a place where he doesn't have to be *on* all the time, and Rocks gives her a chance to come out of her shell a little. I dunno. Regardless, no more burgers and beer at Tom's for him."

"Are *we* still going to meet?"

"I don't see why not. Friday… after work… before the young crowd shows up and kicks us out."

"Ha! We're hardly old."

"Combat ages you."

"It does. Are you doing anything to find those camera blurs? Those creatures?"

"I'm working on it. I've got some servers with a neural net that I'm training… same idea as what some online services use for facial recognition."

"You've got servers?"

"I'm *using* some servers… they were mostly sitting idle… the point is that there's not much of a training set." I noted his careful language. "All I've found so far is false positives. It'll get better if I can spot some more, which, ironically, I'm kind of hoping won't happen. I didn't get to see those things alive like you did, but I saw the bodies… they look like they could do some serious damage."

"All right, well, this old lady is going to get some shut-eye. Keep me posted on whatever you can find."

"Roger that. Take care, Red."

"Sleep well. Be safe." I disconnected and lay down on my cot. I thought for a while about what I *did* know. Alex had taken the bit of knowledge we'd acquired—that the attacks on the buildings were preceded by an evacuation—and used it to build a better security system. One that warned us of The Palace being abandoned. What information did I have that I could use? I knew there were at least three of the attackers. I knew they'd done something in the creepy-as-shit room. How did that help?

And, if I found out they weren't the bad guys, what then?

Chapter 27

Red

I arose the next morning, renewed by sleep and encouraged by my thinking, eager to go for my jog. It was getting colder—and it was still dark—so I ran in my fatigues. An idea had come to me in the middle of the night, and I wanted to test it.

I jogged through North Park and headed south, as had become my pattern. After passing the unsafe section, I turned east, continuing until I felt comfortable turning again, then veered north. Normally I would head back home from there, but that morning I decided to add a loop. When it felt safe to turn west, I did. When I started feeling wary, I cut south, directly into the area that kept causing me angst.

My tension increased with each step and, just as I thought I was surely jogging into a band of cut-throats, when every fiber of my being told me to turn back, I found a tent, nestled in the trees. It was large, like tents I'd seen on military campaigns, big enough to house a small group of people semi-comfortably. Its browns and greens blended in with the woods, hiding it until you broke through the trees. As I approached, an enormous figure stepped out. It quickly looked around, then rumbled with laughter and barked something back into the tent. I slowed, and the troll waved for me to follow him in.

Walking, catching my breath, I eased the knives out of my fatigues. I cautiously entered the tent, but the overwhelming sense of danger had vanished. Ironic, given that I was entering a room with a troll, an elf, and... no dwarf. I did a quick look behind me, but he was not there either. The troll had moved to the far side of the tent, but he saw the knives in my hands, and laughed again, saying something incomprehensible to the elf.

The elf replied and twiddled his fingers, then said, "She can understand you now. Want to repeat that?" The weird dual-voice effect had kicked back on.

"No," he said, amused with himself. "But you," he said, looking at me, "when you come back tomorrow, bring *my* knife." I just stared, which made him chuckle. He was truly enormous—head brushing the top of the tent, which must have hit about nine feet, arms bigger than my legs...rocky, impenetrable skin. My knives were pointless; the elf would just heal him anyway.

When I had come in, I'd found the elf seated behind a makeshift desk—an old wooden door stretched across a stone and a wheel-less shopping cart. Manhattan's finest. In addition to the desk, the tent held a pile of blankets, and an ornate wooden chest which seemed out of place with my world but not theirs. Atop the desk sat paper, pen, and an inkwell—and some alien-looking gadgetry whose use I could not imagine. The juxtaposition of the makeshift desk with the Renaissance Faire decor was jarring.

The elf had risen, and walked around the table, closer to me, while the troll waited across the room. If I had to fight, better to take the Healer out at the start. My first good look at him confirmed what I'd seen in the atrium—he had wavy blond hair that was trying to become curls, strangely high cheekbones, and piercing gold eyes. I would've guessed older than me, but still young. His skin color was darker than his eyes, a close match to mine.

"I'm sure you have a lot of questions."

My eye-roll clearly translated, as the troll snickered and the elf pursed his lips in annoyance.

"I'll explain enough for you to see why you need to help us." The elf spoke arrogantly—he owned the information and would disperse it as he saw fit. That wasn't going to be good enough. I tensed, clutching my knives tightly. They wouldn't hurt the nine-foot troll, but I bet they'd cut into the elf nicely.

"For such a long-lived and long-winded species, elves say remarkably little of consequence," the troll grunted. "Count yourself fortunate that he doesn't insist on telling you the entire *story*. He would start with the First Star and name his way through five millennia just as an *important prologue*."

The elf closed his eyes as though gathering patience. "And," he said through gritted teeth, "in return, you will answer *my* questions. Maybe we will establish some trust and maybe we will not. Let us see. I know you call yourself Red."

No, my friends called me Red. I did not want these... beings?... calling me Red. Neither did I want to give them my proper name, so I said nothing.

The elf filled the silence. "My name is Galad*chirrup* Ara*cry*miel Tera*bra-caw*." Some of that was chirps and tweets without an English sound at all.

I took a half step back and shook my head.

"How about just Galad?" the elf suggested, irritated.

"Galad," I repeated. "How is it I understand your speech, Galad?"

"It is a spell, not simple, but not difficult. It translates for us. But it is not a good place to start. Let us begin our discussion on the topic of those creatures."

"By 'those creatures,'" I said, "I assume you are excluding the present company?"

That comment drew a scowl from Galad and a chuckle from the troll.

"That partly answers one of my questions," Galad said, "but just to be certain, our species are not known on your world?"

"About half the fantasy stories ever written have

creatures—*beings*—like you in them, but they are fantasy, not real."

"Now I'm curious what the other half are about, but I'll save that for another time. As I was saying, those dark creatures, one of which you killed, we call them different things—the Blight, the Corrupted, the Tainted, the Infected. They have been drawn to your world, and we are here to stop them."

"Okay, you seemed pretty effective at that. Or at least *he* did," I said, waving at the troll.

"Grundle," the troll said.

What? I held my hand to my ear. "I don't think that translated properly."

"Grundle," the troll said again. "The effective killer of the Tainted has a name, and it's Grundle." He glared at the elf. "Elves typically aren't so rude as to skip introductions."

Galad blushed, but composed himself and continued. "The gist of it is that large populations of humans draw the Infected. Like a baby to candy or a **chirrup** to a shiny bauble. Your world has become populated enough that large cities draw them here."

Shit. "Where are they coming from?"

"We don't know that, exactly. They have an ability to open portals from other worlds, the same way *we* got here. Sort of. They have overrun many worlds and could have hailed from any of them."

Okay. I took a calming breath and gathered my thoughts. The Palace increased the population density of the upper west side of NYC tremendously. So the monster I'd shot hadn't tried to destroy the building—it had been *attracted* to the building. At least that's what the elf was selling me. "So you're trying to destroy The Palace to prevent more of these things coming."

"I told you she was bright," the troll said.

"You also told me she wasn't worth eating because

118

she was too lean," the elf responded. "I try to tune out most of what you say."

The troll rumbled with laughter. *He eats people?* I kept one eye on him, and he mimed chomping on a giant drumstick. *Okaaaaay.*

"Yes, Red. You've got the right idea. We are doing what we can to keep your population density under control. If we can convince people to spread out, you'll be fine. For a time."

"So you took down the Owaie building in Hong Kong?"

The elf and troll exchanged a look. "We don't know the names of places yet. We demolished another building, far from here. And destroyed a handful of the Infected in the process."

As I processed that, the elf continued, "Remember, we are *trading* information here. I have some questions as well. What exactly is your role in your building?"

To tell the truth or not to tell the truth? I decided on being initially truthful and establishing trust, so I could use that trust later.

"I'm a watch lead, a second in command for building security."

Again, they exchanged a knowing look.

"Those... Infected... why did they run to the light?" I asked them. "What *was* that light?"

"The light was focused magic," Galad said. "I meant it, as you've guessed, to demolish the building. But it also attracts the Infected, like *chirps* to a flame."

Moths, I thought, *like moths to a flame. I wonder what gets attracted to flame on the world they're from... dragons?*

"Now for my next question," he said, as though explaining the rules of engagement. "With whom were you communicating in your building?"

Giving them a connection to Scan was unthinkable. "There are four of us that know about you. Obviously the other man that was in the room, me, and two others."

"See," said Grundle, "they were a *gruunt*," and he looked at me for confirmation.

I just stared back at him, confused.

"Hmm," he said, "a band... a team... a unit."

I nodded.

"You have worked together before, have a common experience and shared obstacles you have overcome together. We have a word for that... something that implies family, or clan, based on shared battles, not genealogy."

"We need to talk with them," Galad said.

"Give it up, Galad," the troll responded. "You don't betray *gruunt*.

Blood brothers?

"She would choose to die before betraying them," the troll said. "On the other hand, if you convince *her* to help, she will bring them in herself."

"These are humans, not trolls," Galad said. "They don't have blood brothers."

So now it translates?

"Ha!" barked Grundle. "She is more troll than I am. Look at her," he said, waving a hand, "standing there with knives bared. I have to keep myself from drooling."

Frowning, I spoke up. "Grundle has the right of it. Whether I'm stopping you or helping you, my blood brothers will be involved."

Grundle waved a hand at the elf, as if to say, "See, I told you so."

"But I have no intention of helping you based on what I've heard so far. The best combat strategies involve deception."

The elf frowned, but the troll raised his eyebrows in curiosity.

I continued on. "You could be trying to decentralize us to make it easier for your own invasion."

The elf looked disgusted while the troll nodded along.

"Or," I concluded, "you could just be taking down buildings for money so you can move out of your little tent."

At that comment, both of them exploded, the elf with anger and the troll with laughter.

The elf was shouting messages of fire and brimstone, "... the most ungrateful... unappreciative... let the Infected have them..." While the elf ranted, Grundle could not stop laughing. He walked over to the fuming elf, slapping him on the back in a companionable manner, but with such gusto the elf tumbled forward.

The elf seethed as Grundle brought him to his feet, saying, "I may yet ask her to play 'catch-the-rock.'" *What in the heck?*

Getting his laughter under control, the troll forced the elf to face him. "Oh, Galad. Does it make you wish you hadn't Healed her after I crushed her tiny skull? She's not wrong to be suspicious. Put yourself in her shoes—that's what you were built for, after all. In the end, you'd finally owned your talent." *In the end? Owned what talent?*

Galad let out a small bark—chirp?—of laughter, but pain etched his face. "I remember," he said. "Would that I could forget. So how do we move forward?"

"Leave the next step to me, *old* friend." The troll looked back at me. "She will either be convinced, or be dead and out of the way." His words were menacing, but his tone wasn't.

"Come back tomorrow," the troll said. "Bring my knife." I started to protest, but he interrupted. "I know you have it. You are dismissed."

I didn't move, and the troll showed his rocky teeth. "Go!" he barked.

A nine-foot troll, sounding like an avalanche, convinced me we were done with civil conversation. I glared, pointing my knife at him from across the room, then slashing the air with a knife as I turned to leave. As I sheathed my knives and started my jog back, I heard a thunder of rumbling laughter.

Chapter 28

Red

I spent the bulk of the day in a surreal catatonia. I had to hurry to get into work, telling myself all the while I had not chickened out, but deciding in the end that I had. But it wasn't about being intimidated by someone bigger than me. It was about everything—the idea of magic, the idea of monsters and aliens, the idea that my world was in danger.

It was a lot to process for a Tuesday.

Tuesday. Why did that ring a bell? Oh, yeah, the gym—I had planned to go that evening. The idea resonated—some sparring would get my mind back in the game.

At work, I found a chance to talk to Bear. I filled him in on what little I knew. He told me that the troll had just toyed with him when they fought; Bear was no match for the troll's speed and combat skills. Trying to be a better person than I actually was, I also asked about his girlfriend, and then didn't really listen to the answer, just noted that things seemed to be going well.

The clock didn't seem to move, and yet somehow the workday finally ended. I walked home and pinged Scan on the computer. He connected me to an encrypted audio chat, and I quickly brought him up to speed. "Trolls and elves, magic and monsters, world invasion. You know, your basic Tuesday stuff," I concluded, feeling giddy.

Scan asked a few questions, which I answered. He told me to keep my phone on me, and that he would fill Rocks in.

I went to the gym after our call—I needed to *do* something. The martial arts class was warming up and joking together. I dropped some things in a locker and joined them. Not a single Asian female among them—so much for spying out Bear's girl. The leader of the group, Carol, introduced herself, then started the class with self-defense warm-ups. She had paired me with a white guy about six inches taller than me—Mike—and I dutifully marched through the exercises as expected, falling prey when I was supposed to fall prey, and "learning" and applying the technique to defend myself. Then we switched roles, and I gave my buddy the opportunity to learn the same. It was a slower pace than I had hoped for, not providing the outlet I needed.

After we'd finished the lesson, Susan invited the class to go over what they'd learned in previous classes. Mike and I stood awkwardly—I had no idea what they had learned, and Mike recognized my predicament.

"If you want to just spar, we can," I offered.

Mike agreed, and we squared off. He attacked with hesitation, probably concerned about hurting or embarrassing me. So I moved in. I feinted with a kick to his right, then did a backspin and took out his left hamstring. His eyes grew round, but he still attacked cautiously, his movements clumsy and slow. I deflected them, then battered the side of his head. He stumbled and I backed off.

Carol noticed Mike needed a breather. "Let me take your place for a minute." She looked at me and smiled.

Carol was a challenge. She had speed *and* experience. From the corner of my eye, I saw students stop and watch. We went at it, and I landed a few hits, but I wasn't great without my knives. She kicked my ass. I ended the workout battered and bruised but mentally invigorated.

We broke for the night, and I strolled home, showered, and fell into a familiar and comfortable sleep of exhaustion.

I was riding a horse at my grandfather's farm as a

young woman ending my teens. As I rode through the field, my horse became an ostrich. Then a bird-like creature with a much thicker neck and the mass of a horse. I whooped as I crossed the finish line ahead of the other riders. An attractive blond girl with pointed ears and high cheekbones pulled my face down for a kiss.

Chapter 29

Red

The next morning I put the troll's knife in a backpack and jogged down to their camp. I used the "stay away" discomfort as a homing beacon and ran straight there. The spell was flawed—once you recognized the foreboding sensation, you could actually use it to home in on the source.

They had a firefly-like illumination lighting the camp. When I arrived, Grundle was waiting for me outside the tent. The dwarf kept him company. Galad stuck his head out, cast a spell in my direction, and tucked himself back inside.

"My lady," Grundle rumbled, "did you bring my dagger?" I took off my backpack and reluctantly pulled out the blade. Just like before, I felt an increase in energy when I held the hilt. My Spidey-sense signaled danger. Spinning, I dodged Grundle, who swiped at me with the partner blade he had kept.

Using the dagger I held, I deflected his blade to my left, jumping to the right. I rolled and came up in a crouch. The troll was waiting for me, smiling, and I used the pause to pull one of my normal knives out for my left hand.

He came at me again, swiftly. But knives were my specialty, and despite the length, Grundle's dagger was light and well-balanced. I exchanged blows with him and snagged his ribs with my knife. His skin was thick, tough to cut through—my knife couldn't do it. But I soon scraped the troll's blade along his rocky exterior and saw a trickle of green blood stain his shirt. He smiled and engaged me again.

He moved in with the same attack, and I countered, ready to draw blood a second time, when he grabbed me with his free hand. My bell was rung, and I felt a horrendous force in my gut. I looked down. Grundle's blade stuck in my belly up to the hilt. I turned my head as far as I could. The blue etching of the blade stuck out of my back. I gagged as Grundle slid the blade back out.

Blood dribbled through my hands as I dropped to my knees, blades discarded. My heart was pounding in my head, and I could not hear a sound as the world slowed. The dwarf approached me at a turtle's crawl and touched me with his hammer. It glowed blue, and my skin pulled back together. The pain receded. I ran my right hand down the skin where there was a hole in my fatigues. Not even a scratch remained, though my hand smeared plenty of blood.

"Take it easy, Grundle," said the dwarf. "Remember where we are. I cannot Heal frequently on this world, and I wish to be able to when we truly need it."

The troll grunted and waved for me to pick my blades back up. While I stood, heart still hammering, the troll mimed what he had just done, showing me where he had fooled me, and I'd taken the hit.

"So, we are training," I commented.

The troll grunted again.

"You could have told me."

The troll shrugged and grinned.

We trained another twenty minutes, and I learned how to use Grundle's dagger. Without the extra speed it granted me, he would have eviscerated me several times over. Even with it, I had a few more cuts that needed Healing before we finished. He took a few minor cuts as well and smiled every time.

Grundle sheathed his blade, declaring us done, and the dwarf spoke. "I was absent when you made your appearance yesterday, my lady. Let me introduce myself. I am *Harisidogle Darriunminer**, or something to that effect, "but you can call me Harry."

"A bit on the nose, isn't it?" I replied, eyeing his waist-length beard.

The dwarf reached up and touched his nose. "I think something got lost in the translation."

"'On the nose' means a joke that is obvious. Harry... and hairy..." I said, pointing at my hair.

Harry looked at Grundle. "See, I told you. Any world where my name translates to my fine physical characteristics has got something going for it."

The troll's rumbling chuckle ensued. He trailed off with a question. "When can you disappear for a day without too many questions being asked?"

"Saturday," I said, but the troll shook his head and waved at his ear. That worthless translator.

"Three days from now."

"Okay," he said, nodding. "Be prepared to spend the day with us."

"What will we be doing?"

"More fighting." He smiled. "*Much* more fighting. Yesterday, you mentioned deception and war. Tell me more of that."

The question caught me by surprise, and I fumbled for words. "I, uh, well, it is conventional wisdom that numbers of troops and effectiveness of weapons can determine the victor in a battle or a war. It is how leaders often determine budgets and whether to enter a conflict."

The troll grunted understanding.

"But reality is very different. If you study our past, the numbers do not always determine the victors. Perception matters, and some of our best military leaders used it very effectively—often with purposeful deception. We have a saying—all is fair in love and war."

"Love and war," the troll mumbled. "I think I like that. It has a poetic ring to it. Tell me, among humans, how is deception used in love? To trick someone into mating, or to keep one's mate?"

My eyes went wide. "I never thought that saying meant either of those things... But, I won't deny there are people who work that way. No, I think the phrase was meant to convey that deception with competitors for the same... mate... is fair."

"Ah, then I do like this saying. Very poetic."

"I think my time is running out for today," I announced, a little sadly.

"I assumed so," he said. "We will train more tomorrow. If you have any books on war and deception, bring them. I would like to read them."

"Um, okay," I responded. I had zero books, but I knew where to find some.

"Bring your big blood brother also. He will train as well."

I squinted at him suspiciously, but he was right. Having Bear train in the fighting styles of those fantasy creatures was a good idea.

I jogged home, showered, and got myself into work. People were coming back to The Palace, their fears of an attack on our building slowly diminishing after speeches from civic authorities and local leaders. Paychecks were also a big draw.

Rocks was prominent in the media. He was a natural smooth-talker, and he looked good on camera. *He was born for this*, I thought.

I touched base with Bear and asked him to meet me in North Park in the morning for fairytale folk combat training. After work, I stopped by "The Corner Bookstore" for the second time in my life, found the book I was looking for, and bought two copies—one to keep and one for

Grundle.

When I arrived at my flat, I put my copy of the book by the computer, pinged Scan, and brought him up to speed. He said he would let Rocks know about the latest intel, and I signed off and crawled onto my cot. The world was under attack, with beings from other worlds living in Central Park, and yet I felt oddly comfortable, back in my own skin for the first time since entering civilian life. I sank into an easy sleep.

Chapter 30

Rocks

I hobbled into my makeshift office, sighing. Worn down, I hoped for respite, some time to call my wife and think about something other than the *building* for a time. Night had snuck in, hidden behind a gentle rain. The windows reflected the dim interior lighting while still revealing lights on structures outside, distorted by rivulets of water meandering down the glass. I should have been *heading* home, not *calling* it.

My office was occupied. Of course it was.

"Reginald," my father said, not unkindly, but neither did he sound happy to see me. Next to him my oldest brother, Jonathan, nodded in greeting.

"Father," I said, matching his tone. "Jonathan. To what do I owe this pleasure?" Of all the roles I was playing, keeping my family at bay had been the easiest.

"Just checking in on you, son," my father said. He and Jonathan both held glasses of scotch. "Join us in a drink?" He raised his glass in invitation.

He wasn't drunk. He drank occasionally, but I'd never seen him drunk.

I nodded, moving closer. "Are we toasting something?" I waited as he poured.

"Your fortuitous return?" my brother offered. "Right when we need a wolf, you rejoin the flock."

"Great metaphor," I said, laughing lightly as my father handed me a glass. I raised it. "To the wolf among sheep."

My brother laughed and drank, but my father just frowned. I took a sip. I had to be careful—alcohol affected

131

me more quickly since the accident. I wasn't among friends; I was among family.

"All these public relation expenses, Reggie, what are they buying us?" Jonathan knew I hated that nickname, but I didn't bite.

"Feeding the insatiable media monster," I replied. I had built a small team whose purpose was to find opportunities to better the community. The overall goal was to improve anything in the upper east side and associate that with either my family or The Palace. Fundraisers, elementary school appearances, new business initiatives... anything. "Those expenses are a much-needed distraction. Without them, we get the full attention of the media on our building security." I thought that would be enough explanation.

"They're not cheap, Reggie," Jonathan said, "and they're coming out of the family's pocket." Distant thunder rattled the windows.

I didn't know exact numbers, but I had a sense of the depth of said pocket, and that the expense wasn't a genuine issue. I had to remind myself that, for Jonathan, any dip in the numbers was a personal affront to his abilities as the next head of the family. "It's cheaper than the cost of slowing completion of The Palace, *Johnny*." I intended my jab to bring my father back into the conversation—The Palace was his baby.

In that respect, my return had been fortuitous. I had learned that my father was having some health problems. He had kept a heart attack out of the news, which would have caused a panic among stockholders. He actually suffered from a rare blood condition, and had not experienced a typical heart attack, but he needed to take it easy while he adjusted to his new normal.

"Reginald is right," my father said. "He's buying some goodwill and distracting the media all at once. But be

132

careful, Reginald; the public eye is fickle." My father had enlarged his empire quietly, not in front of cameras. The media fiasco with the attack on the Owaie building—and the attempted attack on ours—was not giving my father the stress relief he needed. I didn't thrive on being in the spotlight, but I didn't wilt under it either, and I could ride the roller coaster ups-and-downs without losing my lunch.

Thwarted, Jonathan emptied his glass and poured another. His way of showing us he could still enjoy one of life's pleasures that neither of us could anymore. "The media is one thing," he said, "but will you be able to keep the government out of our hair? That's your value here, right?"

I sighed—that was where things got hairy. A quick mental review: the government knew there were "creatures" involved—they'd found the bodies—but they didn't know I knew. Neither my father nor brother knew anything about dead monsters in the atrium.

"They're not releasing information. I've shown them what we're doing to beef security, and they're signing off on it—if you have other ideas?"

"Oh, no…" my brother said, wagging his finger at me—how much alcohol had he consumed? "This is *your* problem. Everyone else in this family carries their own weight." He waved at my artificial leg and chuckled at his own joke.

"Jonathan," my father said quietly, but with authority, "I'd like a moment with Reginald, please. Wait for me downstairs. Have the car ready."

Jonathan scowled. Downing the contents of his glass, he slammed it down hard on the desk, and started for the door, pushing me out of his way. He left the door wide open, and my father closed it. "Not exactly what I'd hoped for," he said with a sigh.

"I don't remember the older brother appreciating the

return of the prodigal son," I said with a half-smile.

"He's just like I was in my youth," he said.

"So you were an asshole then?" I asked, grinning.

"You are your mother's son, through and through," he said. My mother had died when I was very young. Cancer, caught too late. My only memories of her came from photographs around the house.

"I loved your mother dearly," he said. "She brought out things in me I have missed. Things you should have had. Things that would have made you feel less of an outsider in your own home."

I'd never heard my father speak that way. He still didn't crack; his expression was as unreadable as ever. But his words had always been clear—until that night.

"You know," he said, his mouth twitching. "She had a tattoo on her ass. Right here," he said, tapping his left butt cheek. "A Phoenix."

My eyes went wide.

"God, I miss that bird."

"Dad!" I said. And for the first time I could remember since my early childhood, I heard my father laugh.

"Well, it certainly helped me *rise from the ashes* on more than one occasion."

"Dad!" I sputtered out, laughing and apoplectic all at once.

Our laughter faded into a companionable silence as we explored the edges of a new relationship.

My father took a deep breath and moved on. "So, does Cynthia like her new home?"

"It's a beautiful apartment. Who wouldn't like it?"

"You may not be like us, but you've learned our ways well enough—that wasn't an answer. In private, your mother was always honest with me—sometimes brutally. So I ask again. Does Cynthia like her new home?"

"No," I said. "We preferred our old life. But I can't

influence the people I need to influence from a flat in East Harlem."

My father nodded in agreement. "Good. Good. You're right that you needed to move to be effective, but you also need someone who will keep you grounded. I feel bad for Jonathan."

Whoa. Feelings? Who is this?

"That Claudia of his cares only about appearances. There's not enough money in the world for someone that wants her life to look perfect all the time."

Jonathan's wife was a truly snooty piece of work, and part of the wedge between my brother and me.

"I dread to think what I would have become if not for your mother."

I said nothing, wary, even with my father—*especially* with my father—of revealing ill feelings toward family members. Maybe my mother was open and honest with him in private, but I wasn't there yet. It could be a trick.

While I was still thinking through how to respond, my father moved on, looking at me a little glassy-eyed. "Family is important, son. I'm glad you found one, *Rocks*."

And with that, he turned and left, closing the door behind him.

I simply stood for a minute. Then two. The rain itself had paused to appreciate the significance of my father's visit, even if neither of us understood it. I pulled out my phone, called Cynthia, reminded her I loved her, and let her know I was on my way home.

Chapter 31

Red

Bear met me in North Park as planned, and we jogged south from the west side of the park. As the sense of danger to my left ratcheted up, I veered in that direction. Bear put a hand on my arm, "Are you sure this is the way? This doesn't feel right."

"It *is* right. That 'something is wrong' feeling is exactly what leads me to them."

He came along in silence after that, still scanning the flora for whatever was causing the foreboding air. We eventually reached the camp, and the troll and elf were waiting outside, a faerie-magical light illuminating the scene.

"Greetings, Red. Greetings, blood-brother of Red," the troll began. "It is a pleasure to meet you." He introduced himself and Galad, and he mentioned Harry, who was once again absent from the camp.

Once he had completed introductions, Grundle got down to business. He pulled out his knife and extended the hilt to me. "You're going to need them both today. You'll be sparring with Galad, while I work with your friend."

"This plan is ill-considered, Grundle," Galad insisted, looking irritated.

Grundle turned to me. "Galad still believes numbers and efficient weapons win the war." And he winked. The troll *winked*. Then he pushed me off toward Galad and moved to meet Bear in what I presumed would be hand-to-hand combat. I didn't envy Bear. At six feet, six inches, and loaded with muscle, he was an incredible beast for a human, but the troll was almost nine feet tall, had rocks for skin, and his muscles were enormous.

I approached Galad. "You're a spell-caster," I said. "Are you going to teach me how to fight spells?"

Galad sniffed in scorn. "You can't fight my spells. No, we are not doing that pointless exercise." Then he sighed and drew a slim but sleek sword. It flared with a blue light as it left the scabbard, and Galad did some quick, light maneuvers with it. "We shall instead do *this* pointless exercise. Let us begin."

He came at me, moving like a dancer, teasing me with thrusts and slices as fast as lightning. The increased speed the daggers granted me enabled me to keep up, but just barely. He danced with the sword with an expertise that I'd never before seen, and I had a sense he was holding back. We circled one another, and I was facing Bear and Grundle. As I watched, Bear lunged in for some gut punches, and Grundle took the punches while grabbing one of Bear's shoulders and getting his other arm behind Bear's back. Then, the troll yanked, and I cringed to the noise of a sickening "pop." Bear screamed in pain. Grundle spun Bear around and did the same with the other arm, then dropped him to the ground.

Galad danced to the side, giving him a view of the other combatants while keeping me in his sights. "Pardon me," he said with a head bob to me. He looked at Bear, who was on his knees and clearly... well... broken. Galad said a few words with a slight wiggle of his fingers, and Bear's shoulders mended themselves. Bear stayed on his knees, fascinated by the sensation of being Healed, just as I had been.

Galad looked at Grundle. "I believe Harry already spoke to you about wasting our magical essence on unnecessary Healing."

The troll shrugged. "I needed to make a point."

"What point was that?" I asked. "That you can cause

ridiculous amounts of pain?"

"More or less." Grundle, done talking with me, started back in on Bear, but I lost sight of them as I deflected an attack by Galad. Galad moved like water around rocks, smooth and efficient. I could not touch him. I had assumed he was the "intellect" of the bunch—and maybe he was—but his ability with a sword was astounding.

Galad would occasionally stop, shake his head, and say something akin to "try that again." He would attack again the same way, sometimes much slower, in order to give me time to think. We would repeat the maneuver multiple times, until he seemed satisfied with my progress, or gave up in frustration... hard to tell.

Eventually we had to stop. Breathing hard, we regrouped. I cringed when I saw Bear, bruised to hell with one eye completely swollen shut and blood leaking out of several places.

"He can't go back to work like that," I told them.

Galad mumble-gestured, and Bear Healed back up, eye suddenly reappearing like the moon from behind a cloud.

"Thank you," Bear said, looking grateful.

Galad nodded in response. "I think that ends our training session for today."

It had been a good one. Brutal, but good. We gathered up our things to jog back.

Grundle walked over, hand out, palm extended. "My dagger."

I pulled both out and presented the hilts. He took one.

"Hold on to the other for me," he said.

"Oh," I said, remembering my gift for him. Out of my backpack I pulled Sun Tzu's *The Art Of War* and gave it to him. "How will you be able to read our language?"

"Galad?" the troll questioned. Galad came over and examined the book. He performed one of his incantations. Grundle flipped a few pages. "This did not translate well…"

"It is a translation of a translation," I suggested. "The original language is not my own."

"Humph. Even worse, Galad's spell translates to elvish, so I have to translate the flowery nonsensical curls into my own… *beautiful*… language."

Galad laughed.

I took the book from Grundle and flipped to a line in the first chapter. "Here," I said, "try reading this."

"All warfare is based on deception," he read slowly. He smiled at me. "Very good. I will give this a try, and you can help me where the translation breaks down."

With that, and some parting words, Bear and I started back at a slow jog.

Bear waited until we were clear of the camp to talk.

"That was bad," Bear said. "So very, very bad."

"You did okay," I reassured him.

"That thing tore my arms out of their sockets like I was a plastic toy. I've never encountered such physical strength."

We jogged on. "Come to the gym tonight," I said. "You don't get this because you're stronger than everyone else, but there's a way to fight when you are the weaker opponent. Let me teach you how *I* would fight *you*, and then you can use it on the troll."

Bear sighed. "What time?"

"Eight pm. And bring your girlfriend. I'd like to meet her."

We went our separate ways at the northeast corner of the park.

After work I touched base with Scan, let him know that Bear had trained with the fantasy trio, and that we would do the same the following day. In turn, Scan informed me he hadn't had any luck identifying more of the invaders from the video feeds. We signed off.

I met Bear at the gym as Carol started up her class. He was alone.

"No girlfriend?" I asked him.

"Not tonight," he answered. "Her daughter had a school thing she had to attend."

"She has kids?"

"Just the one. Second grade." A child. I hadn't pictured that. I suspected that Rocks and Cynthia were going to start a family soon, but I hadn't considered jumpstarting the parenting role by dating someone with kids.

I walked Bear through some tactics for fighting a much larger opponent. Carol thought it silly to teach Bear, given the slim chance he would ever encounter a larger opponent, but she had lots of tips and tricks I could add to my repertoire. I played the role of a nine-foot-tall beast and let Bear practice using a person's weight against them.

I wasn't exactly sure what I was doing, strategically. It made sense to prepare Bear to fight the troll—he might have to do so without it being practice. But a moment's introspection revealed to me that I *liked* the troll. Was I being tricked? The troll embraced deception—was he telling me about the importance of deception in order to gain my trust? That was a pretzel of a thought. Grundle had killed that monster and saved my life. On the other hand, they wanted to *destroy* my building.

Torn between trusting and not trusting them, I climbed into bed and *dreamed of an elf, smiling and sincere, a young man explaining why I was being ridiculous, though I knew in my heart I'd been deceived. Then it was my beloved Murphy, explaining what he'd never had a chance to explain. And then the elf again, the images twisting around and spinning me until I awoke in a sweat.*

Chapter 32

The next morning, when we reached the camp, the troll and dwarf were there, but no elf. The troll beckoned Bear over, and the dwarf waved me over to him.

"My lady, I fear you and I have not much we can do to spar together. A war hammer versus knives would lead to a lot of Healing, and we wish to conserve exactly that magical energy."

Yes, I could not really deflect a blow from the hammer, just dodge it. I would be forced to try to take out critical pieces of him, like arms or legs, to stop him swinging and thus end the fight.

"If I may suggest," he offered, "we have not seen a great deal of your world. I would like to hear more about it. Would you be willing to use this time to share with me some of your planet's wonders?"

He beckoned me over to some rocks where we could sit. He twirled his hammer, as one might twist a screwdriver, and the hammer began to produce enough light that we could sit around it like a small campfire. I tried to think through how he could use the information he'd asked about... terrorist attacks against our worlds' wonders? I could limit the talk to some more natural, less populated, wonders.

Harry waited patiently, settled back against a rock, one hand on his hammer like a child with a blanket. A short distance away, Grundle and Bear exchanged blows, and it was clear that Bear would need another Healing before we left. Ouch.

"There is a place called the Grand Canyon," I began.

"It is a canyon carved out by a river for many millions of years and stretches miles across."

The dwarf shook his head. "The translation spell has no calibration for the time and distance terms you are using."

Just then, Bear grabbed one of Grundle's arms in a move he had learned the night before, and locked the troll into a position where the troll would have to break his own shoulder in order to free himself. The troll stopped struggling, then turned to look Bear in the eye. "Well done," he said, and nodded for Bear to let go.

Bear took a step back as he released Grundle, but the troll made no sudden moves. The troll gestured toward us and said, "Let us join them. I would hear of these wonders as well."

As they walked over, Grundle put a massive arm around Bear's shoulder, and I flinched, foreseeing some treachery, but the troll just squeezed him in a sideways hug. "Learning you are not the biggest and strongest is not easy," he said. "Your treachery was well done. I imagine you have her to thank." Grundle nodded to me. "It feels *good* to best a larger foe."

"That canyon I mentioned," I said, trying to steer the conversation in a different direction. "Water carved it out for a very long time, much longer than our own recorded history. To hike from one rim to the other takes about a third of a day, and there are only a handful of places where it is safe enough to cross."

"Niagara Falls," Bear piped in. "My family drove there once when I was little. Great falls of water. *Unbelievable* amounts of water. They've built a viewing deck where you can get close. Talk about feeling small. People used to go down it in barrels, but some died, and now access is restricted."

That was one of Bear's longer speeches.

"So humans create rules to stop people from heedlessly putting their lives in danger," said Harry.

"Yes. It isn't universal though," I said. "We have smaller groups that have deadly rites of passage."

"Rites of passage have a purpose," the troll argued.

"Maybe," I said, "but they often become traditions and lose their purpose."

The troll grunted his acknowledgement.

"This is not what we have been told of humans," the dwarf considered out loud, then reverted to his previous topic. "Are there other such wonders in this world?"

"Mount Everest is our tallest mountain. People climb it as a challenge, though I'm told there is a mountain on Mars," and I waved off to the sky, "that is three times its size."

"And people do not climb this mountain on Mars?" asked Harry.

"Mars is a nearby planet," I explained. "We have only sent unmanned ships there so far."

The dwarf's eyes got big. "You travel to other planets? But you don't have enough magic to open a portal."

"We use ships," I said.

"There is no air to breathe," he countered.

"*Enclosed* ships with ways to produce air."

There was a long pause as the fairy tale creatures pondered my claim. "Truly, that is wondrous," said the troll. "I would like to see one of these ships that travel through space someday."

I considered showing him pictures on my phone, but I couldn't shake the suspicion that he was looking for targets.

"Rain forests," I said, moving to wonders that mankind was destroying all on its own. "Blue whales. Kangaroos."

"*Kangaroos*?" Bear asked. "*Really*?"

"What?" I said, defensively. "They're weird. All hopping around with built-in pouches. Who came up with that design?"

Bear shrugged. "Butterflies then."

My eyes widened—mostly in amusement.

"They start as worms, then get wings," Bear explained.

That *was* pretty amazing when you stopped to think about it.

Grundle chuckled. "*You* sound like an elf," he told Bear. "And, *you*," he said to me, "with your healthy distrust of hoppy things with pouches—I still say you're a troll."

"Can we get back to the mountains and canyons, please?" Harry moaned, sounding put out. "I don't really care about your butteroos and kangerflies. Any deep, mysterious caves worth seeing?"

Bear and I exchanged a look. We both shrugged. "Well, probably," I said, "but I wouldn't have any idea about them."

"Tchuh!" the dwarf said in disgust, disappointed with our lack of information on holes in our world.

"The caves on your world are something special?" I asked.

"Aye," Harry said, sighing. "They are indeed. The surface of my home is not worth seeing, but the subterranean marvels definitely are. Phosphorescent pools. The Teeth of Dagmar. The Maze of Shifting Stones. Lava geysers and frozen pockets of ore." He sighed, caught up in his daydream.

I wished I had something to offer. We may have had interesting caves on Earth—I just didn't know. We sat in silence for a time, each of us lost in our own concerns or memories. Eventually I noticed the morning was brightening. I stood and looked at Bear, and nodded toward the entrance to the camp.

"Thank you for sharing some wonders of your world with us," the troll said, recognizing the end of our visit. "Remember, tomorrow we will spend the day together. Bear, are you joining us? I think we would do better to focus on Red alone and work with you another time, but we can probably manage if you wish to stay together. If you both get hurt, we could run out of the magical energy we need to Heal you before we can recharge it."

Bear looked at me to answer.

"Let's train one at a time then," I said, and Bear nodded.

The troll rose and pulled Bear to his feet. Harry grabbed his hammer, extinguished the firelight, and Healed Bear. "The worse the injury, the more magic is required. Healing these minor wounds costs little," he explained.

"Oh, your book," Grundle said. "The translations are proving... difficult. Often, with books like these, there are other books that build on them. One in your native tongue. Would you look for one for me? It would probably be an easier starting point."

I nodded. A book popped into my mind, but I couldn't think of the title. Bear and I got our packs and started the trek back out to get started on our days.

At my flat, I poked a little online, and found the book I had remembered. I ordered two copies. *I'm going to need a book budget if this keeps up.*

That evening I met Bear and Scan in person at our old haunt, Tom's Tavern. It was entirely different without Rocks. The conversation didn't flow, and the mood wasn't as light. I asked questions about Bear's girlfriend, but the conversation went like a bad first date.

"Remind me, where is Akira from?" I'd asked.

"She's second generation Japanese, but grew up here in New York." He smiled proudly, though he'd probably told me that before.

"Oh!" I said excitedly. Pause."Um, what does she do?"

"She's an investment banker."

"Oh, that's nice." Pause. And so on.

The relationship sounded healthy for him, compared to our dynamic as a threesome, which was off to a bumpy start. I felt certain we would have talked longer and laughed more had Rocks been there.

Bear had plans with Akira in the morning, so we said our goodbyes, and I went back to my flat. I wrestled with sleep for a long time. The possibilities of what could happen in a whole day with the otherworldly trio—mind-blowing.

Chapter 33

Red

I met the fairytale creatures at their camp the next morning. By myself. All three were armed and ready to fight. I wondered what sort of training I should expect, or if I had just walked into a trap. They were hard to read.

"You're sure about this?" the elf asked the troll.

"As sure as I can be," the troll shrugged. "Here," he said to me, handing me his other knife, "you'll need this." He had his axe clipped to a pack he carried.

"Let us get started then," Galad responded, waving everyone to come close. Mindful of a potential trap, I moved into their circle. They faced outward, so I did likewise, the dwarf to my left and the troll to my right. There was a flash of light, and with a subtle wrenching in my gut, I was suddenly somewhere else.

***

I wasn't alone. The others scanned for danger, but they showed no surprise about our sudden appearance in a different location. I had seen the trio disappear from The Palace, so I knew they had some way to jump from one location to another. What an insane tactical advantage.

We stood in a location not unlike the one we had left, some trees for coverage, but there were clear signs that the area had once housed industrial works. Plants grew over and through some old machinery, nature reclaiming the space. It was dark, like our previous location. The elf cast a spell, and instantly I could see everything more clearly—the infrared spectrum became visible.

Relaxing slightly, the dwarf and troll discarded their backpacks and moved away from the elf, who was using the trunk of an old vehicle as a table. He pulled out four small, corked bottles. My phone pinged in my pocket. Scan.

> You ok?

I didn't recognize the number, but it was not unusual for Scan to ping from an unknown number.

I'm ok, but this date has taken an odd turn.

The reply came immediately.

> I can imagine. It isn't everyday you travel to Manila for a date.

I was in *Manila*? The *Philippines*? We had traveled halfway around the world in the blink of an eye. I put my phone away. Galad had finished setting up his bottles, and they began to emit a soft glow and thrum, reminding me of the room in The Palace where Grundle had first knocked me out.

"Be ready," the elf told me. The dwarf and the troll already had their weapons out and at the ready. Oh, crap. He was using those bottles as a beacon. We weren't in a training exercise. Thinking back, the troll had never said it was for training. He had said, "More fighting."

Daggers drawn, I kept my back to the beacons and faced the night, waiting. The first of the beasts came charging between Harry and Galad, and Harry let loose his war hammer, sending the dark creature flying into a tree and shattering its chest and a branch of the tree. The hammer pulled itself out of the mess and started its magical return trip to its owner, but it would not be fast enough. A second beast was coming between Harry and me.

I moved with magic-enhanced speed, thanks to the daggers I wielded, intercepting the Infected on its path to the beacons. It swiped at me, and I removed its left hand above the wrist. Not giving up, it turned to swipe at me with the other hand. I caught the swipe with my blade and used the creature's momentum to cause it to sever its other arm. *What else is dangerous on this thing?* It had no mouth, which begged the question of how it ate, but at least it could not bite. A clawed foot raked my leg in an ineffectual swipe as it toppled from its own struggles. So the feet were dangerous too. I was in an excellent position to slice one of its quads as I moved back into formation, leaving it in the throes of death.

Grundle was engaged with two of the Blight, and Galad was slicing up one of his own. Harry had moved to cover the gap I had left. I moved in closer to Grundle, using surprise to embed one of my knives into the flank of an Infected and driving upward, playing all kinds of hell on whatever internal musculature they contained. Another beast used the same tactic on me, battering me away with a rip of a claw down my right side, sending me tumbling. Even worse, my speed-enhancing blade was still embedded in the dying creature.

I was not swift enough to deflect the next blow, and the creature injured my right side. Rolling, I hoped to put some distance between us, but it didn't work. I wouldn't be able to avoid the claw of the beast standing over me.

Chapter 34

Scan

Crazy. She'd jumped cell towers, going to the other side of the world, within seconds.

Sure, I tracked Red, just as I tracked all my friends. Keeping an eye out for them was important.

My system had flagged me—it happened occasionally when Red climbed down into the sublevels of the Tower and lost her signal, but it was a Saturday, and she was with the WoW team, so I paid attention.

When the WoW team had disappeared that night in the atrium of The Palace, I'd assumed they'd futzed with the video feed somehow. But that wasn't the case. They'd used magic—a spell of Teleportation. What were the rules? How far could they go? How did they pick a destination? How did they not Teleport into some random car driving by?

And why did they go to *Manila*? Red had thought they were training. Was it a baptism by fire? *Oh, shit, that makes sense.* They took her to a newbie site to fight some spawns. And that meant...

I scrambled to gather feeds in Manila. *Shit, I'm not ready for this.* Did I know anyone... Zane101? Kill3rb33? I would have to reorganize my database if she was going to be popping around the world. Lokust? Yes!

I pinged him, then sent him info to connect on a secure channel. Secure enough anyway.

I typed, "Lokust, what video feeds have you got in Manila?"

"Whatever you want, Zkan. City-cams, some business security, dog-cat porn..." *Dog-cat porn?*

"City cams," I clicked in response.

"All yours, boss." He sent some IP addresses and code snippets. The code snippets let me into the systems. I stuck them in my cheat sheets. The IP addresses connected me to specific cameras, but they didn't provide me physical locations. I modified a script I'd picked up elsewhere that let me trace back to nodes associated with locations.

From the towers Red's cell had pinged, I had her rough location. I built the tightest ring of cameras I could around her site, an abandoned steel company or something similar. To the southwest, I found water, so I concentrated on cameras in the other directions.

There! The camera had frakked, just like the ones in Hong Kong and New York. Then I spotted another distortion.

The WoW team was drawing 'em in. Sweet. I'd get lots of videos. New videos would greatly advance the training algorithm for my neural net. I started annotating and feeding in the training sets as fast as I could find them.

Good job, Red!

Chapter 35

Red

A blast of fire, as from a focused flame-thrower, tore a hole in the beast that was slicing at me, and then a red line formed, moving up through its body as the fire moved. Hot gore splattered me as the creature's body ripped open. Moving more slowly than I would've liked, I climbed to my feet. There was a lull in the fighting, and I quickly retrieved my dagger and returned to position, as did the others. I felt a wave of Healing and nodded thanks without looking at Galad. I didn't take my eyes off the horizon.

"What more should I expect?" I shouted.

"Likely there will be one more round," Grundle answered, "coming from a greater distance. Hard to say on the number. To the southwest is water, so the next round should come on my side, roughly."

"Help me understand," I said. "How are we in terms of Healing spells, or that fire blast you did?"

The elf did not answer at first, and after a pause the dwarf chimed in, "I've probably got a Heal left in *Be*z*y**." The last word hadn't translated well—had he named the hammer?

"It depends," Galad said reluctantly. "I could do a few minor Heals or one big one. Alternatively, one of those fire blasts."

"Got it," I said. "Bottom line, don't get hurt."

Grundle laughed. We continued waiting. Harry and I shifted positions to get closer to the expected direction of attack, while not leaving our former positions completely open.

"How often do you do this?" I asked, and thought to

myself, *this purging of creatures I didn't even know existed.*

"Oh," Galad answered snidely, "whenever our social calendars are open. You know, when humans with delusions of self-importance aren't forcing us to revise plans."

Grundle chuckled. "About once every seven to ten days we do a bigger expedition, like this," he said. "Judging by today, I think we are losing ground. Also, either Galad or Harry do a daily trip to various places, but they bring only one canister of magic. Less flame for the moth. They insist I stay behind, because I am the brains of the operation and to lose me would—"

"Ha!" barked Harry. "Grundle is the only one of us with no ability nor enchanted artifact with Healing. While he may not be the brains, I would miss his massive presence on days like today."

At that point, the next of the Blighted charged into camp, followed on its heels by several others, and we became too busy to talk.

Chapter 36

Red, 4 years earlier

I was expecting some shit, and I was not disappointed. It was a man's world, and I knew that the bastards would not be happy to have a woman join special forces, but I had done what it required. I had gotten through the programs, and I was there, and they would have to deal with it.

Those smug-asses, "Rocks" and Reed, were the worst of them. Blatantly overcompensating for something, all bravado—they'd be the first to disappoint in the field. And what the hell was up with the little guy, Stanley? How had he even passed the physical exams? Unlike him, no one could say I hadn't earned my place there.

It was hot, dryer than Texas, but it didn't bother me. There were eight of us sitting in the back of an old MTV, with another MTV following behind, going to relieve some soldiers assigned with training the locals as resistance fighters. Including me had been a gamble. They hoped I might have a positive influence on establishing comms with the women of the city. Hard for a man to be a positive influence when half the time his blood wasn't even flowing to the right organ.

While listening to general joking and chatter inside the MTV—excluding me of course—I heard a sudden shout from the front of the vehicle, followed by an explosive force, and then the world turned upside down.

For a few seconds, my brain checked out as the world spun out of control.

I couldn't hear anything meaningful—just a ringing—and most of our crew lay on the ceiling of the MTV, while the bed of the truck hovered above us. Several soldiers weren't moving. The two guys at the back may have been dead. I could faintly hear some Arabic, as though from another room, but I soon realized someone was tearing a hole through the canvas, making their own side entrance.

The next few minutes were a blur. I suspected I had a mild concussion, as I was having trouble focusing, drifting in and out of consciousness.

By the time my brain reassembled reality, I was outside, under gunpoint. I could see several friendlies from my vehicle, and the hostiles had the second vehicle pinned between ours and some Jeeps with mounted machine guns. It looked like the hostiles were using us to convince the second vehicle to drop their weapons, but my hearing was only just starting to return. I had my helmet on, but I put my hand up and found a trickle of blood around the rim on my left side. Yup, I'd hit it hard. They hurriedly tied our hands with some thin rope, gathered us into the Jeeps, and pulled burlap sacks over our heads. We soon rolled out. I hadn't even counted how many vehicles—I blamed the blow to my head—but I was pulling things together.

Fifteen minutes later, they drove us into an enclosure—from the sounds, I believed it to be a camp not in a city proper. They herded us into a room and searched me for weapons, burlap sack still on my head and hands behind my back.

They yanked the sack off. Three hostiles pulled the burlap off the others, and a fourth—the leader?—oversaw the operation. I counted fourteen of our guys. Shit! We had lost the two men at the end of my MTV.

The leader said something I didn't understand, and Reed—that total ass that had made a move on me the day I arrived—answered. He *would* be the translator. Probably learned other languages just to talk about himself more—or bed women. Reed continued to answer the leader's questions. I had Rocks on one side of me, and that little guy

155

on the other.

"Kingpin is a real capitalist," Little Guy whispered. "He wants to know how much our nation will compensate him for returning us with our heads still attached to our bodies."

My eyes widened. So Little Guy spoke multiple languages too. I understood a word here and there but couldn't follow. "Reed is making promises... geez, promises we can't keep. Dumbass."

Like everyone else, I was watching the men with guns, and listening to Reed and the leader negotiate.

"Oh," my diminutive neighbor said in alarm. "Oh, shit. You're toast."

Before I could register what he meant, a hostile pulled my helmet off. I knew immediately what Reed had done. He'd let them know I was a woman. We were in a culture where women were dirt, and Reed had bought himself favor by turning me in. And paid me back for rejecting his advances.

The guards were cutting friendly soldiers' hands loose. They left the ropes around my wrists. I was the only one still tied. I wanted to kill them all.

The one they call Rocks had a coughing fit next to me. The guards focused on him a minute, but it wasn't a trick; it wasn't a diversion. Nobody there was going to help me.

A guard pushed my shoulder. Reed just leered at me. Hands tied behind me, I couldn't stop Rocks when he put a hand on my shoulder. He said, loud enough for everyone to hear, "I read your profile. I know what your skills are," and he slapped me on my ass. "You'll be okay." Reed and the guards chuckled. Total fucking pigs.

As they marched me across the room, I heard a roar. A behemoth of a soldier charged the enemy leader. The guards at my end of the small room raised their rifles, but a guard next to the giant clocked him with the butt of his rifle, smashing the large man's nose in a spray of blood, and sending him to his knees. His charge stopped. The rifles trained on him kept him from rising again.

One guy. One man in the entire crowd willing to fight for me.

The guard pushed me forward again, then turned me around and marched me out of the room. I felt, in the lurching movement, something unexpected—a weight in my back pocket that hadn't been there a minute before.

He led me out a door, turned me to the right, and marched me through an open area in a fenced compound to another building. I walked into a long hallway with doors on both sides, caged by rusty corrugated metal walls. A metal door opened, and they shoved me in, where I fell on my side. The hostile mumbled something and left. I heard the door bolt from the outside.

Rolling onto my back, I looked around. The room had a table, a light, and enough gaps at the corners and floors that I could see even with the light off. There were a couple of chairs, and a footlocker along one wall. An interrogation room?

I backed up to the wall, opposite the door, so I could have some warning if it opened. Having my hands tied behind me couldn't stop me from reaching into my back pocket. I felt a handle—a *knife*. Specifically a switchblade, nothing army regulation. It was someone's toy. Rocks. Okay, maybe *two* guys worth their spit were in that room. I used it to cut the rope. Hands free, I dropped the rope in my pocket. No clue left behind.

Just then, the bolt on the door moved. I put my hands behind my back, pretending ropes still bound them, as their esteemed leader walked in. He closed the door, but didn't lock it, shooing the guard away. Face fixed somewhere between a scowl and a smirk, he approached me slowly.

The blood from my head wound ran down the side of my face. It wasn't as bad as it looked—head wounds bleed a lot—but it still hurt when he grabbed my hair and pulled me up to my knees. Still smirking, he started working with his robes until he got to what was underneath, and made it very clear what he expected from me.

There I was, dressed in men's clothing, doing "men's" work, but what did he care? He was just looking for a mouth. He could have called his buddy in there to the same effect. But I knew it was more about degradation than sex. I lifted my right leg so my foot was on the ground. While that distracted him, I brought my left hand up and grabbed his robes, pulling him down while I stood up. The knife in my right hand plunged into his throat.

I covered his mouth with my left hand to keep him quiet while I continued to push through his neck with my blade. His blood pulsed out in spurts onto my camo, drenching my chest and arm. I held him there for a minute, then tucked the body behind the door.

Time to get everyone else.

I cracked the door and looked out. No one that direction. Pulling the door open a little more, I looked the other way. No one in the hall. As near as I could tell, the compound was two buildings with an open area in between. They had brought us into the compound through a gate between the structures, then into the building on the right of the entrance. They had then taken me, alone, across the open space and into the other.

My best bet would be to get weapons to my fellow soldiers and unleash hell on those guys. But getting across that open area was a problem. Could I wear the robes of the guy I'd killed? Maybe at night. I judged we were hours from that, and I doubted I could wait that long. Fate proved me correct. The door at the end of the hallway—the door leading to the courtyard—was opening.

I ducked back into the room as footsteps approached. Someone stopped outside the room, then gently rapped the slightly open door. I didn't answer, so they pushed the door open more, but the body and I were out of sight behind it. When he pushed his way in, I struck before he could make a sound. I slowly lowered his body to the ground and dragged him behind the door with his buddy.

I took his rifle, and he had an even better knife. His clothes would work as a disguise. I dressed myself in his tunic and turban.

It was only about 25 yards between buildings, enough room to pull in a truck, unload it, and turn it back around.

No point in waiting. I walked to the courtyard door and pushed it open.

The courtyard fence snaked around from my right, leading to the gate for vehicles, and then continuing to the far side of the other building. I needed to get back to the door that was twin to this one, across the yard. I immediately turned left as I exited the building, starting the trek across the courtyard. None of the Jeeps that they'd used to waylay us were there. Good, that meant many of the hostiles had left. But a truck was pulling in just as I started across. There were two guards near the other door, but a guy jumped out of the passenger door of the truck and called them over as he walked to the back of the truck to open it.

I kept moving, like I belonged, and strode into the far building. We had been in the second room on the right; I hoped they had not moved their prisoners. I was approaching the door when I heard rifle fire from outside. The door I was approaching swung open, and a hostile stepped through, turned to me, and asked me something in

159

a language I couldn't understand. I replied with a knife—the newer one—in the gut. I removed the knife quickly, pushing his body down as I walked into the room. Not the subtle entrance I was hoping for, but at least one more hostile was down. There were two more in the room. One near Reed was trying to get his rifle up. I threw the knife, and it caught him squarely in the torso. The other had managed a little better, but that massive guy who had tried to defend me earlier pounded the hostile in the face with a fatal blow.

The big guy took the hostile's rifle, and I gave Rocks mine, while removing my turban. "I'm keeping this," I said, brandishing the switchblade.

"It was going to be a birthday gift. You spoil everything," he replied, as though we'd known each other for longer than the ride in the MTV.

I chuckled.

"She does have a sense of humor," he said with a wry smile.

"Touch my ass again and I'll be giving you the knife back." I glared at him.

He opened his mouth, then closed it and nodded.

"How did you sneak it in?" I asked.

"Um… let's just say they thought I was excited to see them."

Ewwww! And risky! It was a switchblade, for god's sake. Guess he earned the name "Rocks."

I walked across the room to the other downed hostile, removing the nasty shirt I had borrowed. Reed had picked up a rifle but left the knife protruding from the hostile's chest. I pulled the knife out and wiped the blade on my sleeve, though the sleeve wasn't exactly clean.

The gunfire exchange outside had died down.

The door burst open, and two soldiers in U.S. Army fatigues pointed their rifles into the room. They scanned the room and found all the hostiles down. One spoke into his headset. "We've found them. Proceeding to evacuate. Roger."

I couldn't hear the response.

"All right, let's move. You, with the rifle," he said, pointing at Rocks, "you're with Hendrix," pointing at the soldier who had come in with him. "You," he pointed at Reed, "you're with me holding rear guard." He scanned the room again. "You, Red." He was looking at me. Red? Oh, all the blood. "You okay?"

"Mostly their blood, sir."

"Very good. You get in the middle somewhere. I take it you know how to use those knives. Let's roll." He signaled with his head for Rocks and Hendrix to move.

We moved in groups of twos. I left more or less at the same time as the little guy who could speak Arabic, and the big guy with the broken nose, purple already forming under his eyes. We quickly loaded into the back of a truck, and it started moving.

I was sitting in the truck bed, with the big guy and the little guy, but the man who had pulled us out of the building kept looking my way. Finally, he came over. "You've got a head wound. It's still bleeding." He grabbed a rucksack from the front of the truck and came back with some tape. "Let's wrap that until we get to camp." He started wrapping my head, and we hit a bump. It freaking hurt. "What's your name, Private?"

I felt dizzy. "Garnet, sir. Garnet Hernandez."

"Garnet? What the hell kind of name is that? Well, I'm just going to keep calling you Red. Private Wilkins says there were a couple of folks already dead in the other building. Knife wounds."

"That'll happen, sir. The wrong cutlery can really spoil a dinner."

The man laughed dryly. "I think you'll pull through this dinner engagement. I'm Murphy," he said, finishing his

161

work. "Sergeant Murphy O'Shay."

Chapter 37

The attacks of the Infected were peculiar. They swarmed like mosquitoes to a bug-zapper, but once they were there, they snapped out of their obsession enough to attack us. They responded to our defenses as though they were more interested in us than the magical essence that drew them out. That suggested they were not completely mindless, though neither did they appear organized.

So our advantage did not last long. Grundle used his axe to put an end to the first attacker. The rest did not charge in mindlessly; they surrounded us, spreading out. I counted six. To the four of us.

We backed up to tighten our circle. Harry did not throw his hammer—that would have been tactically unwise, making him a sitting duck. Galad did not use his fire—trying to conserve his magic, I assumed. Grundle's axe would become difficult to use if we got much closer, but I'd seen an Infected swipe at him earlier, and I knew his thicker skin and astounding strength gave him a solid chance in hand-to-hand combat without it.

"Close ranks!" I shouted, sprinting toward the one directly in front of me. The Infected yelled, its skin-covered mouth stretching wide, ready for the fight. At the last instant, I dropped to the ground and slid between its legs, slicing with force just above its ankle. I popped up on the other side as the beast began to topple, and I kept running.

I spun around. The fairytale trio had closed ranks and fought in ways familiar to them. I was taking a chance out on my own, betting that they were all coming from the same direction and I could risk my back being exposed. On the other hand, the Infected were not paying attention to their own exposed backs. I cut into one of the two taking on the dwarf first. Rapid defense maneuvers with that hammer would be a struggle. The elf had only one focusing on him, and I felt good about those odds, having sparred with Galad, so I moved on to Grundle. I struck out of the dark, disemboweling one before the other realized it was on his own, then slicing deeply into the side of the one remaining.

I danced to my right, slicing into the arm of the one Harry was fighting, then moving on, slicing the quad of Galad's opponent when he drove it close to me.

Shortly, it was over, and I moved back into position.

"I think we are done for the night," Galad said, heading for his bottles, irritated.

"Galad..." began Grundle.

"That was stupidly reckless!" Galad said in barely controlled fury. "She could have gotten herself and all of us killed!"

"Galad..." Grundle began again.

It was my turn to interrupt. "What the hell is wrong with you? Moving outside their line was a calculated risk. It kept them off balance and gave us an advantage."

"Whoever calculated that risk is a fool!" Galad spat.

The humming was dying down as the bottles were sealed. Galad began to put them away.

"Galad," began the troll for the third time. Pausing, he breathed deeply before continuing calmly. "This war is not going to be won by playing by the rules... by playing it *safe*."

"This war is not going to be *won*," Galad said, eyes downcast, a morbid pallor having taken hold of him.

"Galad. I know what you see," Grundle said. "I know what this dredges up in you. You see it all happening again. You see only loss, and you fear it. But she... *Red*... she sees what can be saved. She has a world to save. *Her*

world. Not yours. *Not yours*, Galad. Honor *her*, old friend."
And I knew the "her" Grundle spoke of was not me. "You
see the reflection of her. As do I. Honor her memory."
Grundle put an arm on Galad's shoulder, and they stood
silently.

Galad came back to himself and began to pack up
his equipment. Harry and I helped Grundle gather bodies
into a pile. When we were done, Grundle said, "Stand back
from the bodies, and prepare for one last fight. It is unlikely,
but sometimes this spell will attract a straggler."

Galad cast a spell, and the pile crawled with little
snakes of light, then collapsed inward and left a pile of
smoldering ashes. No further attacks came. The spell was
not strong enough—or the enemy was not near enough—
but no more Blighted arrived. Galad told us to gather close,
then popped us home.

Chapter 38

Galad took the backpack with the vials—canisters, vases, whatever—into the tent for safe keeping, leaving me with Grundle and Harry.

"Are we done for the day then?" I asked. "Because it's only been..." I checked my phone. "Less than two hours. The sun is barely up."

Grundle chuckled. "You wish to spill more blood?"

"I'm just asking. You said you do that once every seven to ten days. By the way, we call a seven-day period a week."

"You go by seven-days?" the troll rumbled. "How gloriously uncivilized. The elves have been trying to convince the rest of us uncivilized races to switch to a ten-day period for eons. 'It makes the math easier,'" he said in a singsong voice meant to imitate Galad. He chuckled some more. "We will rest here for a time. Normally, we would be done for the day with the one excursion. Let us talk for now. You are asking multiple things. Why do we do this purging at all? And why every *week* or so?" he said, amusing himself.

Grundle settled himself on the ground, resting against a tree, then continued. "These Infected, they will continue to grow in number. We don't know if more are getting pulled through the void, or if they multiply once here."

"Some of both, I suspect," said the elf, rejoining the conversation.

The troll nodded. "What we do know is that, if they reach some critical number, or get triggered to attack, they

166

multiply insanely quickly." He paused. "Perhaps with greater numbers they can open a larger portal." He waved his hand dismissively. "Doesn't matter. Once that happens, your world is done. Their numbers are beyond comprehension. They have taken over so many worlds, have such vast resources to draw upon, there is no stopping them."

"So, we keep their numbers low," Harry picked up the explanation. "We use those vases of mana to draw them in and thin their numbers. All the while we work on more permanent solutions to reduce that which draws them. Which means keeping you humans from bunching up."

I wasn't ready to talk about their "more permanent solution" of taking down The Palace. "Why a week? Why the day trips? What are your limiting factors?"

"Ah," said Grundle, smiling. "Excellent questions. There are two limiting factors at work. One is that we have to recharge those vases. On our worlds, that is a trivial exercise, but your sun is dead and so—"

I held up my hand to stop him. "I don't think that translated correctly."

The troll pointed at the sun, still rising on its daily journey. "Your sun. The star that warms your world. Where we come from, we would call it a dead star."

I was baffled, and it must have shown.

"It produces no magical energy," Grundle said. He looked puzzled at my puzzlement. He waved at the heavens. "We have to rely on all those distant stars to recharge the vases."

Say what?

Galad haughtily stepped in. "It's why you've avoided the notice of the Blighted for so long."

"Hmph." the troll grunted. "I shouldn't have gone there yet. Let's go back to your questions and work our way back out on grounds you are familiar with. She doesn't know about magic," Grundle said, speaking more

167

confidently. "Think about it, Galad. Their whole world doesn't know."

Galad's face became thoughtful, and Grundle returned his attention to me. "For reasons hard to explain, there is little ambient magic in your world. Because of that, the magic in our weapons, or the vases, or us..." he waved at Galad, "recharges more slowly." He nodded his head at me, asking if I followed.

I could at least accept that it might be true. "It's hard to deny there might be magic when I'm staring at beings from fairy tales."

Grundle shrugged, accepting my answer, and carried on. "So your dead sun limits how often we can use the vases, which is about every week or a little longer." I nodded again that I was following. "And the same lack of magic limits our ability to cast Healing spells, which is sometimes the more critical factor."

"So, if Galad's Healing spell, or the hammer, runs out of energy," I said, "and you get mortally wounded, it's game over, and this world has one less defender."

"That's the gist of it," the troll said. "There are nuances—Galad can meditate and recharge faster than a vase. Vases cannot meditate. Galad can recharge *from* a vase, but that obviously depletes the vase, which recharges more slowly than he. There might be ways to recharge the vases more efficiently, but we haven't worked them out."

I held out my hand to halt his rambling soliloquy. "But we are done for the day, while Galad meditates and he and the *vases* recharge?"

Grundle gave a questioning look to Galad, who sighed, his exasperation clear. He then said something that sounded like it should have made him joyous—what was with the attitude? "You were right, Grundle. With four of us, we were more efficient. We could go out again."

Grundle smiled and clapped his hands, the sound

168

like two boulders colliding. "Wonderful!"

"But!" Galad shouted over the noise, and Grundle curbed his enthusiasm. "But, not for some time. The vases—and I—must still recharge."

"Okay," I said. My mind had been churning, and a few hours might be time enough. "I have some ideas," I said decisively. "Let me get my friend."

"Bear?" Grundle asked.

"No. One you haven't met." I texted Scan a series of terse messages.

Did you try to call me earlier? I don't think my phone is working right.

Hey, let's meet at the Apple Store by Central Park. I wanted to look at their iPads.

I'll be waiting.

He would know what I meant.

When I looked up, Grundle was looking at Galad, who waved dismissively back at Grundle, saying, "No one likes a know-it-all. I'm going to go meditate." He wandered back to the tent.

"I'll be back in about an hour," I said. The troll smirked and waved at his ear. Of course "hour" wouldn't translate. "I'll be back in less time than our last trip."

Harry spoke up as I was leaving. "I don't know how things work here, but, if it matters, leave your weapons and clean some of that black gore off." He held out a jug of water.

He was right. I cleaned up, getting the worst of the gore off. But I tucked the daggers into my boots, and, heck, in NYC, no one would give me a second glance with just a little gore.

169

The troll nodded his agreement that I looked okay, and I headed to the Apple Store, off of the southeast corner of the park. As I walked up, a young woman approached me. "Excuse me, could you help me?" she asked.

Under normal circumstances, I would have ignored her, but I was expecting something like that. "Sure," I said, "how can I help?"

She set her bag down and showed me her phone, asking something about the Museum of Natural History. I pointed her in the right direction and made a show of giving directions through the park. Nodding happily, she started off. I picked up the bag she left behind and headed back, pulling out a burner phone and tablet.

I called Scan as I walked back.

"Welcome back to New York," he said.

"Thanks, Scan." I jumped right into it. "These guys are fighting with ancient weapons. I wanted to show them some more modern toys before we go back out."

"What did you have in mind?"

"Can you find me an isolated place?"

"Does it matter where?"

"I was thinking desert—Arizona? You tell me what's convenient. Here's the deal—I spent my early morning fighting those beasts, the Blighted. The Infected. But our fantasy friends are struggling to resource their hunting missions."

"Got it. You're hoping to augment their resources with some 21st century munitions."

"Yes, but just stuff we can easily get our hands on."

"Roger that."

It wouldn't help them recharge their magic, but better weapons could help them use less of it. I found myself already back at the camp. Apparently, that uneasy feeling could even guide me subconsciously.

The dwarf and troll were more or less in the same

170

state as I'd left them, though the troll had a book in his hand—the one I'd given him.

"Your blood brother would not come?" the troll asked as I walked toward him.

"He's right here," I said, wiggling the phone at my ear.

The troll looked amused and perplexed. "He is smaller than I expected."

"Har dee har har," I replied. The troll's look of confusion only deepened. I put the phone on speaker. "Say hi, Scan."

"Hi, Scan," Scan said, the comedic ass. He missed my eye roll over the phone.

"That was gibberish," Grundle said, approaching the phone with interest. "I don't understand what you're showing me. We are talking to him while he is elsewhere? But magic doesn't work here."

"It's not magic, just technology."

Scan said, "I heard some grunting, but that's it."

Crap. The spell that translated languages wasn't working over the phone.

"Red, can you set up the tablet?" Scan asked. "I've got some software on there that will enable encrypted video, and I think we're going to need it for some better pics of landing sites. Ask them if it matters where they Teleport."

"Grundle," I said for Scan, "I have an idea to help you with resourcing your battles. I need to know, does the Teleportation spell cost Galad a lot of energy? Does distance matter?"

"I'm no magic wielder," the troll said, "but my understanding is that distance traveled, on a given world, does not greatly affect the magical energy used. The work, and spell energy, is in traveling to a location the first time. Galad creates a mystic world map that he uses to triangulate a destination, and then he has to work to find an

171

isolated target location—not simple tasks."

"Okay," I said. "I'm trying to get you to a secluded area. I want to show you some weapons. Secluded areas should be easier?"

He nodded agreement.

"Scan," I said, "he says if we can get him a world map and image, he can go wherever, as long as it's secluded."

"Okay, it looks like I can actually do this better in New Mexico." I turned the tablet on, and Scan popped up in a video feed, racks of computer equipment behind him.

"Well, hello," he said to the camera. "There's a troll behind you. So cool."

Grundle shook his head. "Amazing. You... your *people...* worked out how to do this without any magic."

"Still all grunts for me," Scan said.

"I still can't understand him," Grundle said.

"Galad's translation spell must only work in person," I said to both of them. Harry came over to look at the phone.

"Hi, dwarf," Scan said.

"His name's Harry," I told him.

"His name is also Harry?" asked Harry.

"No, no." Eye roll. "I was introducing *you*. Harry, this is Scan."

Harry nodded to Scan, who was typing away, but looked over and waved, then went back to typing.

The troll shrugged. "I've witnessed the translation working over long distances in our spell-bound equivalent of these artifacts, but clearly yours don't operate the same way."

"How long until you'll have some weapons set up where we can test them?" I asked Scan.

"It'll take some time. Any specific requests?"

"Think stealth with firepower. An M60 with suppressor... or an Uzi with silencer for me or the elf. Other than that, let's show them something bigger so they can have an idea of options—and some handguns like the one I used in The Palace."

"I'll see what I can find. Give me a few minutes to get this started and then we can talk about setting up the location."

"Are you telling me," grumbled Grundle, "that, like your tiny little long-distance talking devices, you have magic-less long-range weapons?"

"You saw what I did to that Infected in the building, right?"

"No, I did not, in fact. I know you used one of your weapons on Harry, but his enchanted armor protected him. After that, I was busy trying not to hurt your friend, while waiting for the Infected to arrive. I did *hear* it. I assumed you got lucky in hitting that despicable blighted creature. We know mechanical devices without the aid of magic are clunky and unpredictable."

"You're not entirely wrong," I told him. "I was a little lucky when I managed to shoot the beast, but the luck was that I aimed accurately enough from lying on my side after *Harry* had smashed my ribs."

Harry shrugged.

"There are chances for the mechanics to go wrong, but we've spent a lot of time getting the mechanics to almost always work right."

"Okay," Scan said. "I've got some equipment being gathered. How do we work out the location?"

"Is Galad going to kill me if I disturb his meditation?" I asked.

"Hard to say," Grundle replied and walked over to the tent. "But he won't kill *me*." Grundle poked something out of sight with his foot. "We need your vast intellect out here." Galad's response was inaudible to me, but Grundle chuckled, coming back to us.

173

Galad followed Grundle out, sour as ever.

"Sorry to awaken you, Your Highness," I said with mock sincerity.

Everybody froze mid-step. Galad glared at Grundle. Grundle groaned. "My lady," Grundle said, "what, may I ask, led you to choose that particular turn of phrase?"

"It's just a phrase we use when someone is acting high and mighty; you know, like they're royalty or... holy crap, you're *royalty*, aren't you?"

"I'm not the only one," he muttered, looking at Grundle.

"You are mistaken," Grundle said. "There is no concept of royalty among trolls."

Galad rolled his eyes and shook his head.

I looked at Harry.

"Not me," he said. "Somebody has to do the heavy lifting."

Grundle snorted. "Again, a tale for another day. Her Majesty here," he checked to see if he had used the phrase correctly, and I nodded my approval and gave him the thumbs-up, "would like us to Teleport to a new location, to show us some things she thinks will help."

Galad sighed. "It isn't as easy as that. I have to understand the location relative to us, and I need to *see* it." I waved him over. Another sigh. *Man, is there anything that doesn't irritate this royal pain-in-the-ass?*

"Scan, this is Galad," I said.

Scan looked away from his computer long enough to wave and wink. Galad mumbled a spell—I had learned to recognize when he was casting—and nothing happened.

"How are you doing that?" A perverse smirk crept over my face at his astonishment. "I don't see any mystic aura ... at all."

"Glad I could surprise you," I said. *Royal twit.* "Scan, can you pull up the globe with the source and destination

174

points?" The tablet screen popped up a 3D model of the world, with the earth spinning slowly on its axis, the whole thing transparent, with the continents outlined in green. One red dot showed where we were, in New York, and a second red open circle marked the destination.

Galad stood, open-mouthed, and even the troll and dwarf watched with eyes wide, transfixed. "Amazing," the elf muttered. He cast a spell, and a similar image appeared in the air in front of us, only it was truly three-dimensional. It actually took up space. It wasn't a green stick model of the Earth, but neither was it exactly globe-like. I could see the continents, but it seemed to mark things I could not recognize. It impressed me, and I found myself irritated that his royal highness could do something so interesting.

I moved the tablet so Scan could see. A bright white light appeared on the magical orb, marking our location. The elf studied the image on the screen, and placed a second magical dot where the destination was… presumably in New Mexico, though I couldn't tell state lines.

"That was… eye-opening," Galad began, "but I also have to picture the destination, in some detail, with the current topography. The topography can change some over time, after traveling there once, but the first time has to be accurate. The spell I must cast to see the destination—it takes a great deal of magical energy."

"Scan, he's got the general area. Can you bring up some satellite images?"

"You betcha." The screen shifted to images of the terrain in New Mexico from some height—brown and green clumps, a mountain range to the northwest. "You know how to operate this," he told me.

I showed Galad, touching the screen and swiping my finger to move the camera. Then two fingers spreading apart to zoom in, two fingers coming together to zoom out.

Galad hesitantly touched the screen, like it was a

175

snake ready to strike. He first moved the image around. Then he tried zooming. "Mother of..." he said. I felt palpable pride that our world without magic held surprises for him.

A red outline on the screen showed the boundary of where Scan thought we should go. Galad kept moving things until he finally paused. A bluff, mountains in the distance, a distinctive rock formation on the bluff, and lots of sand, rocks, and cacti. "Here," he declared. "I can take us here."

I nodded. "He says here, Scan."

"Okay," he said, "I have placed your order. Better write down your confirmation number." He snickered. Geeks. "Your shipment should arrive in about two hours."

Chapter 39

Red

There was nothing to do but wait. It was lunchtime, and I was getting hungry. "What do you guys eat? Wait, let me ask that differently."

Before I could correct myself, Grundle was already groaning. "Don't remind me. We mostly live off of grains summoned magically by His Highness. Horrid stuff. I'm wasting away."

"Okay, magically-summoned food," I said. "The elf doesn't eat meat. Have I got that right?" The disgust on the elf's face was enough of an answer. "What about you, Harry?"

"I eat most anything, I suppose. I mean, not other *people*, of course," the dwarf grunted, "but I eat meat, plants, rocks… the usual."

"You eat *rocks*? Never mind. Of course you do. Let *me* summon this meal. Scan, can you order me some pizzas? I'm guessing three meat-lovers for the troll. A supreme for the dwarf. Something veggie for the elf, and I'll just eat with him. I'm guessing he eats like a bird."

Galad shot me his "go to" look—perplexed and slightly offended.

"You betcha, Red," Scan said. "Ray's pizza is about a ten-minute walk. Can you carry five pizzas for ten minutes?" *Dang, they'll be cold by then. Too bad they can't Teleport me there, or the pizzas here.*

"I've done worse," I answered.

"Okay, I placed the order. They said about half an hour."

"Thanks. We have a little time to kill, so let me kick it

177

off with this interesting topic—our sun is dead, Scan."

"I don't remember having a son with you, but I mourn his passing," Scan said, his voice grave and serious.

"Har dee har har." *What an eye-roller of a day!* "The sun in the *sky*. They're telling me the sun in the sky is missing something that produces magic. It is, in their terms, *dead*, which I interpret as lacking something they believe fundamental to life."

"The sun is a big ball of fire, Red."

I repeated Scan's answer, and Galad said, "That's exactly the point. Your star is *just* a big ball of fire. It lacks any of the *essence* that makes it a true star. That is why we call it dead. We didn't believe it could even sustain life."

I relayed the information to Scan, who replied that "all the stars are just big balls of fire," which I told the others.

"Your blood brother has been to so many stars then?"

I intended to echo Galad's snarky remark, but Galad interrupted me. "This is ridiculous. We have some talismans imbued with the translation spell. Can you get one to your blood brother?"

"Of course," I said.

Galad entered the tent. While he was out of earshot, I explained Galad's snide comment to Scan. He laughed and said something about hoping his lack of interplanetary travel was correctable.

"I'd love to understand more, Red," he told me. "You know that about me."

I did. His thirst for knowledge was unquenchable. The downside being he tended toward obsession and an inward focus. We sometimes had to kick him to take on real-world problems.

Galad returned carrying a pair of necklaces with symbols on the pendants. He handed them both to me.

"Get one to your blood brother. Keep the other for yourself, in case anything should happen to me."

I thanked him and put one around my neck. Nothing seemed different, but why would it if I already had Galad's spell working on me?

"But Galad," Grundle said, all milky innocence, "you don't even know the lineage of those necklaces."

Galad tensed and gave Grundle the stink-eye, but Grundle just chuckled, neither of them letting me in on the joke.

"Well, it's time for you to start hoofing it to those pizzas," Scan said. "Location is in your phone."

"Thanks," I said. "Scan, can you have someone meet me at the pizza place to take this necklace back to you?"

Galad frowned his disapproval, but I knew my suggestion was a proven way of delivering things to Scan.

"Sure. Well, given that I can't talk to them, I guess it is time for me to sign off, unless one of them wants to play chess online."

I chuckled and Galad scowled in displeasure at my laugh; what a surprise—hypersensitive elf. So I explained, "He just said he would disconnect, since you can't talk, unless you want to play chess—a strategy game."

"I would play chess," Grundle said. I should have known.

"Scan, bring up the chess."

"Su-weet!" he cheered.

I handed Grundle the tablet and showed him how to touch the screen to move the pieces. His sausage-sized fingers were oversized for the tablet, like a grown man playing with a baby's toy, but he managed the delicate movements with some care.

"I'll be back," I said, and Grundle looked up.

"What was that?" he said, eying me strangely.

"What?" I shot back. He stared at me a few seconds,

and I began to become self-conscious, looking down at my clothes for something out of place, like a giant spider or two-headed lizard.

But he shook his head. "I thought I saw something move across the gemstone in your necklace. A play of the light." He waved it off and returned to the tablet. I self-consciously tucked the necklace under my shirt—it would draw attention anyway—and left to fetch the pizzas.

Scan

I played chess with the troll. People often called chess a game of strategy, but when one was first learning, it was much more a game of tactics. Trying to show the troll the valid moves nonverbally had been tricky, but he caught on soon enough. We played several quick games, where I trounced him soundly, but he learned to use his pieces, and the final game, though I still won, proved much more interesting.

While I played, I got a few other things done. I arranged a pick up for that "Necklace of Tongues +3." I played it down, but I was keeping a tight eye on that. Did they not realize the implications? I already had access to an entire world of camera feeds. Add to that the ability to understand all the foreign feeds. *Sweet Jehoshaphat.* Plus, I'd know everything that little Japanese firecracker of Bear's was saying when she rampaged. On second thought, did I *want* that?

I also had some lab equipment shipped. I'd fibbed a little about those guns for Red. I could have found more—and faster—in Afghanistan, and since location didn't matter, that would have made sense. When I said New Mexico would work better, I meant better for my intentions—I had access to guns *and* some lab equipment. I wanted to have some measurements on site when they Teleported.

I had been waiting for something marvelous my entire life—magic was real, and I would not stop until I figured it out.

Chapter 40

Red

Pizza panned out. *Ha!* Galad ate like a bird—a veggie pizza filled the two of us. The troll took a tentative bite of the carnivore, then scarfed all three of his. He would have eaten the boxes if I hadn't stopped him. Harry ate his, perhaps longing for a little sediment. I should have thought to toss some gravel on his supreme.

"Thank you," Galad said. "That was so much better than I expected."

"Better than anything I've eaten in *ages*! Since before we arrived here," Grundle said, his eyes traveling the table for leftovers. *Okay, four pizzas next time? I wouldn't mind a beer either.*

"How's the delivery coming?" I asked Scan.

"Which... oh, the weapons... um... let me check the delivery time on the website..." Smart ass. "The packages are being dropped off now. Red, I sent some telemetry equipment as well. I want to see if there's any kind of signature from these Teleports. Just keep them clear of that stuff if you can."

I frowned. It made sense for Scan to understand better how they managed to move between distant locations in a blink of the eye, but I didn't enjoy finding out after the fact. I wished he'd told me upfront. "So, how long?"

"Five, ten minutes. Something like that. Depends on how quickly the delivery boys move on."

"Scan says we're five to ten minutes out." At their puzzled expressions, I muttered, "We have got to figure out how to scale for time."

Galad smiled. "Units of measurement are a particular

problem for the translation spell. Do you mind if I touch you?" He reached toward my cheeks but kept his hands from touching them.

"Ohhkaay."

He cast a spell, then put his hands on my head. It felt... odd. "What do you call the time between your star's cyclic appearances in the sky?"

"A day."

"And you break the day up into...?"

"Hours."

"How many hours in a day?"

"Twenty-four."

He wrinkled his face like he smelled something foul. Oh, yeah, the elves were apparently metric nazis, even with time. "And that further breaks down to...?"

"Sixty minutes in an hour. Sixty seconds in a minute."

"A second is the smallest unit?"

"After that, we go by tens. Decisecond is a tenth of a second, but nobody says that. I guess there's a centisecond, a hundredth, and then the actually *used* term, millisecond, which is a thousandth of a second."

Galad smiled thinly, perhaps pleased with our metric units for times that were really short. "And the next time unit *longer* than a day?"

"A week is seven days. A fortnight is two weeks, I think. Months vary from 28 to 31 days, and a year is 365 or 366 days. Just for reference, a year is the time it takes for our planet, Earth, to go around the sun. You know, our dead star."

Galad released my head. He uttered a new spell. "All right, I have updated my spell. It should now be able to handle time."

That was actually pretty cool. How would the necklaces know about that?

"Okay," Scan said, "almost ready. My necklace just

183

arrived. Let's give it a go." He put on the necklace. "Have your boys say something."

"You get that?" I asked Harry.

"Still gibberish." he answered.

"Gah. It doesn't work." Scan's face sank.

"I guess it only works in person," Galad said.

Scan began to pull the necklace off, huffing with disappointment, but stopped himself, and let it fall back into place. "Fair enough. I'll find a way to test it in person. Shipment is on site and the delivery service has left the area. You ready to roll?"

I repeated for everyone. "Are we ready to give this a try?"

They all gathered close together. Galad looked nervous. "You're sure about the location of the site, and that the image you showed me is accurate?"

I showed Galad the satellite image of the site, complete with boxes that were just delivered and equipment that had been set up. "Those are the toys Scan just had delivered," I informed him.

"Okay, let's try. Get close." But we were already together, and Galad began his spell. It seemed to take longer than the previous Teleports, and I began to worry. A second later I saw the familiar flash, felt the subtle disjointed sensation, and suddenly, we were somewhere else.

Chapter 41

I waved them toward the boxes. The delivery boys had left a crow bar, which I used to pry open the lid. *Oh, this is going to be fun.*

I pulled out an M60—just what I'd asked for—suppressor already attached. I added an ammunition belt to my pile, turned, and handed the M60 to Harry. I let him hold it while I loaded the ammo and set the rifle to burst mode. I pointed out a cactus at the bottom of the bluff, roughly 80 yards away. I took the gun from him for a second. "Here's how you hold it. Use this 'sight' here to line up your shot. Gently squeeze the trigger. I've set it to fire in bursts. It'll kick back on you." I handed the gun back, pointing at the cactus again.

The dwarf took a second to take aim, then squeezed the trigger. *Pop, pop, pop!* Dust flew up from behind the cactus, and the dwarf said something; I assumed dwarvish had swearing. Then he took aim again and—*pop, pop, pop!*—he blew the head off the cactus.

"Yes!" I said with a fist pump. The dwarf was already beading on a new evil cactus and blew that one's torso up.

"Yes, you've taught that evil plant not to mess with the likes of you," Galad uttered with a sneer.

"This is unbelievable," the dwarf whispered in awe.

I was already fishing through the pile for something for Galad. Yes, an Uzi. They were smaller than the M60s. Something better for my size or Galad's. I loaded a magazine and took a shot at a rock—"save the cactus" and all. I handed it to Galad, who obediently fired a few rounds at the unsuspecting rock. He turned to me and shook his

185

head—he wasn't interested.

I pulled out a handgun and showed them how to load the cartridge and fire. "Eight shots in this magazine. That can vary. Best to know how many bullets you have in the chamber at all times."

I set the handgun down, grinning at what would come next. "Okay, we can't actually use this in a city, but I wanted you to have an idea of what's possible." I pulled out an M32 grenade launcher, loaded it, then pulled out another and loaded it as well.

"This is for me," Grundle rumbled, smiling knowingly.

I showed him how to hold it. "This is a semi-automatic grenade launcher. It can unload six rounds in three seconds." I had something in mind but... "Try a round with this first," I said without explaining myself.

He lifted the weapon in his enormous arms, making the grenade launcher look small. He fired off a round. The poor, innocent rock got annihilated.

"The other one, if you please," he requested politely. He'd read my mind. Smiling, I held out the other grenade launcher, and holding one in each hand, he pointed at another outcropping, not quite the size of the one we were on. In approximately three seconds, he unloaded the eleven remaining grenades into the rock formation. The rest of us ducked from the rock flying back our way, but Grundle just made a deep growling/rumbling noise, standing like a wall amidst the flying debris. Smiling, he put the grenade launchers back in the box. "Thank you for showing me this."

Peering up at the sky, Grundle added, "I have seen your flying vehicles. I assume they can also drop such weapons from above."

"Oh, yes. Much more powerful."

"I see," he said. He picked up the Uzi and the M60 but put them back. "I think my large fingers will not work with these smaller weapons. And this other is too destructive for city use, though I am glad to have tried it."

"Well, I can use this one." Harry had not set the M60 down. "I'll call her Emma." He turned his head, as though listening to someone behind him. "Don't be silly," he said. "I'm just being friendly." *Who is he talking to?*

I grabbed some cartridges for the .45 and the Uzi. "Okay, I'm ready." The elf waved for us to get close and Teleported us back to the campsite in Central Park.

We'd killed some time, but it was not yet dusk.

"I am going to go meditate some more," Galad said. "We may need the spell energy."

I set down my new weapons and was thinking through how best to use them. The troll came up behind me and placed a hand on my shoulder. "Very impressive," he rumbled. "I'm not sure we can use those in close combat, but it is good to know our options."

"Maybe I didn't show you those just so you'd know your options," I replied. "Maybe I wanted you to know how I'd be coming after you if this proves to be a trick."

The troll's eyes grew large, and he walked away bellowing with genuine laughter, muttering something about she-trolls.

Chapter 42

Red

We Teleported to our next location. It was the middle of the night. Galad cast his night vision spell and began setting up the vials. We were again in a wooded area, but a city glowed through the trees.

"There is a river that way," Galad said, pointing. "I will take position opposite the river. Red and Harry, flank me. If you're going to use those weapons, point them far in front of me, please."

Well, a wooded area at least meant stray shots were likely to hit only trees. On the other hand, it would be harder to see and hit the enemy. I positioned myself on Grundle's left, and I put the Uzi down behind the line of our circle. I thought the handgun would be better suited for the terrain, as long as I spotted the enemy far enough afield.

"There's a small trail along the river, so don't get cocky about that direction being safe," Galad commented. I presumed the others had been there before, on their week-to-ten-day trips, and that Galad's messages were solely for me.

I felt a ping on my phone and saw the text from Scan.

Mumbai

Okay, I knew nothing about Mumbai. I waited while Galad set up the vessels, scanning the grounds just in case. I finally heard the thrumming begin and Galad's warning: "Be ready."

We waited in silence, scanning the woods. I saw the first movement coming from Grundle's direction. One of the monsters came rushing from the woods, and I fired. I caught it in its side. I didn't kill it, but I weakened it before it reached Grundle, who dispatched it with his axe.

The next one came between Harry and Grundle, and Harry let loose a small burst but didn't correct properly for movement and fired behind the monster. Grundle's axe again met his enemy.

Then two came into our makeshift camp almost at the same time, from the same direction as the previous attack. Harry fired a round and downed one, leaving one more for Grundle's axe. Harry had backed himself closer to Grundle. It made sense—armed with a long-range weapon, he needed to be close to the troll in case something escaped past him.

I did the same and moved in closer to the troll. We managed a semi-stable rhythm. Harry and I pulled some down before they got close, wounded others, making it easier for Grundle. Some we missed, but Galad was getting bored.

We finally won a pause. "Round two they will be more grouped, right?" I asked.

"Yes," Grundle answered.

I swapped out my .45 for the Uzi. If they were coming in a group, I wanted a weapon meant for that. We stood waiting. When they broke through the trees, there were a lot of them. Maybe ten? No way to get a solid count. Especially while they were getting torn up by bullets. One slipped through our rain of fire and raked Harry across his upper arm before getting axed—literally.

With no enemy in sight, Harry unslung his hammer and touched it to his arm. Nothing happened. "Oh, it's that way, is it?" he complained. The wound wasn't grievous, not an emergency, but I wondered why the hammer hadn't Healed Harry. Galad came closer to do the honors.

Feeling overall satisfied with the job we'd done, but

still on the lookout for stragglers, I was surprised by a girl's scream in the direction of the river.

I ran toward the sound. "Close formation!" I yelled. I dropped the Uzi and pulled out my knives, giving myself the speed boost I needed to sprint faster.

"Stop!" Galad shouted. But I didn't stop. I found the trail, and not far down it, the source of the scream. A young girl, around twelve years old, lay on the ground. Torn up bodies surrounded her, and standing over her was one of the creatures. It was holding her down, and she was screaming. As I ran closer, intending to plunge a knife into the beast, I saw the girl's body turn black.

As I plunged both knives into the back of the beast, the girl's body elongated. It grew talons, and the face disappeared into an eyeless, mouthless monster with just a nasal cavity.

I pulled out my daggers and jumped back from the dying beast I'd gutted. But… *oh shit. Oh shit oh shit oh shit.* Where the girl had been, a beast threw off the dying carcass of its compatriot, and started toward me.

No no no no no. I ran back the way I had come. Though I hadn't gone far, it seemed like an eternity to get back. I was afraid I had missed the camp—grim death pressed in from all sides, like I was drowning. Seeing Galad felt like popping my head above water and sucking in life-giving air. As I tore past him, he swung his sword.

No. No, wait! But when I turned back, he had already taken the head off the beast. The beast that less than a minute before had been a young girl.

Oh shit. That phrase kept repeating itself in my head. I couldn't catch my breath. The *Infected*—they transformed living beings into themselves. Everyone becoming either dead or Infected—that was what would happen to my world if invaders kept coming. The fairytale trio wanted to stop the draw of those creatures to my world. They thought The

190

Palace, full of people, would beckon more of the horrible monsters to Earth.

Heart hammering, fighting nausea, I felt an internal shift from which there was no going back. If destroying The Palace was what it took to stop those creatures from taking away our very humanity, then I would take down The Palace myself.

Chapter 43

Red

I sat on the ground, stunned. I still kept a wary eye out for the enemy, but Galad had shut down the magic that lured them in. We were waiting for him to finish packing things up so we could leave.

Grundle came closer, still scanning the horizon in case there were more attackers.

"What happened?" he grumbled.

What happened? I'd seen a frightened young girl transformed into one of those damned beasts. "Did you know?" I whispered up at him, then louder. "Did you know that those... *things*... use *us* to create more of *themselves*?"

Grundle sighed and gazed into the past. "I suspected. The way their numbers grow. Red, they destroyed my entire world, within days—even opening a large portal to march in an army would not give them that kind of advantage." Shrugging helplessly, he continued. "I have also entertained the possibility that there is a mastermind behind their attacks that opens multiple portals." He pounded a fist into his hand, creating a crack of thunder. "Red, we don't know a lot about them, because once they get a foothold, there are no survivors to explain what happened."

"*You're* alive," I accused.

"I was off world. As was Galad when his world was attacked. There are very few survivors from any world that is attacked, and they are all people who got out early, so they don't have solid information on the invaders."

Grundle left me alone then. He started gathering the

bodies of the Infected. Of the names that were used to describe the creatures, Infected seemed the best. They literally infected people—not just humans if I was understanding Grundle—converting what they could into more of their horrid species. I didn't help Grundle, but just sat and tried to digest my new reality.

When I left to enlist, my youngest sister, Jade, was thirteen. Though I knew she was an adult, I still sometimes thought of her as that thirteen-year-old girl. The girl from the trail, whose life had just been ended by a monster, could easily have been Jade. I pictured my sister, trapped and scared, becoming Infected, becoming a monster that had no personality, a destructive force of evil.

This is my *world!* Grundle, Galad, and Harry had *lost* their worlds.

Was fighting, in our current stealth mode, really the right strategy? Didn't the rest of humanity deserve the chance to protect themselves?

Harry and Grundle had finished piling up the bodies. Galad was getting ready to incinerate them.

"Wait," I breathed.

He paused.

"I'm not sure keeping this secret is the right move."

I pulled out my phone to take a picture.

Grundle put a gentle hand on my shoulder. "I can appreciate that you want to warn people. That's good. But consider that, right now, *we* are the only ones who can draw these creatures out to fight them. There's no way to track them. If you reveal us in a way that prevents us from doing these tasks, the war is lost. Think through how you'll do this. I'm not saying you're wrong—just think it through."

He had a point. "Can we take a few minutes here?" I needed to think.

"We can," Galad said. "I will place a ward on this space." He cast a spell, which I assumed was like the one on their camp in Central Park, to drive people away.

I brought out the burner phone and pinged Scan, asking him to call me. A minute later it buzzed.

"Hey, Red. How's Mumbai?"

I ignored the question. "Scan, I've learned some things tonight that make me question our approach. I think we need more people to know about this. But I also think it would be a mistake to, say, flood the internet with what we know. We would cause their current methods to get screwed up and risk the whole ball game."

"So, what do you need?"

"There's an FBI agent I'd like you to get in touch with. Hold on a sec." I pulled out my other phone, found her number, and read off her info to Scan. "I'll send you a pic. You get it to her with this location. Get the info to her anonymously. She'll get someone out here to check it out. I'll send a note to clue her in without being entirely open. I think she'll meet with me, and we can go from there."

"Roger that, Red. Just send me the pic from *this* phone."

"Roger that. Scan, can you join us tomorrow? I think I need to dig deeper into some other options. And translating everything for you and for them... I'm worried we don't have that kind of time."

"Yeah, Red, I can do that. 6am, North Park?"

"Thanks, Scan." I hung up, used the phone with its light to take a pic, and sent it to his number.

"Okay, let's go," I told everyone.

"Leave the bodies then?" Galad asked.

"Yes."

"And the ward spell? Should I remove it?"

"Can you make it weaker? I want the FBI to find these bodies, but not random joggers."

"I can do that," Galad said. He re-cast the spell, then had us gather, and he *bamf*ed us back to NYC.

194

"I'm going to head home," I said, my heart and soul running on empty.

Grundle patted me on the shoulder but said nothing. The walk back to my flat seemed very long. My sleep was troubled with dreams of my younger sisters, running from those monsters, then cornered. I woke up, drenched in sweat, as my sisters transformed into the Infected.

Chapter 44

Red

I awoke to my phone alarm, feeling more tired than when I'd gone to bed. How many times could a body do that in one lifetime, I wondered. I made a cup of coffee, but it did not have its usual effect on me. I envisioned the hot liquid filtering not through coffee beans, but ashes, and the resulting brew seemed devoid of its usual flavor.

Nevertheless, I had to keep moving forward. I felt a sudden, gut-wrenchingly deep sense of loneliness, and I wished Murphy were there. He hadn't seen me lose hope often, but his quick and reassuring smiles, his light jokes, brought me out of my funk like nothing else. Knowing I would not have that, ever again, made my despair all the greater.

And yet, I did still have to move forward. Murphy may have been all those things, but he was also practical. Not knowing completely how to fix something was not an excuse for not trying to do so. I needed more information. Bringing Scan in, trying together to understand more of the pieces of the puzzle, was my best next move.

I met Scan in North Park. We walked toward the camp and talked.

"Rough night?" Scan tried to make the question casual, but it annoyed me. I ran a hand through my hair, trying to remember whether I'd brushed it.

"Didn't sleep well. Nightmares," I said, shrugging.

"So what was the recent information you learned that has you so... wrought?"

"Those creatures we've been fighting, we call them the Infected. I had assumed it was a general name for a monstrous enemy… I mean, they also use terms like the Blighted to describe them… I guess I thought they were like a plague of locusts…"

"I can't see what you're getting at."

"Scan, I was watching as one of those creatures attacked a young girl. It transformed her into another of the creatures. They are Infected… they *become* Infected. Their army grows by taking over their victims, converting them into more of themselves."

Scan and I walked in silence for a minute.

"That can't be right," he finally said.

I knew how he felt. "Grundle, Galad, and Harry all come from worlds that were taken over by the creatures. They only survived by being off-world when their homes were attacked. They said their entire worlds were gone within days."

"That makes more sense."

I scowled—Scan's words were very dry and clinical, as though entire planets being killed off was all just an algebra problem to be solved, and I found myself angry at his callousness for the lives lost. Everyone the otherworlders knew was gone—every place they called home was unreachable. That girl in Mumbai was gone—transformed, then beheaded.

Scan saw the anger on my face, and he explained himself. "I just meant that the math doesn't work out on our world—I would expect much more rapid growth than we are seeing, like what happened to *their* worlds. I mean, if you started with just one of those creatures, and he *turned* someone, now you'd have two. Each of those turns someone, becoming four, then eight, sixteen, thirty-two, and so on. That's an exponential increase. If they transformed people whenever they found them, our world would already be toast."

I felt the slightest, tiniest spark of hope. There was

something we were missing. If nothing else, I at least felt I'd done the right thing by asking Scan to come in and talk through things.

"You sure this is the right way?" He was eying the trees like they were about to grab him. "My Spidey-sense is tingling."

I chuckled. Which felt good. We were getting closer to the camp. "They call it a ward. It's some kind of spell that makes you feel uncomfortable, worried, even scared, as you approach it. It's a vague feeling that makes you want to head in another direction. Once you know about it, you can use it as a homing beacon, which seems like a bit of a flaw in a spell meant to keep you away."

"Oh, okay. Cool." But despite his knowledge, he checked over his shoulder every thirty seconds.

When we reached camp, they were all there. I introduced Scan to everyone and vice versa. He pulled the necklace out from under his shirt and said, "This is... amazing. Like Google Translate running live on audio, but also muffling their original language, or amplifying the translation or something."

Galad was the first to respond. "I didn't understand some of those words, but you got the gist of it."

I interrupted. "What did you have planned today?"

"Not a lot," Grundle replied. "The canisters need to recharge. Someone will take one and do a smaller hunt, but there is no fixed time for that."

"So we can spend time talking," I said. I wanted to know more.

"Learning. Planning. Yes," Grundle rumbled with a smirk.

"Okay, let's start with the discussion Scan and I were just having. You said those Infected overran your worlds in a matter of days. I saw the Infected convert a little girl into an Infected. But they're not doing that all the time, or we would see a lot more of them."

Grundle rumbled, shifting uncomfortably. "I'm sorry. I'm gnawing on old memories like the leg of my enemy." *Did that translate right?* "The people who are lucky enough to get out tell of slaughter. I do not doubt what you saw, but I am saying there must be more to what happens than taking over new bodies—why slaughter people when you can transform them?"

"Your world," Galad pondered. "More specifically, your dead sun—perhaps they suffer from the same limitation we do, and cannot recharge their magical energy. Maybe they would replicate more rapidly if they had more energy."

"I want to understand that better," Scan said, "but I also want the answer to the question 'why now?' I mean, how did *they* get here? How did *you* know they would come here?"

Grundle turned to Galad, who considered how to answer. "Some of that answer is very complicated, but the easiest way to understand is a metaphor I learned as a child. I know you have oceans here. Do you have beaches, or is everything harsh cliffs?"

"We have beaches." I had many wonderful memories of beaches from my childhood.

"When I was a child," he said, "I used to collect sea shells that washed up on shore. But I learned that those shells were often broken, and by going out into the water a small distance, I found better shells."

I nodded along. That was something I remembered from my adventures on the beach as well.

"However, if I waded in too deep, the ocean floor became too difficult to see. On top of it all, the ocean was constantly moving things around, so I might see a promising shell, but as I reached for it, the ocean would snatch it away."

199

Grundle chuckled, "I am excited to hear how your idyllic childhood ties in to our current questions."

Galad curled a lip in a half smile while rolling his eyes. Okay, so the elf did have a sense of humor? "The gulf between worlds is much like the ocean, at least in a mystic sense. All you see, when you gaze at the stars, is their physical separation." Galad stopped when he saw our blank faces. "That didn't go well," he acknowledged. "You," he said, pointing at Scan. "Have your people learned that light can behave in entirely different ways with different principles?"

"Wave-particle duality, you mean?" Scan answered. I'd heard of that throughout my life. Something about being able to tell that light came in particles—photons?—but that it also diffracted like a wave, like when you saw light split into many colors through a crystal, or a rainbow.

"That sounds roughly right," continued Galad. "It didn't all translate well. The point is not to understand the details, but the broader concept that things can have dual natures."

"Okay," Scan jumped back in, "related concepts exist in math. We describe signals in terms of their wave characteristics, and we can create circuits based on those concepts, to filter in or filter out certain signals."

Galad started speaking directly to Scan—it reminded me of when teachers would focus their lectures on the one person who seemed to get it. "Right, so now imagine there is a transformation you just don't know yet. Can you do that?"

"Sure, there are wavelet transforms that people come up with for specific problems. They're just out there, waiting for us to find them."

"Okay, so I am just talking about a transform. The worlds we live on map to a totally different space, where how close or far apart they are is changing much more dramatically than what you see in physical space. In this picture of the universe, the planets are like shells at the beach. There is a tide that pushes them around, moving them in and out of the shallows, and closer and farther from one another, all the time."

"Hey," I said, "even *I* followed that! You should have started your explanation with 'shells at the beach.'"

Galad smirked at me. "Duly noted, Your Highness."

"Ass," I said, to a chuckle from Grundle.

"Okay, keep going," Scan urged. "I'm guessing you're going to say our worlds were pushed close together, making travel easier."

"Not so much that. I think your world has never been far from ours in the *chureep*."

Crap, I had no concept to map that to… how about "mystic ocean?" I knew from experience that the interpretation spell would start mapping Galad's spoken word to my choices.

"No," he continued, unaware of the derailment of my train of thought, "I think, rather, your world was too deep to be seen, and recently washed closer to shore, combined with one other factor I haven't explained yet."

Oh, goody. More new vocabulary words.

"Usually, as a child, I would go searching for a specific kind of shell. I might find other interesting shells, but I'd be looking for, say, a shiny round one with small dots on it."

Perplexed, I squinted at him, wondering again where he was headed. I noticed Grundle's similarly puzzled expression. Harry, uninterested, had started cleaning little bits of dirt from his hammer. Scan stared in rapt silence.

"All life has some magic and a mystic signature," Galad continued. "Worlds occupied by humans are like a specific kind of shell in the mystic ocean, let us say a simple sand-colored disk. Worlds dominated by elves would appear different, perhaps an elegant spiral cone of white and purple, and troll or dwarf worlds would, again, look even different from that."

"Perhaps an ugly brown ball with spikes?" Grundle suggested. "I think that's called species profiling. I suggest trolls are tiny soft shells that glow gently in your oceanic setting."

Galad sputtered, and I enjoyed his discomfort. He cast a spell and the sky above us darkened. Little pinpricks of light began to glimmer, stars of different colors swirling in his paranormal picture. "The more magic, the bigger the shell," he began again. "So your world," and he pointed at a tiny spot that grew brighter to join the rest, "though devoid of magic from your dead sun, has increased in population enough that the tiny bits of magic inherent in life have accumulated to the point that you are just barely noticeable in the shallows of the mystic ocean."

"If our sun wasn't dead?" Scan asked.

"If your sun wasn't dead," Galad said, "your world would have been noticeable at a fraction of your current population. There are still human habitats out there." He waved vaguely to the stars. "But when they become too occupied, at around fifty thousand inhabitants, they get attacked by the Infected." He let some stars blink out. "People on planets orbiting a living sun must absorb some magic, creating a larger fingerprint." He let his illusionary spell fade.

Absorbing magic from the sun—did they have the equivalent of SPF 50 for protection?

"So, let me see if I've got this right," I began. "Our seashell," I said, waving my arms to indicate the entire world, "washed up close to the shore, and it is finally big enough to draw the attention of elven children searching for baubles, *or* the equivalent in evil hordes of monsters, *but*," I didn't let Galad interrupt, "because our sun is *dead*, instead of having fifty thousand people on our planet, we have almost eight billion people, which doesn't sound bad for a planet orbiting a dead sun."

"I'm so happy to see your usual *chipper* self has begun to re-emerge," Galad said. "I was growing weary of your quiet—whatever that was—hopelessness?"

"My chipper self is about to give you opportunities to use your Healing spells in creative ways."

Grundle chuckled. "My understanding is similar to yours, tiny she-troll."

"Also," Scan continued my train of thought, "because of the dead sun," he said, waving toward our sun in dispute of its demise, "those creatures are not growing in number as quickly here."

"Though their numbers do continue to increase," Galad pointed out. "If these creatures primarily increase in number through replicating themselves into other beings, then we will lose control very quickly. All we've been doing is Teleporting to places with high population density and using stored magical energy to draw them to us. What if we ignore a population center for too long? We won't know until we get there and find we cannot stop their number."

"Is there any way to detect them?" I asked, but didn't pause for an answer. "How do you find the population centers? You said every living creature has a fingerprint—can you search for that?"

"Finding dense populations relates back to the shell metaphor," Galad said. "With enough people close together, it's like looking in a shallow puddle with a few shiny rocks. Nothing is very hard to see, and the shiny rocks stand out. As for the fingerprint of the Infected, they don't have a normal fingerprint, not like elves or trolls or," he pointed at a bird that landed on a tree and sat watching us, "birds. But you can see the Infected by the shadow they cast. It is a little hard to explain. On my world, we have some creatures

203

that can blend in with surrounding objects. Do you have such creatures here?"

"Chameleons," Scan answered.

"Imagine shining a light on a chameleon that had blended into its surroundings. You would still see the shadow of the chameleon, so you would know it was there, despite not being able to see it."

"So you can see them by their shadow?" Scan beat me to the question.

"With enough magic, we can," Galad said. "But that much magic would also draw them. So practically speaking, no."

Scan was nodding his head, thinking. He retrieved his backpack and pulled out a laptop. "Just give me a few minutes. Keep talking. I've got something I think will help with detection."

Chapter 45

Red

Taking Scan up on his offer, I marched ahead. "One question that keeps nibbling in my mind, is why, now that you see that this world is different, haven't you called home to get help? Surely you see the value in this opportunity to learn more about your enemy."

Galad's eyes sank to the ground. It was Grundle who answered. "Oh, we see the value. The problem is… this was a one-way trip."

My eyes grew wide. "Wait a minute. You came to a planet where you knew the Infected would at least potentially be attacking, knowing the Infected take over planets within days, and you had no escape clause? You're on a suicide mission? No," I said, frustrated, "suicide missions at least provide some perceived benefit. This was—what—just you three coming to die?!? Some last flick of the finger to the universe on your way out the door?"

Grundle, for once, didn't chuckle. "There is an element of truth in what you say. But, don't forget, there was at least one difference for your world—your *sun*." He paused. "We each lost our home. There was nothing to stay for. Our choices were rather limited."

Harry nodded his head in agreement.

"At least here we have a chance to learn something," Grundle concluded.

"A chance to learn something implies a way to get the information back to someone who can use it," I rebuffed him.

"The information, yes," Grundle replied, "but we ourselves cannot return."

"Okay, so you have a phone line. Phone home, and your people can help."

"Maybe, though it is doubtful," Grundle said. "And the price of making such a 'phone call' is high."

"The alternative is losing my world. Is the currency something we can come up with on this planet? Or is this a 'dead sun' problem?"

"The price is one of our lives, and there is no guarantee that they would listen to the message," Grundle said with a frown.

"Okay, higher than I expected. What the *hell*?" I barked in frustration. "Why are you being so cryptic?"

Grundle chuckled a little at that. "I don't mean to be cryptic, tiny she-troll. We just do not have a common background in this area, on which to build ideas. Let me try my hand at a metaphor, though I have not the skill of Galad in bringing in wistful imagery of childhood treasures."

He earned himself a scowl from Galad.

"That might have been a compliment, you know," Grundle said.

"Doubtful," Galad replied.

"Indeed," Grundle chuckled. "Red, you have fought with other soldiers, and yet you are better with knives than most. Your specialty is knives. But it is so through a combination of natural ability and practice. The same is true of magi. They have areas of natural ability and areas of interest, and so they can develop strong specializations."

I nodded. It made sense that there would be specialists in magic, I supposed.

"One such specialization is intra-world travel— making bridges across that metaphorical ocean. That speciality is tightly controlled. As you can imagine, opening up a tunnel to a world overrun by the Infected would be catastrophic on a world-ending scale."

I nodded my head—that much I followed.

"Another such specialty is something we call Empathy, which is the ability to get into someone else's head. That's Galad's specialty, and at the extreme end, it allows him to transfer you, your memories, into an object where it can be stored."

"How do *you* know that?!" Galad asked, "The making of Elder Stones is a tightly guarded secret!"

"It pays to know your enemies."

"Enemies? I thought you two were friends," I said. Wow, the relationship between these two was *odd*.

"We are friends now. It has not always been so. Again, a story for another day. Knowing me," he asked Galad, "does it truly surprise you that I would have knowledge of your people's secrets?"

"*Offends* is perhaps the better word. It *offends* me that elves would betray such a secret."

The troll shrugged. "Let's get back on topic. My point is that we have no way to go back. If we determine at some point that all is lost, we can transfer someone's memories into a crystal, where somehow, someday, it *might* be found and used to transfer whatever little wisdom we have obtained in this endeavor."

"So your coming here was essentially a death sentence." I was a little shocked.

"That seemed likely," Grundle answered.

"Why did you do it then?" I needed to know what was motivating these people, the thin thread of hope for my world.

"I can only answer for myself," Grundle said. "I had two reasons. One was that I had nothing left to fight for— my people were gone. Utterly gone. To my knowledge, I am the last living troll. The second reason was to see that Galad did not throw his life away." Galad's eyes lit up in surprise. "It promised to be an interesting challenge."

Chapter 46

Red

"Okay," Scan interrupted, waving us over. "You're stuck here with us. For now. So let's focus on how to find the bad guys."

When we had gathered around Scan, he directed our attention to his screen. "We noticed that, when one of those creatures moves near a camera, we see this distortion effect." He pointed at one of the earliest videos—the attack in Hong Kong—illustrating the strange imagery.

"That's rather surprising," Galad commented. "On our enchanted equivalent—an *Observalisk*—the Infected, they just... don't show up."

Scan shrugged. "We already know your translation spell doesn't work over our audio and video connections. Maybe the effect of their magic is similarly messed up. Whatever keeps these things from having a mystic fingerprint, maybe it doesn't work right through technology. Or maybe it's just a dead sun effect. Anyway, I have been training my neural network to recognize those distortions. Before yesterday, I had only false positives. Yesterday, I tracked you while you fought, and found a few more camera images as the hostiles moved toward you. Using those, I was better able to train the system. It will continue to get better as I feed it more images with positive identification."

I didn't know what he meant. The puzzled expressions of the otherworlders told me that the information confused them even more.

Sighing, I realized my role as Scan-translator would be continuing. "So what you're saying," I tried, "is that you're feeding videos to your computer to spot those distortions, and the more we capture the Infected on camera, the better your computer will get at spotting them?"

"Well, it's not my *computer* that gets better—it's the neural net weights that get adjusted—" He stopped when he saw my irritation. "Yes," he started over, "my *computer* gets better at finding them," he said mechanically, rolling his eyes.

"It *eats videos*?" Harry's eyes were wide.

Scan cocked his head at Harry, then nodded. "Sort of, yes. I can connect to cameras all over the world, and the computer takes them in, something like food. And I'm trying to convince it that it really likes eating videos of the Infected and telling me where it found that video."

"And it does all that while just *sitting* here?" Galad asked.

"Technically, this isn't the computer that's doing the eating and learning and searching," Scan said, patting his laptop. "It just talks to the computer that does all that. But yes, that other one does it all while just sitting there."

Galad shook his head in astonishment. "All without magic," he said. "I never would have believed it possible."

"Let me show you," Scan said. "I have a few hits on sightings today that appear authentic."

"So you're saying we might track one?" I prodded. Things were getting interesting.

"Eventually," Scan replied. "I have to track movement from camera to camera, and there're places with holes—no camera coverage—that make it more difficult. Better camera coverage would help, but I'm not sure how to get that."

He saw from our faces he was losing us again.

"I'm starting to detect them," he said. "Right now, since I cannot track them, I can't tell you if I'm detecting the same one over and over, or multiples. You keep getting me images, and the detection will get better and better."

"Scan, could we use government compute farms to do this better?" I questioned. Explaining to the otherworlders, I said, "The computer that is eating the videos and learning—we might go faster if we had more of them working together."

"Little boxes eating videos on a farm," Harry said. "I'd like to see that."

"Um," Scan said. "That's not quite…" He shook his head, but did not try to explain the incorrect imagery. He turned and replied to me instead. "Probably… if we convince them to let us use their systems. But, that will be a tough sales pitch. They'll want me to bring my model to them instead. I can't exactly do that. Let's just say they wouldn't approve of the systems I'm using."

I rubbed my temples from my sudden headache. "Don't tell me any more, Scan. I don't want to know."

Scan shrugged. He brought up a picture of a globe on his screen. There were a handful of red dots on it. "These are the locations where I have hits on spotting an Infected." He pressed something and yellow dots appeared. "These yellow dots are the highest population density points by city." Scan zoomed in on each red dot, which implied a video sighting, and each corresponded with the location of a yellow dot, the dense population, until he got to one red dot that sat without a yellow partner.

"Weird, that sighting doesn't line up with any big city," he said. "Let's go through the rest." He continued checking each red dot. There was only the one anomaly. "I see no others. Just this one. Let me bring up the video."

Everyone watched as Scan pulled up a video feed from a security camera in a warehouse district. A group of men walked through from left to right. It was night, but there was a light near the camera. Seconds later, the camera displayed the distortion effect we had come to associate with those creatures, moving in the same direction as the men.

"Wow, that looked legit to me," Scan said. "Why is that one so far from a heavily-populated area?"

"I don't know," Galad responded. "We were going to do a little minor hunting today. Shall we go see if we can flush that one out?"

"I like the sound of that," I said.

"She-troll," said Grundle, with his familiar chuckle. I gave him the stink-eye, and he chuckled more.

"Where is it?" I asked.

"Bata, Equatorial Guinea," Scan said.

"Okay," Galad said, "let me work with Scan on figuring out the proper place to Teleport. Why don't you lot do something useful like... actually, I have no suggestions. Do whatever you do when you're not fighting."

I knew what kind of response that would have received in the military, and I was not disappointed. I guess men were men, no matter the species. Grundle was the first to partake in the verbal opening. "There are no women on this planet large enough to handle what I do when not fighting."

"Yes, it takes a woman large in patience to listen while you try to read," I rolled my eyes.

The troll barked his laughter, and the dwarf shook his head, smiling. "If you're going to be reading, I'll just head over here and..."

"Yes, yes," Grundle said, waving at him dismissively. "Go polish your mighty hammer, but do it out of earshot please."

Harry froze mid-step, then waved his hand in a way that I guessed was the same as our middle-finger salute.

Grundle chuckled, and turning to me, said, in a kinder voice, "I thought you might regale me with tales of your childhood to fill the time."

"Only if you do the same," I replied.

"Agreed," he said, clapping his hands together. We moved away from Scan and Galad to give them space to work.

"Hmm, I have two sisters," I said. "We were all named after rocks."

Grundle held up a hand and shouted, "Hear that, Harry? Red and her two sisters were named after rocks!"

He turned back to me. "That will help him finish polishing his hammer."

Ewwwwww. Grundle beamed, proud of his innuendo.

"Okay, big talker," I said. "Your turn."

Galad entered the tent and came back a few minutes later with one of the cannisters of magical essence. *What is he up to now?*

"I have no siblings," Grundle said, "which is very rare amongst trolls. We birth multiples. My parents named me after the sound of breaking bones when hit by a fist."

"Are there different words for the sounds of bones breaking by other means?" I asked.

"Of course. It sounds different if you snap a bone, or crush a bone, or shatter a bone or—"

"Stop, stop, stop!" I insisted, cringing. I couldn't stomach his full list. He stopped, perplexed.

"Okay. Next topic," I said. "I'm the oldest of my sisters. My father was an engineer. My mother was a decorator. My middle sister, Citrine—that's a yellow gemstone—is a dancer. My youngest sister, Jade—a kind of green rock—is an artist. She paints and makes interesting crafts. Now you."

"As I said, no siblings. Both of my parents were gardeners."

At Grundle's words, Galad turned our way. "That can't be true," he said.

"Eavesdropping, *old* friend?"

"Trolls don't have gardens. They raise meat that they

212

slaughter and eat, usually, but not always, in that order."

Grundle chuckled. "Have you seen the carrion-eating fungi from *grrrax*? Or the meat-shrubs from *rumdug*?"

"You're making that up," Galad insisted.

"Prove it," Grundle replied, "But prove it later; for now, we want that Teleport working."

Galad squinted at Grundle's comment, then shrugged and returned to working with Scan.

"Now," Grundle continued, more quietly, "where were we? Ah, yes, my parents were farmers. Most trolls have many brothers and sisters who act as a little protective bubble. I had only myself, and most trolls think gardening is for the birds." Grundle winked. "So I got beat up a lot. I learned to fight; I learned to hide; and I learned how to be devious enough to keep myself alive."

"Wow." I stared at him hard. "I can't tell if you're lying."

Grundle just shrugged.

I didn't *think* he was lying, but he'd said things about the importance of deception—at least in war—that made me wonder if my world's predicament was all a game to him. "My story is not so interesting," I said, moving on. "I did well in school, was good at sports, and the military offered me a scholarship—meaning they thought I was skilled enough that they would pay for my further training and education. That's it."

Grundle chewed on that for a few seconds. "That's not *everything*. But it's a start."

"Okay," Galad announced. "I think we've got it. Call Harry back, please."

"I'll get him," Grundle said, "Wouldn't want you to see his hammer mid-polish. How embarrassing." And he strolled off in the direction Harry had gone.

Chapter 47

Scan

I was talking with an elf. A magic-wielding elf. I knew those non-humans were real; I'd seen enough evidence even before showing up in their camp. But sitting there talking to an elf, and meeting a troll and a dwarf... well, there weren't words to describe my wonder.

We were working out the details of the Teleportation destination. We had done that once before, while I was watching from the other side of a video camera. Seeing the globe appear, like a hologram, in front of me—it was life-changing.

Galad worked on finding the mystic equivalent of the path to Bata, using his orb and my laptop's image of the globe.

"Can you teach me?" I asked quietly.

It was clear he was about to ask me, "Teach you what?" But he stopped himself. I think he saw on my face what I wanted to learn.

I spoke my mind. "Can you teach me how to use magic? You've already said that humans have the potential for magic, but we don't draw on it because of our dead sun. *You* are doing it somehow though."

"I have done this a very long time," Galad told me. "I know how to draw in the trickle of magic from distant stars. It is a very slow process to recharge my magical energy."

"Still, you're saying it's possible. Can you teach me?"

"There is no point. On this planet, with magic so weak, it would be impossible to learn."

"Nevertheless, I would like to understand. If I know how magic works, maybe I can figure out better ways to track these Infected. And then I can figure out better ways to fight them. Knowing *about* programming is not the same as *knowing* programming, understanding its potential and pitfalls. Actually knowing *how* to do something is eye-opening."

"Some of that did not translate well," Galad said, "but I get your point. Wait here, please."

He entered the tent.

Yes! What was he going to bring me—some grimoire of beginner's magic? *Magic Use for Dummies*? Was there a version on Kindle? I felt giddy with delight. But Galad returned with a vial, not a book.

He set the vial down. "This stores magical energy. If you can use magic at all, you would still have little natural storage ability, lacking any experience and no source of magic. To try even a beginner spell under this sun will require such an aid."

The vials were magical batteries? Storing up energy to be used at a later time, when the proper enchanted circuit was connected? I had so much to learn about how magic worked!

"When we are trying to attract the Infected, we essentially uncork the bottle, and magic streams out. For this exercise, we do not wish to release magic in a torrent. You should take hold of the bottle and try to use the energy within it in a focused manner. If you have no capacity for using magic, you will be able to do nothing with it."

I needed to get one of those vials into the lab and perform experiments. There had to be some radiation signal.

"Before you touch the vessel," he continued, "here's how you should prepare your mind. Picture a tiny ball of light." Galad held out his hand, and a ball of light, the size of a marble, appeared in the cup of his hand. It was white, and it had a soft, gentle glow. "That is what you want to see.

215

Picture that in your head. Think about the connection between yourself and the light, your hand and your head. Picture the energy flowing out of you and into your hand, the light being fed by you."

"There's no incantation, no waving of my hands to cast it?"

"No. Not for this. All the words and movements are mnemonics. As spells become more complicated, as you create and transform, you'll need aids to help you step through the spells more easily and consistently. But, for this, you are just returning magic in its natural form, from light to light. Well, on any *other* world it would be from light to light. On *this* world, light from darkness."

He closed his hand, vanquishing the light.

"Okay, go on," he told me. "Take the vessel in one hand. I suppose, in this case, you're thinking of the energy not as coming from within, but from the hand holding the vessel, and going to the hand that will hold the light."

Nervous in a way I had not been in a long time, I took the vessel in a sweaty hand. Galad turned to Grundle, saying, "That can't be true," and busied himself talking with the others about Grundle's upbringing. For once, I did my best to tune them out.

I thought about light. I pictured the little ball of light appearing in my hand. Nothing. I tried to clear my head further, cast out all thought except the light. A minute passed. Nothing. I pictured the energy flowing out of the vessel, through one arm and then the other and out of my hand. Another minute, at least, passed. Still nothing. *I want this. I have to be able to do this.* My hand tightened on the vial. I tried to force the energy out, tried to force the light into existence.

"The energy already exists." Galad spoke with a calm, soothing tone. "The light already exists. You are just trying to call it forth. The magic is a frightened animal, and

216

you are beckoning it to come forth from its hiding place."

Frightened animal. Okay. Beckoning a scared animal... out of a jar... through my arms... Um, no.

I loosened my grip, to appear more relaxed, but I tightened my concentration. *What do I know about light?* Light existed as both particles and waves, and a mysterious something else I did not understand. I imagined pulling on that incomprehensible strand that I knew must exist from Galad's own casting. I tugged at it like a dog worrying a loose thread on a pillow. There were many things I did not understand in life, but my approach to topics was to tug at the pieces I *did* understand and pull them loose. Then I built up and connected those pieces, eventually mastering topics that once had not made sense. But, right then, my head hurt from trying to force the light out.

Galad put a hand on my arm. "Enough," he breathed, but without room for argument. "You can try again later. This is easier for a child. Their minds are not yet formed. I do not know if you are capable, but allowing your own mind to accept that it *might* be—that's your biggest battle. Enough for now. We need to do other things."

I loosened my grip on the vessel, and Galad took it. I didn't have to cling to it if I was going to get another chance. I *would* figure out magic.

"Okay," Galad announced. "I think we've got it. Call Harry back, please."

Mind like a child. Who had a more childlike mind than I? I would figure it out.

Chapter 48

Red

Grundle returned with Harry. I couldn't help but notice that Harry's hammer was a little shinier, and Grundle chuckled when he caught me looking. I shrugged and shook my head. *Men.*

Galad waited, ready to go, as we gathered together.

"What time will it be when we get there?" I asked.

"About 2:30 am," Scan answered.

I caught Galad's attention and pointed at my eyes. He cast the night vision spell. I'd come more prepared that time and brought some flashlights, but the spell worked so much better.

"Whoa," Scan uttered. "So cool." It was like wearing night vision goggles, only better, because the bright light didn't hurt your eyes. With the spell, your visible spectrum broadened.

"All right," Galad said, "gather around." He turned to Scan. "You're going?"

Scan was smaller than most men in the military, but he had seen combat, and he could use a gun just fine. "Wouldn't miss it," he said.

We got close, and, like the previous time we had gone to a new location, the spell seemed to take a little longer. It might have been my imagination, but I thought the Teleports to new locations took more effort and concentration from Galad, and so took more time. Or maybe it was away versus return trips? I noticed, while I waited, that Harry had left the gun behind, switching back to his hammer as his sole weapon. Then there was that telltale feeling of disconnection and a burst of light.

Suddenly we were in the dark and heard the gunfire of automatic weapons in the distance. I panicked, my mind dropping me back on a desert mission. A quick glance showed me an ocean off to my right, and large docks ahead. The noise came from there. It *wasn't* a desert. But it *was* two in the morning with a gunfight.

"Be careful," I said. "It sounds like they've spotted our Infected. You'll get shot at, the same as the Infected, if you're seen. Let's move in."

I started forward, intending to cover the several hundred yards to the docks.

"Hold," Galad said. "Stay close."

In the blink of an eye, we were at the docks, behind a warehouse that had been just visible from our last position. While I recovered from my disorientation, Galad stuck his head around the corner. *Guess he is taking point position. Okay.*

He nodded to me and Scan. "You two, with me. We will come in from the other side."

Scan and I moved close, and in an instant we appeared at the far side of the dock. The sudden change was again disorienting, but I couldn't afford the time to be sick.

We ducked behind a building.

There was a scream near us. A man's scream, and it cut off suddenly, as did the gunfire. "Sounds like one man down, but there could still be more with guns," I said. We were on the ocean side of the industrial-sized dock. The scream had come from a collection of giant Lego-like shipping containers stacked near the docks.

We entered the maze of stacked shipping containers, running as swiftly as we could on quiet toes while trying to find the source of the sounds. I expected my enhanced vision to reveal the heat signature of a person, even a recently deceased one. I took the lead, with Scan between me and Galad. Running in bursts between the short ends of the containers, I poked my head around each corner, quickly inspecting each direction, searching for a heat signature. My knives were drawn, and I purposefully had to slow my pace for Scan to keep up. I didn't want to get separated in that labyrinth.

It was the fifth car in, to the right—I saw a body, just a couple of cars down. I signaled to the others that I was going that way. One car length. As I approached the intersection, I saw that the body was human, but not moving. He had fallen with his back touching a shipping container, facing the doors of the opposite pod. I peeked around the intersection. Nothing.

Dashing across the intersection, I slowed as I approached the body. His gun was on the ground. The size was right for an automatic weapon, though I could not tell the model with only my night-vision spell. Scan grabbed my arm, stopping me. He pointed. I had been studying the body and the far intersection for an ambush. Scan pointed in the direction the dead eyes were staring. The door to the shipping container was open. Inside were more heat signatures, but from my angle, it was impossible to tell what they were.

Shit. It felt like a trap. Anything inside that container would just need to step out and it would have a clear shot at us. I motioned for Scan and Galad to move back to the intersection and cover me. Well, *Scan* would cover me—he had a gun. Galad's beams of fire might also do the trick. I crept toward the door. There was movement inside. *Aw, hell.*

I took three quick steps toward the door, and, with the enchantment of the daggers, they were quite fast. Moving one dagger into a throwing position, the other I kept ready to strike. I jumped into the shipping container, and saw some movement, but a quick survey showed me nothing was about to attack. Yet what I saw made no sense. Strewn around the shipping container were bodies of the Infected, shot and dead or dying, their heat not yet faded. The smell was horrific—feces and urine, blood, and gore—and the smell of the blood from the Infected was not like ours. It smelled rotten.

I stuck my hand out the door and waved them over. I moved closer to one of the bodies, sheathed a dagger, and pulled out my flashlight to get a better look. Someone had chained the body to the wall by a shackle at its feet. Moving the flashlight around, I saw more chains. There was also a second automatic rifle among the gore and body parts of the Infected. A second guard then. Had he run off? He would bring reinforcements, which meant time was ticking.

There was a sudden loud crash against the side of the shipping container, followed quickly by a few gunshots—semi-automatic, not fully automatic, so probably Scan. Moving back to the door, and clicking off my flashlight so as not to broadcast my position, I stuck my head back out the door. I saw Scan standing over the body of an Infected, which lay unmoving. And a third body lay on the ground. *Aw, hell.*

Galad was down.

"It came from behind us as we moved to the door," Scan said.

I risked flipping my flashlight back on, and saw Galad was bleeding from deep gashes in his side, but worse, his head was smashed open where it must have hit the side of the shipping container.

"I have to find Harry, fast, before we lose Galad," I told Scan. "Harry can Heal with his hammer." *Please let his hammer be working.* "Stay with Galad." I dashed off in the direction I thought led to the other end of the docks, being less careful than I'd have liked.

Galad's life hung in the balance.

Chapter 49

Scan

Red moved with impossible speed when she was holding the daggers. It was like watching a movie run in fast forward. She was never quite where your eyes expected her to be. I didn't have any skill with daggers, but I knew how to use a gun. Could a gun be enchanted the way the daggers and hammer were? Were Galad's swords enchanted?

Red waved us to the door. Galad nodded to me and I went first, Galad following a few steps behind, covering our backs. I thought I saw movement at the end of the shipping container and froze. Galad bumped me and turned his attention to where I was looking. I squinted into the dark, but saw nothing. No movement—it might have been my imagination.

Crash!

I turned back to see one of those creatures fling Galad into the side of the container, and it was moving toward me. I let it have a couple of 9mm in the torso, and one in the head for good measure, and it dropped.

Red popped back out of the pod, did a quick triage, and left me with Galad while she fetched the enchanted hammer of Healing. *Crap!* I hoped the movement I *thought* I saw wasn't another one of those Infected running free. Red would have said if there was any danger from within the shipping container. It would be safer to get out of sight, hide in the box, but I wasn't sure moving Galad was a great idea.

Damn, damn, damn. I prayed she found help in time. After all, Galad was my only lead to learning magic. If he died, so did my chances at using magic. And there was the whole saving the world thing to consider. *Hmm,* I hadn't managed to use magic, but it couldn't hurt anything to attempt to help Galad, could it? Galad's backpack lay exposed, so I wouldn't have to move him to get to the vial.

Opportunity knocked—I opened his backpack and fished inside for the vial. I pulled it out and held it in one hand and placed the other on Galad. *Heal!* I willed it, trying to pull the magic out of the vial and into Galad's shattered head. *C'mon, Heal, damn it.* I concentrated, trying to force magic to start closing his wounds.

It was frustrating and ridiculous. I hadn't even been able to create a tiny light with magic—why was I trying to do something more complicated? Because I wanted to keep my potential teacher alive, that was why. *Okay, okay... back up.* What had Galad said? Mind like a child... allowing myself to believe that magic might be real. Well, that shouldn't be too hard. I still played all those fantasy online games. I played mages that blasted fire, enchanters that mesmerized their foes. Admittedly, I rarely played the cleric, the Healer, because what fun was it just Healing the tank during every battle, not participating in the fight? But it wasn't difficult for me to conceive of magic being possible. Plus, I'd *seen* it. I'd Teleported around the world.

So, mind like a child—check. I refused to believe I wasn't capable. I'd go back to the simple magic. Just call forth light. I closed my eyes and concentrated on making light appear, the pure form of magic, drawing it out of the vial. I felt silly at having my eyes closed. How would I know if the light appeared? And it was stupidly dangerous if there was another of those creatures still out there.

My eyes opened, and I thought I saw, in the hand touching Galad, a faint green light! *What?* Ripping my hand up, I saw I was wrong—there was nothing. I had just wanted it so badly I'd fooled myself. I glanced around, sighing, and put my hand back on Galad. The coast was still clear. At least nothing had attacked us.

Looking back down, I saw the light again. I squinted, trying to see it more clearly. The light was not coming from where I thought—it was coming from *inside* the elf. Concentrating on the light, I tried to make out what I was seeing. It was like a vine, an old vine, thick with tendrils wrapped around one another, and some had been sliced. New shoots had sprouted where the old vine had been severed, but they were not growing rapidly enough. The light was fading faster than the vines were growing.

Dang. Come on, little vines, you can do it, I willed them. I saw the little vines twitch, and, encouraged, I tried to pull energy from the vial to feed the vines. *Grow, little vines!* As though they heard my encouragement, they responded. Slowly, still too slowly, they reached across the gaps of the severed vines. Why only one side? I encouraged the ends of the vines on the other side to start growing as well. There, that was better. Once they started touching, wrapping around each other at both ends, the vines appeared healthier, but the light still faded. I found more places with severed vines and started them regrowing.

Then I found a spot where there was a cascade of flowers, but the injury had taken a swatch out of them. There were no "two ends" of the vine to grow together, so I encouraged the one end to grow blooms. There was a pattern to the flowers, and they seemed to know where to grow to continue the pattern, but occasionally I had to help a little. A vine or bloom had grown too strong, and I had to hold it back while its brethren caught up. Amazing. All those vines had been for different flowers. I hadn't been able to tell when just encouraging the vines to reconnect.

Finally, nothing more appeared to be out of place. And, spent, I released my hold on Galad. As the green light faded, and the mundane world re-intruded, I saw Galad's eyes open, then widen. He jumped to his feet, grabbing his sword and swinging, severing the arm of the beast that was swiping at me, then kicking the torso back against the opposite shipping container, and with another leap, swiping the head clean off. I was still crouched on the ground, tired beyond explanation.

I glanced up—some sense of being watched, or a noise perhaps. Atop the container opposite me, blocking the stars, I saw a form, crouching, staring at me, white hair framing a face that wasn't quite human.

The severed head, eyeless and mouthless, bumped to a stop on my foot, drawing my attention down. Then, I turned at the noise of Red running from around the corner, daggers drawn, with Harry, then Grundle, close behind.

"What the hell?" was all she said.

When I looked back atop the container opposite me, I saw only the stars.

Galad studied the bodies, quickly putting the pieces together. "He *Healed* me," Galad said, pointing at me with his sword. "He must be a natural Healer."

Red walked over to me, saying something like, "Is he okay?" but I wasn't sure, because I was having trouble staying alert. A *Healer*. I rarely played the Healer... not my thing.

Damn.

Chapter 50

"He's just exhausted," Galad explained, walking over and taking the vial from the hand of my sleeping friend. "He performed an admirable amount of Healing for a beginner. It is tiring. Also impressive."

"What does *natural Healer* mean?" I asked. "Does that phrase have some significance, or are you just saying he has a natural skill or tendency?"

I'd fetched Harry as fast as I could, throwing caution to the wind and running out in the open, shouting "Harry!" until, with looks of astonishment, they stepped out from behind a building. It was risky announcing my presence so openly, but it was Galad's best—possibly his *only*—chance.

I had returned in the same reckless rush, only to find him alive and well, Healed by some means, while Scan looked like he'd been hit on the head with a frying pan. I was still trying to wrap my mind around it.

"Everyone has natural abilities," Galad explained. "Some are athletic, some are skills with painting or drawing." I waved impatiently—I understood that much.

"Within magic, there are also areas for which magic wielders can have a natural ability. Scan cannot yet do a basic spell that we start children learning, but he performed a complicated Heal spell. That suggests a natural ability for Healing, different from my own ability in the area of Empathy, but similar in concept. I can Heal, but it took many years of study, whereas I picked up Empathy spells like they were child's play."

I nodded, "And he's just sleeping?"

"Yes, he will awake soon enough. He overextended.

I can Heal him, but we have learned it is best to let the body rest for a few minutes before doing so."

I continued nodding. "Okay. Can we get him out of here? Is it safe to Teleport him?"

"Yes. So we are leaving the bodies again?"

"I think so. This is… puzzling." I pulled out my camera and took a picture of the dead creature and shipping container, making sure Scan was not in the frame, then entered the open pod and used my flashlight and phone to take a short video. Grundle ducked and followed me in, and I shined my flashlight around again for his benefit.

"Most strange," he grumbled, and left.

I joined them outside, where Grundle was already picking up Scan's insensate body. We gathered close to Galad, who whisked us back home in a flash of light.

As soon as we arrived, Grundle rumbled, "Harry, would you do me the kindness of bringing a blanket from the tent?" Harry nodded and disappeared into the tent.

I pulled out my knives, then returned them to their scabbards. I hadn't used them. No need for cleaning.

I paced. Then stopped myself and examined my daggers a second time. I paced again.

"He will be all right," Galad reassured me. Harry returned with the blanket and laid it on the ground, where Grundle then placed Scan.

"If I may say, the two of you seem… unlikely allies," Galad said, into the quiet. "Your personalities are quite different. How did you come to care so much for him?" I narrowed my eyes at him, wondering what he was implying, but I saw no guile in him. It was his attempt to distract me, which was, like the retrieval of blankets, a kindness.

"Scan does have a certain moral ambiguity when it comes to ownership of things. But his moral compass on people is dead on."

227

"That's unsurprising. Healers have a very strong sense of what truly belongs to someone and what does not. It is, at least to my understanding, what helps them be so skilled at putting someone back together. Possessions, to most Healers, are part of a system 'imposed by the delusions of society.'"

Grundle chuckled softly, and Galad shot him a dirty look.

"Hmm," I said. "That fits." I paused, leaning against a tree. "When we first met, I didn't think much of him. In fact, I thought quite *poorly* of him. 'What is this little guy doing in the military?' On our first deployment, we were ambushed, captured by the enemy. The situation was grave. Especially for me. A couple of folks stepped up to help. Bear was one of them."

"And Scan was the other," Galad concluded.

"No, you haven't met the other."

Chapter 51

Red, four years earlier

We had to report out on the ambush. Unfortunately, I had been unconscious upon our return. Apparently the head injury had been worse than I thought, and I experienced continued swelling that led to a prolonged nap.

When I came to, I found myself in a makeshift army field medical hospital and rather isolated. When I started moving, a medic came over, did some quick checks, then left. I assumed it was in order to let someone know I was awake. I wasn't sure why I had been isolated.

I tried to piece together my memories in the short time I was given. We'd been ambushed, and I'd been separated from my unit. The enemy had intended sexual assault, but Rocks had slipped me a knife. I'd used it to escape my bonds and kill my captors. I then helped free the remaining captives, and another force had come in and done a more thorough rescuing.

I was still struggling to pull the last threads of my memory together when a full-fledged First Sergeant came in, sighed, and walked over to me.

I tried to salute and found my hand shaking as I held it up. That was no good. The First Sergeant rolled his eyes and returned the salute. "Private Garnet Hernandez." It wasn't a question. So I didn't answer.

"I'm First Sergeant Nettles. I need you to tell me what you remember about the ambush where you got your head injury." He found a chair nearby, pulled it over, and straddled it with the back facing me. Very casual. Weird. Trying to be my *friend*? "So, please, in your own words, what happened?"

"We were ambushed. My MTV flipped. I hit my head." I already disliked my questioner—gut instinct. I felt zero desire to be particularly helpful.

"Is that all you remember? Anything of what happened after they captured you?"

"Of course. I thought you were asking about my injury." That was a lie, but my gut told me to play dumb. So I just lay there waiting.

"Private Hernandez, what do you remember from after your capture?"

"I was separated from my unit, singled out to become part of the special harem of whoever ran that facility. One of our men slipped me a knife as the enemy led me out. I got free and killed my almost-rapist and one or two guards as I worked my way back over to my unit. Then another of our units snuck in on a delivery truck and got us the hell outta there."

He let time tick by. Long seconds passed, where he waited for me to say more, and I stubbornly refused to do so. Finally, he broke the silence. "Do you have any idea why you were separated from the men?"

"Because I'm… not a man?" I offered. Okay, so he was checking whether I was going to call out Reed when I had no proof that he'd told the enemy I was a woman. In my combat fatigues, with my hair cut short, it wasn't an obvious conclusion. All I had was the word of that little guy— Stanley?—that Reed had turned me over, though it was pretty evident if you'd been there. Damn. I'd had a feeling there would be a situation like that eventually, but day one? Well, I guess it *happened* on day one. *Who knows what day it is now? Two? Three?*

"How long have I been out, First Sergeant?"

"Two days, Private Hernandez. But the doctors assured us you would be okay with rest. The swelling just needed to go down." There was another pregnant pause. I didn't help him get started again. "Private Hernandez, do you know why the enemy thought you were… not a man?"

Okay, that phrasing. That suggested something. You wouldn't say that unless someone had made a claim that there was a reason other than "the enemy just figured it out."

"I suspect Private Reed told him I was a woman, sir." I hoped I was right that I was corroborating someone's story, or I was headed for a court martial and a very short career. It must have been either the big guy or the guy who gave me the knife. Geez, my thoughts were still sluggish. I had trouble digging up their names.

"Why do you suspect that, Private Hernandez?"

"A couple of reasons. The main one being that Reed said something to the enemy, and they came right for me."

He nodded. "And the second reason?"

"There was a little guy—Stanley, I think. He spoke Arabic. Said Reed told them I was a woman, that Reed used me as a bargaining chip." Well, that was that. If Stanley didn't back me, they'd screw me over for sure.

"Okay, Private. Get some rest." He stood up and left me in a state of total inability to rest. My head still hurt, and I was worried as hell. But I did, eventually, drift off to sleep.

Chapter 52

Red, four years earlier

The next time I awoke, I felt much better. The doctor pronounced me well enough to leave and sent me packing. It was the morning after I'd been interviewed, and, well, I didn't even know where the barracks were.

Sighing, I waited a few minutes and watched where people were going. At that time of day people would be going to the mess hall, and I was hungry. Seemed like a good place to start.

Sure enough, it wasn't hard to pick out a common destination and departure point for people. I headed that way and was not disappointed. I mean, anyone would be disappointed when they saw the actual food, but I'd found the mess hall. Some MREs were better than what I was looking at. But the coffee smelled great. So I grabbed some less foul-looking grub and some coffee and sat in an isolated space with my back to a wall. A spot from where I watched people.

Just then, Reed and a small group of hangers-on came strolling into the mess hall like they owned the place. My stomach churned, threatening to regurgitate the only good thing I'd had in days—that coffee. I kept the cup near my lips to make it harder to see my face.

He grabbed some food as I picked at mine. He turned and, of course, looked right at me. A flash of anger crossed his face, then a jack-assy smirk settled in. He headed my direction. What a total snake. Were we in high school?

As he moved closer, someone got up from a nearby table, and sat down across from me. I wasn't even watching the new guy—I had locked my eyes on Reed.

"Good to see you're out of the hospital, Red." I pried my eyes off Reed, who had stuttered to a halt.

Red? Oh, yeah. New Guy was the man that pulled us out of the enemy camp—Murphy. Reed had stopped entirely, turned, and gone back to the food line, rejoining his posse. Dang, it was *totally* like a fight scene from high school. *Bully thwarted by tough Mr. Nice Guy.* Okay, that wasn't terrible. I stood and saluted, and he casually returned the salute.

"Murphy," I said, glad I remembered his name. I corrected myself. "Sorry, *Sergeant* Murphy,"

"Sergeant Murphy O'Shay, to be exact. You just get out of medical?"

"Aye, Sergeant Murphy O'Shay," I said. With a thick, and badly done, Irish accent. I followed with, "And now I'm after me Lucky Charms."

What the *hell* was I saying? Maybe my head was still swollen?

"Wow," he said, staring at me with interest. Or confusion? An awkward pause ensued, and I hid behind my coffee. "*I* don't even *have* an Irish accent," he chuckled, and I blushed. "I'm from New York—the Bronx—but I've been gone long enough that I've lost even *that* accent for the most part."

"I'm so sorry. I don't know what... head injury..." I covered my face with my hands.

He smiled. "Don't worry about it. Hey, you took a nap while I gave the other newbies a tour of the base. How about I show you around?"

"That would be great, actually." It would save a lot of fumbling. "I also need to find my Sergeant." *What* was *his name? Okay, this is ridiculous, I'm not usually bad with names. Head injury.* "Sergeant... Billings?" Yes, that was it. "I need to let him know I'm out."

233

"I'm sure he will be thrilled, as are all Sergeants, all the time. He will bake you a cake to welcome you to the team." He rolled his eyes, and we laughed in unison.

I was done with the only things I cared about eating, so I stood and grabbed my tray to deposit it. Murphy nodded and turned so his back was not to the room, and waited for me. We left together.

He showed me the general layout of the makeshift base. Somewhere during the walk, I found the nerve to ask, "Do you know what I should expect regarding the ambush you pulled us out of? They asked me some very specific questions while I was still in the hospital."

"I do. I do indeed." Smirking, he said no more.

"Ass," I commented.

He chuckled, amused with himself. *Stupid men.* "You'll find out soon enough," he said. "Come on, let's find Billings."

He took me back to the mess hall and led me to a man in his mid-thirties who had been frowning for the past forty years. We exchanged salutes.

"What are you playing at, O'Shay?" Billings said, his frown somehow deepening.

"I thought you should be the one to tell her. As far as she knows, she reports to you."

Billings nodded. "Private Hernandez, it was my pleasure to have you serve in my unit." Sergeant humor— I'd only just met him. "First Sergeant Nettles has re-assigned you to Sergeant O'Shay." With that, he seemed done with me, so I saluted and departed.

O'Shay followed me out of the mess hall. I wasn't sure how I felt about that. He had been jerking me around. He had known I reported to him and hadn't told me. But he had also been kind and friendly. That was fine in general, but it worried me from a higher-up.

"Okay, Red..."

I interrupted and corrected him. "Private Hernandez, sir."

He raised an eyebrow. Yes, we needed some more formality.

"Okay, *Red*," he said again, drilling home the name he was going to call me, "come with me. It's time to meet your new unit."

I'd learned during the tour that the base had been formed by taking over some existing buildings, and there were multiple buildings used as barracks. I marched behind him to one of them. Inside the building, we passed some doorways to sleeping quarters, and he marched me—okay, *I* marched; he was still casually walking—into a makeshift conference room.

"Wait here," he said.

"Sir, yes, sir," I said, saluting smartly.

He rolled his eyes. "At ease. Have a seat." Eyeing my stiff posture, he added, "Or stand at attention if you wish. It's all the same to me. I'll be back shortly."

I stood there, seething. What the hell was wrong with me? He had done nothing untoward or spectacularly deceitful. Yet I felt a betrayal.

Aww, shit.

All it took was the briefest of soul-searching to realize I liked the guy. And I was pissed at myself for being so stupid.

True to his word, O'Shay returned in short order, with three men in tow. First was the guy who'd given me the knife—Rocks. Second was the big guy who had moved to defend me and gotten the butt of a gun in his face—I didn't think I ever caught his name. Finally, there was the little guy who understood Arabic—Stanley.

I saluted again as the Sergeant came back in, with the others coming in around him. He gave a half-assed salute back and muttered, "At ease, soldier." Everyone moved in to flank O'Shay, and my first thought was that I was about to get the crap beat outta me.

Then Rocks smiled. He had a charming smile. He held out his hand, and I shook it. "Glad to see you came through okay," he said.

"I don't know how well you know any of these people," O'Shay began. "So, this is Rocks. He gave you a knife when you needed it." I nodded. "This is Bear." He pointed at the large guy. How appropriate—a bear of a man. Bear nodded to me. "He apparently attempted physical combat despite very poor odds."

Finally, Stanley stood there, not ashamed or flustered, almost curious why he'd been included.

"This is Stanley," O'Shay introduced. "You don't know this, but his report was very clear about what Private Reed told the hostage-taker. He wouldn't back down or retract his statement, despite *pressure*."

My eyes widened, and I nodded my recognition and appreciation to him.

"Let me explain," O'Shay continued. "Stanley has an interesting background. As far as I can tell, he hacked into a government system and got dealt a deck of cards that landed him in jail or in service of the government. They set the deal up to try to pull him into the CIA, but he followed the letter of the deal, instead of the intent, and joined the Army."

"Damned idiots," Stanley commented. "I would have chosen jail if they hadn't left me another option. I needed to learn to do a push-up anyway." He flexed a muscle the size of my wrist. "Look," he told me, "I couldn't be any help in that camp. I'm not terribly strong or fast. I'm not great in a fight—though I plan to get better—but I can help in other ways."

"Stanley was quite insistent," O'Shay said, "but it wasn't going to end well."

Stanley cocked his head. O'Shay's message was news to him.

"I pushed to get you all together as my new team," O'Shay said. "We will get tough missions, ones that require a certain amount of discretion, even internally."

He locked eyes with Bear. "We've got heart and strength." His gaze moved to Rocks. "Guts and slight-of-hand." Looking at Stanley, "Brains and relentless drive." Then he turned to me. "And execution." We waited for his next words as he let his statements sink in. "We've been given an opportunity. An opportunity to get some shit done. It won't all be by the book, but more about why the book was written in the first place."

I liked that phrase. Rule books were written to codify some kind of behavior. If you truly valued why the book was written, you shouldn't need to codify the rules.

"Our first job is to stop a local mob organization that's involved in illegal gun acquisition and sales. Conventional, by-the-book approaches have not worked. The first step is cracking a code that combines two problems, a language barrier and an algorithm. I need you, Stanley, to scan the radio and figure out what they're doing. We don't know where or when to intercept them."

Stanley nodded.

"But," and he took a deep breath, "in order to do that, you've got to stop pushing about what happened with Red."

Stanley raised an eyebrow. "Why can't I do both?"

"Because I told our leadership that, if they gave you to me, I could get you to drop your story."

Stanley and I turned identical stink-eyes on him.

O'Shay just sighed again. "Hey, you keep pushing on this, and it keeps you and Red in the spotlight. Whether you win or lose, I can't use you. I know Red is skilled, from what I've already seen. I suspect you are too. We have a chance to do some real save-the-world shit here. But, to do that, you've got to move past your current situation." He ran his hand through his hair, then held up his hands like he was reading a news blurb. "Army turns over woman to enemy as bargaining chip," he said. "If that hits the news, give up on anything but a political career. The response will not be 'How can we do better?' It will be "I told you women should not be in the Infantry.'"

He stopped, staring at me. I understood what he was saying, and I never intended to push on charges against Reed. I wouldn't trust him, but I didn't need a formal declaration of his guilt. However, I also didn't like being told I *couldn't* move forward if that had been what I wanted. Then he went and dangled a carrot in front of me— mysterious work that required special skills. *What* do *I want?*

I locked eyes with Stanley. "I can let it go."

Stanley shrugged. "Okay, then I can too. Shit happens. Let's make the best of it."

"Like fertilizer?" Rocks said.

I rolled my eyes. *Idiot.*

O'Shay nodded. "Okay, let's get started then. Come with me, and I'll show you where the radio is, and you can scan."

Chapter 53

Red, present day

"No, Scan came through for me a little later," I told Galad. "And many, many times over the years since then. He's our 'behind the scenes' man. He's our eyes and ears, and the brightest of us all. Losing him would be losing family. I don't know why I let him come along."

My eyes flicked to Galad. The curves of his elvish cheekbones maintained their unsympathetic and aristocratic aloofness, but his eyes melted ever so slightly, with just a hint of warmth. "We have let him rest long enough."

He cast a spell. "I'm doing two things to help him recover," he said. "One is a spell that encourages his magical essence to recharge more rapidly. His capacity for using magic—this is true for anyone who is new to magic—is very low. He drained himself—he tried to squeeze magic out of his physical body, even though he had the vial. This can be deadly, and I will have to teach him how to recognize the signs. He was, fortunately, also pulling magic from the vial, which kept him safe. At least as long as the vial had energy, it would have."

A spell to recharge spells. Similar to a portable charger used on a phone?

"Now I will cast what we consider an endurance spell. It will give his body the physical energy it needs to finish recovering. And to handle what he's about to do."

I watched perplexed as he cast the second spell.

Scan's eyes fluttered open. He smiled at me, then raised his hands to see them. The tiniest pinpoint of light flickered into existence between his hands. It lasted about two seconds, and then he passed back out.

Galad smiled whimsically. "He's fine. That little spell drained the resources he had just built. Knowing what he would do, I prepared his body with a regenerative spell."

"But why did he do that?" I asked.

"He had to know, to remind himself, that magic was real. He will wake up again soon. My spells are still recharging him."

True to Galad's prediction, Scan's eyes fluttered open again. When he lifted his hands again, I grabbed one of them.

"Welcome back," I said, distracting him. "Yes, magic is real, and you seem able to use it." I gave him a mischievous grin. "But we have work to do, and I need you to stop playing with yourself 'til you pass out, at least for long enough to finish the *job*."

Scan barked a quick burst of laughter. "Gotta make sure the woman's needs are satisfied before sleeping—got it."

Grundle chuckled in the background. "Sometimes I feel sorry for you... *advanced*... races."

I shot Grundle a puzzled expression.

"Please don't ask him," Galad said, rolling his eyes dramatically. Grundle chuckled again, but I decided I didn't want to hear about the elf and troll's debate.

I gave Scan a hug. Not something we did in the military, but we'd left that behind. It was time for new protocols. And Bear had hugged *me*. I was learning that the idea of losing my team scared me as much as losing a family member would. And family hugged. Scan hesitated in returning my embrace, like I was covered in mud. Change can be hard.

I helped him get to his feet. "How do you feel?"

"Tired and super-pumped at the same time. Like I just finished a marathon."

"The spell I cast will continue to energize him for a little while," Galad said, "and he will keep improving on his own after it fades." He looked Scan in the eyes. "But you cannot use magic for the rest of the day. After today, your body will self-regulate better under normal conditions. Do you understand?"

"Um, not entirely, but I get that I shouldn't use magic until I've rested. Is that good enough?"

"That's good enough," Galad answered.

"Okay," Scan said. "So what's next?" His mind seemed to be clearing of its sleepy fog.

"Get the pics from my phone to the FBI," I said to Scan, "same as the last batch. Give 'em the location. Oh, I have a short video this time... is video a problem?"

"Not in terms of a data upload, no," he said, "but I thought video didn't work on these things."

I pulled out my phone, and the video seemed okay. No distortions. "I guess once they're dead, they show up on video just fine," I informed him.

He took my phone to his laptop. Every once in a while he would stop and stare at his hands, as though contemplating trying to make light appear, but then decide against it.

"So, what did we learn?" Grundle asked.

"Well," I began, "there was an entire train of the Infected, all dead, and they were chained to the walls or each other." An image of the dead human outside the shipping container flashed through my mind. "I imagine the guard was someone surprised by what he found in the pod and opened fire, but also took a fatal hit in the process."

"Had somebody captured some Infected and brought them there?" Grundle suggested. "The guard, going to check on them, found to his surprise, that one had gotten loose?"

"How would you capture an Infected?" I asked.

241

"I do not know," Grundle admitted. "Maybe they can be knocked unconscious, or asphyxiated? Before your world, their sheer, overwhelming numbers prevented any such attempts."

"Okay," I thought out loud, "so what if someone captured the Infected, but one got loose? The guards were surprised and—"

"Guards?" asked Galad. "I saw only one human body."

"There was a second gun inside the shipping container," I told him. "I assume one dropped his gun and ran."

Galad nodded, but he didn't seem convinced. "Let me propose another theory. What if the guards were surprised because they weren't expecting Infected? What if... what if they were expecting to find a container full of *humans*?"

Scan stopped typing. "*Humans* in a *shipping container*? Hold on." He popped up something on his laptop. "Equatorial Guinea is a hub of human trafficking."

"Okay," I picked back up the discussion. "So theory one is that someone captured a bunch of Infected, but one got loose. Theory two is that there was a container full of people, chained up, and they all transformed into the Infected." I shuddered, thinking of what that might have felt like, trapped and watching as those around you transformed into inhuman creatures, knowing your turn was coming. "Then the guards were surprised, not that a creature had gotten loose, but rather by the existence of these creatures at all. They were expecting humans and found monsters." Sighing, I concluded, "Theory two seems more likely."

"So the second guard..." Galad began.

"Probably did not run off," I concluded. "The gun in the shipping container was from the first guard that entered.

He fired off a few rounds, but one of the chained creatures transformed him. He probably killed his buddy and then moved on, but came back when Scan used his magic to Heal you."

"It fits together," Grundle rumbled, "but I would caution you not to jump to conclusions. We don't know enough. How did the original Infected find these chained captives? Was it before they left, or after they arrived? If they came from a densely populated area, it would explain how they'd encountered an Infected. But it doesn't explain how the Infected would have entered a shipping container, infected one person, and left. Someone would have noticed the panicked yelling. On the other hand, why would an Infected have been at the destination to transform them? The population density was low there."

I wasn't sure I followed what Grundle was saying, but I got the jist—many unknowns still needed explanation.

Scan stopped typing and stood up. "The data is uploading," he explained. Then he started walking around the camp, searching the ground intently for something, but I couldn't spare the brainpower for that distraction.

Returning to the conversation, I said, "Neither makes sense."

"Nevertheless," Galad concluded, "I adhere to the theory that the guards were expecting people and found more than they bargained for."

I nodded and turned to Grundle.

"Agreed," he rumbled.

"So, that's our working theory."

I turned back to Scan, who crouched on the ground, scooping dirt into a ziplock bag. "Scan, for whatever reason, we found some Infected outside of a major population center. How do we help your program find more?"

Without glancing up, he answered, "One thing that would help is more videos where we know we have seen

243

one. When you all go somewhere to fight one, let me know where you're going. The bigger the training set, the better the identification algorithm will become."

"How do we do that?" Grundle asked. "We don't know the names of the places we go."

"I'll get all of you phones and chargers that I'll swap out for you, seeing as you don't have any electricity here. Should we consider moving you somewhere with power?"

"I prefer staying outdoors," Galad said.

"Me too," Grundle echoed.

"I wouldn't mind a nice cave somewhere if you've got one." Harry muttered.

"Second," Scan carried on, ignoring the relocation dilemma, "we need more cameras. That means I need access to more systems, and to do anything with that data, I need more compute power and disk space. Red, if you want things to scale quickly, do what you can to convince the government to let me into their systems. It would be so much easier."

"Will do," I answered. "You've sent those pictures to Agent Smith?"

He walked over to his laptop, pocketing his ziplock baggie. "It's done, yes."

It was early afternoon by then in NYC. I had things to do. "Are we otherwise done with traveling and fighting for the day?"

"Scan depleted an energy source, and I am drained. Doing another trip would be risky to our overall magical resources," Galad responded. "We need to let the vials and myself recharge more, or we risk running dry and getting stuck wherever we go. I say we are done."

Pulling out my phone—not the burner—I texted Agent Terry Smith. I wanted her to know it was me who sent the pics.

> Can you meet for dinner?

No. Some shit has hit the fan
here. Can't get away.

> You sure? I had a craving
> for Mumbai Palace, or
> Cassava House.

I'd searched the web for food from Equatorial Guinea to come up with Cassava House, while Mumbai Palace was a bit on the nose. My texts could not be too condemning—I needed plausible deniability—but I wanted to be sure Agent Smith made the connection.

After several seconds, I received a text back.

> I suppose I do still have to
> eat. But I think I've had my
> fill of foreign… unless you
> know of anything outta this
> world.

Oh, nice one. I texted back.

> I do. But let's save that
> for another day… if you
> want local, let's do Tom's
> Tavern. I hope to have one
> other with me. 5pm?

"Scan, see if you can get Rocks to Tom's for a meeting with the FBI. I think I'll need him. I need some people skills. Bring him up to speed as soon as you can."

Okay, that would take care of the people who would be talking. I needed security.

"Troops," I started, then wondered about my particular word selection—what were these guys to me? They were more to me than they were two weeks ago. Gaggle? Posse? Gang? For all I knew, whatever word I picked would translate, through the spell, to the same word.

245

Realizing I had paused too long, and everyone was looking at me strangely, I started over. "Um, sorry, I took a mental wrong turn there. I just brought in the fourth guy from our old unit. We call him Rocks. He's got people skills."

"He is coming *here*?" Grundle questioned.

"No. Getting him out of the public eye is difficult. I hope he will help me deal with our, um, organizations that control infrastructure."

"Ah," Grundle rumbled, "he works with people like Galad and is the grease that keeps the wheels spinning."

I nodded. "And gets them pointed in the right direction."

"Would that I had been able to do the same," Galad said, regret clear in his tone.

Grundle grunted and put a consoling hand on Galad's shoulder. "In the end, you did the best anyone can do."

"I can bring him up on video," Scan said, oblivious to their odd exchange. "He should see you all in person before we move forward. The translator won't work, of course, but there's something to be said for seeing you all in more than pictures." Scan kept tapping away on his keyboard as he spoke.

"Okay," I said, hesitantly. "If you can get him alone…"

Scan continued to click away, and a video popped up.

"Hey, Scan," Rocks said.

I moved behind Scan, so that I could be seen on camera.

"Red," Rocks acknowledged.

"Hi, Rocks," I said. "Things have escalated. Scan will explain in a minute, but we wanted you to meet the team we are working with. They won't be able to understand you, nor you them, but we thought you should see each other anyway."

Rocks nodded. "Not the first time I've needed a translator." True. Rocks had managed a great deal in places where he did not speak the native tongue.

Grundle was the first to move forward. Scan slipped to the side, as did I, to make room for Grundle. "This is what he sees?" Grundle asked, pointing at the image of himself.

As Scan answered, "Yes," we heard Rocks on the other side saying, "Holy Mackinoly! Please tell me that *thing* is on *our* side."

I heard an "eep" in the background. Cynthia, his wife, was somewhere off screen.

"It is a pleasure to meet you, O' Grease in the Wheels that Mash People into an Oppressed Paste," Grundle said in a formal tone.

"Excuse me?" I said, offended for Rocks's sake.

"You said he couldn't understand me. What difference does it make what I say?" Grundle replied.

"*I* understand you!" I told him.

"But *you* thought I snacked on humans when we first met." He smirked. "I like to make a strong first impression."

Galad chimed in, "Have you not heard me complain of his oddness?"

"What are they saying?" Rocks asked.

"Grundle", I said, "—the big guy—is being a drama queen." Grundle rumbled with laughter, looked pointedly at Harry, and walked back out of sight of the camera.

Harry walked up and hefted his hammer in a kind of salute. "I'm Harry." Then he turned back and walked off, leaving Rocks with a raised eyebrow.

"He said he is Harry," I told Rocks.

"He is that," Rocks replied, and Scan snickered.

With the snickering, Harry narrowed his eyes at Scan. The last thing I needed was a fight, so I patiently reminded Harry of his homophonous name. He grinned and got back to work on his hammer.

Galad, the last, moved into the view of the camera. He politely nodded. "It is a pleasure to meet you. I am Galadrindor Arafaemiel Terebra'an, but you may call me Galad."

Sensing his formality, Rocks replied, "I am Reginald Penbrook, and the pleasure is all mine. My friends call me Rocks, and any friend of Red's is a friend of mine."

Galad gave a slow, but polite, nod of the head and moved away from the camera. Rocks's statement got me to thinking—I *was* starting to see the otherworlders as *friends*. Scan and I moved back into the field of vision of the camera.

"I've set up a meeting with the FBI at Tom's," I said. "Just the one agent."

Scan barked a short, disbelieving noise. "I'll make it as secure as I can, but your agent won't be alone."

"Agent Smith?" Rocks asked.

"Yes," I said, confused as to how he knew her name. I should have known Rocks had been paying attention when I'd been interviewed.

"I liked her too," he said. Then he rolled his eyes and said off-camera, "I meant I had a sense she was trustworthy. But I'll be happy to illustrate how much I *like* you, on or off camera."

"Ewww. Get a room! Hi, Cynthia!" I shouted and waved.

Cynthia stuck her head into view, her blond hair flowing straight down while her head came in sideways. She waved and blushed, while pushing her glasses back up onto her nose, then disappeared.

I continued my overview. "We've been feeding the FBI pics and locations of the monsters that are invading our world. We need to get some more compute power to help find these creatures, the *Infected*. I hope to use our intel as a bargaining chip. I hope you can be there, Rocks. You know I don't do slimy political work well."

"Thanks for acknowledging my sliminess. This is *why* you don't do slimy political work well, by the way. You have to save the word 'slimy' until you've hung up." I would have blushed if I'd had any decency, but I knew my weakness in that area well—my unfiltered statements had created many problems in my past.

"I'll be there," Rocks concluded. "Scan, you'll send me details?"

"Roger that," he answered.

"Okay, I'll sign off then, and go remind Mrs. Slimy how much I *like* her."

"It's two hours 'til the meeting. What will you do with the other hour and fifty-eight minutes?" I teased.

Rocks chuckled and hung up. Realistically, I would have bet he needed to clear a spot on his calendar to meet with us, even on a Sunday.

I was going to hit the FBI up for resources. I had Scan covering my electronic back, and Rocks by my side— all I had to do was show up. And not screw up.

Chapter 54

Scan

What a day!

I learned about traveling between worlds without a spaceship, learned that I could use magic, learned I had a natural ability for Healing spells, Teleported twice, and a creature from another world almost killed me. Waiting for an Uber driver at the southwest corner of Central Park felt anticlimactic.

I needed to get back to my home base; my compute capability was limited because I was stuck on a laptop with a poor LTE connection in the middle of Central Park. Red wanted to meet with the FBI agent at Tom's. I wasn't so sure that was a great idea, but great idea or not, I would have eyes and ears ready. The elf and company wanted to be close. I hadn't worked that out yet. A radio wouldn't do the trick—the translator spell didn't work over the radio. A truck could get them close, but I needed some way to communicate.

Ah, *Bear*. He could drive, and, with the aid of a magical translation, he could get any messages to and from the elf. I knew who to call to borrow a truck. Radios and cameras were next—I had the radios, and I'd tapped into the tavern cameras before, so things were pretty well set up. I just needed to get the pieces ready.

Okay, Bear responded that he would help. Excellent.

The Uber driver dropped me off, and I paid him through my phone—well, not *my* phone, but *a* phone. I told the driver to drop me a block from the back entrance to the old office where I had set up shop.

As I walked in, though I knew Galad forbade me from

doing it, I made a tiny little light glow in my hand for just a second. Amazing. How had that ability been inside me all my life?

Once inside, I did a quick check of my security, both physical and online. No hints that anyone had approached my base, and only the usual random attempts to hack the system. I'd set up a few nasty surprises for anyone who got in deep enough, but no one had triggered them. Just as well. That would have cost me some time to clean up.

First thing was to procure the physical equipment needed for the meeting with the FBI. Get the truck, have it ready for Bear, get the radios inside it. We would want a jammer to make the conversation private. That was illegal, of course, but it was necessary. Some more burner phones for the otherworldly crew, in order to locate them when they Teleported. No other equipment came to mind.

Moving on to the electronics, I double-checked my access to the cameras near Tom's. I also did a quick recording of the vehicles along the streets to get a feel for whatever the FBI rolled in.

Okay, the pieces were in place. I popped up my program for identifying sightings of the Infected. They all mapped to populated areas and had low hits, except Bata, but we had just taken care of the ones there, so I filtered it out.

I turned to the other pet project I had brewing. The equipment I'd used in New Mexico had picked up some interesting data. The video itself showed a flash of light and a distortion that was very similar to the distortion seen when filming one of the Infected. It must have had something to do with the magic involved—the type, the intensity, something.

The other piece of data was more obvious when they'd Teleported out of New Mexico. The dust on the ground after they'd left was from New York. The colors were noticeably different—the dark earth from Central Park vs. the lighter sand in the desert—but I had since done some soil analysis and verified my assertion.

I pulled out the samples I'd collected earlier that day from the Park. I had sand from the desert in New Mexico, and dirt from the pavement where we had Teleported into Africa. I'd also picked up soil from the Park that had never seen a Teleportation spell—a baseline reference. I put that under a microscope first. The image that greeted me was what I expected—some single-celled organisms moving around, bacteria and archaea "doing their thang."

I placed the sand from the desert under the microscope. At first, the bacteria of the two samples appeared to be similar, but after watching for a while, I spotted a difference.

The bacteria from the Teleportation spot were "twitchy." I couldn't put my finger on it, but it reminded me of the effect of magic on cameras. Maybe an attempt of a single-celled organism to distort an image, but falling flat on its non-existent face?

I made some notes and tried the other sample, the one from Bata, and it seemed similar to the sample from New Mexico, only there were more of the "twitchy" bacteria. Something to do with the time frame of the Teleport? The jump to New Mexico had been earlier and so had experienced a longer time to normalize. I made some more notes and switched gears.

I checked up on the upload of my database to my new site. It made little sense to keep everything I had without backup, and by backup, I meant a whole other site. It was only a matter of time before my abode was compromised.

Okay, what else? I couldn't think of anything, and I needed a little down time, so I set my alarm for an hour, moved over to my cot, and took a much-needed nap.

Chapter 55

Red

I had a radio in my ear as I walked into Tom's. I was sure Agent Smith would have one as well. Scan had equipped radio jammers near the tavern, but we wouldn't use them unless necessary. I figured the FBI would also have a van set up with the equipment to block radio and Wi-Fi.

I was the first one there, arriving just a few minutes early. The tavern showed scant signs of life, so there was no squabble over my favorite booth, where I sat, facing the door.

Agent Smith was the next to arrive. Where I had shown up in blue jeans and a T-shirt, she wore her official government suit. She had undoubtedly come from the office, given all the work I had dropped on her desk the previous two days. I couldn't believe I had killed aliens in Mumbai just the day before.

"Ms. Hernandez," Agent Smith said in greeting.

I stood up, but neither of us moved to shake hands, neither formal nor friendly. I knew I liked her.

"Agent Smith," I responded, and we sat, facing each other.

"Just the two of us then?" she asked. "At least in person."

"I hope we will have one more," I said, "but I can't be sure he'll make it."

"Mr. Penbrook has a busy schedule."

I knew they'd connect me to my old army unit at some point.

Agent Smith threw a couple of books on the table between us. "These came for you," she said. Peace offering or indictment? The book I had ordered for Grundle, with a second copy for me, had arrived after I'd last been at my flat. That book had been the first that had taught me there was more to winning than numbers. I thought Grundle would appreciate it.

I gathered the books from the table as the door opened. Rocks strolled in, baseball cap pulled low, wearing a T-shirt and blue jeans. No one would mistake that guy for Reginald Penbrook, financier extraordinaire. A casual observer would never notice his tailored jeans fit to cover an artificial leg.

Rocks pulled his cap off—of course his hair remained tousled, yet neat—and nodded to the bartender. "Hey, Mike. How's it hangin'?"

"Rocks!" The bartender smiled and leaned forward, holding out his hand across the bar. "Long time, no see."

Rocks shook his hand and pointed back toward us.

"Ah... pitcher of beer? IPA, I believe." Amazing. The bartender hadn't recognized me until he saw Rocks.

I shook my head no and mimed drinking a cup of coffee.

"Make that two," Agent Smith said. I held up two fingers.

"Can you ask the kitchen to put on a pot?" Rocks said to Mike. "Looks like we all need some."

"Sure thing." Mike punched something into his tablet—good thing nobody had jammed the Wi-Fi—and returned to cleaning and prepping the bar.

I made room, and Rocks sat down next to me.

"Mr. Penbrook," Agent Smith greeted. "Should we get down to business?"

"Business, is it?" he asked. "I thought the business aspect was only *my* problem."

"Brass tacks, then. Ms. Hernandez, are you involved in getting me the intel I've been receiving in regard to some

254

overseas activities?"

That was direct enough. Faced with the prospect of answering such a pointed question, when I was sure I was being recorded, I decided it was time to pull the plug. I turned to the house security camera and gave the kill signal.

I winced, as did Agent Smith, as the radio in my ear screeched. We each took out our earpieces, and Mike pulled out a remote and started pressing buttons. "Cable is out." He pulled out his phone and sighed when it also didn't respond.

"You know that's illegal, don't you?" Agent Smith said, tired and a little annoyed. I didn't think she expected an answer.

"I sent you the pics from Mumbai and Bata," I said instead.

"How'd you get them?"

I held up my phone, "I took 'em with this."

She squinted. "The timelines don't work out. The pictures from Bata were just a few hours ago. But I don't care who you are protecting for now. I do care about where these things are coming from. Who is making them?"

"I don't know exactly where they started from, but," and I knew it sounded weird, but she'd hinted at knowing as much herself, "they're not from this planet."

"What makes you say that?" she said.

I wasn't prepared to admit the axe-wielding source of my knowledge. "I can't say."

She stared at me deadpan.

"But I can say that they multiply by taking over our bodies... transforming one of us into one of them."

She froze, then closed her eyes. "That makes sense," she said. Her eyes popped open. "Oh, shit. I have to go!" She jumped up.

"Wait!" I grabbed her arm. "I need something from

255

you."

"What? Be quick."

What the hell?

"We think we have a way to find where these creatures are hiding, but I need access to more compute resources."

She nodded, "You'll get it. Anything else?" I wanted to shoot a puzzled expression to Rocks, but he was sitting beside me, and it would have been obvious. The conversation was not going the way I expected. I hadn't even needed Rocks to negotiate. Agent Smith didn't wait for us to decide, but turned and walked to the door.

"Why are you in such a hurry?" I yelled.

She didn't stop walking but shouted back, "You claim you were there. If so, how many shipping containers did you look in?" And, with that, she was out the door.

I turned to Rocks. His jaw hung as low as mine, maybe lower. We stared at each other wide-eyed. Rock found his voice first. "What in the hell did she mean by that?"

I didn't have an answer. The TV kicked back on, saving me from trying to find words. We weren't facing the set, but Mike had not turned the volume off, and we heard faint voices. Mike picked up the remote and turned the volume up.

"... and we will keep covering this event as long as we can..." Rocks and I looked at each other, confusion and curiosity reflected on our faces, and scooted out of the booth to see the TV behind us.

A live feed of running, screaming people cut back to a newsroom, with a slight scramble because the feed cut sooner than expected... not unusual for breaking stories. The text banner under the live newsroom read: "Breaking News: Monster Attack in Equatorial Guinea." The video box in the bottom corner showed a crowd of people running through the streets, then a familiar distortion of the camera, followed by people dying. Distortion guarded sensitive American eyes from seeing the gore, but the dying and dead were obvious. What was *not* obvious was how many Infected there were.

"I'm told we are going back to a live—" one newscaster said, then got cut off as the camera flipped to an aerial view. The picture was steady—from a helicopter. The cameraman was far off, showing an overview of the city. Fires raged in multiple places, creating pillars of smoke. Lights from emergency vehicles dotted the highways and city streets. A popping noise was getting picked up through the reporter's microphone—the muffled sound of distant gunfire. Waves of distortion smeared the images throughout the city, like the picture couldn't focus.

Oh, my God. The Infected were everywhere! Agent Smith had asked if we had checked the other shipping containers. They must have all been full. Or at least enough of them to wreak havoc. How had they gotten out? I had a panicked thought—if they were reaching such numbers, then we were already too late! Even if they did not multiply as quickly on Earth, they had somehow built up a small army. Were they beyond control?

The reporter tried to describe what he was seeing— hordes of alien beasts running loose in the city, killing relentlessly. He tried to zoom in, but wherever he zoomed, whatever horror he was seeing, we saw just distorted images. The distortions deprived us of the images of live attacks by the monsters.

I picked up my earpiece. Scan had gone back to his flat to orchestrate the meeting with the FBI. "Scan, you're seeing this?" I said once I had the earpiece in.

"I am. Sorry, Red, I had my eye on our mission. There don't... hold on... yeah, there don't seem to be additional sightings in other places. I checked for new hits on my alien-spotter. It's a little hard to read now that there are so many hits in Bata, because that news is getting re-broadcast all over the world, so it's hard to filter out."

My panic rising, I heard myself ask, "What do we do, Scan? How do we stop them now?" The gunfire and adrenaline-fueled panic felt uncomfortably familiar.

"Red, we have to go," Rocks said, staring out the window. "Now!"

Chapter 56

Red, four months prior

I didn't care what Murphy said—First Sergeant Nettles was a tool. Yeah, he kept us busy with missions that cracked down on weapons dealers, ended mafia groups, freed captives from human trafficking rings, and the like. But he also moved us on to new locations just as we were making real headway into transforming the populace into something truly better.

"You shouldn't have provoked him like that," Murphy said, sliding an arm around me and pulling me close, the two of us finally away from prying eyes. My blood still pounded, and I scowled, ignoring the pleasant warmth at his touch that threatened to snuff out my anger.

"*He* shouldn't have provoked *me*," I returned, pushing back, but not hard enough to break his hold on me. I didn't want out.

He smirked. That jackass smirk which I envisioned someday complaining to my girlfriends about. After I slapped dinner on the table for our three boys, who were just like Dad—noble jackasses with too much charm to resist. When he leaned in for a kiss, I pushed back just a little. Just so he'd know the topic wasn't closed.

Having a room—and a door with an actual lock—had its advantages. Too bad for us we didn't have one. But we made do. We had blankets, and there was a lot of understanding in the field.

We killed some time dancing in the sheets, and I dreamed for a while of an increasingly intoxicating future, one so far from anything I had thought I would ever want. A husband. A home in a small town. Kids to raise. Growing old with someone.

"We are moving on too soon," I said as we dressed, picking back up the thread that I'm sure Murphy hoped he had cut away.

He smiled, pulling on his boots. "I should have known we weren't done."

I slammed a boot onto the floor, sliding a foot in. "My point exactly—we aren't done, but we're moving on. Next town. Next problem."

He rolled his eyes. "Weren't done with the *conversation*," he clarified, shaking his head. "Do I need to distract you again?"

I pushed him hard enough that he had to drop his other boot to catch himself from falling. "I will cut you," I said, for the thousandth time.

He grinned, just like the other nine hundred ninety-nine times he'd heard that empty threat.

"I'm serious, Murph. We give people hope. We show them possibilities, but we aren't in towns long enough for roots to take hold. The fruit never grows before someone uproots the trees, and a year later, we are back in the same town—new mission, new hope planted, but never allowed to grow. Don't you ever tire of that?"

"It's a desert," he countered, half-playful, half-serious. "Let's say we stayed somewhere long enough to water your proverbial trees. What happens to all the other places we *don't* visit? When no other town has fruit trees, where will the fruitless go when their towns are overrun by sand?"

"Ass." I hated when he pissed on my metaphors. I knew there was meat to my ideas. Shit, I'd just mixed meat into my fruit metaphor. I slammed my other boot down and shoved my foot in.

Pissed, I walked off. "You're not wrong, Red," he said to my back. Finally, he was speaking sense. "But we have our orders."

"Ugh," I growled and continued out the door. I left Murphy behind, knowing he was never far.

***

We've been here before. This town.

It had been in better shape when we'd left it the first time. It would be healthier when we again left it behind. We had returned to take care of a corrupt mafia that had sprung up. Nettles had given us the mission.

Scan had started hacking into their radio and cyber security. Rocks was using his charm, turning over stones, stones I didn't want to know about, to get information.

We would infiltrate their system and dismantle it. We always did. Usually there was a big event in a mission— something Murphy would coordinate. Meanwhile I worked with the women, the children, the noble of heart, to show them how to protect themselves, and more importantly, to show them how to have one another's backs.

The mission was rolling out like any other, and Murphy was using the combined intel from the three of us to construct a plan. Bear, as always, was our tank.

There were two problems with missions in the same locations. One was that your honorable intentions were less accepted the second time around. You'd left before—why would anyone believe you were committed the next time? The second was that your M.O. was predictable. I should have seen it coming, but it was the latter trap that we fell into. Most specifically, the trap we sent *Bear* into.

"That was a setup," Scan said coolly. "They've got Bear." Scan would stay cool in a volcano. We crowded in a hot room on the second floor of a building near the rendezvous, Scan wearing a headset plugged into a laptop. He closed his laptop and stood. "We need to go." Sliding the laptop into his backpack, he headed not to the door, but to the window. "Now." He peeked out the window and drew back. "And not that way."

The only other way was the door, and Scan shook his head when I looked at it with eyebrow raised.

Rocks walked to a shared wall and used the butt of his rifle to make a new door. The ambient noise was loud enough to cover a little destruction, and we all squeezed into the next room, which got us access to a window along a wall that was not being watched. We dropped into a busy market, where we blended in and escaped watchful eyes.

"We're not leaving Bear," I said.

"Of course not," Murphy said. "But we were sitting ducks back there. And we can't go back to the base." He was staring at Scan, waiting.

I didn't catch on as quickly as the others, but the pieces started clicking for me. "Someone on the inside betrayed us. I told you that rat-bastard Nettles was shit."

"I can't be 100% sure it was someone on the inside, but our room was being watched," Scan said.

Unless Scan had become clumsy covering his online trail, someone had spilled our location.

"Rocks," Murphy started, "where to?"

Rocks nodded once and took the lead. We weaved around a few corners; it wasn't a long trip to the slim alley where he stopped. He rapped a pattern on a side door. The door was plain, but the sounds coming from within suggested substantial metal bars being moved on the other side. There was more heavy movement from inside, and in less than a minute, the door opened.

A figure in a drab thobe stood inside, medium build and gender impossible to guess until she spoke. "Sakhra!" she exclaimed, pleased.

"You know that's a mistranslation," Scan threw in.

"Shut up, Scan," Rocks said, leading us inside. The woman nodded to someone holding the door, and I followed

Rocks in. Rocks and the woman conversed, but Scan was between me and them, and I couldn't hear. A hall with several doors led off one way, but we headed straight and ended in a lounge room with…

"You brought us to a brothel," I stated, my voice flat. Several women rose from their seats as we walked in. "I can't believe you brought me into a brothel. *This*," and my voice cracked, but I got it back under control. "This is what I have been fighting against for *four years*. From town to town, trying to empower women…" A thought struck me. "And you're fucking *married*, Rocks!"

I yelled that pretty loud. The woman who had opened the door was staring at me in the quiet after my outburst.

"I can assure you," she answered in unbroken English with a British accent, "I am *quite* empowered."

"And the first thing she asked," Scan added, "was why he'd been so long, and did it have anything to do with the new ring on his finger. The second," Scan continued with a confused smirk, "was whether he'd still want the Two Moon special."

Rocks blushed but held his tongue.

Murphy, who'd come in behind me, put his hand on my shoulder. "We're just regrouping. Rocks has places all over town." The woman laughed—a light, playful laugh—and Murphy amended, "Not all of them brothels."

That was all the go-ahead Scan needed to pull his laptop out and start connecting up his radio. Rocks pulled a second radio out of his pack and set it next to Scan. The hostess and the other women moved into a farther corner, but none left.

I stared daggers into the group of women. They didn't care. The hostess spoke up. "We don't have children employed here, Ms. Hernandez—at least not in the back rooms." Her using my name shocked me, and I glared at Rocks. "He didn't tell me," she said. "You did. During a presentation at our town hall four years ago. It was quite inspiring."

Shit, she was right. About the timing. I doubt it was inspiring, though I had wished it had been. "But *this* is *not* what I was hoping to inspire!"

"But you inspired me. 'Do what you can, with what you have, where you are,' you said." She paused and moved a little closer. "I was already *in* the business, and my path to getting there was as bad as you spoke of. I didn't think I could stop prostitution, Ms. Hernandez, but I could stop the buying and selling of children for that purpose. 'Do what you can, with what you have, where you are.' Theodore—Teddy—Roosevelt. I don't remember if you told us who said that, or if I learned it later."

Flustered, I paced in tiny circles, clenching and unclenching my fists. *This isn't right. It isn't what I meant. Is it?*

"They've left breadcrumbs," Scan interrupted. "Not breadcrumbs. An obvious trail. They want us to follow it. It's a trap. Another trap." He tapped away at his keyboard another minute. "They have him in a junkyard at the edge of town. Hell, they've got cameras on him." There he was, on video, chained to a metal chair with a pile of metal plates, pipes, and wires as background.

Scan looked at Murphy. Murphy looked at me. They still had Bear.

"Okay, then let's spring the trap," Murphy said. "Let's follow your hunch a minute," he said, locking eyes with me. "Scan, can you bring up an inventory of what we acquired and turned in from our last mission?" Scan started clicking away, but Murphy didn't wait. "Compare it to previous inventories—search for exact matches. Start with missions in the same places, but broaden the search if you can't find anything."

Scan was typing, clicking, dragging—working his

magic.

"Rocks, get us some backup," Murphy said. "We can't go through official channels. Set up a meeting place near the junkyard. Red—"

"I'm with you," I interrupted.

"You're with me," he said, resignation etching his voice.

"I've got a match," Scan announced. "A grenade launcher. It's worse than that though—they've made it look like the item never made it into inventory. They've made it look like *we sold* it, instead of turning it in.."

Murphy sighed. "Damn." He turned to me, "No 'I told you so'?"

"Do you need to hear it?" I asked.

"I think I do."

"I *so* fucking told you so!" I said, shoving him.

He gave me a sad half-smile. "That's better. Okay," he said, nodding. Then, again, "Okay. Make the list as complete as you can, Scan. But you've only got an hour, maybe less. Here's what we're gonna do."

Chapter 57

I hated splitting up, but we needed to enter the junkyard from different points. Rocks had found us some men—paid mercs. I loathed the idea. All it took was a higher bid and they'd turn on us.

But that was what I had. Three men, flanking my position, armed with rifles. They seemed competent, but nothing I would feel safe trusting my life to. I tried not to think about that, since I had no choice but to use them. We swept through the junkyard, moving with care, surrounded by walls of jagged metal that the enemy could be on top of or hiding behind.

I didn't know where Bear was. I had a rough idea where Murphy was. All I could do was keep moving. The setting sun made long shadows out of the piles of metal corpses, but provided enough light for clear vision.

There. I signaled my men to hold. Around the pile to the left, a clearing opened up—a gap in the piles with a larger machine. A compactor? They'd cuffed Bear to a chair, two men armed with rifles standing nearby, one seated at a makeshift table with a laptop, and a familiar face looking over the shoulder of the seated man. I turned to search the general direction I expected to see Murphy coming from, but there was no sign of him. He couldn't be far though, and I didn't want to lose the sunlight.

Hidden behind the pile, I brought my rifle up and sighted that familiar face. That ass-wipe Reed—I should have known any chicanery would involve him. I had an excellent view of everyone, but I could only take out one with surety, and I knew which one I wanted gone.

"Hernandez," he yelled out, still staring at the screen. "I see you and your *troops* back there."

I scowled. He had cameras.

"We just want to talk," he said. "We know what you've been doing, and I have to bring you in."

Whuut? Damn, was it possible Reed didn't know we were being framed? I *so* wanted to believe he was the bad guy, that I could justifiably put a bullet in his pompous, betraying, candy-ass forehead. But what if he *had* been given the job of bringing me in after I'd been framed?

I turned to my mercs and waved for them to scatter; I was relieved to be rid of them. They receded back the way we had come, as I placed my backpack amongst the pile, careful not to make noise. I watched Reed watch his screen through a hole in the debris. "Okay, Reed. I'm coming in. Hold your fire." I bought myself some precious seconds to secure my equipment amongst the debris, hoping my back was to whatever camera was watching me. I checked my knives, handgun, and rifle—it was time to get Bear.

I weaved my way around the protruding metal pile and into one of the main pathways, giving Reed and his men an unobstructed view. I moved slowly—no sudden movements. I dangled my rifle in my left hand, a throwing knife concealed in my right.

Reed's men had no such concerns—their rifles pointed at me.

"Your friends will be here soon," Reed said. "Your geek and Rocks are being brought in now." At the "geek" comment, the man at the laptop scowled, but Reed marched on, oblivious. "I've seen Murphy cross a couple of cameras. He's nearby. We shouldn't have to wait long."

"If you just want to talk, how about unchaining Bear?" I said, stopping about twenty feet away.

"Keys are on the table." His eyes met mine and he nodded toward the keys, then he returned his eyes to the

267

screen. "Once the entire gang is here, we'll talk about letting him go." The keys were on a *Pirates of the Caribbean* jailer's ring.

I heard people approaching from a trail next to mine, and three soldiers brought Scan and Rocks into the clearing, hands tied behind their backs. The soldiers shoved my friends to the ground near Reed.

Reed ignored them and kept his eye on the screen. Rocks and Scan worked their way back to their feet, while Reed shouted out, "Murphy, I know you're close! We've got your team!"

Murphy ghosted in on the same path my other two teammates had just been forced down. Murphy had snuck up behind them. He strolled forward, rifle in his arms but pointed down—as unthreatening as possible while still holding a rifle.

"Ah, good, the gang's here now," Reed said. "Here's your situation. Right now we've made it look like you've been stealing from the U.S. Army."

Dammit! I should have gone with my gut and put a bullet in his head when I had the chance.

"What you've been doing has been very profitable, but you were getting too close to stumbling on the truth. So now you have a choice. Keep doing what you're doing, and we all make a little money, or take the rap for all that equipment that's gone back into enemy hands and spend the rest of your lives locked up."

"I'm not crazy about those options," I said. "How about you admit what you've done, and we'll be free to make the world a better place without you?"

Murphy had continued to move into the clearing. We were all there. Finally, Reed took his eyes off the computer. Step one of Murphy's plan was complete.

Ignoring my barb, Reed started with Rocks. "You're in. You've always straddled the line." Rocks shrugged. I didn't think Rocks was as morally unbound as he pretended, but it wasn't the time to point that out.

"Stanley," Reed continued, "you've never quite grasped the concept of ownership. Would you rather keep redistributing goods, and making a little profit, or spend the rest of your life in prison, framed for things you've never done?"

Scan crinkled his face in puzzlement while maintaining a grin. "There's plenty of things I *have* done—why invent more?"

Reed paused. His jaw worked a couple of times, but he couldn't figure out how to steer through that reef.

Scan saved him. "Locked up is not my preference."

Reed nodded and looked at me.

"I still vote for you turning yourself in," I answered.

Reed sighed. "I knew you'd be the problem. You and the big guy. But we can find another ox." He was wrong about that—there was no one with heart like Bear. "Your skills are harder to replace. You're... convincing. People want to buy what you're selling."

"That's because I'm not selling bullshit," I said. "Which I would be, if I did the same thing knowing it was making a profit for you, Nettles, and whoever else is in on this."

"She's not going to budge," Murphy said. He sounded resigned. I had expected him to sound angry. "And no matter what they say, the others will not be the same without her." His face fell in disappointment. "I'm going to need a new crew." Wait, *what*? "Who does Nettles have that can replace *her*?"

Wait, that wasn't part of the plan. Reed was nodding—he wasn't hearing anything surprising. I saw Rocks and Scan staring at Murphy with narrowed eyes. They weren't in on it, whatever *it* was.

Oh, hell. *Murphy.*

269

"Nettles chose her replacement already," Reed answered.

"That's all I needed to hear," Murphy said. And I knew from those words, despite his betrayal, where his loyalties lay.

Minor explosions echoed off the walls of jagged metal as the clearing filled with smoke from the canisters we'd left behind, mine in the opening by my backpack and Reed's at the entrance to the clearing. I shifted positions and let my knife fly—the noise Reed made as it entered his body being the only satisfaction I would get in the smoky blackness.

The camera I had mounted from my clear shot into the clearing had served its purpose—we had recorded the confession we needed. It had already gone to the cloud. *Now, we just need to get out alive!*

There were rifle shots. We had prepared ourselves, but we didn't know exactly how things would play out, and only Murphy and I had ended up armed. Murphy had triggered the smoke bombs. Whatever his past, Murphy had chosen to do the right thing. He had chosen *us*.

He was closer to Rocks and Scan. I circled to the table for the keys to unlock Bear. Speeding through the hissing darkness, I dropped the rifle in favor of my blade. I found the table earlier than I expected, flipped sideways on a body that lay unmoving. I felt around for the ring of keys, knowing time was of the essence.

There. My free hand found the ring, and I rushed to Bear's chair. Either he'd toppled himself, or someone had shoved him over. I moved to his cuffs behind the chair back and fumbled with the keys, having to put my knife down and use both hands.

There had been no trickery with the keys—they opened the cuffs and Bear untangled himself. I retrieved my knife and took Bear's arm to lead him out the way I had come, stumbling through the smoke along the path.

Our eyes burned, but we made it. Rocks and Scan were already out, untied, but still unarmed. We joined them, and I was trying to decide whether to go back for Murphy, when he stepped out of the smoke.

He moved a step or two closer, and I saw he wasn't alone. Reed, blood coursing down his shoulder, had a handgun to Murphy's head.

My Murphy. My love. Who had been lying to me for who knew how long… maybe forever.

I had my knife. I could have thrown it. I should have thrown it. But I hesitated.

"Over here!" Reed shouted. "To me!" There was a clatter as a few armed men moved to Reed. Their rifles pointed our way as they crowded around him.

"Do what you can, with what you have," I heard Murphy say, as he tossed a small object in the air over his shoulder, "where you…"

The grenade went off too soon.

Chapter 58

Red, present day

"What? Why?" I said. Rocks didn't answer, and I had no choice but to follow him.

They surrounded us the second we got out the door. Six agents moved in, pairs coming from across the street and from each direction on the sidewalk. "Run, Red." Rocks tapped his metal leg—he couldn't run, but he wanted me to. I felt a moment of panic, then the fight-or-flight rush of adrenaline.

A few other people roamed the street. Concern for civilian casualties proved my undoing. When the FBI drew their guns, I worried that, if I ran, they would fire in the streets of New York. I didn't have my daggers, so no enhanced speed. However, I had one more ace up my sleeve. Three more aces, in fact.

Far behind the two FBI agents crossing the street, Galad strolled toward us, not so out of place in his wizardly robes as one might expect. I'd seen stranger things in NYC. I did not spot Grundle or Harry. Okay, just the one ace then?

Rocks put on his baseball cap, and his movements, even though non-threatening, caused the approaching FBI to slow and raise their weapons, like Rocks was going to pull some ninja throwing stars out of his cap or something.

I hadn't run, and the opportunity had passed. I had no weapon, except my hands of course. Rocks's distraction, drawing the attention of the FBI, had allowed Galad to close the distance between himself and the two he was approaching from behind. They were in the middle of the road and he would reach them in about ten more seconds.

"Get down on your knees! Hands behind your heads!" shouted an agent approaching from our left.

Rocks put his hands behind his head, and I followed suit, but he tapped his metal foot on the ground. "Can't kneel... artificial leg."

The FBI agents had closed to within a few feet. From my sides, agents could see Galad continue to approach. One agent turned his weapon toward Galad. "You! Back away!"

Galad did not stop, but instead drew the sword he had concealed within his robes. The sound, louder than I would have expected, caused all the agents to turn to the new potential threat. Oddly, the agent who had yelled at Galad did not fire. He just stood there. Then he re-holstered his gun. The other agents followed suit. The lead turned and walked into Tom's—quietly, calmly—and the others followed.

"What... the... hell?" I asked the world, stretching my words out, staring wide-eyed at Galad.

Galad shrugged, sheathing his sword. "I told you. I'm an Empath."

Scarlet-faced, arms waving, I shouted, "Like I know what the hell that means!" I grabbed him by the lapels of his wizardly robe and got in his face. "What. Just. Happened?"

"As an Empath, I can shift people's perceptions of things." He remained calm, not responding to my agitation. "Alter their priorities. Make them feel like it is of much more import to go into that building and wait for a while, than to point a gun at me."

"What in the *hell*?" Rocks said. "Will they *remember*?"

"As much as you remember a dream, so some will remember more than others."

I tried to wrap my mind around Galad's strange

ability. If I thought of it as a rapid hypnotism, it didn't seem so far-fetched. *Come see the Great Mesmerismo! One week only! Buy tickets now!* But the oddness paled in light of the oddness we'd seen on the TV in Tom's.

"Um, are we safe to go back in?" I said to Galad. "There's something you need to see."

"Should be," Galad answered.

I walked in first. All six FBI agents—I did a quick count—were scattered around the bar, some sitting, some standing, all of them staring straight ahead, at *nothing*.

Mike stood behind the bar, dividing his attention between the TV and trying to get the attention of the agents. "Hey, are you guys okay?" He waved his bar rag in their faces, one by one. "Hello? Anyone in there?"

Galad came in behind me, and Rocks followed. Mike became quiet after Galad entered, and began cleaning the bar in slow, mindless circles.

I directed Galad's attention to the television. He stared, squinting, "I'm sorry," he said. "What should I be seeing?"

"That's where we just Teleported from," I explained. "The shipping container that was full of chained-up Infected corpses." My agitation rose as I again watched the news, my attention switching from my own adrenaline-filled need to escape the FBI agents to the world-threatening scale of attack from the Infected. "Those distortions, they are Infected! They've overrun the city!"

In the time I had been gone, the situation had grown worse. The ground was almost invisible behind a wave of distortion. A plane was drifting to the ground. *How would the Infected take out a plane?* We watched as it hit a building and caused a massive explosion. The feed switched to the inside of a helicopter before that video also distorted, then cut off—there had to have been an Infected on the helicopter.

All the color had drained from Galad's face. "We have lost," he said, grim as death. "There is no stopping them now."

I shoved him. Hard. "Snap out of it! What have you got left in that grab bag of magic? How do we stop this?" I shoved him again. "What do we do?" I moved to shove him a third time, but Rocks stopped me. I turned my wrath toward him, but his calm, sad smile stopped me.

"Red," I heard in my earpiece. I'd forgotten about Scan. "The fight's not over yet, but..." A long pause. "Go back to the camp in Central Park. This battle is over."

"Dammit, Scan, the entire *war* is over," I said, Galad's hopelessness rubbing off on me. "You've heard how they multiply. There's no stopping them now," I repeated Galad's words dumbly. "How can—"

"Red!" Scan interrupted my tirade. "We haven't lost. The rules are different on our world. I don't know why yet, but they are. The Infected didn't move past Bata. I've got nothing in neighboring cities, and Bata is gone."

"I know we've lost Bata," I said, "and the Infected may not have spread yet, but the numbers in Bata are too much. Once they move on..."

"They're *not* moving on, Red. Bata is gone. I mean, *really* gone. Nuked. Someone fired or set off a nuclear warhead. I'm watching the mushroom cloud from a camera in Doula."

Someone just nuked *Bata*? Was Scan *serious*? I believed him and yet couldn't internalize the info. Had somebody had the balls to pull the trigger? Like removing a cancerous organ to save the body?

Sure enough, the news caught up with Scan, showing a mushroom cloud from a great distance. The newscasters were talking over the image. "This just in," a man began somberly from the TV. And as much as I wanted to stay and hear, we needed to scatter.

"Guys, let's go back to camp," Rocks said. Rocks had an earpiece. He had heard Scan. Galad was the only one not aware of Scan's announcement.

"Just go, Galad," I said, "I'll explain on the way. Where are the others?"

"Outside in a truck," he answered, more zombie than elf.

"Let's go," I replied. "Lead the way."

I waited for Galad to lead us out, but he wasn't moving. What he had just witnessed, or something from his past, haunted his eyes. I put an arm on his shoulder, and he stirred, but then checked back out again, giving in to whatever demons tormented his soul.

"It's not over yet," I told him. "It's bad, but it's not over."

"I... I do not think I adequately explained how fast these creatures take over once they have begun." He spoke as a man lost. "Your world has only hours now." We crossed the street and headed to the right, then left at the corner.

"You've forgotten that something is different on this world," I told him. "Maybe the lack of magic, I don't know. But, for now, though the cost was... too high... we contained the Infected."

"I fear you fool yourself," Galad said bleakly.

He pointed to a delivery truck. Bear was in the driver's seat, and he gave me a nod as we approached. The whole truck leaned to the driver's side. I didn't see the others. Galad opened a back door and climbed in. I peeked in and saw Grundle sitting with his back against the left wall. A sliding window opened to the cab.

"You ride with Bear and bring him up to speed," I told Rocks. "I'll ride in back with this lot." I climbed up and in, pulling the door closed behind me.

I slid the two books I'd carried from the tavern toward

Grundle.

"Hello, Red. Why so grim?" Grundle asked in his rumbling bass. He held up the two books, saw they were the same, dropped one, and started thumbing through its twin.

Galad answered for me. "The invasion has well and truly begun. There were more of the Infected in that city we visited this morning. Enough to overwhelm the city. Our time is very short."

Grundle nodded along. "And yet, I think I see some spark of desperate hope in Red." He held up the book and nodded his approval.

"We nuked the city," I confirmed, sitting down between Harry and Galad, opposite Grundle. Our three to one didn't balance the truck.

"Nuked?" Grundle asked, as Bear revved the diesel engine and double-shifted into gear.

Galad sat, alone with his tormented thoughts, saying nothing.

"A nuclear bomb," I said. "One blast destroys the entire city, and leaves it unusable for a long, long time."

"Impressive," Grundle said, "but we also have magic-based equivalents of attacks that decimate cities. I have no doubt that, at some point, some world has tried it, though we don't get much recorded history from invaded worlds."

"But, as you've said," I countered, "something is *different* on our world. Perhaps the lack of magic energy. What I just saw was multitudes of the Infected beyond a scale I can explain. Nothing seemed slow about their ability to replicate, and yet Scan says he sees no Infected in the next nearest cities. That still true, Scan?"

"Still true," he said in my ear. "We're back to the numbers we had yesterday. Hits in the population-dense cities only."

I repeated his words for the others.

"You are sure about this?" Galad wore the expression of one who desperately wanted to believe what he was being told, but didn't dare.

"As sure as I can be," I answered. "For now, let's assume I'm correct. And let's talk about our next steps."

A quiet hope settled over the crew as they sat staring at each other. A shared sense of having gotten away with something buoyed their spirits.

"I think we should assume," Rocks said through the open window, "that the FBI will connect the four of us, and that at least you three are in danger. My family's wealth and notoriety might make me harder to nab. What's your situation, Scan?"

"I'll be moving soon. Getting all my data moved securely will take time. Let's face it—while I think I could do a better job than the government of getting the alien recognition software improved, I would rather the FBI have it than destroy it. So I'm being careful that nothing gets lost."

Rocks turned to Bear. "And you, Bear?" Bear shook his head no. He didn't have a hidey-hole. Neither did I.

With part of the conversation over the headset, I wasn't sure the otherworlders were following, so I explained. "Our government will be after us now, and we have to abandon our homes." I had just started to decorate my flat. *Geez.*

"Your government has recognized the threat," Galad said. "Perhaps it is time to come forward."

I translated for Scan.

Rocks sighed.

"We should consider it," I said. "This isn't like last time."

"You mean it is more public," Rocks replied with sarcasm. "We're not as ignorable and expendable?"

"Okay, fair enough," I said. "We might be even *more*

278

ignorable and expendable than on our last mission. They just nuked a city in Equatorial Guinea. Even if the government captured and executed us in public, they'd get away with it because public tension will be so high."

"I see three options for you two," Rocks said, "Either join in with this lot, if they'll let you, or go hide out in The Palace, or go on the run."

Running—bad idea. We'd lose all influence over the situation. Hiding in The Palace would get us stuck. Sure, there were rooms well suited for that purpose, but the cameras in the halls would be a real pain in the ass.

Galad was the one who finally answered. "Staying with us gives you the most freedom. We should be able to accommodate two more."

I nodded. "That's settled then. I think it's time to finish our conversation with Agent Smith."

Bear drove us to Central Park. Scan told him where to stop the vehicle, and we all climbed out. The four of us dashed into the woods, and Bear and Rocks followed more slowly, Bear keeping Rocks safe. Scan had someone ready to get in the truck and drive it away. We started moving back to *our* camp.

Chapter 59

Red

"Agent Smith... it's Hernandez."

"Ms. Hernandez. Hello." Then nothing. She was getting someone to trace me.

"Ms. Hernandez," she repeated, "you pulled quite a number on my agents at the tavern. Reminds me of what happened at The Palace. People dazed and confused about why they'd made the choices they did."

Crap, she was right. I hadn't put that together. Galad must have worked that same magic in Hong Kong and in the Palace tunnels. Wow.

"Wasn't me," I said, "but I get why you'd think so. Listen, I'm calling to give you information, but I have a healthy distrust of how you'd welcome me if I turned myself in, so let's just keep the relationship long-distance for now."

"Not smart to hide," Agent Smith said. "It makes you look guilty."

"Enough already. You've seen what those creatures can do. I have a way to find them and get to them, but not if I'm locked in a—"

"Yeah, you did a bang-up job in Equatorial Guinea."

"And I will not risk getting locked up where even more of those monsters can get out of control!" I yelled. Speaking of getting out of control, I was spiraling.

"If you've got something you can *do*," she shouted back, "then *share* it so we can have more than a vigilante crew trying to stop a world invasion!"

The conversation wasn't going well, but then I hadn't expected it to. *Breathe, Red.* She hadn't hung up. Probably because she still hoped to trace the call.

"You already know they can take over bodies," I said, more calmly—resetting the tone.

"Yes, like Gremlins in a swimming pool."

"Beg pardon?"

"Like Gremlins in a pool… *Gremlins*… the movie?! Though I suppose they're more like *The Borg*."

"No idea what you're talking about." I think I'd heard my mom mention *Gremlins*—not *The Borg* though. "Anyway, you've seen how they distort camera images?"

"Yes."

I waited for another movie citation. It never came.

"We've got an algorithm," I continued, "a trained neural network, that can find sightings of these creatures."

Silence on the other end.

"We want more camera access and more compute power to handle the extra videos."

"You should give the neural net to us," she said. "Wouldn't that make more sense? I know your guy, Stanley Ashcroft—Scan—is one of the best at what he does, but we have a lot of bright people here too."

"If you know Scan," I said, "you know he doesn't like you. You in the general sense. For you, specifically, I'm sure he'd be quite impressed with your folkloric movie references."

"Ha ha," she said. "Don't blame me for your poor education. Scan may not like government agencies, but is he willing to risk the entire world because of it?"

"No, he is not. Which is why he won't risk letting you control that information. We've had some pretty shitty experiences working with government agencies. On the other hand, have *you* had any shitty experiences working with *us*?"

"Nicely said, *Red*. You're going to have to tell me where you picked up that nickname some day. But there are privacy laws. We can't just give you access to cameras."

"We were afraid you'd say that. Scan will send you the info for the system he is using to build his neural network, but he won't give you the system itself. You'll have to rebuild it on your end."

A long pause. "The guys here are impressed—they can't trace this call." Agent Smith sighed. "So let's assume we duplicate your ability to locate these creatures. How are you able to get to them and destroy them?"

"You wouldn't believe me," I said. "How do you *think* I do it?"

"I think you teleport."

I needed the little surprise emoticon from my phone.

"We know those monsters can teleport," she said, matter-of-factly, like we were talking about one of her *classic* movies. "We had a couple of them captured, but they disappeared, or so their captors reported before we lost contact. Or they cloak themselves and appear suddenly, but teleportation seemed more likely. Assuming they can teleport, I'm guessing you've figured out how to do the same. Our scientists are pretty sure these things are not from our world. They can't rule out some kind of biologically-crafted super soldier, but we don't think there's anyone on Earth advanced enough to do this."

I attempted a coherent response and came up with, "Erk."

"So, if they came from another world," she said, "it is possible someone else did too. Someone helping you stop these things."

"Erk," I repeated, then coughed to give my brain time to catch up. "You're seriously entertaining that idea?"

"Me? Sure. I grew up watching the X-Files. The entire government? No way." There was a pause with some shuffling. "My guys are telling me that, if Scan shares his neural net setup, they will share some resources. Something about being able to tell if the resources are being used for what he says, and that they'll be able to catch up faster watching how he uses—" She talked with someone away from the phone then came back. "I can't repeat the whole explanation—I don't really get what they're saying. I think they'll work it out. Yeah, they're giving me a thumbs-up. I guess they're already talking or whatever."

I related to her dilemma. I understood what Scan would tell me up to a point, but yeah. So Scan was trading his intel for more resources. He was not so naïve as to believe that the door to additional resources would remain open, but I left that to him. Scan and the government were both preparing to fight a better battle.

"So," said Agent Smith, sighing, "I now think you were telling the truth when you said you were taking pictures in Mumbai and Bata. I think you've got some alien tech that enables you to teleport, and you're hopping to other cities and killing these invaders. Can you prove me wrong?"

A strange accusation. Wasn't I innocent until proven guilty? No, I couldn't prove her wrong. But that provoked a thought—was there anything I could do to prove her *right*?

"I'm sure Scan can patch you back through to me if you want to connect. I have some work to do." I hung up.

One of the biggest lessons I learned in the military, working to improve life for communities around the globe, was that people didn't respond well to being scared shitless. Nor did they change just because they'd been shamed.

People changed—communities changed—when they found something to *hope for*.

"Grundle, we need to talk."

283

Chapter 60

Agent Terry Smith

I had never felt so out of control.

Ever since Garnet Hernandez had become a person of interest, my life had been one confusing piece of information after another. We had flagged her after the initial incident because of her military experience, a minor player. I'd done the bit that was in my power to help her— I'd kept Peters away from her. It bothered me that, with all the training we underwent as federal agents, and the yearly classes on harassment, a misogynistic ass like Peters still managed to get his name assigned to the two women relevant to leading security at The Palace. I blamed Agent Rogers for his failure in leadership more than Agent Peters for being the womanizer he'd always been. Regardless, I had intervened for her and had her re-assigned to me, someone who had little to show for her 20 years in the FBI.

Then Hernandez had turned out to be the key, making me wish I'd let Hernandez go with Peters, and I'd taken Staci Wei instead.

We had sent scientists to examine the original corpses found in The Palace. They had verified the obvious—those things weren't from Earth. Their molecular composition was wrong, their DNA was completely foreign. The brainiacs wouldn't rule out that someone might have biologically engineered them.

"The same geniuses," I muttered to myself, "wouldn't rule out advanced technology in Wakanda from an ancient vibranium meteorite crash."

Then there was the incident in Mumbai where someone handed over a whole pile of dead aliens, connecting up to me through a text. I was just doing my job—I wasn't freakin' Fox and Scully—and then everyone started coming to me to discuss aliens from outer space. But I had prepared everyone for the next drop, and we were on site in Bata quickly. First agents were there in an hour—guarding the bodies, waiting for backup—when one of the agents decided to check more shipping containers. Nasty shit happened fast after that. We managed to capture a couple of the things, which is how we learned they can teleport. It didn't end well for us. The nuke was the right move. Near as I could tell, it hadn't come from us. Not sure how that was possible. Not sure I believed it was true.

But I didn't voice that, because it was Rogers's case. I didn't like Rogers—he was on his way up in the agency while I was on my way down and out. In some ways, I didn't mind. I couldn't remember when I last felt any ambition for my work... or anything. The job had become rote for me—nothing but a paycheck. Why should I resent someone who still had ambition? Yet, I had to admit I did, while still not being able to muster that drive in myself. It didn't help that he was a micromanaging, controlling a-hole, but that was just icing on my resentment cake.

"Smith," he said, poking his head into my office, "have you finished the paperwork on your bungled operation with Hernandez?"

He'd wanted to bring Red in. Hernandez had latched onto me, so they had sent me into the tavern. I'd left in a hurry to deliver the vital intel about those creatures taking over human bodies, using them as hosts. I'd only learned later that Rogers's trap had failed. A small part of me cheered to see his arrogant micromanagement fall apart, even if he was trying his hardest to pin the blame on me. My bungled operation. Ass.

"Already filed it," I told him, not even glancing up from my computer.

Crazy to think that, at a time when we were nuking our own world to save ourselves from an alien invasion, I was so petty as to care whether some selfish prig stumbled in his attempts to achieve his career ambitions. But what exactly would Rogers or the FBI do with Hernandez or her supposed partners if they captured them? And was that what the world needed?

Rocks

That had not gone how I had expected at all. They had prepared me to negotiate for access to computers. I wasn't ready to tell Red we didn't need them. I'd arranged a few strategic business losses in The Palace and opened up some space that we had plumbed for incoming tech companies. Their servers were being redeployed for use by Scan. There was a skeleton crew to do some manual labor as needed, but otherwise a compute farm for one man.

I'd acquired a small microbiology lab as well, replete with technicians who knew how to use the equipment. They had ongoing work from before they'd become part of the Penbrook corporate body, but I had the authority to influence their priorities, as long as I kept them profitable.

After all, locating those creatures was not enough. Even if we established armed squads near the locations of the creatures, we had no way to draw them out except through the otherworlders, or at least the magical tools Red had mentioned.

Scan had handed me soil samples and asked me to get them analyzed. "The bacteria seem to behave strangely," he'd said. "Just tell me if they find anything interesting."

A strange request, but we needed some answers to some strange issues, so okay. Explaining that to the lead microbiologist at PharmLabs was a little more vexing. In the end, I'd had to hint that the samples related to the situation in Bata; I didn't know what they should search for, but they should do it for the safety of the world. Motivations are personal. I'd missed the target on the "safety of the world" comment—that wasn't a motivator for the scientists. But the idea of doing something that might relate to a problem on the world stage appealed to them. That was fine by me, as long as they did the work.

We had nuked Bata, and it had to have been U.S.-launched. We were the only ones likely to have perceived the threat, with the means to respond, *and* the willingness to act on it. The idea that the U.S. had nuked Africa was surreal. On the other hand, I had seen the elf put seven people into a dreamlike trance with just a look. Just a *thought*. Super powers, magic, whatever it was, it felt very tangible. *It's funny how the mind works with experiences versus visual input*. Magic—an idea that should have been laughable—felt *real*. Nuking a city, though I was sure it had happened, had only been on TV, and it felt like a dream.

I focused on financing the problem-solvers. We needed to track the creatures, to draw them out, or figure out how to stop them from getting to Earth in the first place. Scan was working on tracking. I was quietly setting up teams to work on the other two aspects.

I did so because there was a tipping point where those creatures multiplied faster than we could stop them by conventional means. And I'd done it despite what the otherworlders had told us about how much slower the Infected multiplied on Earth. I didn't trust the otherworlders—what did we know about them? I didn't trust the government—I knew them well enough to know better. They'd cost me a leg; they weren't getting a chance at the other. I didn't trust the people I worked with to build The Palace—their motives were all monetary. That didn't prevent me from working with all of them to make things better.

I texted Cynthia.

> Tell me something
> important.

Cynthia and I had worked out a system. When I involved myself in the twists and turns of motivating people—the financial maneuvering, the backstabbing—I sometimes got lost. Ages ago, a glimpse of myself from the outside drove me to leave the family business for the Army. I saw how I would do almost anything, including hurting people, to prove I could outmaneuver everyone else. It wasn't the man I wanted to be.

Cynthia anchored me. She would remind me of purer motives. She shot me three quick texts in a row.

> That bad again, eh? I'm sorry,
> Babe.

> You're helping people you care
> about.

> Who are trying to save the
> world.

I sighed. That should have been good enough. It *was* good enough. I decided it wasn't lack of motivation that was bothering me—it was my inability to influence things. It was so much effort to work political and financial strings, particularly when you had a conscience, and yet my ability to change things for the better had been abysmal. I stood there too long, not replying, wrestling with my inner demons, and Cynthia came to my rescue.

> Meet me for dinner. I'll have
> some more for you then.

I smiled. Cynthia was my rock.

> That sounds great. You

pick - text me place and
time and I'll be there.
ILU.

ILU2

Chapter 61

Red

I'd explained what I was thinking to Grundle. He'd nodded along and taken a genuine interest in how I thought about the problem, asking questions that prompted me to be daring, deciding what we could do with what we had. "Accelerating change" he had called it. We spoke long into the night until my massively long day overcame my enthusiasm.

I nodded off and awoke to a gentle nudge from Grundle, who had set up blankets for me on the ground. Some trinket pulled from their enchanted storage chest created a warm but smokeless nightlight. My eyes closed to Grundle settling in, his back against a rock, the book I'd given him open in his hands. I could not see the title, but I knew what he was reading. *Certain To Win,* the book that had changed how I thought about fighting—it called out like horns before a battle.

Monday began my first day of living in Central Park. Day one, and I longed for my morning coffee. Then I thought of baths and clean clothes. I sighed. It was like being back in the field.

I also found it dissatisfying not to go to work. I had gone from working as a security lead at the newest building in the world, to being on the lam, hiding out in Central Park. It wouldn't be good for my résumé. Realistically, none of that mattered—the world needed saving. If I didn't make the effort, there wouldn't be a job to go to. I still felt like a total failure. I needed coffee.

From my phone, from the tiny screen and constant scrolling, I struggled to digest how the world was reacting to the previous day's events. I wanted my laptop, but it was back in my flat—off limits. My mind drifted back to the evening before.

After Bear had driven us to the Park, we had all walked back toward camp. At one point a jogger came close, but ran right by us. A bit later an approaching couple stopped and kissed, giving us time to move by.

"How does that work?" I had asked, waving back at the lip-locked duo. "No one seems to notice us."

"It's a variation of the warding spell Galad uses," rumbled Grundle, his mind elsewhere. He had pulled a necklace from beneath his leather tunic—a yellow stone placed in a silver partial moon. "This necklace contains a 'look away' spell. The spell is not as strong as a ward. It distracts people so they don't notice what is in front of them."

"Weird," I had said. "Wait, why aren't *we* distracted then?"

"That would be funny, wouldn't it, putting on a necklace and then being distracted until the wearer died from forgetting to eat." Grundle had chuckled.

"Such things exist, I assure you," Galad had piped in. "An experienced spellcaster imbues the spell in the stone and connects to the wearer and the wearer's intent. One that distracted the wearer, we would call a curse. And, before you ask, it is possible someone might make such a thing with the intent to hurt someone, but more often it is a spell gone wrong. Creating enchanted artifacts is difficult."

"Could *you* make them?" I had asked. "I mean, are you capable of it?"

Galad grimaced. "That one? Maybe. Not the translation necklace."

"Only a natural can imbue items with spells," Grundle had elaborated, "and only in their area of natural ability. So Galad can create Soul Stones, or imbue Warding spells into

291

an object—strengths of an Empath. I would have thought translation fell in the strength of an Empath."

"It does," Galad said. "But I've never heard of anyone imbuing translation into an artifact. I don't know how it was done."

"And yet we have a whole box of them," Grundle said.

"The room where I found them," Galad said, "contained some really ancient items." He sounded bitter as he continued. "Undoubtedly the secret of their making sits on a world now inhabited by our friends with the eyeless faces and long claws."

We had entered the camp, and Galad strode off to the tent while Grundle, Harry, and I slowed. "You keep calling Galad an Empath, but he doesn't seem very empathetic. Am I missing something?"

"Hmmmm," Grundle had groaned. "Let me ask you to picture something." He gathered his thoughts. "Imagine being able to feel… *everyone*. To be connected to everyone you encounter, feel their joy and their pain. A stronger feeling when physically or emotionally closer, but natural Empaths pick up on the emotions of people they have not seen in years, even when far away."

He raised an eyebrow, and I nodded that I was following.

"Now, imagine that, in a matter of days, those connections fill with fear, rage, grief—and then, at a rapid rate, the links to everyone you know are snuffed out. Total silence. All the lights in the universe go out. Galad says a wall went up; he can no longer feel others' emotions."

It was an odd thought—I was feeling empathy for an Empath who couldn't seem to muster any himself. The idea of that much loss was disturbing.

***

Pulling myself out of my reverie, I realized there was no

292

way to get to a real computer, so I contented myself with crawling through media feeds from my phone.

"U.S. Denies Nuking Bata."

There were ramifications to nuking another country. The people had elected President Rushman on a platform of "return to normalcy" after the shenanigans of our previous president, and nuking a country was not "normal." Nevertheless, the world court of opinion believed the nuke was from us. I kept reading.

"What are you learning?" Grundle asked. Hard to believe I'd been so absorbed I hadn't noticed a nine-foot-tall walking rock approach me.

"The world's response is mixed. Because the Infected distort videos, the footage of the attacks in Bata are very confusing."

I held up my phone for him to see, and he nodded agreement.

"There are occasional shots of dead Infected; *their dead* appear on camera readily enough. But get this— 'Videos of Bata Fake!' Some people think this was a hoax set up as an excuse to nuke Bata—"

"For what purpose?" Grundle interrupted.

"That's not clear—but people in that camp are sure there's a money trail."

"Mmm," Grundle rumbled as I scrolled through other headings.

"Viral Outbreak in Bata," I announced. "We've got people thinking there was a viral spread, a deadly sickness, of some kind. They suggest the nuke might have saved the world from a pandemic. 'Footage of planes dropping out of the sky are convicting for a rapid viral outbreak.' But they can't explain the video distortions."

"So, hoax or virus," Grundle summarized. "What are the responses that your world might take?"

"The hoax theorists don't have a common—or

293

believable—explanation for *why* someone would fool them."
I paced as I thought it through. "There's nothing they can do other than point fingers, so I predict no significant change to anything from them."

"And those that believe it is a virus?"

"They'll want disease-protection actions—heightened airport security, suspended travel from places with suspected outbreaks, and getting out of high population centers where the virus could spread more rapidly."

"Hmmph," Grundle said. "That's good."

That *would* help. Dense populations attracted the Infected, so, if people scattered, there would be fewer attacks.

"But," I said, "no one has a rational idea of what happened, and there's no explanation from those who had perpetrated the nuking. There's way too much speculation, combined with distance from the problem, for most people to react. The bottom line—there will be heightened tensions with no tangible actions or release."

"Scared people with no outlet," Grundle commented. "Always a delightful combination."

"Indeed." I gave up on trying to dig more intel from my phone. "Let's talk about our own next moves." I needed to understand more—I had some questions.

Grundle chuckled and opened his hands in welcome.

Where to start? Harry sat nearby, cleaning grime from carvings on the shaft of his hammer, his movements careful and attentive.

"Are these magic weapons just 'normal' in your worlds?" I wondered aloud. After all, they seemed to have quite a few.

"No, they are rare, and *these* are exceedingly rare," Harry said. "Recall that we had entire worlds to choose from after the Infected destroyed ours."

"Wait, what?" I hadn't considered any of that. "You're

telling me that, after the Infected destroy a world, they *leave* it?"

"No," Grundle answered, "they go into stasis. They don't have eyes, so it's hard to say they are sleeping. They don't lie down, though they do crouch. And they twitch. It is very unnerving."

I didn't like to think of what that Goliath found unnerving. "They *crouch*?" I asked.

Harry took over the narrative. "They crouch," he said shrugging. "And they don't defend themselves or help each other if natural events strike." He watched his hammer as he related that information, but then tore his eyes away and looked into mine. "A single person can walk around, and if you do nothing else, they do not revive. But the more people, the more likely they are to stir. Use of powerful magic also gets them moving, as well as direct interaction or loud noises caused by the living." He shrugged, not able to explain their behavior. "But this offers some opportunity to do small raids on overrun worlds. Along with not eating or drinking, the Infected don't use weapons—we take back what we can."

Scan and Galad were near us, but doing their own Wizardry 101 class. Scan was clearly listening, though, as he piped in, "I don't see how something like that *evolved*. If they don't reproduce except by taking over bodies, there would never have been a first."

Grundle nodded agreement with his logic. Harry, as usual, did not seem invested. Galad was the one who answered. "While I generally agree with your statement, you have seen little of the universe." Pompous ass. "There are beings that change between two significantly different forms—one humanoid and the other animalistic—and we cannot explain how they do it. They use magic, but such transformation defies our understanding. There is a planet where fish can fly, but only at night, where they light up and create small nebulas of dancing stars. It is amazing to watch and totally defies logic. There is some way that magic is imbued in their very function. Not like us with sporadic capabilities to harness magic and some basic potential."

"Come on," Scan scoffed. "I'll buy that these Infected are magical creatures—no question—but they have to have been *created*. I mean, just look at them—they are the stuff of nightmares. Eye holes covered over with skin; no mouth, or nose, or ears. Just nose holes, and ear holes. Fingers and toes disproportionately long with claws. These things were designed to be frightening as hell."

"But as I think about it," Scan continued, "many animals have developed characteristics to look frightening—puffer fish expand themselves to appear bigger; the viceroy butterfly mimics the poisonous Monarch so predators will stay away." He shrugged and returned to his studies, pulling Galad's attention back with a question about magic.

After a day of thinking over what Grundle and I had discussed, I let him in on what I believed our next moves should be.

He laughed—that monstrous, grumbling roar of genuine laughter he emitted on occasion. "Oh, Galad is going to hate that. This will be so much fun." He clapped his hands together once in glee, producing a small crack of thunder.

"So, you think we should do this?" I needed confirmation that the idea wasn't insane.

"Yes. In fact, we must!" Grundle couldn't control his enthusiasm. "What do we have to lose?"

Just the world, I thought. *Just the world*.

Chapter 62

Rocks

The lead scientist at PharmLabs had frayed my last nerve.
He talked down to me, using long, scientific terminology to
tell me why the assignments I gave him were a waste of his
time. I'd seen him roll his eyes when he thought I wasn't
watching. But, with very few leads on stopping the alien
invaders, I kept pushing the guy, and absorbing his disdain.

So the excited voice mail pleased and surprised me.
"It's Dr. Manusov from PharmLabs. Come by when you can.
We've found something." I'd gone in as soon as I could,
feeling somewhat vindicated regarding all the crap I'd put
up with. Nothing set me off quite like someone thinking they
were better than me. But, still heady from Cynthia's news
during dinner the night before, I would have taken even
more abuse well.

"We're going to have a baby," my sneaky librarian
had said through happy tears.

The idea of having kids had excited us when we
were newlyweds, but that was several years ago. On my
furloughs we'd done our best to get a family started, but it
hadn't happened. Testing revealed difficulties. Just
difficulties, not impossibilities. We'd planned to take steps
toward fertility, but life had become rather complicated, and
we'd agreed, without discussion, to wait.

So, instead of "baby steps," we'd focused on the
effort with building The Palace and easing Cynthia into the
public eye. She'd been a real trouper, battling her own
shyness, and had slowly been learning the ways of her new
role. But I'd also wanted her to remain who she was, the
woman I'd fallen for. And so the pizza place she'd chosen

as the venue to tell me about our next big adventure in marriage was exactly the right choice.

I swiped my badge to get in the lab. Dr. Manusov didn't keep me waiting. He dressed the part of a lead scientist—rumpled white lab coat, spectacles, disarrayed black hair, and a laptop.

"Thank you for coming in, Mr. Penbrook," he greeted me. "Please, let me show you what we've found." He led the way, bubbling with excitement, and I followed, to a small conference room.

The room seated six, a clinical rectangular table surrounded by ergonomic, adjustable chairs. Ergonomic for people with two legs, anyway. I stood up, waving at my leg as explanation.

One wall was glass, overlooking the lab where fancy, expensive equipment was being sparsely used by a geeky crew. Two of the walls in the room bore whiteboards. One displayed handwritten chemical compositions and diagrams. The last wall held a large monitor.

He opened his laptop and set it on the table, connecting his screen wirelessly to the monitor on the wall.

He popped a video onto the monitor—an image from a microscope, centered on one of the little germs. It moved around and the camera centered on it, while other germy things moved into and out of the shot.

"These are the bacteria you asked us to watch," the doctor reported.

I waited. The priggish scientist wanted me to be curious, and I was, but I refused to give him the pleasure of knowing that. I berated myself—*I need to be better than this.*

"As we've told you," he began, "the population of these cells, the ones you wanted us to learn about, seem to decrease over time, dying without replicating, and eventually the normal, 'non-twitchy' ones are all that's left."

"Yes," I said, impatience seeping through. "You've told me that many times."

"Well, we were wrong," he said, as the cell-thingy suddenly vanished, the ones around it moving along as though nothing untoward had occurred.

"What the hell?" Had it disappeared? "They shouldn't do that, right?"

The doctor harrumphed while backing the recording up a few seconds and playing it again. Poof, it repeated its vanishing act.

"Well, what happened to it?" I asked, having no idea what to expect.

"We have no idea," Dr. Manusov answered. I narrowed my eyes at him, and he hastened to explain. "We set up this system—the one following the cell around—with some difficulty. These scopes," and he waved out to the lab, "were not made to trail bacteria. It is incredibly difficult to do so at the scale of magnification needed to see them." His cheeks turned a slight red. "We set this up because we thought, if we showed you a video of the lifecycle of one of these bacteria, you'd let go of your obsession. Instead we found *this*," he said, waving his hand at the monitor.

If only I knew what "this" was.

"We've learned a bit more since then. First, there's no energy dissipating on any spectrum that would explain the sudden annihilation of the mass. I know these things seem tiny, but there is a law about the conservation of mass. If that thing had converted to light—visible or ultraviolet—the amount of energy released would be measurable."

I was confused. He tried again. "Our first thought was that the cell had somehow converted spontaneously into pure energy, but we were wrong. Again."

Dr. Manusov concentrated on his feet for a moment, then looked me in my eyes. "Mr. Penbrook, I apologize for how dismissive I've been of these requests of yours. They seemed... well, they seemed ridiculous... but I was wrong. I treated you poorly."

Wow. Who woulda thunk it? A part of me wanted to smack him, but he'd made a ballsy move, admitting he'd been a dick. I had to give him credit.

"You did, but I get it," I told him. "I'm some corporate asshole with more money than brains. Look," I stopped him from his polite interruption, and repeated, "I get it. You're right—I don't understand most of this. My only value is to help others connect the dots. But I do have reasons I'm asking for this. I appreciate what you've done and how you can help."

My brief speech encouraged him, and he picked back up his narrative. "The other odd piece of data is that the twitchy bacteria vanish more rapidly when they're on their own. The more there are, the more they seem to stick around. So large groups of them seem to be more stable than individuals." He said that like it was meaningful, but I didn't get why. "You see," he said, patiently, "bacteria reproduce by asexual reproduction." *Poor bastards.* "A process called binary fission. Basically, splitting—they don't need other bacteria. As far as we know, they know nothing about other bacteria nearby. So the idea that they behave differently in groups is... not normal."

He waited to make sure I was tracking. I nodded that I understood.

"But, we were also correct in part of our original assumption," he continued. "Bacteria reproduce by splitting, every twenty minutes or so. These don't. I'm not saying they don't split at all—we suspect they do—we just haven't caught one in the act."

"Camera shy?" I offered with a grin. Dr. Manusov grinned back. We were practically buddies at that point.

"Well, that's all we have so far," he said, clasping his

hands. "I'm not sure how that's helpful or what else to look for. I suppose we will continue to watch for splitting or cell death, unless you have another direction."

"No. No, I don't. Thank you for the information." I sat in silence for several breaths, thinking. "As I've said before, you cannot publish this data yet."

"I understand," he said. "I'm sure we are racing against someone, but I will tell you again—*this kind of work is what we do*. When you can let us in on the bigger picture, we will do even better."

I thanked him, shook his hand, and left, wondering if Scan could use anything I'd learned.

Chapter 63

Scan

Rocks had provided some interesting information. I'd stitched together a theory in my head but didn't know how to apply it.

I had a more pressing, though less important, problem to solve. Paranoia convinced me that people were trying to follow me, that I would be the one that blew the cover on the alien camp, or my hidden computers, or both. Galad had given me a "look-away" charm, but it only worked on bystanders. I'd also started training with Galad on the Teleportation spell, but it would be a while before I mastered it.

There was a simpler spell—the one Galad had used after we had Teleported into Bata. It teleported you over short distances to destinations visible to you. The fundamentals of the real Teleportation spell required a different way of thinking, like doing a Fourier Transform in your head, and operating in that mental-mathematical space to find the shortest path among multiple vectors. Your brain did all the work automatically when you were operating within visual distances. The Blink spell prepared your brain for the more complicated spell, and would be enough to stop anyone from following you. Round a corner, Blink to the other end of the street, then rinse and repeat until you've put large distances and multiple turns between you and your tracker.

Even with the reduced need to hunt down the Infected—at least temporarily—Galad had not agreed to let me use a vessel of magic for practice. Too risky, but it sure would've been nice. He assured me I was building up my capacity for magic, and would soon be ready for the Blink spell.

So, there I was, trying to get myself from my main server room down the hall to the bathroom. Galad had said a need to be at the target location helped your brain get in the right frame of mind, so I'd set up my own little Red Bull and coffee situation to provide some urgency. I felt silly, but the urge to be in that bathroom was strong.

I stared at the location where I wished to be, used the incantations and finger movements Galad had taught me to focus my mind, and *bamf!*

Except no *bamf*—I was still in the computer room. The trick was to get your mind to do more than one thing at once. Finger movements were a mnemonic device to trigger your brain to think of one thing, while words were another trigger. Getting them each right separately came first. I worked on the incantations and finger motions, then tried the combo again, and *bamf!*

Dammit, still no *bamf*. I desperately needed to pee, so I tried it again—*bamf!*

I was going to have to walk to the bathroom or pee my pants. C'mon, *bamf, bamf, BAMF!*

Time seemed to slow, as something *very different* happened than when Galad Teleported me. For a split second, I saw tiny little threads connected between, well, *everything* within sight. Some were thicker and longer, some brighter and some dimmer, different colors, with some full of little nodules like a well-fed snake, some splitting and fanning out, and some connecting threads to other threads. It would have been overwhelming, but my brain latched onto what I'd needed and yanked, and I was just *there*.

Whoa!!! I'm outside the bathroom. I didn't have time to celebrate. I rushed inside and took care of business. Close call.

I tried to make sense of what I'd seen as I Teleported. The myriad of connections between objects was beautiful and complicated, beyond comprehension. Galad was right—there was some part of my brain that just "got it."

Galad said the two biggest things someone needed to succeed in magic were, first, figuring out how to tap into that "got it" part of the brain, and, second, feeding your conscious brain with information the intuitive part found usable. After that, it was just like building any muscle. Your endurance and capacity grew, and so did your efficiency.

I knew I would have to rest and recharge my magical energy before trying the spell again. At some point, I would have the skill to gauge my energy level. Quick self-review— I'd learned the spell to bring forth a ball of light, a spell for Healing, and most recently, the Blink spell.

Interesting observation: what Galad told me about casting the Healing spell was not right for me. The way he described it didn't mesh with what I saw when I tried to use the spell. When I mentioned that to him, he was not surprised—Empathy spells worked differently for him than when non-Empaths used them. He believed it had something to do with natural abilities.

Anyway, it was time to shift gears. I couldn't practice the Blink again for a while, not without one of those vessels to help recharge me. So back to studying bacteria. And recent learnings about spells gave me a clue.

"How do you prevent tragedies like Teleporting into objects, or appearing too high and falling to your death?" I'd asked Galad.

"It's built into the spell once you learn it," he'd said. I hoped he was right.

Part of the spell was grounding it and making sure the source and destination were compatible—you could, in fact, Teleport into the air if you started in the air. He'd also

304

told me, "Going back and forth between the same locations gets easier over time. Those same Teleportation points become easier for everyone to use. Worlds developed Teleportation hotspots, where even those with very little magic moved between the two points." He said that, when he Teleported from Central Park, he would do it from a different source location near the camp for each destination.

He himself wasn't a natural at Teleportation. The Teleportation naturals, he explained, hopped between worlds with almost the ease that I cast Blink.

All that information, and what I'd seen when I Blinked, led me to a hunch about those bacteria. Testing my theory would be tricky. A video image wouldn't work; I needed to *see* a bacterium disappear. I set up my microscope and pulled out a sample that was a few days old. There were less twitchy bacteria, though, which made them harder to find. I did eventually find one and tried to follow it, but I lacked fine motor control of the microscope to keep it in view.

I needed help.

Chapter 64

Red

Grundle was right; Galad was the least excited about my plan. However, he reluctantly agreed. Harry lit up, coming out of his usual solitude to help us with details. It had been about a month since Africa had been nuked, and people were trickling back into the cities. Galad had been casting his "population detection" spell, and we had witnessed the slow return of people. No virus had broken out, despite many false scares, and the hoax theorists were becoming more credible.

People returning to the cities, and the resulting population density increases, meant our brief respite was ending. It seemed like the right timing, so for our next four-vial trip, we kicked off our new strategy.

We Teleported into Karachi, Pakistan, one of the most densely populated cities on Earth. Google maps had revealed a solid patch of ground in the Mangroves that was perfect for our efforts.

It took us longer than usual to get everything ready. In the past, setting up our assaults had been almost entirely Galad's effort, with a little work from Grundle to clear visual obstructions, which I hadn't even realized he was doing on our early trips. In contrast to the previous battle preparations, Harry invested his time and energy, paying special attention to our battle gear. He made sure everything in the field of battle was just right. At one point, he even snapped at me with some weird-ass comment about my hair. I made a mental note to stop involving Harry in my plans.

Actually, as anal as Harry was being, he was right.

Galad activated the vials, and we waited. The first few Infected came in, and Harry was all over them, crushing skulls with that hammer, bellowing ferociously at the slain corpses before jumping in to help me with the one I was working on, who was already missing one arm from my knife-work. Harry even dropped his hammer on the skull of an Infected that Grundle had torn apart, dramatically splattering the brains. There were no guns involved.

When the second round of Infected came charging, Harry positioned himself at the forefront. He struck, his hammer flying out of his hand and plowing through three of the Infected, letting off small sparks of lightning as it traveled. I didn't even know the hammer was capable of that, but the enemy that survived became easy targets for the rest of us. Grundle tore them limb from limb while Galad and I dismembered the rest.

The battle was over more quickly than usual. But cleanup took longer—besides the usual work, we had the extra equipment to pack up. I took pics of the final body pile for Agent Smith, and we Teleported back.

The extra equipment—lights and cameras and costumes—was worth it. The video we posted of the battle went viral.

Chapter 65

Red

The stone-skinned colossus walked past an abandoned van, the top of his shoulder higher than its roof.

"Grundle," I said.

The light glistened off the metal rings in the straps of his gear. His brown leather tunic and pants, though still marred from use, had been cleaned to make a better impression on camera. "This Warlord stands nine feet tall, with skin hard as rock."

He stopped in the junkyard clearing, bracing himself with his war-axe poised to strike. The two-headed axe was taller than most humans, with a heavy knob at the end to balance the weapon. His rumbling growl reverberated like a Harley engine.

An Infected charged in, and Grundle's axe glowed blue as he swung it with inhuman speed into his attacker. The Infected split in two, its legs tumbling to the ground as the upper body flew past, black gore spraying through the air.

"The Infected are no match for his strength and speed."

Another darted in to attack. *Damn, those things are fast.*

Grundle spun and ended it just as swiftly.

"At a hundred years old, he is middle-aged for a troll. On his home world, he was a leader. But the Infected overran his planet."

Grundle waved his gargantuan axe over his head and roared.

"Now he is here, a guardian of Earth."

308

We settled into something of a routine—an odd one, but a routine nonetheless. Teleport and kill Infected during the week—single-vial excursions. Every seven to ten days go on a bigger excursion and kill more—four-vial excursions. And every day or two a visit from Scan for magic school. Grundle and Harry taught Bear how to use a long-sword. Like the other enchanted weapons, it enhanced his speed and gave him a better chance against the enemy.

We kept releasing videos. Scan was phenomenal with the technical content, software, and engineering. Harry surprised me by being *The Man* for getting the lighting and scenery right. He understood how to capture the feeling, the essence, of a battle. He was the one who nixed the guns— said they wouldn't play well on camera.

But connecting the filming to the social media, releasing videos with a cadence that kept people interested—-that was all about communicating a theme and, ultimately, a big picture. *This is my domain.*

***

"His name is Harry," I said.

He stood in the clearing, head held high, long hair and beard blowing in the wind. The brown and black braids curled about his wide body, draping almost to the ground. His garb was sturdy—thick black leather tunic and pants, studded in places with metal spikes. His tall boots reached almost to his knees.

"From a subterranean world, his race carves tunnels and moves stones with the ease that we plant crops."

Reaching behind him, he flexed a bicep as big as a human's quad. His hand came back wielding his Mighty Hammer. The head was elegant marble overlaid with a pattern wrought in silver, the handle polished wood engraved with runes. He thrust the hammer to the sky, and the air lit up with blue arcs of electricity.

"At fifty years old, a young man by dwarven standards, he left his home world for a higher calling."

Harry began spinning his hammer, and when the Infected rushed out of the trees, he set the hammer free. It whistled through the air and crushed the chest of the assailant, knocking the monster away. It arced back to his waiting hand, and Harry smiled wickedly.

"He found that calling as a guardian of Earth."

***

I posted the first video, the one filmed in Pakistan, through a YouTube channel I called GuardiansOfEarth. It repeated through tweets set up by Scan solely for information propagation. We received half a million hits on the first day—not breaking any records, but not bad. There was plenty of scepticism about the video's authenticity. The idea that we would film a spoof on a topic that involved so many deaths disgusted some people. After all, what people saw was the distortions on the video when the creatures attacked, but once they died, the distortions stopped. So the entire world—or at least those connected to the internet—got to see the dead Infected up close.

We video-taped every battle. Even Grundle—who normally did not do the one-vial trips because he lacked the means to Heal himself—did his share. Since Harry involved himself in the filming, we had his Heals handy. One problem with our little plan was that I was the only one who spoke any human language, so as we introduced Galad, Grundle, and Harry to the world, I had to narrate. My voice became the voice for #GuardiansOfEarth.

***

Galad stood, proud and regal, his normal irritation pasted across his face. His golden curls matched his golden skin, but when I zoomed in on his face, the golden pupils in his eyes declared him more than a California surfer boy.

310

"Galad hails from a truly long-lived race," I said.

I panned back again, capturing that day's dark green elven robes patterned with lighter green leaves and symbols. The robes swayed gently in the breeze as he drew his sword. He swiped the sword, loosening up, and it glowed a dim blue.

"Once they reach adulthood, elves no longer age. Galad has eons of experience to draw on."

When the Infected came out of the woods, Galad spun to the side, letting it move harmlessly past. He toyed with the Infected, showing off his skill with the sword. Skill that came with thousands of years of practice. With a rain of blows, he sent the Infected tumbling to the ground, where it let loose a horrendous yell of fury from its skin-covered mouth.

"But Galad's skills are not only martial," I said. "He is also a master of the arcane arts."

In an elegant motion, Galad sheathed his sword, and moved his hands to cast a spell. As the Infected struggled to rise from its multiple slices, Galad blasted it with a beam of heat, cutting into, then through, the neck of the beast, ending it in a puddle of molten gore.

"He came to halt the invasion of the Infected. He *is* a guardian of Earth."

***

Even Grundle and Harry did not know Galad was that old. With a little work, we estimated his age to be around fifteen *thousand* years. Perhaps it wasn't relevant info, but fascinating nonetheless. The troll and dwarf wanted to hear about life before The Infected, and Galad obliged with stories of people exploring other worlds, magical discoveries, and even monsters that predated the Infected.

As interesting as it was, I'd never intended to be a video narrator.

While Scan managed the internet technicals, Harry's

aptitude for our endeavor surprised me. Once I learned more about him, it made more sense. He'd left everything— he and his family had been miners—to become an actor. Leaving his parents at his young age was a big deal, and Harry had cut all ties to pursue his dream. He'd met and befriended Grundle in his travels. Shortly after, the Infected destroyed Grundle's world, and Harry cast his lot with Grundle and Galad.

Introducing one of the world's protectors as an actor didn't seem wise. The decisions about what information to reveal were difficult. I introduced their alien "species," let people see and experience their fighting skills, and their intentions to stop the Infected. I did not show everything.

***

I panned the camera around in a circle, showing my friends' backs as they awaited the Infected. "Galad, Harry, Grundle, Bear," I said.

"Bear is from Earth." I flipped the camera around and waved. "As am I. Call me Red."

I began mounting the camera on a drone and continued my narration.

"The Infected attack high population densities," I explained, as the camera clicked into its mount. "But on Earth, our sun weakens them, giving us a chance that the Guardians did not have on their own worlds."

I started the drone, knowing the noise would prevent any more speech from being captured. It rose into the air, and I monitored the feed from my phone. I positioned the drone so we were all in view and set my phone down, drawing my daggers with a blue flash of light.

We had used all four vials for the fight, though we hid them from the camera floating above. The battle went well, and our watchers gained some knowledge of my crew and the war they waged.

***

The information about the Infected being weakened by our sun received a lot of follower comments—paradigms from the Superman/Red-Sun comic books. That wasn't what I was aiming for, though not too far off the mark. Heroes, yes. Comic book lack-of-reality, no. It didn't help that Harry had garbed me in a mask when I'd told him I worried about the safety of my family if anyone recognized me. It was a small mask that just wrapped my eyes and part of my cheeks, black around the eyes and some red swirls underneath.

We didn't showcase the vials but clarified that something was being done to draw the Infected out. We did not allow any humans to become Infected, and thought it best, at that time, to keep hidden that horrid ability to transform. Such information had the potential to drive people to take desperate measures.

We were trying to build up sentiment that these otherworlders were heroes and protectors of our world. It seemed inevitable that, at some point, we would have to go out in public, and I didn't want the world greeting my friends with pitchforks and torches.

Chapter 66

Rocks

Sneaking Scan into The Palace—and PharmLabs—was not easy. Building security kept an eye on The Palace, and the FBI hunted for Scan. Scan had learned some tricks since our previous operations, but we still struggled to get him past the double-whammy of safeguards.

Scan shrugged off concerns about his ability to avoid those searching for him. But we had beefed up The Palace security, and while Scan had access to the computers in PharmLabs and the data center I had set up, there was no direct tie into The Palace security servers. Alex's guy, Phillip Roswell, was top notch. Scan had gotten in once, but Phillip had filled those gaps in security. Scan doubted his ability to get back in, or stay in long enough to knock out camera feeds.

Another option was to fake a security badge and walk right in. Many people walked in on a given day. Since I needed to get someone into the building unnoticed, I silently thanked the business investors of The Palace who had prevented a significant increase in security, complaining of the cost.

The badge creation process was online, making their design possible from any security station. You needed access to the secure intranet of The Palace, which I had. You also had to enter your own ID for badge creation, so there was some traceability in case anything went wrong. Using my ID for that would have been risky—I couldn't afford someone tracing the misuse back to me—and I doubted I even had the correct permissions to add new hires. Ironically, I had access to all the security feeds, and there were several cameras where the keyboards of the security stations were visible.

It took a little time, but I figured out one of the guard's passwords. *Thanks, Gil Rosenberg.*

My conscience gave me the stink-eye over that move. "Cynthia wouldn't approve," it reprimanded me. I raised an eyebrow and reminded it who was boss, and if it wanted to stick around, it'd better watch its tone. Still, it had a point—I just didn't see any other way.

Creating a badge took a couple of hours. Scan and I spun up a crew of six workers for the new data center—the right number for a believable backup shift to the existing crew. Scan fed me the information, and I entered it in. He darkened his hair—a simple addition that got some mileage as a disguise—and we took his picture as one of the six.

We didn't have to get Scan a separate PharmLabs badge. I had Dr. Manusov arrange for a junior lab technician to be available for Saturday morning, when the labs would be fairly empty. I told him I had a colleague that thought the videos were fake, and he wanted to see with his own eyes that the bacteria were disappearing spontaneously. Dr. Manusov arranged the PharmLabs guest badging himself.

With the preliminaries taken care of, it was time to put the plan into action and get Scan into The Palace and PharmLabs. Overseas, that type of work was my bread and butter, but I had been doing an entirely different song and dance since coming back, and I found my nerves were more rattled than I'd expected. The stakes had always been life and death, but the scale had increased—and I'd always had Murphy to direct my efforts. I didn't enjoy being the one making the questionable calls, though it hadn't bothered me terribly to implement someone else's, as long as I thought it was for the greater good.

But, when I next awoke, I would sneak an FBI

315

Person Of Interest into a secure facility that was mine to protect. Risks be damned.

Chapter 67

Agent Terry Smith

As often happens, after enough blood, sweat, and tears, we caught a break.

The entire investigation had been a fiasco. Rogers caught hell for fumbling the capture of Hernandez, and that shit had rolled downhill. I had thought Rogers was an arrogant prick before, but he became an intolerable, arrogant prick after that. He did everything he could to hold on to the case himself—pulling strings, using up favors—and I overheard all the random petty comments he used to make me smaller and himself bigger, which gave others permission to join in.

"Explains why they have a connection," I overheard Peters say as I passed an open door to a conference room. "They both play for the other team."

Yeah, sure. My rejection of you is because I play for the other team, not because you're even uglier on the inside than on the outside. I kicked myself for that thought. The reality was I preferred men who were not… classically attractive. Knowing a man had been through some tough shit gave me some hope that he would understand the tough shit *I'd* been through. But Peters had directed life's abuse back outward, spreading his venom as though that would free him of the poison.

I walked past the conference room window, and saw Rogers in there with Peters, both abruptly mute save for a sniffle from Peters as I continued by. They needn't have worried on my account; I didn't want to deal with HR.

I'd be off the case except it seemed Hernandez played only with me. Rogers wanted to run the effort, and I had no problem with that, but the bigwigs upstairs kept pushing things back to me. We'd dug into Red's army squad and, once the nuke went off, they gave us access to even the redacted material. When I saw her records—well, Hernandez had reason to distrust her government.

We'd been following her old squad. The big one, Barry "Bear" Higgins, had gone off the grid after the nuke. Reginald "Rocks" Penbrook was easy enough to follow in a general sense, as he was often in the public eye, but he had money enough to pay for diversionary tactics that gave him time off our radar. Thomas "Scan" Ashcroft and Garnet "Red" Hernandez were the most irritating failures for us. Ms. Hernandez would just disappear—we couldn't track her hidey-hole, and she didn't come out often. Ashcroft was covering her electronic trail, in addition to his own, and was likely providing some help for Penbrook as well.

Ashcroft was infuriating. He was helping, giving information that would enable us to spot the aliens, providing digital links that *had to* be useful for locating him, and yet, our experts could not find him. His digital fingerprint led nowhere.

Ms. Hernandez had added to the insult by creating videos of fighting the alien invaders, alongside... what else but *other aliens*. She was making those *aliens* look like heroes, defending us from distorted images that coalesced into hideous beasts upon death. She somehow uploaded and published the videos, undoubtedly via Ashcroft, and yet we found neither of them. The locations of her films were not obvious, but timestamps and embedded locations were visible, so we knew she was world-hopping. Technically, she had time to reach the different locations via jet, which Penbrook might have been paying for, but we had no evidence she was doing so. I was convinced she was teleporting, though I'd given up arguing that point, as it gave Rogers ample opportunity to make me look ridiculous.

But our luck had changed.

We had suspected that Penbrook and Ashcroft were still in contact, and we had embedded some eyes in the security system at The Palace. That morning, we had a hit in facial recognition—an ID had been created that resembled Ashcroft. We were just waiting for him to use the card, so we would know exactly where he was. "And then I'll get you, Ashcroft." *And your little dog, too.*

The question that gnawed at me, despite my assigned job—was stopping them the right move?

Chapter 68

Red

Some feedback from viewers was that the videos seemed staged. We marked the locations on the videos, but the places were always remote and "those markers could be faked," one commenter noted.

"Truth is stranger than fiction," some old guy said once.

Fighting the Infected in a location that was *not* remote was more dangerous to everyone involved. Bystanders might get hurt, or we might mess something up trying to protect them. We got the point though—the locations needed to be recognizable. Harry had an idea. For the bigger fights—the four-vial ones—if we Teleported to recognizable locations early, and Galad used his Empathic skills to clear the area, we would protect the innocents.

Harry was super excited about the idea of fighting the next battle *in* The Palace, in the same spot where we had fought before. We would have our own cameras, but all the security cameras would get the footage as well. Rocks could ensure they released the footage before there was any kind of government interference. The location was very distinctive, and, if we cleared the building, there was no risk to people. I tried to get ahold of Scan, but he'd warned me he would be out-of-pocket for a little while that morning. Scan was my only means to double-check with Rocks, though I didn't think Rocks would balk on filming in his building.

Still, it would take some time to get the building cleared, and Scan thought he would only be offline for an hour or so. We decided to get started; we would back out if Scan or Rocks had doubts.

"So, how do we get in?" I asked.

"We Teleport in, of course," Galad replied with a puzzled expression. "You *know* where I go in and out of that building."

I didn't know he had a Teleport spot in The Palace, much less where it was. *Why would he think… oh… oh!* That room, in the tunnels, where Grundle had first attacked me. Of course! Wow, did I feel stupid.

"You're blushing," Galad said, smiling. "You didn't know."

I shook my head. Geez, sometimes I thought I was so clever, with my ideas on popularizing my alien friends, and then I had times when the glaringly obvious escaped me.

"Okay," I started, trying to recover, "how do we avoid cameras once we're inside?"

"I have a spell for that, too," Galad said. "It creates the distortion you are familiar with."

"You mean like when we film the Infected?"

"Yes, just like that. It's something of an illusion. Not my strength, but I can manage. The Infected seem to have it as a natural part of their existence. They aren't the only creatures in the universe with such a thing. It is how we learned to create a spell for it after all. There were some lizards on a—"

I waved my hands at him to stop. "It's okay, I don't need to know the origin of your spell right now."

He nodded in acquiescence.

"So we Teleport in," I reasoned. "You start your spell to get people to leave. You camouflage us to avoid the cameras, then we work our way up to the atrium and set up shop. Is that the essence of the plan?"

Harry, Galad, and Grundle all looked at one another

quizzically, then nodded in unison.

"It seems so," Grundle rumbled.

Bear also nodded—he was in too.

I nodded back, thinking aloud. "Since the last time you attacked The Palace, they've upgraded security. If too many people leave the building, it sets off phone calls to the heads of security."

"How do they know if you've left the building?" Galad asked.

"Badges." I formed a rectangle with my fingers. "A little card people wear around their necks or attached to their clothes. We can track those cards within certain areas of the buildings."

Grundle had his own question. "Can we trick the system?"

"I don't think so. Scan said he would have a tough time cracking their security again. Wait, can you make people want to take off their badges before they leave?"

Galad thought about it, but shook his head. "I can't think of anything that would make a person do that. You could get a few people to do it if you convinced them their necklace was shocking them or their clothes were on fire, but I doubt the response would be consistent."

I raised my eyebrow.

"What?" he said.

"I'm just wondering how strange your world must be with people rushing around trying to take their clothes off for imaginary fires."

Galad blushed. *Yes! Score one for me.*

"Okay, so once Galad does his Empathy thing, we will have a limited time before security flags it and returns, either from too few badges in the security offices, or from reports of people running around outside the building naked."

Galad frowned at me, and I enjoyed it.

322

"Do we need to get back to that room to the tunnels to Teleport out? No, never mind, you Teleported out of the atrium before."

"Teleporting from the room is easier," Galad said, "but I can 'Port us out from the atrium."

"Well, let's mount up then," I said.

Blank stares. I sighed and rephrased. "Let's gather our stuff and go."

Chapter 69

Scan

A Dr. Manusov met us at PharmLabs in The Palace. It was my first time to enter The Palace in person, though I'd wandered its security systems and used its cameras to help Red and Bear. Seeing the breadth of the thing from up close—spanning four blocks at the upper levels—was a bit awe-inspiring. It was like the first time boarding a battleship. Sure, I'd played games with battleships, and I had an idea of their size, but the first time on board was really something.

One thing my friends didn't get about me was that I mostly did nothing "new." They all thought I was a genius, but my actual strength was seeing how things could fit together. However, other, more creative people, came up with those "things." I was a great coder, but my strength was reading other people's code and knowing how to use it. I was great with hardware, but only in connecting what other people had already done in ways they hadn't considered.

So when I saw something like The Palace, something truly creative and new, it took my breath away. I sometimes wished I had that creativity, though there was also something special about my strengths—seeing connections and possibilities others did not. It was part of the reason I had such a small online fingerprint. Nothing was mine—I was just reusing other people's algorithms in different ways.

Dr. Manusov had apparently thought Rocks's alibi for bringing me into the labs was important enough that he didn't want to leave it to a tech. Rocks looked surprised—

even bothered—by that. I'm sure he thought it was a failure on his part to minimize my observability. I didn't mind. Dr Manusov had some interesting thoughts on how to activate more reproduction in the odd bacteria. The theories were wrong, based on things I knew that he didn't, but they were interesting.

Ultimately, I still insisted on seeing the bacteria disappear myself, despite having watched the video. Dr. Manusov saw that I was only skeptical—I played the role—and not hostile, and he explained how they had set up the micro-rotors to move on a scale appropriate for moving the sample under the camera. He called them micro-rotors, but they were not rotors at all. His guys had designed new hardware that worked off of small inductive currents to create magnetic fields that slowly moved the plates in two dimensions and let the height recalibrate/refocus independently. They had used—surprise surprise—neural networks to better anticipate movement. Very similar to what Tesla used for autonomous driving but on a much easier scale. The cool thing was that, any time they lost the bacteria they were tracking, they used that as training data to improve the neural net. He showed me a list of patents they'd filed, minus the details of course.

It was all meant to wow me, and it did. They'd done outstanding work, and I found myself eager to see the bacteria disappear for myself. Dr. Manusov got me set up, and then the strangest thing happened. I felt a tug accompanied by a sudden desire to be sure I'd turned on all the safeguards when I'd left home. That was crazy. I was sure I had activated my safeguards before leaving, but, wracked with doubt, I wanted to double check.

I started to excuse myself when Dr. Manusov beat me to it. "My apologies, Dr. Ashford." I checked the name on my badge, self-conscious about the lie of holding a PhD. "I've just remembered that I promised to take my daughter to soccer this morning. It was a big game for her, and it slipped my mind from all the recent work. I apologize, but I must run. I've shown you how to get this going. Are you okay on your own?"

I nodded, noticing Rocks eyeing his watch and the exit door himself. What was going on? Something wasn't right. I relaxed my mind, turning off my own concerns about my home, and just *looked*. I saw it. There was a spell at work in The Palace. As Dr. Manusov left, I put a hand on Rocks's arm to stop him from following. "It's a spell, Rocks. It's making you want to leave."

He protested, but then stopped himself, believing me, and nodded.

I smiled. People leaving meant I had time to work with the equipment unobserved. Had Red arranged the spell on purpose to buy me some time? I took advantage of it.

I set up the equipment and fished around on the sample Dr. Manusov had put under the scope. The first step was to find a bacterium I wanted to observe. That took a few minutes, panning around, searching for the characteristic jerky movement of the odd bacteria. I found one, but, in the time it took me to work through activating the tracking system, I had lost sight of it. So I had to fish again for several more minutes, but had a better feel for the equipment the second time around and activated the tracking.

"Scan," Rocks interrupted, "I think we have a problem. Do you have a way to contact Red?"

I handed him my phone. "Look for 'Santa Suit' in the contacts. I need a few minutes undisturbed, Rocks."

He nodded and took the phone, heading toward the lab entrance while he scrolled.

At that point, the key for me was to relax my mind and focus on "seeing" with more than just vision. I didn't understand how it all worked yet, but I tried to activate that same mental shift that enabled me to see Galad as a bunch of vines that were growing together, or see the Otherness of the magic my light spell produced, or tell that a spell was being used to vacate the building.

Shifting my mind did not take long, and the bacteria was still being tracked. What I saw as I peered into the scope—which was just lenses, not an image run digitally through a camera—was that the bacteria seemed to pulse when they twitched. Like the magic from the light spell, these pulses had an Otherness about them. I had expected that, hoped for it, and I was excited to think I was probably right about what I would see next.

It took several minutes, but the bacteria finally disappeared, and there it was—the answer I needed.

Chapter 70

Agent Terry Smith

Ashcroft had used the fake ID to get into The Palace—or it was just some guy who resembled Ashcroft, and I was about to make an utter fool of myself. *Yay, high-stress job!*

The FBI was willing to go all out to nab Ashcroft. We had people securing the entrances of each of the four buildings—about twenty per building—and Alex Handell had given us access to the security feeds. We had tracked the man presumed to be Ashcroft into a laboratory. Penbrook had joined him, solidifying our theory. Rogers ran the mission, but made it clear that the crap—my word, not his—would fall to me if I was wrong and it wasn't Ashcroft. Big surprise.

"All units, move in," Rogers barked over the radio. Rogers made the calls from on-site, so we didn't have "a repeat of the café failure." Agents moved into the building nearest me, and I poked my head in the van to confirm that the same was occurring at the other three buildings.

I watched the monitors as our agents entered all four buildings.

A disturbing thought popped into my head. I'd forgotten to set my streaming capture to get the new episode of *Big Bang Theory*. There'd been that software patch, and I'd been unable to interact with the system while it was patching. I'd started breakfast and forgotten to get back to it. Aw, hell, I hated to miss that. I could take off for a bit and get that done. *They have this under control, right?*

I'd ridden in someone else's car from our building. The nearest subway was… oh, it didn't matter—walking would be fine. I started heading toward my house, a day's walk from The Palace, plus the swim across the Hudson. That thought gave me pause—it was discordant. But then I remembered there would be a ferry, so I wouldn't have to swim. Relieved, I told myself the important thing was to start on the trek.

I looked around and saw other Agents also leaving The Palace and heading off in different directions. Wait, that wasn't right. *They couldn't have all had the same software patch this morning, could they?* The ridiculousness of that thought made me pause. I stuck my head in the back of the van and saw people were emptying out of every entrance of The Palace, all four buildings, and not just my agents, but lots of civilians.

Still, the desire to leave pulled at me. *They're all leaving. Shouldn't I go too?*

Convinced by that sound logic, I pulled my head out of the van and gave a last glance at The Palace before embarking on my journey home. Everyone was leaving. Except that one man, who was making a beeline for the FBI van, waving his hands frantically. *I should go before I have to deal with that!*

I shuffled down the street, away from The Palace, hoping the lunatic had not paid me any special attention. Sadly, I was wrong.

"You!" he said, frantic. "Um… Smith! Agent Smith!"

Never liked that name. Time to pick a new one and ignore Lunatic.

As I walked away, the man got in front of me. "My name's Richard. Richard Wales. You interviewed me after I left my post at The Palace the last time this happened."

He was right, but I failed to see the relevance.

"You have my friend, Gil, in custody."

That we did. He had been the one to create the IDs we believed to be fake. *Again, relevance?* I moved to go around him.

"Ugh!" he groaned, examining his watch. In a decisive move, he popped back in front of me, removed his watch, and held it on my arm.

Bzzzzzt!

"Frakin' hell!" I shouted, "What the frak, skinjob?" He'd *shocked* me! That wasn't a watch; it was a shock collar!

All of a sudden, the situation made sense to me. Whatever had made everyone leave the Owaie building—or the first attack on The Palace when it had emptied—was happening again!

Richard was blushing, but the removal of the shock collar from his wrist had not returned him to a zombie state. He hadn't kept the collar on my wrist, and I hadn't re-lost my marbles.

"You've been wearing that since the last attack?" I asked him.

"Yes," he said, blushing even more. "I made a promise to Ms. Hernandez that I wouldn't abandon my post again. Gil helped me hook this up to the software that is monitoring for a mass exodus from the building, and it just went off!"

Ms. Hernandez again. She had made some very loyal friends. Gil, whom we had in custody, had clearly known her, though he hadn't shown evidence of knowing Ashcroft.

"How did you know getting a shock would help?"

"I didn't. I just—" he shrugged. "I had to try *something*!"

My head nodded in agreement. Richard's loyalty had certainly paid off for me. "Go zap some more FBI agents. Most will have stun guns—tell them to zap others."

"You want me to go zap FBI agents?" His eyes were like saucers. "I'm pretty sure that will land me locked up with Gil!"

I grabbed my stun gun and jogged to a departing FBI agent, zapping him on the arm without using the firing mechanism. He jerked away with a "Hey!" but then, rubbing his arm, he looked around like he had just awoken from a strange dream.

"Go do the same to other agents!" I shouted to him. "Let the civilians walk away." No point in having more people at risk.

He nodded and started off, and I followed suit.

I set about waking agents out of the trance, then giving them the task of waking other agents. Richard was using his shock collar too. We lost some in the crowd, but we still had enough to move in.

Chapter 71

Rocks

I called Red, aka Santa Suit, as I walked out of PharmLabs.

"Red, it's Rocks."

"Rocks. Good. Everything okay with Scan? He's been out of contact longer than I expected him to be."

"He's okay. Still out of pocket for a few more minutes. Red, what's going on? I just got the security alert that people are leaving The Palace. This is your doing, right?" I felt a wave of mild anger that they hadn't involved me in whatever plan was in play.

"Yeah, that's why I've been trying to reach Scan, so I can confirm that what we're doing won't mess anything up for you. We decided we would do the next filming in some place more recognizable. We can still back out if it's a problem."

"You decided you had to do that *today*? You couldn't confirm first and do the filming tomorrow?" I was trying to keep my voice down. I didn't think the cameras had microphones, but I wasn't positive.

Red hesitated. "I didn't think there would be a problem." She didn't say more, probably halting "her people" in case I said there *was* a problem. I asked myself why I was so bothered. I was tired of everyone constantly running things by me. So many stupid little decisions where someone wanted my sign-off, as though that abdicated them from all responsibility. And then, when given a reminder of a fully functional team, I got upset. What was my problem?

"Sorry, Red," I said, sighing. "This is just for filming, right? You're not attacking the building?"

"Just filming. We're still trying to build some credibility so we can get people to listen."

Just filming. Using my *building for PR, without my consent.* Wow—when had I started thinking of The Palace as *my* building? But, if I was honest with myself, I felt it. I had taken on a leadership role just to help Red, but I'd invested significant time, and my heart followed. Ironically, I'd not influenced Red's security improvements at all, and it wouldn't have mattered if I did, given the nature of the attacks. Even more ironically, Red was the one causing the increased security to trigger.

I asked myself, *What's the big picture here, Rocks?*

We needed to canonize Red's allies. In that context, filming a fight with the Infected in The Palace was a solid PR move for Red. We also needed to disperse the population—doing so would be bad for the finances of The Palace. So, my options were to either make some money and put the planet in danger, or save the planet and lose the family business and the very heart of what my dying father had dreamed of.

Damn.

Knowing I had Cynthia, who was carrying my child, made the decision easier. It wasn't about proving I could get the building done and increasing the family legacy—it was about being sure there was a world left in which to raise my family.

"Do your film," I said. "I'll swing by Sec Ops and be sure they evacuate it and that the cameras are running."

"Okay," Red responded, hesitation in her voice. "You sure you're okay with this? You sound... reluctant."

Reluctant. Excellent word choice. "I'm good, Red. Do what you need to do." I hung up. She would call back if she needed anything.

Scan was okay—he was in a lab, far away from the proverbial shit that was soon going to hit the fan in a spectacular fashion. I marched toward Sec Ops, pondering the short-term publicity boost that would become a PR nightmare. Scan's phone kept drawing my attention. Was there anything I could text Red that would change the course of events in a way that would save The Palace—and my family—without sacrificing the human race?

I continued on to Sec Ops, attention on Scan's phone, though it gave me no answers.

Red

That was... weird. I wasn't sure what was bothering Rocks. We needed a heart-to-heart. But later. Promising myself I would circle back to understand Rocks's angst, I moved forward with our plans.

Harry was setting up the portable lights and camera. We cleared the four key passages to the stage, in order to allow the Infected unimpeded access to us. We set the camera behind one of the half-walls that concealed the staircases in an outer corner—the southwest corner. Harry manipulated the existing lights at the northwest and southeast corners, to provide stage lighting without being visible to our camera. We knew well that all of our actions were being captured on the security cameras. So we were trying to be professional yet not uptight. It was our "coming out"—our chance to reveal what was going on, to get people to appreciate that they were watching a reality show and not a web hoax.

Despite my intent to move forward, my mind returned to contemplation of Rocks's perspective. He'd been evangelizing the construction of the building for some time. How could you do that and not grow attached? *Well, hell.* We needed the world to admire Galad, Grundle, and Harry. For them to be heroes. And we had to get people to move out of the cities—that would at least buy the world some

334

time. Saving The Palace had been off my radar since…
well, since I'd realized the Infected transformed people into
more Infected. I had been incapable of viewing the world
through any other lens since then.

Ultimately, while I sympathized with Rocks, it didn't
change what needed to happen. So with his reluctant okay,
I'd quickly decided to move forward with our plans. I felt like
a jerk, taking what I'd wanted without considering his
feelings. Sighing, I picked the phone back up and called the
number he had just used to reach me.

Chapter 72

Agent Terry Smith

After losing about half our team, I decided I needed to participate more actively. I moved with the remaining agents into the nearest building, and my crew of three targeted Sec Ops, the eyes of The Palace. If that massive evacuation was any indicator, there was no one managing security.

We were nearing the door to Sec Ops when we heard the stairway door open, and a distinctive "clap-tap, clap-tap, clap-tap" of irregular footsteps came down the hall toward us. From around the corner Mr. Penbrook appeared, the younger one who ran the tower, looking at his phone. His head down, he didn't notice us there until he got close.

The three of us were armed, but we pointed our guns toward the ground as he stumbled into our midst. His phone buzzed, and in the movement of raising it to answer, he spotted us. He clicked it off, and said with enthusiasm, "Oh, great! You're here." He held up his phone. "I got an alarm that security had evacuated. Since I was in the building, I came to check it out."

I gave him the stink-eye. No way was he there to help, at least not help anything but his own ends. How had he even overcome the feeling of needing to flee? Still, there was nothing specific of which I could accuse him.

"Get behind us," I told him, as I motioned for an agent to move forward into Sec Ops proper. He pushed the door open and went in, and the other agent followed.

"All clear," one called, even as Mr. Penbrook and I walked in. The room was devoid of other people.

I scanned the images on the monitors, spotting

movement on a camera showing the atrium, the open space on the 12th floor where we'd found the first alien bodies. I corrected myself—the FBI was not known for its openness—those were just the first alien bodies *I* knew about. Moving closer to the monitor, I saw it was Ms. Hernandez, along with her alien friends, and I felt relief that I was right about their being real. They had set up lighting to stage one of their "close encounters."

"You two," I said, pointing at the agents whose names I hadn't bothered learning, "you stay and monitor things from here. Let me know if anything unusual happens—that I can't see for myself, I mean. Hold the room, okay? This is command central now."

They nodded. The lanky dark-skinned agent pointed at the monitor showing the atrium and said with a Jersey accent, "What exit?" He prodded tentatively at a console, watching the monitors for some sign that he'd produced a result, to no avail.

The shorter light-skinned agent rolled his eyes, sat, and tapped on the keyboard. "We've got this," he said. "Go."

I spoke into my radio. "We've got eyes in the building. Sec Ops is secure. Rogers, Ms. Hernandez is in the atrium with her crew from the videos. What do you want to do?"

Rogers came back on the radio, "Peters, keep the exits covered—I don't want anyone slipping through our noose. All other units converge on the atrium. If you encounter Ashcroft, detain him, but Hernandez is the primary target now."

I turned to Mr. Penbrook, "You're with me."

"Do I get a gun?" he asked, a mischievous grin on his face.

"No, you do not," I replied, though I knew he knew the answer. "I'm not bringing you for backup. I'm bringing

337

you to keep an eye on you... and because I might need to use you."

He smiled. "People aren't usually so upfront about their motives. I appreciate your openness." He turned and started for the door. "But there's no way I can climb ten flights of stairs in a reasonable time with this leg."

Yup. I knew that. That's why I needed him. The elevator would be much faster, and, "Somebody has to walk out of the elevator first."

He frowned. "I thought you were supposed to protect citizens."

"Ms. Hernandez is your friend. I think you'll be okay. Let's go. I want to talk to them."

As we walked toward the elevator, he said, "Thank you for responding to the security alarm so quickly." He was fishing. He wanted to know *how* we had done it.

"We've had a crew here for weeks," I lied. "We don't have a lot of leads." That was the truth. "You can help me answer the biggest question—why destroy buildings?"

"My understanding," he replied, "is that dense populations attract those creatures. Halting the progress of new residential buildings—"

"That would slow urban growth. Okay, but why such violent means? And, if those creatures are attracted to big cities, why Bata?"

"My sources tell me Bata was an aberration. As for less violent—seems like they're making an effort to be sure human casualties are low. My sources—" he began.

"I'd like a word with your *sources*," I mumbled.

"My *sources* tell me," he tried again with a laugh.

That guy, I could have gotten into—lost his leg serving the country and still found joy in life. But married. And rich, which put him out of my league. But his roguish good looks were hard to ignore, even if they weren't my norm.

"The good guys don't speak any human languages, so their conversational abilities are limited to a certain distance where a translation device can help them. And, let's face it, most of us, upon seeing those aliens, would shoot first and ask questions later, right?"

We entered the elevator, and Mr. Penbrook pushed the button to take us to the atrium. "Right now, they're the only means we have of drawing out the bad aliens, so—and I say this as one of the billions of people who have no planet but this one—we can't afford to have the world's defenders out of action. I suppose 'Ms. Hernandez' is helping them with their public relations. Establish them as the good guys, and then maybe—doubtful, but just maybe—the world will listen."

I heard what Mr. Penbrook was saying, but my role was to capture the aliens. I had my assignment. I was closing in, and, with the agents storming the buildings, the net would soon be drawn.

Chapter 73

Scan

Okay, that was a little weird—I hadn't expected Rocks to leave me there alone, without a phone. I assumed he would be right outside the lab, but after waiting a few minutes, I became nervous. Something wasn't right. I could flee the building, which was probably my safest path. I'd felt the effects of Galad's Empathy abilities though, and that suggested they were close. If so, where would they be?

My money was on the same place they had been before—the atrium.

I had no phone, and didn't know the layout of the building that well, but getting to the atrium would be simple enough. I'd just take the elevator up and see for myself.

Rocks

As we rode up the elevator, I considered the wisdom of trying to overpower Agent Smith and take her gun. She didn't consider me a threat and kept her gun holstered, though her hand was on it. I could shift my weight, fake a fall from the bad leg, and get close enough to make a move. But it didn't seem necessary. She was going to the atrium to talk—at worst, try to force a conversation with that gun—but it wasn't overly aggressive compared to my past.

The door opened, and we walked out. The elevator doors faced the outside of the building. We would have to walk around the elevator shaft, and the small shops surrounding it, in order to see the center of the atrium. Red and company would not be able to see us until we moved to

340

the wide corridor between the elevators.

As we started around to the right, the elevator next to us opened. Scan saw us and hesitated. Oops. I'd hoped he would bail when I didn't come back. I should have known better.

Agent Smith, looking at Scan in the elevator, muttered to herself, "Before we get started, does anyone want to get off?"

Scan chuckled and raised his hand, saying, "Hitting does not solve everything," which got a wry bark of laughter out of Agent Smith. I had no idea why that was funny.

"Ashcroft," she said, nodding her head, smiling, but keeping her hand on her holstered gun. Scan exited the elevator, but stopped his forward progress before getting too close to Agent Smith.

Scan nodded, "And you are...?"

"Agent Smith," she answered. Scan squinted, and Smith sighed. "Agent Terry Smith."

Scan smiled, "Oh! Right! Sorry, I thought we might still be doing movie quotes. I pictured you much older from Red's description."

Agent Smith scowled, then shrugged off the comment. *And movie quotes? What movies? These two are speaking their own language.*

That made me think of the texts that Cynthia and I would send, so immersed in context it was like our own secret language. I felt a heart-wrenching worry—if the situation went badly, what would my wife and my child do without me?

"Are we all here to see Red then?" Scan said, plowing through the discomfort he'd caused Agent Smith—and me.

Agent Smith nodded, and Scan started forward. She waved me ahead, too, and followed soon after. Red had something staged, so I kept close to Smith. If Smith was going to try to stop Red, I'd have to take her out.

Chapter 74

Galad had placed the four vials in the center of the stage. It was what he had done the first time he'd performed magic there, but that first time, I had been too preoccupied to notice the canisters. Harry had griped that we didn't have a small table to put them on—he said, irritated, they looked like *toys* on camera. Ignoring Harry's rant, Galad activated the vials. We had placed a person at each of the compass points of the circular stage, facing outward to wait for the Infected to come up any of the four staircases leading to the stage. Galad was facing north, Harry west, Grundle south, and Bear east. I was behind them all, batting cleanup, though it was unlikely they would need me. Our camera was filming.

Unlike the last time I was there, actual seats filled the sloped amphitheatre. They would confine the battle to the stage and the large pathways leading from the stairs. We waited, alert but calm—we had been through many battles together—prepared for the first Infected to show.

"Um, Red?" Grundle rumbled. "I need you over here." I had been watching over Harry's shoulder, because trying to see around Grundle was impossible. It took a few paces for me to get visibility.

What the hell?

"Stay back!" I yelled. "The Infected will come up those stairs any second!" Rocks and Scan, along with Agent Smith, were coming down a hallway from the outside elevators. They had not yet reached a point where they would be between the Infected and us, but they were close.

The three of them stopped, and Agent Smith yelled,

"Wait, what?"

Then the screams began.

They started in the south stairway, with accompanying gunshots, and within seconds, an Infected came charging up the stairs. Rocks, Scan, and Agent Smith had stopped behind the stairs and were out of the way, but it sounded like several people in the stairway had not been as fortunate. Grundle made swift work of the Infected with his war axe, matching the speed of the monsters with the magically enhanced speed his axe granted him.

More shouts and gunshots from the other stairways, and more Infected made it up, only to find their advance suddenly halted by sword, hammer, and axe.

The first round ended quickly. During the pause, some humans trickled in from the side of the stairway. Hopefully, the Infected had just charged through the humans, slicing up the ones in the way, but not bothering to stop and kill or convert those that stayed clear of them. Maybe no humans had even perished. I wasn't expecting anyone to be there, so I had no idea of their initial count. FBI jackets on all of them—not normal building security, which made me feel marginally better. It was the FBI's call to try to pull a fast one to nab us. I wasn't happy about anyone getting hurt, but it wasn't on me.

"Stay out of the way!" I shouted. "There's going to be another round!" The FBI responded swiftly to that, both clearing the corridors and pointing their weapons in the direction from which they had just arrived. I was frustrated. I hadn't been in any fighting, and I couldn't see how to help. "Should we stop?" I asked my team.

Galad shook his head. "No. We've likely drawn them out now, awake and moving. Kill the ones we've called, or we risk losing it all."

"We can't stop this yet!" I shouted to the room. "We have to kill the ones we've drawn out!"

People continued to move out of the corridor and into the seating area, getting clear of the passage, but keeping their eyes on the stairways nearest them.

I looked once more for my friends and spotted Scan leading them toward our camera. He was planning ahead. I couldn't think beyond the upcoming second wave of Infected.

They didn't keep us waiting. Several came up the western stairway I was facing, and out of the corner of my eye, I saw similar movement in the northern corridor. Grundle's enormous frame cut off a portion of my view of the room.

There were just a few gunshots. I hoped the agents were disciplined enough not to fire once the Infected got too close, risking the other FBI agents or us.

Harry pounded the first Infected in the chest with a swipe from his hammer, crushing its chest and sending it colliding with another Infected. I dispatched it with my knives, freeing Harry to move in to take the next one.

At a quick glance, Grundle was covered in them, but held his own. He was a magnificent wall. Galad, with his thousands of years of experience, was also holding the line well. Bear, not so much. He'd cleaved through one with that mighty long-sword, but while he fended off another, two more worked their way behind. Bear was the farthest from me, but he needed help.

I ran, jumping over the open canisters in the middle of the stage. A stupid move, but I didn't vanish in a blast of magical force.

One of the two Infected behind Bear knocked him forward, throwing off his swing at the one before him. It slashed his arm, drawing blood, while another knocked him down from behind. They piled on top of him. I drove my knives into the closer of the two from behind it, making a mess of its internal musculature as I dragged my blades

345

down and out of its body. Jumping off of the falling corpse, I ducked and rolled backward as one of Bear's opponents vaulted them both to get to me.

The Infected impaled itself on my blade, and I pitched it past me as I finished my roll. I smoothly returned to my feet, knowing that the one I had stabbed may not have died. Looking back to the most immediate threat, I saw not one on top of Bear, but two, rising from the ground. *And no Bear.* As the pieces of what had happened clicked in my brain, my world went red.

Chapter 75

Oh, shit.

Bear was *gone,* and Red had lost it. She coated herself in black gore as she slashed through the Infected in a rage the likes of which I'd only seen once before. Soon she stood there, breathing heavily, nothing left to kill, and she let out a blood-curdling scream. Of all people, it was Galad who moved closer. From the wild look in her eyes, it was obvious she wasn't thinking clearly, and she took a slash at Galad. But he was ready and deflected her blade. As though being invited to dance, Red moved in, and Galad gave her an outlet, keeping his distance and letting her spend her energy.

The FBI moved closer to the stage, still staying clear of the center of the aisles, slowly—and not surely—moving down the rows of seats.

I saw Rocks with a rictus of anger that matched Red's, and Agent Smith looked sad and weary. I had moved near the camera, thinking I might need to get it out quickly once the fight was over, and Rocks and the Agent had followed me.

Red was wearing down. No less angry, but energy spent, she was slowing. Galad made a swift move, snuck in under her guard, and foolishly pulled her into a hug. Red still had her daggers free behind Galad's back. Did he have protection or a Heal spell at the ready?

He whispered something down to her, and her hands wrapped around him, as she let loose a massive, wailing sob. She never dropped her blades.

Seconds ticked by. Galad let her loose, and Grundle

347

moved in, swooping her up with one arm and squeezing her tight. Her body shook as she continued to sob.

Galad moved toward the canisters. Time to clean up and get out. I turned off the camera and removed it from the tripod. I would do my part.

A voice from the audience startled me, a latecomer exiting a stairway—"Freeze!"

An FBI agent stood, jacket ripped and head bleeding, with his gun trained on Galad. He limped up the stairway to my left along the side of the stairs, clear of the main passage. Heads spun, and all eyes locked onto the speaker—there was a tense silence, the air between the agent and his target palpable.

There was a sudden flash of light opposite me in the atrium. A woman robed in white stood where moments before there had been no one. Her fiery red hair streamed behind her as she jumped atop the chairs and started running down toward the stage. She was beautiful and graceful, her feet lightly touching the chair backs as she raced into the fray—definitely not human.

Galad had eyes only for the canisters. One down, three to go.

"I said 'freeze,'" the agent said, firing a shot that hit the stage inches from Galad's feet. Galad looked up at the man, raising an eyebrow. The rest of the room stood, transfixed, attention torn between the interactions of the agent and Galad, and the woman descending toward the stage.

"Wait," Agent Smith choked out. Then more loudly, "Rogers, wait!"

But Galad moved, grabbing the second canister and deactivating it, while moving swiftly to the third.

The agent fired again, and the bullet shattered the canister Galad was moving toward. A bright light formed where the canister had stood. Galad locked eyes with me, a look filled with meaning, then moved back toward the team, cast a spell, and they vanished in a flash.

I glanced back up toward the red-haired woman, but she was gone.

A wind rushed toward the remains of the canister, and the light continued to grow brighter. I looked around for a way out. I couldn't Teleport like Galad. We were twelve stories up, so I couldn't Blink. I could see out the window, but that way led to death by splatter on the streets below. Still, that look in Galad's eyes—remaining in the atrium was about to result in death by some means I didn't even understand.

I grabbed Rocks and the agent and concentrated on the sky outside the window. I adjusted my mind and— Blink!—we were on the other side of it, in a terrifying free fall.

Chapter 76

Scan

Out of the frying pan, into the... crash-dive? As if it wasn't enough that we were falling, the building we had just vacated exploded with a massive burst behind us. The heat rose rapidly while pushing us down and away, and—Blink!—I got us farther away from the building.

Still falling, but with the explosion farther behind us, I had a few seconds to think. We were speeding up, and Teleporting us to the ground would just bring us to a massive splat faster. I figured I had one or two more Blinks left in me before I was out of juice, though I felt energized—was there magic in the explosion?

The look in the agent's eyes was a combination of terror and excitement. Rocks's mischievous grin was priceless—asking me what the hell my plan was.

I took my eyes off Rocks and found the edge of the skyline and, beyond that, the Bronx. The Harlem River! If I could just make it to the river! I had enough juice for at least one more Blink.

The water was rushing at us, and I focused on myself and my passengers with my special sight. I wove some strength into the vines that defined us, bolstering us for the impact. I knew we had fallen from high enough that even hitting water, we would go splat. My bones grew stronger, my skin thickened like the outer layers of an ancient oak.

Hitting the water still hurt, but it was stones hitting the water and not the big water-balloons our bodies actually were.

It took several seconds for the three of us to pop

350

back to the surface, but I undid my own changes so I could move more readily, and swam to the other two and did the same. Put on your own oxygen mask before assisting others and all. Rocks had lost his artificial leg in the impact, but even with just the one leg, he stayed afloat. It crossed my mind that I might be able to Heal his leg. I promised myself I would scrutinize it when I wasn't so tired.

From miles away, floating on the Harlem River, we watched, with mournful eyes, the fire that burned The Palace.

Epilogue

Grundle

The mood at the camp was somber. Galad had retreated into the tent where Red lay sleeping. I suspected there was a reason Galad needed to retreat—something I had been hoping for, but the cost was high, maybe too high.

The tiny, fledgling wizard had made it back to camp. He and the one-legged man, who had lost his metal leg and was using a tree limb as a crutch, would hopefully bring some measure of joy to Red. When she awoke.

He had also brought a new human—a woman tasked with capturing us. "Keep your Clan close and your Border Brethren closer."

For a woman surrounded by enemies, she bore herself well, at home in her skin—she eyed me with curiosity and not fear. And she respected the dark atmosphere instead of pushing her own agenda. I liked that.

Harry showed some life when the little wizard appeared with the camera, but crashed back down into his dark mood when informed that the camera had been ruined in the river. Wizardling believed the video had survived—he would just have to take the "microSD" card out and put it in something else to watch it.

Those two were the only ones with any energy, fiddling with some electronics, trying to piece together something to get at the video.

I left them alone and walked over to the one-legged man. "Rocks," Red had called him. He was in charge of the massive construct we had just inadvertently destroyed. "I am sorry for your loss," I told him. And I was. I'd had enough loss, both large and small, to know it was never easy.

His eyes seemed tired, but he grinned. "Which loss is that? There are several to choose from—my friend, my building, or my future?"

Ah, so he had realized. He was a sharp one, like Red. And he hadn't mentioned the leg. "Which pains you the most?" I asked, hoping to draw him out and understand him a bit more.

The question caught him off guard, and he gave it some thought before answering. "I will miss my friend; that one will be a hole for a while." Another pause. "I realize now I cared very little about the building. It seemed important, but..." He shrugged. "Those canisters though... that was the only way we had of drawing out the Infected. We cannot track them at a level where we can hunt them. We can only draw them out. Can we do it with the two that remain? Do you have more?"

I sighed. "We had one more beyond the two that Galad saved. But, no, we will not be effective enough at drawing them out now."

He had hit the heart of my own concerns.

"We will manage for a short time," I said, "but we cannot keep them charged enough to manage long term."

We both pondered the future in silence.

"That," he said, "is my biggest loss. The idea that we are all going to die or, worse... *become...* those things. Those Infected."

The new woman listened in silence.

There was noise as the computer the little wizard and the dwarf were working on kicked to life. I heard audio that sounded like our recent visit to the one-legged man's building. So they got it working. I wasn't interested. The video only mattered when we were trying to build a reputation.

The little wizard said something to the dwarf and

353

came to speak to me.

"Don't give up yet," he told me.

I'd noticed he had a knack for listening in to other conversations while seemingly busy.

"I have an idea," he said, looking up at the stars, "on how we can get some help."

Acknowledgments

First, I thank my family—my wife, Dina, for being patient and my kids, Sienna, Citrine, and Jade, for putting up with my insanity. Questions like, "what's another word for decapitated?" and "do you think a living rock would have a good sense of smell?" Also, my mom, who has been my cheerleader throughout this endeavor, and who, let's face it, started my addiction to reading so many, many years ago.

Second, I thank my editor and writing teacher, Marla Taviano, who has been exactly the person I needed in order to write the story I wanted to write. Without her help, me no writes goodly-ish. She will kill me for that, but maybe she will finish editing the rest of the series, and it can be published posthumously.

Third, thanks to my friend Rafael Rios, who wrote a book out of the blue, and rekindled a flame that had burned to ash and scattered on the winds.

Finally, thank you to all those authors whose books my mother introduced me to. A couple that inspired me the most: Stephen R. Donaldson's *Mordant's Need* and Barbara Hambly's *The Darwath Series*. Many more moments and characters inspired *The Guardian League*— the damn threads that attacked Pern, shooting the kneecaps of an angel who guarded the pearly gates, magic capacitors fighting for fairydom, super-power-stealing succubi. Thank you all for your worlds!

Author's Note

Hate cliffhangers? Good news! Book 2 of the Guardian League, *Stars in the Sand*, will be available by June 1, 2021! Expect four books in total, but the third book is almost twice as long as the rest, and might end up becoming a part1/part2 release.